SECRETS *on*
MERSEY SQUARE

BOOKS BY PAM HOWES

A Child For Sale

Fast Movin' Train
Hungry Eyes
It's Only Words

SECRETS *on* MERSEY SQUARE

PAM HOWES

bookouture

Published by Bookouture in 2024

An imprint of Storyfire Ltd.
Carmelite House
50 Victoria Embankment
London EC4Y 0DZ

www.bookouture.com

ISBN: 978-1-83790-998-8
eBook ISBN: 978-1-83790-997-1

Dedicated to the memory of Elvis Presley, 1935–1977
And Lisa Marie Presley, 1968–2023
Father and daughter reunited.

1

SAN FRANCISCO, FEBRUARY 2001

Livvy closed the birthday card and traced her finger around the cute cartoon bear gracing the front. He carried a pink balloon and wore a matching ribbon sash across his shoulder inscribed – *To a Special Daughter*.

She jumped as a sharp rap at the door preceded a deep masculine voice, 'Ten minutes, Miss Grant!'

'Be out soon.' She put the card in a pink envelope and picked up a dog-eared photograph of a dark-haired, brown-eyed baby girl. 'You're the image of your daddy, Harley. Not a day goes by that I don't think about you.' She blinked rapidly. No tears tonight. The make-up girl had spent ages on her face. Mustn't spoil it. But tears were never far away, especially at this time of year. In two weeks' time her firstborn would be sixteen and she wouldn't be with her to celebrate. She'd never wished her girl a happy birthday. Never helped her choose a new outfit, or welcomed her friends into their home. Those privileges belonged to Harley's father, rock musician Roy Cantello, and his all-forgiving wife, Sammy.

It had seemed the right thing to do at the time, sign Harley over to her father and get on with her life. The Cantellos were fabulously wealthy and would give her daughter everything that she couldn't – well, certainly nothing quite as grand as she could offer today. But as far as she knew, Harley had no knowledge of her existence. In spite of the Christmas and birthday cards she sent, there'd been no contact from the family after the first year. Maybe it was better that way, although Roy *had* promised he'd tell Harley the truth when she reached ten years old.

Livvy kissed the photograph, slid it into her handbag and checked her appearance in the full-length mirror. She fluffed out her blonde curls, smoothed down the full skirt of her dress and hurried backstage in time to hear her band Juice playing the opening bars of their latest hit. A deep breath, a smile fixed in place, she walked on stage to tumultuous applause for the final show of their West Coast tour.

* * *

Daniel McVey was deep in thought as he drove down the dusty lane on the last few miles of his journey home. Livvy would be flying in tomorrow and no doubt the quarrels and conflict would start all over again. Daniel was growing tired of his wife's mood swings and he dreaded the next few weeks. They'd reacquainted in their native Glasgow almost sixteen years ago when Livvy was recovering from a broken heart. Good friends at school, they'd dated off and on, then gone their separate ways. He to London to pursue a career in property and she to Manchester to escape the clutches of a controlling adoptive father, who'd left her with a lasting fear and little trust in men.

Someone though had managed to break down those barriers. She'd fallen in love and given birth to a daughter. All she'd divulge was that the child had been adopted by a wealthy couple and she had no further contact with the baby's father. Daniel had wanted nothing more than to love and protect the petite, blue-eyed blonde who'd walked back into his life. He suggested he sell his business and they move to the States on the condition she married him.

Within the year they not only moved to Los Angeles, but also became the proud parents of Courtney. Livvy became depressed following the birth, which put a strain on their relationship. The more he tried to understand, the further away she withdrew. She didn't want more children, she said, and avoided intimate contact as often as she could. Daniel was desperate for a son and heir, but those dreams had faded as time moved on.

Livvy joined the country rock band Juice and was now a successful recording star. Daniel started a property development company and as the money rolled in, they'd made their home in wealthy Orange County.

He spotted Courtney sitting on the front porch steps of the sprawling ranch, twiddling her curls around her fingers. He waved and caught his breath as she jumped up to greet him. She was so pretty, so like Livvy with her blonde hair, blue eyes and petite stature. But Courtney was desperately lonely. Her close friends from school lived too far away to drop in. She needed companionship, a sister to gossip with and share her secrets. *No chance of that*, he thought as she flung her arms around him.

'Hi, sweetie.'

'Hi, Dad.' Courtney sighed into his linen jacket. 'I'm so glad you managed an earlier flight. I missed you.'

'Missed you, too. Mom's home tomorrow, so we'll spend some time together over the next few days.'

'Good! The housekeeper's okay, but not as much fun as you.'

'Is that right, Goldilocks?' He ruffled her curls. 'I'll take a shower and then we'll eat supper and watch an episode of *Friends*.'

'Can we watch the one where Phoebe has her triplets?'

'If you like,' he said, thinking, *thank God Livvy's not home.*

The *Friends'* character was a surrogate mother and he didn't want Livvy reminded of giving her baby away. Things were strained enough as the time of her lost daughter's birthday drew nearer.

* * *

Livvy lay on the huge bed in her plush fifth-floor suite, staring at the ceiling. The final show had been a success and the end-of-tour party, as always, drunken and rowdy. She'd made an excuse to leave after the first hour, claiming a headache. A chauffeured limo had brought her back to the hotel. She'd showered, ordered a tray of English Breakfast Tea and toast and her thoughts turned once more to Harley and Roy.

Since handing their daughter to him, she'd closely followed Roy's band through MTV, and chat shows, where he and his drummer and songwriting partner, Eddie Mellor, were often guests. Her heart still leapt at the sight of Roy, rocking on stage with The Raiders. She shivered, remembering back to that long-ago afternoon when he'd stolen her virginity and the passionate affair that ensued. She could almost taste his kisses; feel his hands on her body. She moaned softly, turned on her side and curled into a tight ball. Daniel had never been able to excite her like Roy had done.

She lay awake for most of the night and climbed out of bed at seven, head thumping. The flight home wasn't until two thirty. She pulled on faded denims, a loose cotton shirt and slipped her feet into trainers. A jog in the hotel's landscaped grounds would help her feel better. She scraped her hair into a ponytail, popped on her shades and set off down the long, carpeted corridor.

Outside, Livvy took a deep breath of the cool early-morning air. The already bright blue sky was peppered with fluffy white clouds. Another hot day looked certain. Back in

Glasgow, it would be cold and wet, maybe even snowing. She jogged along the path at the back of the hotel and towards a man-made lake, where a flock of geese were squabbling. She smiled. Probably males fighting over a female. It wouldn't surprise her if even geese were prone to affairs of the heart. She stopped beside a white-painted bench by the lake and sat down. An overwhelming feeling of loneliness crept over her and tears ran unchecked down her cheeks. Unbeknown to Daniel, she'd recently made steps to try and trace her own natural parents. Until she could find her roots, Livvy was certain she'd never find true contentment with Daniel and Courtney. She wished she was closer to her youngest daughter, but found it hard to show her how much she loved her. She wiped her tears on her shirtsleeve and strolled back to the hotel.

'Message for you, Miss Grant,' the receptionist greeted her. 'Will you please call home?'

'Sure.' Livvy headed for the elevator. What was so important that it couldn't wait till she got back? She sat down on the bed and dialled her home number. 'Danny, what's wrong? Is it Courtney?'

'Nothing's wrong, sweetheart. There's an urgent email for you.'

'Who's it from?'

'Sheena. She wants you to call her as soon as possible.'

'I'll try her now. Thanks, Danny, see you later.'

'Okay, honey. I love you.'

'Yeah, me too.' Livvy hung up with a rush of both excitement and apprehension. Sheena had emailed. That could only mean one thing: news of her birth parents.

Her hand shaking, she dialled her old school friend's Glasgow number and lay back on the pillows.

Sheena answered almost immediately: 'Livvy?'

'How on earth did you know it was me?'

'Because the caller display flashed up International. I don't know anyone else who lives abroad.'

'I see. Well, it's almost eight fifteen in the morning here. Danny just called me with your message.'

'You're not home then?'

'Still in San Francisco. We've just finished the West Coast tour. I'm flying home later. We're taking a six-month break now. So, have you got some news for me?'

'Yes, are you ready for this? I've found your father.'

'Oh my God!' Livvy shot upright and could hear her heart hammering in her ears. 'Are you sure it's really him?'

'Dead sure, Liv! I wouldn't have mailed you otherwise. I placed the ads in the local paper last week as we agreed. Yesterday, I had a call from a woman claiming to be his daughter. She questioned me a little. I think she thought I was you, but pretending not to be, if you know what I mean. I explained that I was trying to trace family for my friend in the States.'

'Oh, Sheena, did you tell her who I am?' Livvy held her breath. If this man was indeed her father, she'd prefer them to meet first without he or his family realising she was famous.

'Course not. I told her that my friend, who was adopted as a wee baby, was looking for her natural parents.'

'What did she say?'

'Well, like I said, at first she thought I was you.'

'And then?'

'Turns out she knows all about you. Your father told her and her brother that his first girlfriend had given birth to a baby girl, who'd been adopted. Afterwards, your mother and her family moved to Canada.'

Livvy wiped her tears with her hand. 'So, I've got a dad and a half-sister and brother?'

'Yes. And you've got cousins, aunts, uncles, a nephew, nieces and a granny to boot! What do you think of that?'

'I can't believe it. Is there any news of my mother?'

'Sort of. Your father knows the whereabouts of her sister, who's back in Glasgow so we can get in touch and see how the land lies. We have to tread carefully though. Your mother may be married and her hubby might not know anything about you.'

'I understand. So, what should I do now?'

Sheena was quiet for a moment. 'I'll ring the family and let them know I've spoken to you. Why don't you come home for a couple of months? Then you can contact them yourself.'

'I'll have to tell Danny about this first, but yes, I see no reason why not. I can take Courtney out of school. I need to spend some time with her, I hardly ever see the poor kid from one week to the next.' Livvy took a deep breath and continued. 'There's someone else I'd like to see when I come to Britain, but I'll explain when we're face to face. It's too risky to tell you over the phone in case there's a crossed line.'

'Sounds intriguing! Will Danny be coming with you?'

'I'd rather he didn't. And the risky thing I mentioned is definitely taboo in front of him.'

'Have you got yourself involved with another man, Liv?'

'You could say that, but it was a long time ago.'

'Who was it? Someone famous? Mick Jagger, Rod Stewart? Oh, come on, tell me, please.'

'Can't tell you now, but I will when I see you. I need to talk about it – I've bottled it up for far too long and it's eating away at me. I'll call you tomorrow from home and let you know what I've decided to do. Can we stay with you? I can keep the visit really low-key then, for everyone's sake.'

'Of course you can.'

'Thanks a million, Sheena. Can't wait to see you again. I'll talk to you tomorrow, goodbye.' Livvy hung up, smiling. The whole thing was amazing and it had been so easy. Why hadn't she done this years ago? Fear of rejection, probably. She imagined the look on her daughter's face when she explained to her that she had a grandpa *and* cousins.

* * *

'Here you go.' Livvy handed Danny a beer and sat down beside him, clutching a glass of white wine. It was her second night home and they were enjoying the cooler air of the late evening on the back porch. They'd eaten supper together as a family and now Courtney had gone off to bed, happy to have both parents under the same roof for a while.

'Are you absolutely sure this guy is your father?' Danny asked.

'Yes. Sheena spoke to his daughter at great length. All the details are correct.'

'So, you're definitely taking a trip to Glasgow?'

Livvy looked at him and then across to the Santa Ana foothills. The setting sun was colour washing everything in a soft red glow. It looked beautiful, so peaceful. On the surface she had everything she'd ever craved – a good and loving man, a pretty and healthy daughter, a successful career and more money than they knew what to do with. But she needed to find her roots.

'I have to, Danny. I hope you understand why.'

'Think I do.' He was quiet for a long moment. 'What about *him*, Harley's father?'

She shrugged. 'What about him? That part of my life's over.'

'You loved him once. I know you still have feelings for him. I see it in your face whenever this time of year comes around. What's there to stop you contacting him? Go home if you must and sort yourself out. If you can't come back and tell me that you love me – and mean it – then there's little point in this marriage continuing.' He stood up and went inside, shoulders hunched.

Livvy finished her drink then followed him indoors to the bedroom, willing herself to show him a little of the tenderness she knew he deserved.

* * *

'More juice, Courtney?' Livvy smiled at her daughter.

'Please, Mom. So... tell me again, how many cousins do I have?'

'Four!' Livvy answered for the umpteenth time. 'Three girls and a boy.'

'*And* I've got a grandpa,' Courtney said softly.

'You have. And *I've* got a dad!' Livvy said, grinning. 'This newfound family will bump up your status at school.'

'Well, I hope they don't reject you both,' Daniel said, emerging from behind his newspaper. 'Because *I* won't be there to mop up your tears and pick up the pieces.'

'There won't be any tears,' Livvy said. 'Why do you always have to be so negative? You were the same when I joined Juice, telling me it would be too much for me. I'm quite capable of running my life, you know. I managed fine before I married you.'

Daniel stood up sharply. His chair screeched on the tiles. 'Did you? If I remember rightly, you were suffering from rejection then. Who picked up *those* pieces and dried *those* tears? It certainly wasn't *him.*'

'Do you have to bring him into every conversation? Courtney, go to your room, please. I need to speak privately to your father.'

Courtney's lips trembled as she looked at her warring parents. 'Can't I stay here, please?'

'No, sweetie. Go and choose your clothes for Scotland. It's going to be very cold. You'll need sweaters, scarves and gloves. Go on, quickly. I'll be up soon to help you.' Livvy pushed her gently towards the door and turned back to Daniel. 'Why did you mention him in front of Courtney? Can't you just leave it?'

He grabbed her arms above the elbow and stared into her eyes. 'When I made love to you last night, you wished I was him, didn't you?' He shook her gently. 'You're *always* wishing that.'

'That's not true.' She wriggled out of his grasp. 'You know why I can't relax – I don't want to get pregnant again.'

'In that case, I'll have a vasectomy.'

'There's no need.' Livvy was touched, but knew she couldn't allow it. It was time they faced up to their floundering marriage. If they divorced, Daniel might want to start another family with a new partner. A vasectomy would put paid to any dreams of him having a longed-for son. Anyway, it wouldn't make any difference; she would still struggle with her feelings. Daniel was tall, blond, blue-eyed and handsome, but she just didn't fancy him physically, no matter how hard she tried. She was grateful he'd helped her pick up the pieces of her life after Roy, but she knew it wasn't fair and a lesser man would have played around before now.

'Another coffee?' he asked, an air of defeat settling around his shoulders.

'No, thanks, Dan. I'll supervise Courtney's packing then we'll exercise the horses before it gets too hot.'

'Okay. I thought the three of us could take the yacht out later. We've only a few more days and then you'll be gone.'

'It's only for a couple of months. I'm coming back, you know.'

He shrugged. 'Maybe you will – maybe you won't.'

2

ASHLEA, CHESHIRE, FEBRUARY 2001

Harley opened her eyes and stretched her arms, cat-like, above her head. Today was Saturday, no school until Monday, and in one week's time she would be sixteen. Grown up at last, she couldn't wait.

She smiled, recalling last night's conversation with her dad when she'd announced she was getting her belly button pierced for her birthday.

'Not a chance!' He'd coughed and spluttered on his single malt.

'Well, I'll have my nose done instead.'

'School will never allow it,' he'd said, looking smug.

'I'll wait till I've left school then. Only four more months and I can do as I please.'

'And that's what *you* think, is it?' he'd said – then, 'Get your ears done instead.'

'Dad... hello!' God, he was naïve at times. She shook her head at him, revealing neat black opals, set in gold drops that swung from her lobes. 'Are you going senile, or what? Remember, you had these made for me in Oz.' She'd spoken slowly, as though to a child. She'd no intention of having any more piercings at the moment, but she loved winding him up. He fell for it every time. She climbed out of bed, pulled on her dressing gown and went downstairs to the kitchen, where her parents were eating breakfast in front of the patio doors.

'Morning.' She slid into a vacant chair next to her dad, helped herself to a glass of orange juice and a slice of toast.

'Morning, darling,' her mum said. 'Do you fancy shopping with me later? I'm meeting Jane and Jess for lunch in Wilmslow.'

'No, thanks, Mum. I'm going into town with Jack to buy a couple of CDs. Can someone give me a lift to his house when I'm dressed?'

'I'll take you,' her dad offered. 'I'm seeing Ed. I'll spend the afternoon with him at Hanover's Lodge and bring you home with me later.'

Harley's heart sank. 'Okay.' Damn it! That would screw up their plans for a romantic afternoon. Jack's house was in the same grounds as Uncle Ed's place. Maybe they could sneak back into Jack's when no one was looking.

Her mum looked across and frowned. 'Are you okay, love? You're looking pale this morning. And is that blood on your dressing-gown sleeve?'

'Yeah. Had a bit of a nosebleed last night. I'm just tired – I watched a scary film then I couldn't get to sleep for ages. I'm okay though.' Harley finished her breakfast and pushed her chair back. 'Right, I'll take a shower. Are you ready to go out, Dad?'

'Not in my boxer shorts and T-shirt,' he replied. 'I'll get ready in a bit.'

* * *

Roy finished his coffee and lit a cigarette. He stood up and held out his arms as Harley sauntered back into the kitchen. 'Come and give me a hug, princess.'

'Put your ciggie down then. I wish you'd pack in smoking, Dad. I hate the smell.'

He stubbed the cigarette out in the ashtray and she went to him. He kissed the top of her head and she did a twirl. 'Do I look okay?'

'Well, you would if you went and put a proper skirt on.' Harley's slender legs were topped with a black leather skirt, shorter than the minis his wife Sammy had worn in the sixties and that was saying something.

'Dad, chill for God's sake!' Harley shrugged and flicked her long dark hair over her shoulders.

'Don't you think it's a bit too cold for that outfit, Harley?' Her mum was more diplomatic. 'Jeans and a sweatshirt will be warmer.'

'But we're going into town, Mum. Everyone dresses up on Saturday to go into town.' Harley turned to face Sammy as Roy exploded behind her.

'Harley, what the bloody hell is that on your arse?'

'What?'

'That, that *thing* on your arse.' He pointed, his face going purple. 'That tattoo!'

'It's a Japanese J… for Jack and it's not on my arse, Dad.'

'Bloody looks like it to me!'

'It's on the top of my leg, for Christ's sake! You're getting to be such an old fogey. And I'm not changing my skirt for you or anyone else.'

'Well, you're not leaving the house dressed like that. I hope you haven't shown Jack that tattoo either!'

Harley stomped out of the kitchen and up the stairs in her clumpy boots. Roy scratched his head and looked bemusedly at Sammy, who smiled, both eyebrows raised in amusement.

'Did you know she'd got that tattoo?'

Sammy nodded. 'It's only henna, it'll fade in time.'

'Oh, right. Well, she can't go out dressed like that – she'll catch her bloody death.'

'You sound like my mother,' Sammy teased. 'I caught many a cold for you in the sixties.' She put her arms around him and gave him a reassuring kiss.

'Well, it was different then,' he said tetchily.

'Why, *what* was so different?'

'You were my girlfriend. *She's* my daughter!'

'And I was Molly's daughter back then,' she reminded him.

'I know. I just worry about her, she's growing up too quick. I promised Livvy I'd always take good care of her, but she runs rings around me now.'

'You *do* take good care of her, Roy, but you have to let her grow up. Jack Mellor's a good lad. I don't think they're getting up to anything. But if they are, well... she knows what's what.' She lowered her voice. 'And talking of Livvy...'

'Don't even go there, Sam!'

'But you promised you'd do it six years ago.'

'I can't do it. Drop the subject.'

'Suit yourself.' Sammy shrugged. 'But the longer you leave it...' she tailed off as he stormed out of the kitchen and slammed the door.

* * *

Jack and Harley turned right at the bottom of the lane instead of left towards the bus stop.

'We'll go into the woods for ten minutes, then sneak around the back and into our house,' Jack said. 'Your dad and my pops won't see us that way and we should be okay for a couple of hours. Then we can go out the back later and round again and walk up the lane like we've been into town.'

'What about the stuff we're supposed to be buying?' Harley said. 'They'll wonder why we've come back empty-handed.'

'It's sorted. I've done a deal with Nathan – he's getting the Green Day CD for you and Eminem's for me. He promised to be back at the house before we leave. I've given him the money and enough for a McDonald's for the favour.'

'You're not so dumb, Jack Mellor.'

'I'm not.' He smiled and slipped his arm around her shoulders as they made their way into the woods. In a small clearing, he took off his parka jacket and spread it out over the remains of a large tree trunk. 'Don't want you getting splinters in the tattoo.'

'Should have heard Dad on his high horse when he saw it.' Harley laughed. 'Gave him the shock of his life.'

Jack grinned. 'Bet it did.' He drew her close. 'I love snogging you, Harley.' He placed a kiss on her lips. She kissed him back and he sighed with pleasure. 'Can't wait for later, hope I don't mess things up.'

'We'll be fine, Jack. If Nathan and Faye can do it, so can we.'

Jack smiled, glad of her reassurance, and kissed her again.

Harley moved out of his arms and glanced at her watch: 'If we walk back slowly to your place, we'll have been more than ten minutes.' She pulled him to his feet and he picked up his jacket. 'It's freezing out here,' she said, shivering.

'I'll soon warm you up,' Jack said. He slung his jacket around her shoulders and took her hand.

* * *

'Do you want Coke or juice?' Jack asked as they stood in the kitchen of his bungalow home. He suddenly felt awkward and sensed it in Harley, too. They'd been planning this since Christmas, but something always got in the way. Nowhere to be private being the main problem. It was a stroke of luck that his mum was out with Harley's mum today.

'Nothing, thanks, Jack.' She slipped off her jacket and hung it over the back of a chair with Jack's parka. 'I'll just nip to the loo.'

Jack hurried into the bedroom he shared with his twin brother, Nathan. He tutted and kicked Nathan's discarded clothes and sports gear over to his side of the room. Mum was always saying the large room should be divided into two bedrooms and today, Jack wished it was. His side was tidy with his books and CDs filed neatly on the shelves. He tweaked the Manchester United duvet cover straight and shook the pillows. What a pity he had to bring Harley in here – it wasn't very romantic and it smelt faintly of Nathan's sweaty socks. He supposed he could borrow one of Mum's scented candles. Then a thought struck him. Dare he...? He hurried back into the hall as Harley came out of the bathroom. He grabbed her hand and smiled.

'What are you doing?' she asked as he opened the door to his parents' bedroom and pulled her inside.

'My room's a tip, thanks to Nathan. Mum and Dad won't know we've been in here if we tidy up later.'

Harley's eyes opened wide as she took in the spacious room with its huge four-poster. 'Nice bed.'

Jack drew the curtains and switched on a bedside lamp that cast a soft, seductive light on the cream satin bedspread. He was thankful the room was at the back of the house and not visible from his grandparents' home. Last thing they needed was Pops and Harley's dad coming to see what was going on in a supposedly empty house. He sat on the bed and pulled Harley down beside him; he held her tight and kissed her. He could feel his heart hammering and she was shaking in his arms. He stroked her hair from her face: 'You nervous?'

'A bit.' She nodded and looked into his eyes. 'Have you got the...?'

'Yeah.' He patted his pocket. 'Slide over and lie down.' He put the condom packet on the bedside table.

She kicked off her boots and lay beside him. He slid his hand under her top and she moaned softly as he caressed her breasts. She ran her hands through his thick, dark curls and reached to pull his T-shirt off. They rolled together, kissing, caressing and slowly undressing each other.

Jack leant up on one elbow and looked into her trusting, brown eyes. He traced round her face with his fingertips and she smiled. She smelt fresh and clean, of talcum powder and her favourite Issey Miyake perfume. Her dark glossy hair fanned the pillows. She was lovely in clothes, but naked here beside him she was beautiful, as he knew she would be. Her skin felt soft and smooth to his touch. He was the luckiest boy in the world to have her. Everyone at school fancied her and he knew Nathan would give his right arm to be in his place now.

He felt breathless and nervous and terrified all at once. What if he made a fool of himself and couldn't do it? He'd never live it down. He willed himself to relax, because it had to be perfect: Harley deserved only the best. Her face, gazing up at him, told him that she was scared, too. They'd petted many times, mainly in the woods, but she'd always stopped him going too far.

Jack rained kisses on her face and over her body. He reached for the condom and Harley helped him roll it on while he held his breath.

'You're still sure?' he whispered.

'Yes,' she whispered back as he lay on top and fumbled to get inside her. He felt all fingers and thumbs, but she helped guide him in. He took a deep breath and moved slowly and then faster as his confidence grew and he realised he wasn't going to come right away.

Harley moved in rhythm and ran her hands up and down his spine. Jack knew he was going to explode soon and when he couldn't fight the feeling any longer, he cried out and told her that he loved her. She nibbled his ears and told him over and over that she loved him too. He rolled off and lay flat on his back, staring at the ceiling while his heart stopped hammering and his breathing became normal.

'Jack, are you okay?' Harley was prodding his shoulder. 'You were in a trance,' she added as he turned and flung his arms around her.

Lost for words, he shook his head, feeling almost tearful. He wanted to spend forever just lying here and holding her. 'That was the most wonderful thing that ever happened to me,' he mumbled into her shoulder.

'Aw, Jack. It was for me too.' She stroked his cheek and they lay in one another's arms for a few more minutes. 'We'd better make a move and get out of here in case your mum comes home early,' she said, eventually.

He groaned. 'Yeah, I suppose we had. Nathan will be back soon, too.' He reached over and grabbed a handful of tissues from the bedside table. He sat up and his euphoric mood vanished instantly: 'Oh no!'

'What?'

'Shit!'

'What's wrong?'

'The condom's leaking. Fuck, it's split!'

Harley stared at him, her eyes wide. 'No! Are you sure?'

'Yes.'

'Oh God, Jack.' She burst into tears. 'What can we do?'

He shook his head. 'Don't know.'

'Well, think of something, quick!'

He chewed his lower lip for a long moment. 'Nathan told me Faye took the morning after pill when they took a chance.'

'Where did she get it from?'

'Aunt Kate got it for her.'

'Call her then, see if she can help us.'

* * *

Jack pulled on his clothes and left the room. He came back with his mobile phone and dialled his aunt's number while Harley got dressed.

'Aunt Kate, it's Jack. Where are you?'

'On my way home,' Kate replied.

'Come straight to our house but hurry, before Mum comes back from shopping and don't say anything to Pops and Uncle Roy if you see them first. I'm not supposed to be here, you see.'

'Sounds mysterious! Be with you in five.'

'She'll be here soon,' he told Harley, who nodded and wiped her eyes.

Jack hurriedly straightened the bedspread, turned off the lamp and opened the curtains. He led Harley through to the lounge and they sat huddled together on the sofa.

There was a tap at the back door and Kate walked in. 'Hello, you two. What's wrong?'

Jack told her what had happened. 'Please can you help us?'

Kate sat down next to Harley. 'You'll need to take the morning after pill.'

'I can't go to the doctor,' Harley wailed. 'Can you get it for us?'

Kate nodded. 'Yes, but not until tonight. Jack will have to give it to you tomorrow. You'll need to take it within 72 hours. Why don't you wait till you grow up a bit more before you do this again?' She looked pointedly at Jack, who hung his head. 'Uncle Roy will annihilate you if he finds out and your mum and dad won't be too pleased, either. You told me that you're not supposed to be here, Jack. So where exactly *are* you supposed to be?'

'Shopping,' Harley sniffed, 'in town.'

'Right, get in my car and we'll go across to The Lodge together and you can say I picked you up on the lane.'

* * *

'Thanks, Ed.' Roy took the mug of coffee from his mate and swung his legs down off the mixing desk. He'd been deep in thought, absent-mindedly blowing smoke rings into the air.

'You okay, Roy?' Eddie asked. 'Got something on your mind?'

'What? Not really. Well, actually... yeah, I have.' Roy stubbed his half-finished cigarette out in the overflowing ashtray.

'I'll take a guess. Harley's forthcoming birthday?'

Roy nodded. 'Sammy was giving me earache again this morning, saying I should tell her about Livvy.'

'Sammy's right. You've got to do it, and soon.'

'I'm scared of her reaction, Ed. She's a volatile little monkey at the best of times. I tell you, when she stands in front of me with her arms folded, giving me what for, it takes me back to that night Livvy took exactly the same stance and refused to have a termination. She has the same defiant air, not to mention the guts to put *me* in my rightful place.'

'Are you still worried she'll reject you?'

'Terrified, it would destroy me. I love that kid to bits.'

'And *she* loves you. But the longer you leave it, the more it'll hurt. You made a promise to Livvy that you'd tell Harley the truth when she was ten,' Eddie reminded him. 'I'm surprised Livvy hasn't made it her business to get in touch when she's toured Britain. At least she's honoured *her* part of the deal. Can I ask you something? Tell me to back off if you like.'

'Ask away, Ed.'

'Do you still have feelings for Livvy? Are you frightened of re-opening old wounds?'

Roy stood up and walked over to the window. He stared as Kate's silver Peugeot 206 hurtled up the lane. 'Your Katie's in a hurry!'

'It's Kate now and she always is. Stop changing the subject.'

Turning, Roy nodded slowly. 'What if Harley wants to meet her? What then, for me, I mean? If I clap eyes on Livvy Grant, I might do something stupid. I love Sammy – you know that, I always have. But Livvy did things to my head that no woman's ever done before.'

Eddie groaned and shook his head. 'Roy, you can't get involved with Livvy again. Besides, she's happily married to that property magnate and she's got another daughter. You saw the spread in *Hello!* magazine last year.'

'Yeah, I remember – happy families! She and Danny looked the perfect golden couple, posing on the yacht. Harley will be sure to want a slice of their lifestyle.'

'Well, she's already used to the good life. She's not been deprived of anything.'

'I suppose you're right.' At the sound of crunching gravel, Roy looked out the window again and smiled. 'Here she comes, the cause of my grey hairs! Kate must have picked her and Jack up on the lane. Shall we call it a day, Ed? I haven't been a very productive partner this afternoon.'

'No problem, I'll see you at yours tonight. You'll feel better after a couple of single malts.'

'Alright, you two?' Roy greeted Harley and Jack as they strolled into the music room, clutching the CDs Nathan had just arrived home with. 'Get everything you want? You look a bit pale again, Harley. Don't you feel well, love?'

'Dad, stop fussing. I'm cold, that's all. And don't start moaning about me wrapping up warm either!'

'Okay. It's only because I care about you. Where's that bruise come from on the back of your leg?'

Harley looked down and studied the large purple bruise. She shook her head. 'Don't know, it wasn't there earlier. Must have banged into something.'

'See you tomorrow, Harley.' Jack kissed her chastely on the cheek and squeezed her hand. 'Try not to worry,' he mouthed as Roy turned his back for a second.

'You ready?' Roy turned back to Harley. 'Let's get you home, see if your mother's spent all my money. Come for lunch tomorrow, Jack. Sammy's promised roast beef and Yorkshire pudding.'

'Thank you,' Jack mumbled, looking down at his feet.

'Cheer up, mate,' Eddie said and ruffled his grandson's hair. 'You look like you've got the world on your shoulders.'

3

Jack polished off the last roast potato and leant back in the chair with a contented sigh. He was feeling mellow from the glass of red wine he'd been allowed. 'That was lovely, Aunt Sammy.' He smiled and patted his stomach.

'Thank you, Jack. More beef?' Sammy held out a thick slice of top rump over his plate.

'No, thanks, I'm stuffed!' He felt much better for eating the huge Sunday lunch. His nerves, and the inner terror he'd felt when he arrived earlier, sure that Uncle Roy would see the guilt written in his eyes, had gone.

Harley's greeting had been strained at first but thanks to the wine she appeared to be in a more relaxed frame of mind, laughing and joking with her brother Jason and his partner, Jules. She turned to smile at Jack and he smiled back.

'You two go and play some records while we old folks relax,' Uncle Roy suggested. He poured himself a fourth glass of red wine and gestured the bottle towards Jason and Jules.

Jack silently thanked God for alcohol. He'd seen Uncle Roy down a couple of large single malts prior to lunch, which had obviously helped.

'You mean in my bedroom?' Harley said.

'Well, we don't want Green Day on down here.'

'Okay, c'mon, Jack.'

Jack scraped back his chair and stood up quickly, before Uncle Roy changed his mind.

'By the way, Dad,' Harley called over her shoulder, 'we in the modern world don't call them records any more, they're compact discs! And *you* a recording artist, too!'

'Cheeky little madam! Get out of here before I make you sit in the lounge and listen to The Raiders!'

* * *

Jason chose that moment to make an announcement: 'Dad, Mum, Jules and I have something to tell you.'

Sammy put down her glass and touched his hand. 'What is it, son?'

'We're going to be parents,' he announced.

Roy spluttered into his wine goblet. Sammy removed the glass from his hand and slapped him hard on the back, digging her fingernails warningly into his spine.

'You're what?' Roy choked, his eyes watering as he got to his feet.

'You heard,' Jason replied, looking him directly in the eye.

'Well, who, err... how? Oh fuck, you know what I mean!'

'Roy!' Sammy said. 'Don't be so personal, it doesn't matter how. Which of you is the father?'

'I am, Mum,' Jason replied proudly.

'Oh, Jason!' Her eyes filled with tears. 'When's the baby due?'

'Beginning of November. We only found out for sure this week. I wanted to wait for the right time to tell you, which isn't always easy.' He raised an eyebrow in his father's direction. 'Our surrogate's six weeks.'

'Who *is* the surrogate?' Sammy asked. 'You *have* vetted her properly?'

'Of course. She knows about Dad's band and having to keep things private and all that stuff,' Jason replied. 'Her name's Elena. She's twenty-eight, dark-haired with brown eyes. In fact, she has Italian blood like Dad and me, so she's a pretty good match. We've known of her for quite a while – she had a little boy for friends of ours four years ago and a baby girl last year for friends of theirs.'

'For fuck's sake, what is she, a one-woman baby factory!' Roy sat down heavily and poured another red.

Jason ignored the comments. 'She'll live with us until the baby's born. Her name will appear on the birth certificate and so will mine. But then Jules and I will raise the child. Just like you brought Harley up for *him*, Mum.'

The jibe washed over Roy and he smiled. 'You've got it all planned, haven't you, son? Well, good luck. I'm very pleased for you both. Hope it all goes smoothly. Dare I ask... did she use a turkey baster?'

'Roy, how could you?' Sammy groaned.

'It's okay, Mum. He might as well know and then he'll shut up about it. Yes, she did, but don't you *dare* embarrass her when you meet her or I'll never, ever forgive you.'

'I won't. I'm thrilled, honestly. We'll have a flesh-and-blood grandchild. That's something your mother never thought she would have. Isn't that right, sweetheart?'

Sammy nodded, blinking away tears. 'I can't believe it. I'm so proud of you, Jason.'

'Can I just ask how you decided which of you was to be the father?' Roy asked.

'If you must.' Jason sighed. 'We took a turn each. Jules was first, but it didn't work. This month it was my turn – I was lucky.'

'Bad luck, Jules old son, you must be firing blanks! Our Jason might be gay, but he's still got that good old Cantello—'

'Roy, get in the lounge and don't you dare open your mouth again!' Sammy dragged him mid-sentence from his chair and pushed him towards the door.

'But I was only...' he began, as Sammy raised her fist. 'I'm joking, Sam, honestly.' He ran from the room as she turned to face Jason and Jules.

'I'm sorry, boys. I know he's a pain in the arse but you just wait till the baby arrives, he'll be the proudest grandpa in the world.'

* * *

Jack lay on Harley's bed, watching her chew the ends of her hair as she paced up and down.

'You'll wear a hole in the carpet. Come and lie beside me.' He patted the bright yellow and orange patterned duvet cover.

'I can't relax with you,' she said.

He leant up on one elbow. 'Why not? You're usually *very* relaxed when we're together so what's changed?'

She shot him a meaningful look. 'Do you really need to ask? You know what's changed. We're lovers now, remember?'

Jack nodded. 'So, what difference does it make? Apart from the mess we might be in, of course?'

'Well, you won't want to settle for a kiss and cuddle any more. I'm not sure I can do it again after what happened yesterday,' she replied, tears filling her eyes.

'Harley, no, you're wrong. *I* don't want to do it again either. Not for a while anyway. I'm just as happy to kiss and cuddle like we did before.'

She sat down beside him. 'Honestly?' She bent to kiss him.

'Harley, look at that huge bruise on your thigh!' Jack exclaimed, as her skirt rode up.

'I know. It's nearly as big as my hand. I've got that one on my leg as well – it's shaped like a map of India. I thought maybe I'd banged it on your bed yesterday, but I don't remember doing it.' She studied the mottled, purple and red bruises. 'It's a mystery where they've come from.'

'You don't think it's anything to do with the pills, do you?' Jack asked.

'I doubt it. I only took the first pill when you gave it to me four hours ago and I already had one bruise. I'll ask Faye tomorrow if she got any.'

'Give me another kiss then and we'll put yesterday behind us.' Jack held out his arms and she moved into them.

* * *

On Wednesday afternoon Jack was loitering outside the girls' changing rooms at Manor Banks School, hoping to see Harley, when he heard Faye Blackwell shouting. She ran out into the corridor.

'Jack, go get the nurse, quick! Harley's fainted.' She dashed back inside before he could reply. Jack hurried down the corridor, hammered on the sick-room door and, when the nurse appeared, babbled out what had happened.

He followed on the nurse's heels, but stayed outside the changing rooms. Boys weren't allowed in under any circumstances. He leant against the corridor wall, his stomach in knots. Faye came out to find him. She told him they'd just finished playing a hockey match and Harley had complained of feeling queasy and breathless, then passed out when they came back indoors.

'What's wrong with her?' Jack whispered. 'Do you think it's the pills, or could she be pregnant?'

'I don't know,' Faye whispered back. '*I* was okay when I

took them. Surely she wouldn't be fainting after only five days, even if she *were* pregnant?'

'Oh God, I feel faint myself,' Jack muttered.

'Stop being such a wimp, Jack. Maybe she's ill or something. She had another nosebleed this morning and her legs are covered in strange bruises.'

'I know,' he said. 'She looks like she's been kicked by a donkey.'

The nurse appeared behind them, making them both jump.

'Mr Cantello is on his way to collect Harley. I suggest that you both get ready to go home – the dismissal bell rang five minutes ago.'

They nodded and walked down the long corridor.

'I'd make myself scarce if I were you,' Faye said. 'Harley's dad might be suspicious about why she fainted.'

Jack needed no second telling. He caught up with his brother in the playground and told him what had happened to Harley.

'Oh fuck, Jack!' Nathan exclaimed. 'Girls usually only faint and feel queasy for one reason. Maybe those pills didn't work.'

'She took them on Monday and they hadn't worked up until lunchtime today,' Jack said. 'Here's Mum.' He waved as the family Jeep came into view.

'Hi, boys. Jack, you look worried. You okay, son?' Jess said as Roy's BMW screeched to a halt and he leapt out. 'Roy, what are *you* doing here? I thought Harley was coming home with us?'

'I got a call. She's been taken ill, talk to you later.' He sprinted across the playground and disappeared through the entrance door.

'I wonder what's wrong. Get in the car, I won't be a minute.' Jess hurried after Roy and disappeared inside the school.

* * *

Jack stared out of the window as Jess came outside, followed by an angry-looking Roy, who was supporting Harley. His mum climbed into the Jeep and looked directly at him, her face pale and pinched. 'I think we need to have a word, don't you?' She started up the engine and headed towards home, her fingers gripping the steering wheel so tight that her knuckles were white.

Jack sat silent and terrified. Something must have been said. Why else would Mum look and sound so furious? Nathan, next to him, rolled his eyes and drew his hand across his throat. Jess pulled up outside their home and said, 'Inside, both of you.'

They followed her indoors and sat side by side on the sofa. She stood in front of them, arms folded across her chest. 'It would appear that Harley has taken some form of drug. Do you two know anything about this? If I find you've been taking anything at all, and I mean *anything*, I'll kill the pair of you! Do you understand?'

They nodded meekly.

'So, what did she take? Ecstasy or something?'

Jack shook his head.

'Well, in that case, Jack, what was it? Roy and Sammy need to know. Harley will probably have to see a doctor.'

Jack tried to speak but his words stumbled over one another.

'What? Speak up, Jack. If you know which drugs Harley has taken then for God's sake tell me.'

'The morning a-a-after pill,' he stuttered, not daring to look her in the eye.

She sat down heavily on the opposite sofa. 'The what?'

'The morning after pill,' Nathan repeated for Jack, who could feel himself shaking from head to toe.

'Yes, Nathan, thank you. I heard what he said, I just can't believe it. How *could* you, Jack? When did this happen?'

'Saturday afternoon,' Jack muttered, dry-mouthed. He stared down at the scuffed toes of his school shoes.

'I thought you went into Stockport with Harley on Saturday afternoon?'

'We came back here when you went out,' he admitted.

'You stupid, careless boy – after everything your father's told you about safe sex!'

'No, Mum, I wasn't careless,' Jack protested. 'I used a condom. It split. Honestly. We were really scared. Aunt Kate got the pills for Harley, but they haven't worked yet,' he finished, biting his lips.

Jess shook her head. 'Bloody hell, Jack, you're only fifteen and a half! Christ Almighty, your father will go mad!'

He nodded. 'I know. Do you think the pills have made Harley ill? She had a nosebleed today and her legs are full of bruises. Could they cause all that?'

'I don't know. Maybe Harley's anaemic or something. Whatever, she'll still need to see a doctor. I'm going to have to tell Roy what you've told me, I'm afraid.'

'No, please, Mum, he'll kill me, he really will!'

'He won't, but he'll be very angry with you. I suggest you keep out of his way for a few days. He'll be relieved to know that Harley hasn't taken any dangerous drugs.'

'Mum, what if Harley's pregnant, what'll we do?' Jack asked. 'She said she'd be too scared to tell her parents.'

'God only knows! Was that the first time?'

He nodded. 'First and last, probably.'

'Oh, Jack, what will I do with you?' Jess turned to Nathan. 'Now, if it had been you...'

'Yeah, well it wasn't me, was it?' Nathan leapt to his own defence.

'If you jumped in a barrel of manure, Nathan, you'd end up smelling of perfume. If I find out you've been having sex with that Faye girl, you'll be grounded, my lad! Now get to your room, both of you. You're grounded tonight so I can keep my eye on you.'

'But I'm seeing Faye tonight,' Nathan protested. 'It's not fair. Why should I suffer just 'cos he's made a mistake?'

'Your room, Nathan, now,' his mum yelled at the top of her voice. 'Don't you dare speak to me like that again.'

'Okay, okay, I'm going. Keep your wig on!' He stomped off down the hall, glowering at his mother. Jack shuffled slowly behind him, head bent with shame.

* * *

'What was all that about?' Eddie had let himself in at the front door while Jess was in full flow.

'Oh, thank God you're here.' She burst into tears. He put his arms around her and held her close.

'What is it, sweetheart? The boys playing you up?' Eddie led her to the sofa and sat her down. He sat beside her, his arm around her shoulders. 'Come on, Jess, tell your old dad what's wrong. I just got back from the studio. Roy had to dash away – he got a call from the school. Do you know what it was all about?'

Jess nodded, sniffing. 'Harley fainted after a hockey game. She felt breathless and queasy, and then passed out.'

'Hell! Is she okay?'

'She told the nurse she'd taken some pills. The nurse assumed it was drugs, Ecstasy or something. I tackled those two when I got them home, thinking *they'd* know what she'd taken.'

'And did they?'

'Oh, they knew alright. She's only taken the bloody morning after pill!'

'What? Why?'

'Why do you think? She and Jack had sex on Saturday afternoon. Here of all places. Almost under yours and Roy's noses!'

'But they went out on Saturday. I saw them go and they

arrived back with Kate later. They were never on their own for
any length of time.'

'They sneaked back home when you obviously weren't looking. To give them their due, they used a condom, but it split.
Kate got the pills for Harley. Now she's ill and the pills haven't
worked. Jack's frantic in case she's pregnant. I don't know how
the hell I'm going to tell Roy all this, or Jon for that matter.'

'I'll go and see Roy, explain it to him. You go and have a cup
of tea with your mum, tell her what's happened.' He smiled and
kissed her on the cheek. 'And don't worry, love, hopefully Jack
won't make you a grandmother yet.'

'Oh my God, don't!' Jess exclaimed.

'Hey, *you* should worry! What about me? Great Grandpops
Mellor... Now that would do absolutely nothing for my street
cred as a rock drummer.'

* * *

Sammy opened the door to Eddie and led him into the lounge,
where a tearful Harley lay on one of the sofas. Roy glanced up,
a look of defeat on his face.

'Have a seat, Ed.' Roy gestured to the sofa. He poured two
single malts and handed one to Eddie.

'Thanks. I've just left Jess and the boys,' Eddie began,
sitting down next to Roy.

Roy nodded. 'You can tell Jack he's off the hook. Sammy got
a pregnancy testing kit for Harley after she told us which pills
she'd taken. Thankfully it was negative. Not that it excuses her
actions after we trusted her. She's grounded for a month and
she's banned from seeing Jack.'

'No, Dad, you can't do that,' Harley wailed. 'You can't treat
me like a kid any more. I love Jack, I keep telling you it wasn't
his fault. I hate you for this.'

'Harley, for God's sake, you're only fifteen, so is Jack!'

'I'm sixteen on Saturday,' she cried. 'I can get married and have kids quite legally then. And we can always wait until Jack's sixteen too. You don't have a leg to stand on, Dad. I'll leave home if I have to!'

'Roy, stop, you're upsetting her,' Sammy said. 'Oh no, her nose is bleeding again!' She sat beside Harley, holding a wad of tissues to her nose as blood spurted down the front of her white T-shirt. 'This can't be because of those pills. I've never heard of them doing this before, and just look at those bruises. Some of them are fresh today. Call the doctor, Roy. I'm getting worried now, she's been pale and tired for weeks. I just put it down to her age, like you do,' she told Eddie, as Roy left the room.

'Hmm, it's a bit of a worry,' he agreed. 'She should definitely see someone.'

4

GLASGOW, FEBRUARY 2001

Livvy scanned the faces in the crowded arrivals hall at Glasgow Airport and soon spotted Sheena, who was jumping up and down and waving her arms. 'There she is,' she said, waving back. After much hugging and kissing, Livvy and Courtney followed Sheena to her waiting car and lifted the luggage into the boot.

'Thought you'd have loads more stuff than this, a big star like you,' Sheena teased.

'I travel light whenever I can,' Livvy said, grinning. 'I only wear the Dolly Parton gear on stage – I live in shorts and T-shirts back home. Anyway, Courtney and I plan to go clothes shopping, don't we, honey?'

Sheena laughed as they climbed into her Fiat Punto and headed for the Glasgow suburb of Dennistoun. Courtney yawned loudly from the back seat.

'You tired, sweetie? You can have a sleep when we get to Sheena's.'

'Your rooms are ready and waiting, so you can both have a sleep if you like,' Sheena offered. She put her foot down as they left the city behind.

* * *

Livvy gazed out of the window at the lush green fields, dotted here and there with woolly sheep and gambolling lambs. Even in early spring, Scotland was greener than most of America, the air much fresher. It was good to see familiar sights again and she felt her spirits lift. 'Sheena, you still drive like a madwoman.' Her friend's handling of the bends did not involve slowing down in any way.

'Och, you know me, I'm a frustrated Formula 1 driver.' Sheena grinned. 'Oh, it's so good to see you again, Liv. You look really different when you're not all dolled up on stage.'

Livvy smiled. 'I've left Livvy Grant, the singer, behind and brought Livvy McVey, housewife and mother, on vacation.'

'You sound like Dame Edna.' Sheena chuckled. 'I've arranged for you to see your family tomorrow afternoon. They're meeting at your sister Leanne's house for tea at three.'

'Can't wait to meet my grandpa,' Courtney said excitedly.

Livvy looked at her animated face. 'Nor can I, honey.'

'Leanne told me he's really excited,' Sheena continued. 'He's been in touch with your mother's sister and she'd like you to contact her while you're here.'

'Really? Do you think there's a chance I might get to meet my mother?'

'She's still in Canada, so you'll have to wait and see about that. Your family don't have a clue about your fame. Because your adoption was private, your father knew your adoptive parents were called Grant, but he's no idea you're now called Olivia. He still thinks of you as Marie, the name he gave you. It's sad, giving a baby away and missing out on all sorts of things. It would have finished me off if I'd had to part with my two, even though they're now driving me crazy with their noise and messy bedrooms.'

Livvy nodded, silently staring ahead at the road in front.

'What is it, Liv? You're white as a sheet.'

'Tell you later,' she muttered, inclining her head back towards Courtney.

'Okay.' Sheena took a left turn into a road of sandstone Victorian villas. 'Here we are.' She pulled onto the drive of a detached house and turned to Courtney. 'I hope you don't mind dogs? We've two Labradors, Sandy and Fred. They're very friendly, but a bit licky and always overpowering at the first meeting.'

Courtney's face lit up. 'I love dogs. I always wanted a puppy, but our housekeeper has an allergy to fur.'

'Housekeeper?' Sheena raised an eyebrow.

'Yeah.' Livvy nodded. 'Mainly a gem, but sometimes a pain in the butt!'

'I see. Still, there's compensation in not doing your own ironing and cleaning.'

'Mrs Grayson doesn't either,' Courtney chipped in. 'She does the cooking and looks after me when Mom and Dad are away. The maid cleans and irons, but she doesn't live at the ranch with us.'

'Bloody hell, it's another world!' Sheena exclaimed. 'And to think we used to share a manky flat and sing duets in pubs to make ends meet before you did your disappearing act.'

The front door opened and two golden Labradors bundled out, tails wagging furiously. A frenzy of barking accompanied the wags at the sight of Sheena and her guests.

A tall, clean-shaven, ginger-haired man followed the dogs down the steps and he wrapped his arms around Livvy, green eyes twinkling. 'Well, hello, hen! It's really good to see you again, and you too, Courtney. My goodness you're all grown up! You were only a wee girl when we last visited.'

'Hi, Gerry. It's good to see you, too.' Livvy's eyes filled with tears as she gazed up at Sheena's husband, Daniel's best mate from college days.

'Come away indoors,' Sheena said. 'Gerry will bring the bags in.'

Livvy and Courtney followed Sheena down a narrow hallway to the back of the house, which opened up into a comfortable kitchen and family room. Livvy looked through the French doors that overlooked the landscaped garden.

'How lovely, just look at the colourful crocus,' she said to Courtney. 'We don't have anything so delicate as those at home, do we?'

Courtney shook her head. She rested her hand on Fred's golden head as he stood beside her, tail thumping against her legs. 'Such pretty colours.'

'I'll show you to your rooms and then you can freshen up before we eat. The kids will be home from school any minute, demanding food like they've not been fed for years. By the way, they've been threatened with their lives to keep your visit a secret. Cassie's your age, Courtney, and Robbie's fourteen. That wasn't very good planning was it? Only ten months between them!'

'Like Nick and Jason,' Livvy said quietly.

'Nick and Jason who?'

'They're the sons of an old friend of mine. They were also born ten months apart.'

She was saved from having to answer any more questions about Roy Cantello's sons as Fred and Sandy began a barking contest. The front door opened and Sheena smiled.

'Here they are. This is Cassie.' She introduced a petite, dark-haired, blue-eyed girl, the image of herself. 'And this big fellow here is Robbie.' A young, lanky version of Gerry grinned at them. 'Take Courtney to her room and we'll follow in a minute.'

Cassie smiled at Courtney in a friendly manner and led her away up the stairs.

* * *

'What a fabulous room,' Livvy said, sinking into the deep cushions of a red leather sofa. She'd seen a very jet-lagged Courtney off to bed and joined Sheena and Gerry for drinks in the lounge. 'It's so cosy and warm. Not like my place, all white and open-plan.'

The room, with cream walls, stripped-pine floor, colourful rug and blazing coal fire, was a haven of comfort. She kicked off her shoes. Gerry handed Livvy and Sheena a G&T each and helped himself to a glass of whisky.

'Cheers, girls. I know you two have a lot to talk about. I'll join you for this drink and then I'll go and play on my computer for a few hours.'

'Thanks, Gerry.' Sheena smiled. 'For being so understanding, I mean.'

'That's me all over,' he said as the phone rang. He grabbed the receiver. 'Oh, hi there,' he answered. 'How are you, pal?' He handed Livvy the phone: 'Danny.'

Livvy assured Daniel that she and Courtney were fine. The tone of her voice was less than friendly and she saw Sheena and Gerry exchange looks of concern. She finished her call, hung up and downed the last of her drink.

Gerry served up fresh G&Ts before leaving the room.

As he closed the door behind him, Livvy felt Sheena's eyes on her.

'You seem troubled, Livvy. Why don't you tell me what's going on between you and Dan?'

'We're not getting along too well,' Livvy admitted. She picked up her handbag from beside the sofa and took out a pale-blue envelope, which she placed on her lap.

'I gathered that,' Sheena said. 'Is he sulking because you've come to find your family?'

'Kind of. But my birth family isn't my only link with

Britain.' She pulled a document from the envelope and handed it to Sheena, who frowned as she studied it.

'A birth certificate?'

'Yes,' Livvy said. 'My daughter's birth certificate.'

Sheena's eyes registered shocked surprise. 'Not Courtney's then?'

'No, it's Harley's. She's my first child, born sixteen years ago this week. Saturday, to be precise.'

'Well, where is she? What have you done with her?' Sheena was wide-eyed. 'Why have you never mentioned her?'

'I left her in Cheshire with her father and his wife – they brought her up for me.'

'Who *is* her father?'

'Look at the name.'

'Roy Cantello. Musician! Roy Cantello? The Raiders' Roy Cantello?'

'The very same,' Livvy replied. She passed the dog-eared colour photograph she always carried across to Sheena. 'You couldn't mistake her for being anyone else's child, could you?'

'God no, she's the spit of him though her face is heart-shaped like yours. Oh, Liv, she's so beautiful. You must have missed her like crazy. Why on earth didn't you bring her back here to Glasgow when you left Manchester? I would have helped you look after her. How long is it since you last saw her?' Sheena's questions tumbled over one another.

'I didn't think I was capable of bringing her up on my own,' Livvy replied. 'I thought it best that she had a stable home and two parents. I haven't seen her since she was five days old.'

'That's awful,' Sheena gasped. 'How on earth did a timid mouse like *you* get involved with the likes of Roy Cantello? I used to think he was drop-dead gorgeous. He still is, even though he's getting on a bit now. You hardly ever mentioned your time in Manchester, is that why?'

'It was too painful to talk about. I'll tell you what happened, but please don't think too badly of me – I did what I thought was the right thing at the time.'

Sheena refilled their glasses and sat back on the sofa as Livvy began her tale.

'You remember my adoptive father Joe Grant did time for Actual Bodily Harm against me?'

Sheena nodded.

'When I heard he'd been released and was looking for me I upped and left, getting the first train out of Glasgow. It was Manchester bound and I ended up at Piccadilly in the early hours. That was March 1984. Joe's mother had died the previous year and she left me five grand in her will so I knew I'd be okay for a while. I sat on a station bench until it got light, then I found myself a B&B in the city centre. Later, I walked down the main street and saw a sales assistant's job advertised in the window of Flanagan and Grey's Record Emporium. I spoke to Sean Grogan, a nice Irishman, and he offered me the job in the record department. Then I got a train to Stockport, a few miles outside Manchester. An estate agent took me to view a small flat. I signed the lease, bought some furniture, moved in at the weekend and started my new job on the Monday.' Livvy paused for breath and she and Sheena sipped their drinks.

'Jon Mellor was working alongside me. He was lovely. Chatted me up and took me under his wing. He and his half-sister Jess had a band called The Zoo with their mates, Nick and Jason. When he realised I could sing, Jon invited me to a rehearsal one night at his home. Me, being totally thick, didn't realise until I got to the house that Eddie Mellor, The Raiders' drummer, was Jon and Jess's dad. I also had no idea that Nick and Jason were Roy Cantello's sons.

'They were all so normal and down to earth, never bragging about their dads' fame or wealth. Roy was also there that night. He and Ed encouraged me to sing with The Zoo and it sounded brilliant. The boys wanted me in but Jess wasn't happy about it.

Then a few weeks later, she and I had words because she thought I was after Nick – she was so jealous over him. I was upset and realised my singing with them wasn't going to work out, which was a shame as Roy and Ed had written a few songs with *my* voice in mind. Tell me if I'm boring you.'

'You're not! Carry on.'

'I'd gone in Jon's car that night, so Roy gave me a lift back to my place and invited himself in for coffee. We sat and talked for a while, then he made a pass and kissed me. He was very upset afterwards – he practically ran out of my flat, apologising. I couldn't stop thinking about him, the kiss, the way I'd felt when he touched me. It was like an electric shock. I can't begin to explain.'

Sheena nodded, scarcely breathing while Livvy was telling her tale.

'Roy must have felt something too, because he called me first thing the following morning and invited me to lunch. That was my cue to say no, but I didn't. We drove to a place called Castleton. Honestly, I felt like a queen, out in a posh car with a handsome and famous man. We had lunch in a little country pub and he bought me a beautiful teddy bear from a craft shop – I still have him at home.

'We went back to my flat and made love all afternoon. It was my first time and I was so glad I'd waited. Roy was a wonderful lover. I can't begin to tell you, it was like flying to the moon and back!'

Sheena sighed and rolled her eyes. 'God, lucky you!'

'We began seeing one another as often as we could. The Raiders had disbanded then and Roy had lots of free time. He and Ed were still writing songs. They had loads of hits in the eighties. That Perry's Dream group had two number ones for them the year of our affair. I can never hear those songs without being transported right back to that time. Anyway, Roy told me he loved me, but he also loved his wife and couldn't leave her.'

'Why didn't you get out then while you could?' Sheena asked, frowning.

'It wasn't that simple, I was completely under his spell.'

'Who else knew about the affair?'

'Only Ed. He told Roy to end it. Nick was eighteen that May. Roy bought him a car. Nick and Jess got engaged that summer. At the end of August, Nick crashed the car. Jess was badly injured and Nick died. That same week I discovered I was pregnant. I couldn't tell Roy because he and Sammy were in bits about their son so I told Ed.

'Anyway, to cut a long story short, Roy and Sammy split up. He said he wanted to be with me but he was back and forth between us until in the end she forgave him and they re-took their marriage vows.'

'My God! She must be a saint. I'd have castrated him.' Sheena poured them more drinks and threw another log on the fire. She settled back down. 'Carry on. This beats *EastEnders* any day!'

'During all the upheaval The Raiders re-formed. They were busy recording new songs and rehearsing for their tour. I went to stay with my boss Sean and his wife Tina until the baby was due. Before Roy and Sammy re-took their vows, I asked them if they'd be willing to bring up the baby as their own. I couldn't handle the thought of being a single mum, I believe a child should always have two parents if possible. To my surprise, they agreed to take the child and pass it off as Sammy's.

'Harley was born the night of their first show in Manchester. My waters broke in the theatre hospitality room. I'd been in labour all night but I didn't want to miss the show – I wanted our baby to share Daddy's return to the stage. When the group sang "My Special Girl", I'm sure Harley decided she couldn't wait any longer.' Livvy smiled, remembering the night as though it were yesterday.

'I used to love that song,' Sheena said dreamily. 'I always felt as though Roy was singing it just for me alone.'

'Roy and Eddie wrote that song for Jane and Sammy while the group was on its first tour.'

'How romantic! Anyway, carry on. Did they get an ambulance and rush you to hospital with blue lights flashing, or did you deliver behind the drum kit?'

'Neither.' Livvy laughed. 'Ed's wife Jane drove us all to the hospital, only we didn't make it. Harley arrived on the back seat of the Jeep. Jane delivered her, with Sammy and Roy as an audience!'

'Oh, Jesus Christ, Olivia!' Sheena gasped.

'Roy fainted clean away as the ambulance arrived. I handed Sammy her new daughter. The joy in her eyes outweighed the pain I'd seen on previous occasions. I had no doubts that Harley would be adored and pampered all her life – it was far more than *I* could give her at the time.

'I signed an agreement that I would keep quiet. I accepted fifty thousand pounds from Roy as a one-off payment. I've kept the secret to myself ever since. No one knows outside of Roy's close circle. I told Danny I had a daughter who'd been adopted by a wealthy couple. He has no idea who the father is. Whenever we have an argument, which is most of the time these days, he throws Harley's father in my face. He's convinced I'm going to search for her *and* him now I'm home. But I don't need to search, I know exactly where to find both my daughter and Roy.'

'So, have you plans to see them?' Sheena asked.

'Yes.' Livvy nodded slowly. 'Roy promised me that he would tell Harley about me when she was ten years old. She's never been in touch, even though I regularly send her cards.'

'Well, if you don't want Danny to know the whole truth, isn't seeking out Roy and Harley a bit of a risk?'

'I *do* want Danny to know the truth, but not until I'm sure

Harley herself knows. I don't want her life destroyed by Danny playing the jealous husband and threatening to get even with Roy, or whatever. This is why I've never spoken of my time in Manchester. One, because I wanted to protect my daughter from feeling rejected by me, and two, because I'm still in love with her father.'

Sheena sighed and shook her head. 'So, are you saying you want to resume your affair with Roy Cantello?'

Livvy smiled ruefully. 'I'd give my right arm to, but I don't think that's an option after all this time. I presume he's still with Sammy and I doubt he'd leave her now. They're both in their fifties, but he still looked good last time I saw him on TV.'

'There were pictures in *The Sunday Mail* magazine recently of Roy, Eddie and their wives, sunning themselves on a beach in Australia,' Sheena said. 'According to the article, the group had just finished a tour and Roy and Eddie were taking a well-earned break. Actually, all four of them looked in good shape for their ages. You mentioned Jon and Jess before. I remember reading a bit of scandal about those two a few years ago. They're half-brother and sister, yet they had twin boys together and actually got married. How did they manage that? It's against the law to marry your siblings!'

Livvy grinned at Sheena's puzzled expression. 'And there hangs another tale! Jon and Jess fell in love after Nick's death. Jess became pregnant with the twins while I was expecting Harley. Then they discovered that Ed wasn't Jon's father and they weren't related at all. Ed had been duped by Jon's mother into marrying her after she'd told him she was pregnant but she was carrying someone else's child.

'Ed and Jane brought Jon up and kept the truth from him. Jon's gran inadvertently gave him his late mother's diaries, where Angie had secretly recorded her confessions. He and Jess married the year after me and Danny. Jack and Nathan, their twins, are four months younger than Harley is.'

'Bloody hell, what a colourful life you've all led!' Sheena said. 'And Jason, Roy's youngest son, is the gay one?'

Livvy nodded. 'Yes. Jason was an absolute darling. He was so quiet and gentle; nothing at all like Nick, the charmer, who was just like his father. Jason had a friend, Jules, who he was very close to – I wonder if they're still together.'

'Ah, my turn now to tell *you* something,' Sheena said. 'They *are* still together. Jules is a famous sculptor and Jason an interior designer. They featured in *Hello!* magazine recently at the opening of their new gallery in Cheshire. Fancy that, Jason Cantello's your daughter's half-brother! I can't take all this in, Livvy. No wonder it was doing your head in, keeping it all under wraps. I'm surprised you don't need therapy.'

'Being part of Juice has kept me together. We've been so busy over the last few years. The guys are very supportive. They know when I need a shoulder to cry on and when to leave me alone. My drummer, Hank, is wonderful. He and I write most of the songs. He says I'm at my most productive when I'm miserable!'

'That's a back-handed compliment. Has there ever been anything between you and Hank?'

'No, he's happily married and the father of four teenage daughters. At least he understands women and their mood swings.'

'When you came back from Manchester all affluent but sad-eyed and silent, I knew something drastic had happened to you. You couldn't wait to marry Danny and drag him out of the country either, which Gerry and I found a bit strange. We never saw the pair of you as a love match.'

'That move was to put as much distance as possible between The Cantellos and myself, so they could get on with being a family,' Livvy said. 'Otherwise, I wouldn't have been able to stay away from them, no matter what promises I'd made.'

'That was very brave of you. Well, *I* feel as though I've had a really boring life by comparison. The only bit of excitement was getting caught two years on the run with the kids!'

'But at least you and Gerry are happy.'

'For the most part – yes – we are. We have our ups and downs like everyone else of course, but nothing like yours.' Sheena stood up and stretched her arms above her head. 'Let's go and make ourselves a cuppa. I'll let the dogs out and then we don't get up to puddly floors in the morning.'

Livvy followed Sheena to the kitchen and opened the French doors for Sandy and Fred. 'Will you do me a big favour, Sheena?'

'What would that be then?' Sheena asked as she filled the kettle.

'Will you come to Manchester with me next week? I have to go and find Harley – I can't go back to the States and not see her.'

'What about Courtney?' Sheena asked. 'Will we take her with us?'

'Would Gerry be prepared to look after her for a few days?'

'I don't see why not and my mother will stay over to help if I ask her. We can tell Gerry you have business to attend to, or something.'

'Good idea. Tell him I've got to meet a new songwriter and I want to treat you to a few nights away. We'll fly down and stay at The Midland. I'll try and contact Sean or Jon tomorrow morning. I have a feeling Sean still works at Flanagan and Grey's even if Jon doesn't. We'd better go to bed after this cuppa – I don't want bags under my eyes for my first meeting with my new family.'

5

MANCHESTER, FEBRUARY 2001

The junior sales assistant popped his head around the staffroom door and cleared his throat. Jon Mellor looked up from reading *Mojo* magazine. 'What's up, Liam?'

'Woman on the phone, wanting to speak to you or Sean. Shall I tell her you're busy?'

'Who is it?'

'Dunno. Wouldn't give her name. Told her you were both on lunch break. She said to see if you were in the staffroom. She's gorra funny sort of accent! American-Scottish-Irish or summat!'

Jon laughed. 'Double Dutch, more like.'

'You say she wants Jon or me?' Sean Grogan chipped in. 'She actually asked for us by name – as though she knows us?'

'Yeah – like I just said.' Liam spoke with an air of boredom.

'Okay, put the call through,' Sean said. 'We've ten minutes of lunch left, I'm determined to have my full hour today.'

As Liam went back into the shop, Sean offered Jon a cigarette and lit up himself. The phone rang out and he grabbed the receiver: 'Hello there, Sean Grogan speaking.' His eyebrows shot up his forehead and his face broke into a wide smile. 'Fucking hell, I don't believe it! Pardon my French, Livvy, it's the shock. How are you, my little darlin'? More to the point, *where* are you?'

Jon felt his jaw drop as Sean continued: 'Glasgow, eh? You on tour? I see. Well, I'll look forward to that, so I will. Of course he's still here – part of the bloody furniture! To be sure, I'll ask him. Speak to you soon then. Bye.' He hung up. 'That was Livvy Grant.'

'I gathered that. What does *she* want?'

'To meet us next week for lunch or dinner,' Sean replied. 'She's flying in, staying at The Midland for a couple of days and will call us when she arrives.'

Jon nodded. 'Harley's sixteen on Saturday. Livvy will want to see her. We've all been kind of expecting it for the last few years.'

Sean sucked on his teeth and frowned. 'We'd better call Roy and warn him.'

'I'll do it,' Jon said. 'Though, to be honest, I'm low on his list of favourite people at the moment after my wayward son's antics with his precious daughter.'

Sammy took Jon's call. She told him Roy was at a band meeting at Hanover's Lodge. 'How's Harley?' he asked.

'Not so good. The doctor took blood samples, we get the results next week. I'm in two minds whether to cancel the party, but Harley insists she wants it to go ahead.'

'It might perk her up a bit.'

'Maybe, anyway, we'll see. The test results should tell us something.'

'Hopefully. I'll see you Saturday, Sammy.' He hung up. 'Roy's at my dad's place,' he told Sean. He dialled his parents' number. 'Hi, Mum. Can I speak to Roy, please?'

'Hold on a minute, Jon. I'll give him a shout.'

Jon could hear her calling upstairs, then Roy's deep voice following her into the kitchen.

'Hi, Jon, what can I do for you?'

'You'd better sit down. I've something to tell you.'

'What the fuck's happened now?'

'Livvy's been in touch. She's in Glasgow and flying to Manchester next week.' There was a clatter and then silence. 'You there, Roy? Roy... are you there?'

'Jon, it's Mum. Whatever you said to Roy has totally shocked him, he's white as a sheet. What's happened?'

'Livvy's coming to Manchester.'

'What? How do you know?'

'She just rang me.'

'She rang you? But why? After all this time, for God's sake! Did she say what she wanted?'

'I'm sorry. No, she just rang out of the blue and that's all she said.'

'Oh God! Right, I'll get your father and pour Roy a brandy.' She hung up.

Jon turned to Sean. 'That's put the cat amongst the pigeons!'

* * *

'Ed, come down here, please,' Jane called up the stairs. She poured Roy a brandy and bumped into Eddie on her way back to the kitchen.

'Who's that for? Bit early in the day.'

'Roy's had a shock.'

'What's happened, mate?' Eddie placed his hand on Roy's shoulder as Jane handed over the brandy.

Roy looked up, a strained expression on his face. He told Eddie what Jon had said.

'This is it, Ed. This is where I lose my daughter.'

Jane's eyes met Eddie's over Roy's head. 'Go home, Roy,' she said. 'It's time to tell Harley the truth. Ed will make your excuses to the rest of the band.'

'But she's ill. I can't tell her now. It's her party on Saturday, I don't want to spoil things. It'll have to wait till Sunday.'

'Roy, the more you make excuses, the longer you'll put it off, and the harder it will be to deal with. Believe me I know,' Eddie said. 'Livvy will want to see her daughter. Why else would she come? Juice isn't currently on tour in this country. She's coming to see if you've fulfilled the promise you made.'

'Well, I have. I've looked after Harley's every need, I've taken good care of her.'

'I mean your promise of telling her the truth.'

'I have to do it, don't I?' Roy ran his hands through his thick, dark hair. 'Fucking hell, this is a nightmare! I don't even have a clue how to begin. She'll hate me for this, you just wait and see!' He rooted in his jacket pocket for his car keys. 'I'll see you on Saturday night then.'

Jane turned to Eddie as Roy left the house. 'Don't envy him, do you?'

'No, sweetheart, not at all.'

* * *

'You absolutely sure you're doing the right thing?' Sheena said as Livvy replaced the receiver.

'Dead sure. Jon will call Roy now. If he hasn't already, Roy may tell Harley about me this week. I want to see my daughter. You've no idea how much I think about her, she's constantly on my mind. I don't even know what she looks like now. Roy's never allowed her to be photographed by the press. Well, I haven't seen anything in magazines or newspapers.'

'Come to think of it, neither have I,' Sheena said. 'The only kid of Roy's I've seen in the press recently is Jason.'

'The Raiders are very private where their families are

concerned. They've never really courted publicity, other than for the band,' Livvy said as Courtney appeared in the kitchen and announced she was starving.

'Sit down, Courtney,' Sheena said. 'I'll make you both a sandwich before you go and see your family. Cup of tea, Liv?'

'Please, Sheena. By the way, do you have a stamp? I need to post something later.'

* * *

Roy's head whirled as he drove slowly up the long driveway of Jasmine House and pulled up outside the garage block. He felt sick, shaky and not sure that he had the strength to say anything to Harley. He wished he could whisk her and Sammy away to a secret location where Livvy could never find them. He just knew that his comfortable and carefree lifestyle was about to be ripped apart – again.

He looked up. Harley's bedroom window was closed and the curtains pulled across. She must still be in bed. That wasn't like his daughter, he thought, as he clambered out of the car. She was usually up early and bouncing with energy. This virus, or whatever it was, had floored her.

He strolled towards the large Edwardian house that had been the family home since the sixties and surveyed the surroundings. The trappings of wealth, and he was proud of it. He'd worked bloody hard for it, him and Sammy, both. She'd shelved her successful design career and sold her business to be a stay-at-home mum to Harley. Harley was *his* mistake, but it was Sammy whose life had changed drastically, while he continued much as he'd always done – a happy Jack the Lad, or Jack the Old Man, as he now thought of himself.

He found Sammy sitting alone in the kitchen by the open patio doors. He joined her, poured a mug of coffee and topped hers up: 'Harley upstairs?'

'She's sleeping, don't go disturbing her.'

'I won't.' He shivered. 'Bit chilly in here, Sam.'

'It's nice and fresh. I'm boiling hot, as usual.' She looped her long, light-brown hair back behind her ears and fanned herself with a magazine.

He stroked her cheek. 'Another hot flush?'

'How did you guess? When we take Harley for the blood test results I'm going to ask the doctor to change my HRT prescription. The pills don't seem to be working. Jane's got patches. *She's* sailing through the bloody menopause and I'm stumbling blindly through mine!'

'Don't let him prescribe anything that puts you off sex! I read in one of your magazines that some types of HRT can do that.'

She rolled her eyes and laughed. 'Trust you, Cantello! Always thinking of yourself.'

'I'm not. You know how crabby *you* can be if you don't have a regular servicing.'

'You make me sound like an old car.' She giggled. 'Anyway, why are you home so early? I wasn't expecting you until teatime.'

'Something's happened. We need to talk... seriously, I mean.' He led her through into the lounge and they sat side by side on one of the cream leather sofas. He took her hand.

'What is it, Roy? You look very anxious.'

'Livvy's in the country,' he began. 'She's flying into Manchester next week. We need to tell Harley the truth.'

Sammy's face blanched beneath her crimson flush. 'Telling Harley's one thing, the reality of Livvy coming here is quite another.' She squeezed his hand. 'Well, this is it. I guess you can't put it off any longer.'

'I know what you're thinking,' he said. 'I won't be seeing her, I promise. Not unless I'm with you or Harley.'

She nodded. 'I'm not prepared to go through all that again.'

'You won't need to – I can handle it. I love you, Sammy. We're not going to lose Harley to her mother.' A movement by the door caught his eye – Harley in her pink dressing gown. How long had she been standing there? Judging from the puzzled look, she must have heard most of what they'd said. Roy jumped up and walked across the room. He took Harley by the hand and led her to sit beside Sammy.

She stared at him, her brown eyes wide in her pale face. 'Dad, what did you mean just then, about not losing me to my mother?'

He puffed out his cheeks and looked at Sammy for inspiration.

'Dad's got something to tell you, darling.' Sammy stroked Harley's hair back from her face.

Roy sat on the opposite sofa. He cleared his throat and swallowed hard. 'Harley, this isn't easy for me,' he began. 'What I have to tell you will come as a big shock but I hope you won't think too badly of me.' He paused and took a deep breath. 'Back in 1984, I had a brief affair.'

Harley gasped and moved closer to Sammy, who put a protective arm around her.

'I, err... I got the woman pregnant. She gave birth to a baby girl.' He looked at Harley, who was staring at him as though he were mad.

Her frown deepened as he continued: 'She wasn't in a position to look after the baby, so she handed her over to me and your mum to bring up as our own daughter.' Roy looked at Harley's stricken face. A faint pink flush appeared on her cheeks. 'Oh, sweetheart, I'm so sorry. I should have told you years ago, but I didn't know how.'

'So, why have you decided to tell me now, Dad?' Her voice wobbled and she stared, wide-eyed. She snuggled closer to Sammy, who held her tight.

'Your birth mother's coming to Manchester,' Sammy told her. 'She'll probably want to see you.'

'Well, *I* don't want to see *her*.' Harley looked at Sammy in despair. 'Mum, tell me he's lying. *You're* my real mother, aren't you? Everybody says I've got your ways, even though I look like *him*!' She pushed Sammy away, shot across to Roy and beat her fists against his head and shoulders, tears tumbling down her cheeks. 'You're a liar, Dad! Why are you doing this to me? Mum's my mum!'

Sammy gasped, tears flowing freely down her face. Roy caught Harley's hands and pulled her down beside him.

'I'm not lying to you. I only wish I were, believe me. I had an affair, you were the result. We've brought you up since you were a tiny baby and we've loved you more than any child could ever be loved. Sweetheart, it's the truth. No matter how much it hurts, it's the truth.' He held her close and she lay limply against his chest. Shuddering sobs racked her slender body.

He looked at Sammy, who was sobbing too. She went across, knelt on the floor and flung her arms around father and daughter, crying with them. 'It was never going to be easy, Roy,' she said softly, stroking Harley's cheek.

'Can you get me a brandy, please, Sam? Pour a small one for Harley and put some Coca-Cola in it.'

'I think we could all use one,' Sammy said and got to her feet.

'So... my real mum didn't want me then?' Harley choked on her words.

'Harley, she wanted you *very* much. But she was quite young and worried about the future alone. She thought you'd be better off with two parents.'

'She was *young*?' She stared at him. '*How* young, Dad?'

Roy swallowed hard, cringing inwardly. 'Twenty-two and I was forty-two. She was a friend of Nick and Jason's.'

'Dad! Forty-two's a bit old to be slipping up.'

'You're right, it is, but it happened.'

Sammy brought the glasses of brandy in. Roy knocked his back. Harley and Sammy sat side by side, sipping slowly at theirs.

'Did *you* ever not want me, Dad?' Harley asked, a challenge in her eyes. 'You know, with me being so obviously an inconvenient accident!'

'I always wanted you,' Roy lied, pushing the fact he'd demanded Livvy have an abortion to the back of his mind. 'But I couldn't leave Sammy to marry your mother. We'd just lost Nick when she announced she was pregnant.'

'Neat timing!' Harley sniffed and reached for a tissue. 'So, was I your Nick substitute?'

'Of course not,' Sammy said. 'No one could be a substitute for Nick. He was unique, like Jason is, and like you are.'

Roy watched silently as Harley chewed on her lips and stared at the ceiling for a long moment. This was all his fault and he'd only just scratched the surface. He felt totally inadequate to deal with it. He'd already turned his daughter's world upside down and devastated his wife, yet again. He was sure he was about to throw up his lunch at any minute.

Then Harley took a deep breath and spoke: 'You said my mother's coming to Manchester and might want to see me? Why now? How come she hasn't been in touch before?'

'She *has* been in touch,' Roy admitted, putting his arm around her. 'Every single year she's sent you birthday and Christmas cards and letters and photos.'

'What?' Harley pulled away from him. 'So why have you never showed them to me?'

He hung his head. 'Because I was terrified of losing you. I'm not proud of it. People do strange things when someone they love is involved and *I* love *you* to distraction.' He turned to Sammy, tears running down his face: 'Will you go upstairs and get me the box of cards and things, please?'

She nodded and left the room sobbing.

Harley stared after her. 'Oh, Dad, what have you done? I can't believe she's not my mum.'

'Sammy *is* your mum, in every way other than that she didn't actually give birth to you. She watched you come into the world and held you in her arms when you were only minutes old. She loves you to bits. This is really hard for her, too.'

'You mean she was in the delivery room, watching *your girl-friend* giving birth to *your baby*?' Harley gasped.

'No, it wasn't quite like that. You arrived in the back of Jane and Ed's Jeep.' Roy told Harley the details of the events leading up to her birth and she sat open-mouthed, shaking her head. Sammy walked back into the room with the box and he sighed with relief as she took a seat beside him. He squeezed her hand – he needed her there.

'So... does she have a name, this mother of mine?' Harley asked.

'Her name's Olivia,' Roy replied. From the box he produced the most recent photograph of Livvy and her family.

'But that's Livvy Grant,' Harley exclaimed. 'The singer with Juice.'

Roy nodded slowly. 'Livvy Grant is your mother.'

'Yeah, right... course she is! You told me she was young and single. Quit winding me up, Dad!'

'She *was* young and single back then,' Roy replied. 'She's only thirty-eight now. She's married to the property tycoon, Danny McVey. The young girl in the photograph is your half-sister, their daughter Courtney. They live in Orange County.'

Harley looked at Sammy. 'Is this true, or am I dreaming?'

'I only wish you were, Harley,' Sammy said, dabbing her eyes on a sodden tissue. 'Believe me, everything your dad's telling you is the truth. I am so, so sorry you've had to find out this way.'

'Livvy Grant is *my* mother?' Harley shook her head in disbelief. 'Are you *sure* it's her?'

'That's the sort of question usually relating to the father,' Roy answered.

Harley half-smiled. 'How stupid of me! I can't think straight. Will you tell me everything, Dad, right from the word go? I want to know what happened. Why you had an affair in the first place when you love Mum so much and why you haven't told *me* before now. Be honest with me, please. You owe me that much. Mum... you still want to be my mum, don't you?' Harley looked at Sammy with a pleading expression. 'She can't take me away from you, can she?'

'Of course I still want to be your mum. No one can take you away from us, Harley, unless you want to go. I feel terrible that we've kept this from you – I don't know how you'll ever forgive us.'

'I don't want to live in America.' Harley's tears started again. 'I can't leave you and Dad. Jason and Jules need me to be auntie to their new baby. I can't *possibly* leave Jack because *he* needs me, too.' She sobbed into the front of Roy's T-shirt. He held her until the tears subsided.

'And *we* need *you*, Harley.' He tilted her chin with his finger and kissed the tip of her nose.

'Does anyone else know about this, Dad?' she asked eventually.

'Yeah, our close friends and the family all know. Everyone else thinks you're Sammy's child.'

She nodded. 'I can't believe you kept such an important thing from me – all of you. Did you never think that I might want to meet my real mother? Maybe not to go and live with her, but to know her all the same. The very fact she's sent all these.' She indicated the cards, letters and photographs. 'Surely that must mean something? That she still cares about me.'

Roy held his head in his hands. 'I'm sorry, I'm so sorry,' he sobbed. 'I don't know what else to say to you. It was wrong of me to keep the letters and cards from you. I promised Livvy I would tell you the truth when you were ten but I just couldn't do it.'

'Livvy must feel really bad that you haven't let me contact her,' Harley said. 'Maybe she thinks I got the cards and I don't want to know. Well, you know what, Dad? I *do* want to see her.' She jumped up and ran out of the room, yelling, 'I need some space. I'm going to my room.'

The door slammed and Roy stared at Sammy. He made to go after Harley, but Sammy pulled him back.

'Leave her for a minute or two. Let her get her head around things, then go up and see her.'

'She hates me,' he cried. 'I knew she would.'

'She doesn't, but she's a lost and very hurt girl at the moment. She's angry with both of us. I'm as bad as you for keeping it from her. I knew this would happen, Roy. You should have listened to me years ago and told her when she was ten. She might have taken it better then. But no, you always think *you* know what's right.'

'Don't you think I don't know how stupid I've been?' he sobbed. 'Now I've completely fucked everything up. She'll probably come down with her bags packed and demand to be taken to Livvy.'

'She won't.' Sammy wiped her eyes. 'I'm going to make a cup of tea. Give her five more minutes and then go up to her. And get on your bloody knees if you have to.'

* * *

Sammy leant against the worktop, waiting for the kettle to boil. *She* also needed to clear her head. Hearing Roy dredging up the details of his affair was almost more than she could bear. She'd half-hoped Harley wouldn't want to know too much and that simply telling her about her birth mother would be enough. Wishful thinking. Why wouldn't the girl want to know about her real mum? And that's what hurt most. Sammy had always looked on Harley as her own. She'd successfully blocked Livvy out of the equation until Harley was ten – the time Roy had promised he'd tell her the truth. Each year from then on, she'd been expecting contact of some sort. Roy had bought them an extra six years by bottling out. It was wrong of him, but in a small way she supposed she should be thankful for that. She would never be able to truly put his affair behind her. Now that Livvy was coming back into their lives, and despite Roy's insistence that he wouldn't see her alone, she had a gut feeling that it was all going to kick off again and this time she'd be powerless to stop it.

* * *

Roy tapped lightly on Harley's bedroom door. There was no reply so he tried the handle. She was on the bed, sobbing into her pillow. He pulled her to him and cuddled her, crying with her. He sat for some time, rocking her until her sobs subsided. He stroked her hair and wiped away her tears with his fingertips. His stomach was in knots as he looked at her. She was the most precious thing in his life. He'd do anything for her and it was killing him to see her so upset. He thought about how Livvy must feel, each time she sent a card and got no reply, and that made him feel bad all over again. He'd hurt so many people in his life – it was time to start putting things right.

'I love you, princess,' he whispered into Harley's hair. 'I'll make arrangements for you to see Livvy as soon as she gets in touch next week.'

'I love you too, Dad.' She looked at him and smiled through her tears. 'Thank you. I still can't believe that she's my mum. It feels so weird.'

'I'm sure,' he replied. 'Just one thing, don't tell anyone just yet. For Mum's sake, really. Your mum Sammy, I mean.'

'I know you do.'

'Are you coming downstairs now? Mum was making a cuppa for us.'

She nodded. 'I'm a bit peckish as well. Didn't have any lunch.'

'Come on then.' He pulled her to her feet. 'I'll make you a sandwich and get a takeaway later. You choose – Indian or Chinese. We'll have a family evening together, just the three of us.'

'That'll be nice,' she said. 'And maybe we can finish reading Livvy's letters and you can tell me all about her.'

6

GLASGOW, FEBRUARY 2001

'You absolutely sure I don't look like Livvy Grant?' Livvy asked, climbing out of Sheena's car.

'You look fine, stop worrying,' her friend said. 'Without all the make-up, there's a passing resemblance, but that's all.'

Livvy took a deep breath and smiled at Courtney, who reached into the boot for an arrangement of pink roses, tied up with a cream raffia bow. 'See you later then. Thanks for the lift.' They waved as Sheena sped away.

'You ready for this, honey?' Livvy tucked a straying curl behind Courtney's ear.

She nodded. 'I feel a bit nervous. Hope my aunt likes the flowers.'

'I'm sure she will. They're beautiful.' Livvy looked up at the red-brick, semi-detached house with its neatly curtained windows and well-tended front garden. 'Come on, let's go for it.' She rang the bell and stepped back. The inner door opened a fraction and then wider as a tall woman, with a mass of red curls and a tentative smile, reached out and opened the porch door.

Livvy extended her hand. 'Leanne?'

'Marie? Oh my goodness, you're here! Come away inside,

do. Dad, Marie's here.' Leanne stepped back to let Livvy and Courtney in.

A tall, ginger-haired man, with a lop-sided grin, emerged from a door at the end of the hallway. His face lit up and Livvy saw the wonder in his green eyes as he stared at the two of them.

'Marie, oh Marie, how wonderful to meet you at last! Come through, both of you.' He led the way into a comfortably furnished sitting room, where a welcoming fire blazed in the cast iron fireplace. He stood with his back to the coals, shaking his head as though he couldn't believe his eyes. Blinking away tears, he held out his arms. Livvy and Courtney moved into them. Courtney gave her grandfather a hug and a kiss on the cheek, then stepped back to let her mother get closer. As he held her, Livvy had an intense feeling of coming home. She sobbed against his chest, releasing years of pent-up sorrow; she felt no animosity towards this man who'd had no choice but to give her away.

Leanne placed a reassuring arm around Courtney's shoulders. 'Aren't you pretty? So blonde and you've a lovely tan. I look like Casper next to you.'

Courtney smiled at her aunt, whose green eyes twinkled kindly. 'The roses are for you.' She held out the bouquet. 'I chose them specially.'

'Oh, thank you, dear. They're lovely.'

'You're welcome. Where are my cousins?'

'At school, sweetheart. They'll be home soon. Everyone will be here for tea and then you can meet them all.' She turned to Livvy, who was wiping her eyes on her father's handkerchief. 'We thought it best the two of us greet you to start with so you wouldn't be too overwhelmed. I'll make a cup of tea. Would you like to help me, Courtney? We'll find a vase for these beautiful roses – I adore pink.'

'So does Mum, it's her favourite colour.'

As Courtney followed Leanne, Livvy's father gestured to a sofa at the side of the fireplace.

'Make yourself comfortable, Marie. You and Courtney are so like Gina, it quite takes my breath away. Oh, hen, if only things could have been different!'

'Please tell me all about Gina and why...' Livvy hesitated but knew she had to get this out. 'And... and why you had to give me away.'

Her father wiped his eyes and sighed. 'I'd love to, Marie. It's not a long tale to tell, but it's a sad one, nevertheless. Me and Gina were very much in love. Her parents were against our relationship from the start, said we were too young. Gina got pregnant when she was fifteen and a half and I was just sixteen. Well, as you can imagine, all hell broke loose. I was banned from seeing her. Her father threatened me with prosecution because of her age. Believe me, we wanted to keep you. We ran away from home and slept rough in barns for a few days but they tracked us down.

'Gina was packed off to an unmarried mothers' home. She sent me the address. I hitched up there at weekends and she'd sneak out and meet me when she was supposed to be cleaning the church. After you were born, I saw you once before you were adopted. The girls were allowed to take their babies out on Sunday afternoons, you see. Boyfriends appeared out of the woodwork and we all paired off. Someone who worked at the home spotted Gina and me and reported her to the nuns. She wasn't allowed outside the grounds again until the day you were taken away. I took a whole film of colour photographs that Sunday. Would you like to see them, Marie?'

Livvy nodded, tears tumbling down her cheeks.

Her father crossed the room to a built-in cupboard beside the chimney breast and took out a photograph album. 'There's a few photos in there of Gina and me during our courting days,' he said, handing Livvy the album.

She opened the book at the first photographs of her parents – a tall, skinny, red-headed boy with a face-splitting grin, standing alongside an attractive petite blonde who could have been Courtney.

'See how much you look like your mother,' he said softly as she turned the pages.

She smiled at pictures of herself as a tiny baby with a heart-shaped face and wispy blonde hair. 'I do,' she said, marvelling at the likeness. 'I always wondered what you both looked like and who I resembled.'

'Well, you're Gina's living image and so is Courtney. Gina was beautiful, and do you know, she had a voice like an angel. She used to sing her socks off at the youth club dances. She knew the words to all the hit songs. "Bobby's Girl", "Walking Back to Happiness", *and* the rest! She was thirteen when I met her and we were inseparable until that bastard of a father sent her away.'

'Is she married now – to someone else, I mean?' Livvy asked.

'She was, but she's divorced. Her sister told me when she first went to Canada, she pined for you and me and made herself very ill. She wouldn't eat or get out of bed. She was sent to a mental hospital. When they let her out, she got a job waitressing, which her parents hated. She was a clever girl; would have done well at college. I ruined her future. I've never stopped feeling bad about that. Anyway, she married a bartender when she was eighteen. They had a son. Her marriage, like mine, only lasted a few years. She now lives in Toronto – her son Joel's in Vancouver.'

Livvy nodded, hardly daring to let her thoughts run as wild as they were trying to. Her mother was free – there was every chance they'd eventually get to meet.

'I got all this information from Gina's sister,' her father continued. 'Gina wants to come home, but can't afford to. Her sister's trying to raise the flight money, but she's also struggling. Her husband's an invalid, you see, and they get by on state benefits. I injured my back a couple of years ago and I only work part-time now. If it wasn't for Leanne and Peter Junior, I don't know how I'd survive. I'm unable to make anything other than a small contribution for the air fare.'

Livvy swallowed hard, her spirits soaring by the second. This was her chance to help her family, but she didn't want to offend this proud man by flashing her money around just yet.

The sitting room door opened and Leanne appeared, carrying a laden tray. Courtney followed with a milk jug and sugar bowl. They put everything on the coffee table. Courtney flopped down on the rug by Livvy's feet.

'Sorry, we've been ages,' Leanne said. 'We thought you two would like a bit of time alone. Do you want to pour, Dad, or shall I?'

'You be mother, I end up slopping it all over.'

'Courtney's been telling me about your home, back in Orange County, Marie. It sounds fabulous.'

Livvy nodded and looked warningly at Courtney, who'd been sworn to secrecy – for a while at least.

'I told her about the horses and how Mrs Grayson doesn't buy cookies in packets like people here do. She makes them herself from scratch,' Courtney said, blushing slightly.

Livvy smiled reassuringly. 'How old are your children?' she asked Leanne, quickly changing the subject.

'My daughter's sixteen next week and my wee son's thirteen,' she replied. 'Our Peter's two girls are the same age as my kids.'

Livvy nodded. What a coincidence. Her half-sister and sister-in-law had been pregnant at the same time as she'd been with Harley. She could have shared her experience with them if things had been different.

'Peter's collecting them all from school later,' Leanne said.

'His wife Patsy will be here when she finishes work and my husband Jamie will be home around five. That's a full complement, barring Granny. She's in a nursing home. Dad will take you to see her – that's if you want to, of course. She's still got all her marbles. She's keen to tell you it wasn't *she* who insisted on the adoption. Granny was willing to give you all a home in her front parlour, but Gina's parents wouldn't listen. Her wish is to make peace with you before she meets her Maker.'

'Oh, bless her!' Livvy smiled. 'I don't lay blame on anyone, Leanne. Things like this happened a lot back then, still do sometimes.'

'Well, you'd never catch me putting a child up for adoption. It would break my heart.'

Livvy sighed. 'I had a bad time after my adoptive parents' marriage ended. I was left with my father.' She gave them a brief outline of her life history, leaving out the main factors of Harley, Roy and her fame and wealth.

'What does your husband do for a living, Marie?' her father asked.

'He buys and sells property. I suppose you'd call him an estate agent.'

'Obviously a successful one,' Leanne said. 'You look very prosperous. Your clothes are lovely and your curls are so well-cared for. Mine look like they've been put through a mangle!'

'You can try some of my hair-care products,' Livvy said. 'They tame even Courtney's wild mane.'

Voices in the hallway alerted Leanne, who leapt up. 'Coats on hooks and muddy shoes off before you come in here,' she called.

Four green-eyed teenagers, with hair ranging in shades from strawberry-blonde to deepest auburn, peered around the door. They stared curiously at their new aunt and cousin.

'This is,' Leanne began, reeling off names, 'Claire and Simon, my two, and Gemma and Louise, Peter's daughters. And this is your brother.' She pulled a replica of their father into the sitting room. Peter's jaw dropped as his eyes caught Livvy's. She was standing in the middle of the room, grinning from ear to ear.

He composed himself and cleared his throat. 'Forgive me for staring, Marie, but has anyone ever told you that you're the spitting image of Livvy Grant, the singer with Juice?'

Livvy felt her cheeks warming as all four children nodded their agreement.

Gemma spoke up. 'Dad's crazy about Livvy Grant. Because she originates from Glasgow, he thinks he sees her everywhere. You must think he's crackers, but actually, he's right, you *do* look very much like her.'

Livvy felt Courtney squeezing her hand: 'Mom, tell them the truth.'

Leanne and her father stared at Livvy. Her father spoke first: 'The people who adopted you, Marie, they were called Grant?'

Livvy nodded. 'That's right. They changed my first name to Olivia.'

'Oh my God! So you *are* Livvy Grant?' An incredulous Peter crossed the room in two strides and hugged her tightly. 'My long-lost sister is Livvy Grant. Now I *know* I've died and gone to heaven! I can't believe this; wait till your mother gets here.' He turned to Gemma, who raised an amused eyebrow.

'We'll never here the end of this.' She shook Livvy by the hand. 'Welcome to Scotland, Aunt Livvy, and you too, Courtney.'

Leanne stared in total disbelief. 'Why didn't you tell us?'

Livvy shrugged. 'I wanted to meet you all as a normal person – I hadn't bargained on my brother being a fan! Can we keep it to ourselves for now, so I don't get mithered by the press?'

Her father nodded. 'Of course we can. I feel such an idiot

for not recognising you. But then *I* was looking for a likeness of Gina and nothing else. Welcome to our family, Livvy. Do you prefer that name to Marie?'

'It's all I've ever answered to,' she replied, smiling with relief. 'Now my secret's out in the open, can we get down to some serious talking?'

Leanne nodded. 'I'm still reeling from the shock but, of course, we can. Where would you like to start?'

'Tell me everything there is to know about my family. What you all do to make a living, and, Dad,' she said, turning to Peter senior with a smile, 'is it okay to call you that?'

'I've waited all my life to hear it,' he said.

'Please tell me more about my mum – where I can find her and bring her home.'

Her father smiled warmly. 'That would make me very happy, Marie, err, Livvy. I'm sure it would mean the world to Gina, too.'

'Mum, I'm starving. Can we have tea while you lot talk?' Simon said, a bored expression on his face. 'Once you start blethering, you never stop. We've only had an ant-sized pizza and chips for dinner.'

Leanne laughed. 'Cheeky, I never blether! Go through to the dining room. Take Courtney with you. Everything's laid out buffet style. Claire, you take the clingfilm from over the dishes and, Simon, make sure you leave some for us.'

Courtney followed her newfound cousins and Livvy looked at her father and half-siblings. 'Apart from wanting to find you all, I have another reason for coming to Britain,' she began, as they sat forward on the edges of their seats. She explained about Harley, but kept Roy's identity to herself. They nodded with understanding.

Her father spoke up first: 'I wish I'd had the chance to see *you* when you were sixteen. You must make contact with her.

Her father and his wife, were they good people? Presumably you knew you could trust them?'

'I'm sure they'll have looked after her very well. I'm hoping to visit them next week. All I want is to satisfy myself that she's okay, I've no intention of removing her from their care. She's old enough now to cope with the truth. If she'd like to visit me some time then I'd be thrilled to have her stay. That invitation is extended to all of you, by the way. I really hope you'll visit me in LA.'

'We'd love to,' Leanne said. 'But we can't afford that sort of trip, it would cost thousands.'

'It won't cost you a penny. I'll pay for the flights and we've plenty of spare bedrooms at the ranch to accommodate you... really,' she finished, as her brother began to protest. 'You're my family; the thrill of knowing I have you is wonderful. I've felt so lonely all my life, you can't possibly imagine how good it feels to find you after all this time.'

'Well, in that case,' Leanne said, grinning with delight, 'we'll take you up on the offer.'

'Do you live close to the sea?' her brother asked.

'Not too far. We're in Orange County on the West Coast, just south of Los Angeles. We have a yacht moored at Newport Beach. My husband Danny can take you sailing, Peter, he'd love that. I'll make sure he takes time off – he works far too hard and hardly ever takes a break.'

'Selling property can be hard graft,' her father said. 'Does he need to work, you being a big star and all that?'

Livvy felt her cheeks warming again. 'Dan's a property millionaire,' she admitted. 'He's responsible for employing many people across LA. He couldn't just up sticks. Anyway, he needs to do his own thing or we'd be under one another's feet too much. To be honest, we're going through a rough patch in our marriage at the moment.'

'Is that why he hasn't come with you?' Leanne asked.

'Yes... sort of.'

'Well, let's hope it all works out in the end, hen.' Her father patted her hand.

'Shall we eat before the kids scoff the lot?' her brother suggested.

'Good idea,' Livvy said.

7

'You still awake, Sam?' Roy switched on the bedside lamp and gently prodded her shoulder. 'I can't sleep,' he said as she rolled over to face him.

She put her arms around him, snuggling into his chest. 'What's wrong? You worrying about Harley and Livvy?'

'Yeah.' He sighed. 'What if Harley decides she wants to live in the States with her?'

'She won't – she wants to get to know Livvy but doesn't want to leave *us*, Roy. She's adamant about that. We talked when you popped out to get the takeaway.'

'Did you? What would I do without you, Sam?'

'I don't know.' She kissed him and stroked his face. 'I was thinking before about when we first started dating. All those fun and happy early days. Do you remember our trips to Norman's Woods after school?'

'Oh boy, do I! I'm getting horny just thinking about you in your school uniform. My Mersey Square girl!' He stroked her hair from her face and pulled her closer. She always slept naked since the hot flushes started and he loved the feel of her silken skin next to him. 'Don't suppose you fancy making love?'

'Why not?' she said, smiling at his hopeful expression and snuggling into him. She reached to caress his growing erection. 'At least I can still turn you on.'

'The day you can't, I'll be dead!' The expression in her eyes told him how much she loved him as they rolled together, kissing, caressing and murmuring words of endearment.

'Feel better now?' she whispered as they lay together later, totally satiated.

'Much,' he whispered back. 'I'm so scared things are going to change between us.'

'Well, don't be – we won't allow them to,' she said.

* * *

Sammy rolled over and moved Roy's arm from around her middle. She slid out of bed and wiped away secret tears. Roy was snoring softly, but now *she* couldn't sleep. Her mind was all over the place *and* she was having another hot flush.

She pulled Roy's discarded T-shirt over her head, crept downstairs, brewed a mug of chamomile tea and sat at the table next to the patio doors. She watched a scrawny fox making its way across the garden. It stopped in its tracks when she switched on the patio lights. Frozen in the glare, it stared at Sammy and she stared back. Then it turned with a flick of its bushy red tail and ran off. She went to the fridge, took out the remains of a cooked chicken and opened the patio door. She slid the plate outside, locked up and drew the blinds. The fox would be back when it scented the chicken on the gentle night breeze.

Sammy reached for the end of a joint Roy had left in the ashtray. There was just enough for a couple of tokes. She lit up, spluttered and puffed out a small cloud of smoke. It was years since she'd smoked anything. Harley was forever lecturing on the dangers, but with Roy, it fell on deaf ears. She inhaled again and smiled as it hit the spot.

She sipped her tea and tried to envisage a scenario where she would come face to face with Livvy Grant. She couldn't picture it, and hopefully, it wouldn't be necessary. Roy and Harley could handle any meetings well enough without her. Her eyes filled with tears again. The thought of Roy and Livvy in the same room filled her with fear and uncertainty. All she held dear felt threatened. But one thing was certain, she was a stronger woman than she'd been sixteen years ago and whatever happened this time, there was no way she was sharing him.

* * *

Harley pulled back the curtains and stared out at the bright, sunny morning. Saturday – she was sixteen at last.

In her en suite bathroom, she studied her pale face. She still had dark circles under her eyes and rubbed at a spot of dry blood just above her top lip. Last night's nosebleed had been short, compared to others she'd had that week. She brushed her teeth and saw blood when she spat into the basin. She frowned. Why the hell did she keep bleeding? Must be to do with anaemia – whatever that was – like Mum had said.

* * *

Sammy pushed a mug of coffee across the table to Roy. 'Shall I go and wake her?'

'She'll be down when she's ready,' he said, lighting his first cigarette of the day.

Sammy turned to the pile of presents and cards on the table. She rearranged them and tweaked a couple of bows.

'That's the third time you've done that,' Roy said. 'Sit down and drink your coffee, woman. Pity you finished my joint.' He pointed to the ashtray. 'Looks like you could use it now.'

'Shh, don't let Harley hear you saying that.' Sammy sat

down and feigned a smile. She could feel her heart beating. 'Think I'm getting another hot flush.' She fanned herself with her hand as Roy took a swig of coffee. She jumped up again and opened the patio doors, reaching for the chicken plate from last night. The remains had gone and she had a sudden picture of the fox, jaws slavering, picking up the carcass and staring slyly at her. As he turned to run, the carcass became Harley hanging from his mouth. She closed her eyes to block out the scene.

'You okay, love?' Roy's voice penetrated her thoughts.

She looked at him, saw the concern in his eyes and her heart turned over. He was a soft touch at times – Livvy could wrap him around her little finger and he wouldn't stand a chance. *Stop it, Sam*, she told herself. *He's yours and he's going nowhere.* 'Yeah, just a bit nervous in case she doesn't like her pressies.'

'She will. You always get exactly what she's asked for. Here she comes,' he said, smiling as footfalls sounded on the stairs.

Sammy ran to greet her and hugged and kissed her. She laughed as Roy stood up and caught Harley in his arms. He twirled her around and then put her down and sang 'Happy Birthday' to her in his own rock-style. Harley giggled as he flung out his arms and threw back his head in a final crescendo.

'Happy birthday, darling. How are you feeling?' Sammy asked, giving her another hug.

'Better thanks, Mum.'

'Come on, sit down and get your pressies opened.' Sammy pulled Harley's chair out. 'Now, what would you like for breakfast? Bacon and eggs, full English?'

'Juice and toast with honey, please, Mum.'

'Full English sounds good to me,' Roy said.

'Bad for your heart, Roy. You can have grilled bacon and scrambled egg in a minute.' She poured him another coffee and Harley some juice, then sat down as Harley picked up a bulky parcel and ripped off the wrappings.

'Oh, black leather.' Harley held the contents to her nose.

'Love the smell! It's exactly like the jacket Kate bought Jack at Christmas.'

'I expect that's why Jason bought the same one for you,' Roy said. He picked up a neatly wrapped and beribboned package: 'This is from Jules.'

'Feels like CDs.' She tore off the paper and grinned. 'Wow, look at this lot! Robbie Williams, Dido, Westlife – it's the current chart.'

Next, she unwrapped a flat box and lifted out a low-cut, black Lycra and lace dress. 'Wicked, a Chloé dress. Oh, thanks, Mum. I'll wear it tonight at the party.'

'It's very nice,' Roy said, 'but it's a bit short.'

'It's no shorter than I normally wear. Now what's in this last parcel? More clothes. Oh, they're from Gap, brilliant!' She held up a pair of khaki combat pants, a matching padded gilet and a cream, long-sleeved T-shirt.

'Mum's choice again.' Roy smiled. 'She always gets it right.' He grinned at Sammy.

'Glad you like them, sweetheart,' Sammy said as a loud clatter came from the hall. 'There's the post. Nip and get it, Roy.'

'Thanks, Mum, for everything. I'll wear the pants and stuff later when Jack and Nathan come over. Dad,' Harley began, as Roy came back in the room and handed over a pile of cards, 'please don't be horrible to Jack.'

'I've no intention of being horrible to him but that doesn't mean I've forgiven him.' He dug into his back pocket, pulled out a small red book and Sammy snatched it off him.

'An extra gift from me and Dad,' she said, handing it to Harley.

It was a building society book. Harley opened the first page and gasped. 'Five grand! All for me? My own money?'

'Well, sixteen's a special birthday. Now I can come and tap you up when I'm a bit short,' Roy teased.

'Thank you, thank you, thank you,' Harley cried. 'Wow, just wait till I tell Jack! By the way, can I tell him about Livvy yet?'

'Leave it a while,' Sammy said. 'Let's see how things go. Open your cards now, there's quite a lot this year.'

'My friends have posted instead of giving them to me at school.' She opened several of the cards, smiling at the messages of greeting and get well wishes. Then she pulled out a card from a large pink envelope and looked at the written message, which simply stated, *Wishing You Many Happy Returns, With All My Love, Livvy*, followed by a row of kisses. 'It's from Livvy.' She handed the card to Sammy and sat back in her chair.

Roy grabbed the pink envelope and studied the franking: 'Posted in Glasgow. That's how I missed it. I was looking for an Air Mail mark.'

'Well, I hope she doesn't turn up here tonight,' Sammy said, staring at the card with the inscription – *To a Special Daughter*.

'She wouldn't dare,' Roy said.

'Well, turning up unannounced was something she used to be good at,' she reminded him and folded her arms. Trust Livvy to take the shine off this special morning.

'Mum, stop worrying,' Harley said. 'She'll make proper arrangements to meet me.'

'Yeah, of course she will,' Roy agreed.

* * *

'Do you think I'm getting jowls?' Roy inspected his jawline in the dressing table mirror.

'Are you heck!' Sammy said. 'Stop hogging the mirror and finish drying your hair. I want to do my make-up.'

'My face isn't as lean as it used to be though, is it?' He pushed his chin up with both hands and frowned. 'Perhaps I should have a facelift.'

'You don't need a facelift. Why are you suddenly so bothered about your appearance?'

'I need a bit of reassurance, that's all,' he said, wrapping a towel sari-style around his middle.

'Why?'

'Dunno. I'm fifty-nine next birthday. I feel old lately. Perhaps I should dye my hair instead.'

'No way! You look really distinguished with your silver threads. This panic about getting old wouldn't have anything to do with Livvy coming, would it?'

Roy looked put out. 'No, of course it bloody isn't.'

Sammy shook her head. 'Then stop faffing and get a move on. I've still got loads to do. Harley will be in any minute – she turned her hairdryer off a while ago.'

There was a tap on the door. 'Are you decent?' Harley asked, popping her head around.

'I am, but your father's not!' Sammy threw a pair of boxer shorts and black trousers at Roy. 'Put them on in the bathroom.' She turned to Harley, who, in spite of her make-up, still looked pale. 'You look lovely, sweetheart. That Chloé dress fits you like a glove.'

'Do you think Jack will like it?' Harley twirled around, showing off the dress from all angles. Her dark hair cascaded over her shoulders and she'd anchored each side with sparkling silver clips.

'I'm sure he will.'

'You can still see my bruises even through these black tights.' She held out a silken-clad leg for inspection.

'Not as much as you think,' Sammy said. 'No one will notice. I'll finish getting ready and we'll go downstairs.'

Roy sauntered back into the bedroom and whistled at Harley: 'Wow, you look stunning! Better keep my eye on you and Jack tonight.'

Harley blushed, adding colour to her cheeks. 'There's no need for that, we've learnt our lesson.'

'I hope so, princess. There's the doorbell, go and see who it is.' He delved into the wardrobe and pulled out a red silk shirt as she left the room. 'Will this do, Sam?'

'Yes. Red suits you.' Sammy stroked blusher on her cheeks, slicked on lipstick, and ran her fingers through her long hair, leaving it slightly tousled. 'Does this outfit look okay?'

'Very oriental. Same blue as your eyes. New?'

'Yeah. I got it when I went out with Jane and Jess last week. Thought it would look good with my Jimmy Choo's.' She held out her foot, clad in an elegant pewter sandal, toenails painted to match.

'You look bloody gorgeous, but then, you always do.'

* * *

'So, who told you that?' Roy heard Harley saying as he walked into the lounge. She was talking to two girls, who were wearing serious expressions.

One of the girls shrugged. 'No one in particular but it's all round school.'

'Oh, great!' Harley turned to Roy with a look of utter despair.

'What is it?' he asked, putting an arm around her shoulders.

'There's a rumour going round that I'm pregnant.' Her dark eyes filled with tears. 'Tell them I'm not, Dad.'

The girls fidgeted nervously under Roy's stern glare. 'Harley is most definitely *not* pregnant. Whoever started the rumour will be in serious trouble when I get my hands on them.'

'It wasn't us, Mr Cantello, honestly,' one of them said.

'I'll feel like a freak show tonight,' Harley wailed. 'Everyone will be talking about me.'

'They won't,' the girl said. 'We'll tell the others that it's a lie.'

'Thanks, Tasha,' Harley said.

'You see that you do.' Roy looked at Tasha and shook his

head. *Bloody women, they were born gossiping.* 'Get your guests a drink while I answer the door.' He patted Harley's arm reassuringly and went to greet Jason and Jules, who had arrived at the same time as Jane and Eddie. Sammy was taking coats and Roy pulled her to one side and told her what had been said.

'It'll all blow over once she gets back to school next week,' she said. 'I'll get rid of these coats and fix everyone a drink.'

'Okay.' The doorbell rang again and Roy let in Phil Jackson, The Raiders' rhythm guitarist. 'Hi, Phil, nice to see you, matey. Where's the lovely Laura?'

'Not feeling well,' he replied. 'I've come with Kate, Zak and the twins. They're unloading parcels for Harley from the boot. How is she, by the way?'

'We're waiting for blood test results. Should know something next week. So, what's wrong with Laura?' Roy led Phil to the drinks' cabinet in the corner of the lounge where Sammy was mixing G&Ts for herself and Jane. She passed glasses of single malt to Eddie, Jules and Jason and poured one for Phil.

'Thanks, Sam,' he said.

'You're welcome, Phil. Nice to see you, help yourself to ice.'

'Laura's on the change,' Phil told Roy. 'Bad heads, hot flushes and all that jazz. It's doing my bloody head in. She won't do anything about it, I'm climbing the walls with frustration.'

Roy smiled. 'Sam's having a few problems. Laura should see the doc. Make sure she gets the right sort of HRT though, or you'll be worse off than ever. Apparently, some brands lower the sex drive.'

'Bloody hell, if Laura's gets any lower it'll drop out!' Phil said. 'It's less stressful to have a fling than persuade *her* into bed at the moment. The band needs another tour and quick, preferably Germany where the *frauleins* are generous with their favours.'

'I'll see what I can do for you, Phil,' Roy said laughing as Kate and Zak came in.

Nathan strutted in behind them. With his black leather jacket, low-slung baggy jeans and his dark curly hair extended with dreadlocks, he looked like a young rap star. His bright blue eyes scanned the room, eyeing up the girls. Jack, dressed similarly, but with his curls in their usual untidy tangle, like he'd just climbed out of bed, slid in behind him, his arms laden with gaily wrapped parcels.

'Jack!' Harley flung her arms around him and dislodged the stacked parcels as he staggered backwards.

'Steady, Harley.' Zak put out a hand. 'You're knocking him off his feet.' He grinned, looking exactly the blue-eyed, blond-haired, younger version of his father, Phil.

Jack smiled at Harley. 'These are all for you. Shall I put them on the coffee table?'

'Please, then we can have a dance.'

She led him away as Roy's eagle eyes followed. He felt his stomach tighten. In spite of her dark colouring, his daughter was so much like Livvy. The way she walked, the way she held her head slightly to one side as she listened to people talking. The black dress she was wearing, although shorter, was similar to one Livvy had worn while she was pregnant. It had stretched defiantly over her bump as if challenging anyone to dare say a word against her decision not to have an abortion. Roy swallowed the lump in his throat and tried to block out the memory. He turned to greet Sean and Tina Grogan, who had just arrived.

* * *

Nathan spotted his girlfriend Faye at the back of the lounge, standing with a group from school. Holding court was Jamie Donahue, who appeared to be doing his utmost to chat her up. Jealousy reared its head and Nathan homed in, grabbed Faye by the arm and pulled her round to face him.

'I'm here,' he announced, glaring at Jamie, who shrugged and turned his attention to Tasha.

'Hi, Nathan.' Faye kissed him lightly on the lips. 'I've been waiting for you.'

'Yeah, it looks like it.' He glared at Jamie's back. 'What you doing, talking to *him*?'

'*He* was talking to *me*,' she said. 'I like your hair. Who did it for you?'

'Mum's hairdresser,' he replied. 'You know he only wants to get into your knickers.'

'Who does?' She giggled. 'Your mum's hairdresser?'

'Don't be stupid. Let's get a drink.'

'Mrs Cantello told us soft drinks are in the kitchen.'

He rolled his eyes and pulled her by the hand. In the kitchen he poured two half-glasses of Coke and, looking over his shoulder to check no adults were around, fished in his jacket pocket and pulled out a bottle of clear liquid. He topped up the glasses and handed her one.

'What is it?'

'Vodka,' he whispered, slipping the bottle back in his pocket. 'Nicked from home.'

Faye grinned. 'Cheers, Nathan.'

They clinked glasses. Nathan took a set of car keys from his jeans pocket. 'I locked Aunt Kate's car earlier, thought we could use it later. It's parked behind the garages. It's dark round there because the security light's broken.'

'You're on,' she said. 'Better sneak out separately and then it won't be too obvious.'

'Let's have a dance first,' he said and led her back to the lounge, where Harley and Jack were sitting on one of the sofas while Jamie Donahue and two more boys were dancing with Tasha and her friends.

* * *

Harley watched Jamie and Tasha swaying together. She turned to Jack and whispered, 'Tasha says there's a rumour going round school that I'm pregnant.'

'Yeah, there is,' he whispered back.

'Why didn't you tell me?'

'Didn't want to upset you, with you being ill.'

'Did you deny it?'

'No. Told them to mind their own effin' business.'

'Jack, honestly! Now they'll all think I thought I was, which is almost as bad as actually being pregnant. Don't you see? You should have said something.'

'Sorry.' He took her hand. 'Don't mean to keep letting you down.'

She tutted and looked across at Nathan and Faye, who were snogging the faces off each other. Why hadn't she gone out with Nathan when he'd asked her? She was sure she loved Jack, but Nathan was such good fun. *He'd* stick up for her and quash any rumours. Faye always seemed to have a good time with him. She pulled Jack to his feet and propelled him across the lounge towards Nathan and Faye.

'Enjoying your party, Harls?' Nathan asked, tearing himself away from Faye's lips.

'S'pose so. Would have been better if the parents had gone out and left us to it. Still, after last Saturday, there's no chance of that.'

'Not really.' He looked pointedly at Jack. 'Have a dance with *me* later, Harley.'

'Love to.' Ignoring the jealous expression in Jack's eyes, she looked up and saw Jon hovering by the door. 'Here's your dad.' Jack turned and waved at his father. 'Bet he's been sent to spy on us.'

'Happy Birthday, Harley.' Jon crossed the room in two easy strides and kissed her. Harley saw him glower at Jamie

Donahue, who was squeezing Tasha's backside and pulling her closer.

* * *

'Were the kids okay?' Jess asked as Jon reappeared by her side.

'Jack and Harley are the least of our worries,' he said. 'They seem a bit strained tonight. Keep your eye on Nathan and Faye, they're looking very into one another and that Jamie Donahue was all but screwing the girl he was dancing with – it was only her clothes stopping him.'

'Randy little beggar! Nathan can't get up to much with a houseful of people.'

'Let's hope not. Here's Tina...' Jon smiled as Sean's wife wove into view, clutching a large brandy balloon.

'I only wanted a small one,' she said, 'but you know how generous Roy is. At this rate, I'll be flat on my back before the night's out.'

'Sean won't mind that,' Jon quipped.

'What won't Sean mind?' Sean appeared by Tina's side.

'Tina flat on her back.'

Sean raised an eyebrow at his pretty, red-headed wife's blushing face. 'Oh, to be sure! Is that a promise I can hold you to, Tina, my love?'

'Might be,' she said. 'If you behave yourself.'

'Oh, I will. Scouts honour.'

'Have you two heard any more from Livvy?' Jess lowered her voice.

'No,' Sean replied. 'She'll be in touch midweek.'

'Roy and Sammy have prepared Harley,' Jess said. 'They told her yesterday.'

'How did she take it?' Tina whispered.

'She was very upset at first, but she's curious enough to want to meet Livvy.'

'It's not going to be easy for Sammy,' Tina said, 'but it was inevitable that Livvy would come back at some point. Who could blame her?' She turned to find a grinning Jason behind her.

'Long time no see, Tina.' He kissed her lightly on both cheeks.

'And how are the daddies-to-be?' Tina smiled as Jules joined them and handed Jason a large single malt. 'Congratulations, boys.'

'Thanks, Tina,' they chorused. Jason knocked back his drink in one go. 'Dutch courage,' he said. 'In case Dad starts making comments later, as he is wont to do after a few drinks.'

'I don't suppose he means any harm,' Tina said.

'Don't suppose he does, but he can't seem to help himself. I'm sure I still disappoint him, even after all these years.' Jason smiled as Jules put a comforting hand on his arm.

'No, you don't,' Tina reassured him. 'Listen, he'll be pleased as punch when that baby arrives, you mark my words.'

'Let's hope so,' Jason said as Jules smiled.

'Food's ready,' Sammy called from the dining room, where a cold buffet was laid out on the large table.

* * *

Faye stumbled from the car, pulled her short skirt straight and ran her hands through her tangled, blonde hair. She lurched drunkenly across the lawn, negotiated the steps up to the front door, made her way to the cloakroom, dashed inside and locked the door. She leant against the sink, feeling sick and dizzy. All she wanted to do was flop to the floor, curl up and go to sleep.

She stared at her reflection in the mirror: her cheeks were flushed and her eyes red-rimmed. She splashed her face with cold water and wiped away the mascara smudges. Her skimpy top didn't cover the huge love bite Nathan had given her.

Damn, her dad would go mad. She'd have to ask Harley for some concealer. Hand over her neck, Faye left the cloakroom as Nathan slipped indoors.

'You okay?'

She nodded. 'Except for this.' She moved her hand.

'Sorry. Ask Harley for something to cover it.'

'I will, see you later.'

She found Harley dancing with Jamie Donahue while Jack, looking jealous, was sitting alone on the sofa. Faye beckoned her over. Harley slipped out of Jamie's arms.

'What?'

'Have you any concealer?'

'Why do you want that?'

Faye moved her hand.

'Who gave you that?'

'Nathan. We've been in his Aunt Kate's car.'

'You've done it with Nathan outside our house?' Harley exclaimed.

'Shhh!' Faye hiccupped.

'God, Faye, you're such a slapper!'

'Oh, and you're not?'

'You *know* I'm not.'

'Well, it wasn't *me* who thought I was pregnant.'

'And neither did I. I bet it was you who started that rumour at school.'

'It wasn't,' Faye protested.

'What's going on here?' Roy intervened, as he strolled into the room.

'Nothing, Dad, don't worry,' Harley said. 'Come upstairs, Faye.'

In her bedroom, Harley handed Faye a concealer stick. 'That won't make much difference; it's a whopper. Your dad won't be too pleased. I hate love bites you can see, they look so common.'

'I didn't realise Nathan had done it,' Faye muttered, checking her neck in the dressing table mirror.

'You shouldn't get into situations where you don't know what's happening.'

'We had vodka in our Coke. I feel a bit drunk actually,' Faye confessed. She flopped down on Harley's bed and closed her eyes. 'The room's spinning round and round, Harls – ooh – I feel really sick.'

'Don't be sick on my duvet cover, it's new. I'll get you a bucket.'

* * *

Roy spotted Harley running through the hall and followed her upstairs.

'What's going on? Why the bucket?'

'Faye feels sick.'

Faye had passed out on the bed and Roy pulled her into an upright position.

'Get your mum,' he said to Harley. He held Faye's hair back from her face and gently tapped her cheeks.

'Come on, Faye, open your eyes, girl.'

She opened them, stared glassily at him and began to wretch. He bent her over the bucket as she threw up. Sammy and Harley appeared at the door as he was wiping Faye's mouth with a tissue.

'Get her a black coffee, Harley, and send Nathan up here,' he said.

Sammy rinsed a flannel with cold water. 'Hold her head up.' She gently sponged Faye's green-tinged face, tutting at the love bite on her neck. 'No prizes for guessing who's given her that! No doubt he's given her alcohol too; probably vodka, because she doesn't smell of drink.'

Nathan slid silently into the room. 'Is she okay?'

'No thanks to you,' Roy replied angrily. 'Where did you get the booze from? Ours has been under guard all night.'

'Home.' He hung his head.

'Look at the state of her, Nathan. She's absolutely legless and her father will be coming to collect her soon,' Sammy said. 'How much did you give her?'

'Three glasses of half-Coke, half-vodka,' he confessed.

'Bloody hell!' Sammy exclaimed. 'That's about a dozen pub measures. And where have you been? Your mum was looking for you earlier.'

'Nowhere. Faye needed fresh air, we walked up and down the drive.'

'I don't think so,' Jess said, coming into the room. Harley followed, carefully carrying a steaming mug, Jack on her heels. 'I looked everywhere for you. Were you up here in Harley's room?'

'No,' Nathan said.

'So *where* were you, Nathan?' Jess grabbed his arms and shook him. 'And why's Faye in this state? I'm sick and tired of you. Jack, go downstairs and ask your father to call a taxi. I'm taking you both home.'

'That's not fair, Mum. I haven't done anything wrong,' Jack protested.

'Can't Jack stay?' Harley pleaded. 'Please, Jess. It's not *his* fault.'

'Okay,' she relented, 'Jack can stay, but *you're* going home and you're grounded for a week.' She glared at Nathan. 'Now apologise to Roy and Sammy for your behaviour *and* to Harley for spoiling her party.'

'Sorry, Uncle Roy, Aunt Sammy,' Nathan mumbled. 'Sorry, Harls.'

'S'okay, Nathan.' Harley shrugged.

Nathan stared at Faye, who was sipping her coffee. 'I'll call you.' He left the room with no apology to *her*.

'Nathan told me he loved me earlier,' she wailed to Sammy.

'Nathan only loves himself, Faye,' Jess said. 'I'll see you all soon and I'm really sorry,' she apologised to Roy and Sammy as she left the room.

Sammy turned to Roy. 'I'll call Mr Blackwell, see if Faye can stay tonight. I'll tell him the girls are all having a sleepover.'

'Good idea.' Roy nodded.

'I haven't any clothes or toiletries with me,' Faye mumbled.

'You can borrow mine,' Harley said.

'I'll get her sorted and settled in the guest room,' Sammy said. 'You and Jack go downstairs and have a dance. Enjoy what's left of the night.'

* * *

Jack took Harley's hand as Roy and Sammy left the room, Faye wobbling between them.

'I'm sorry I wasn't supportive to you about that rumour,' Jack began and stroked her cheek. 'I promise never to let you down again.'

'It's okay, Jack. I'm sorry I was off with you, at least you don't get me legless. You won't believe this either: they did it in Aunt Kate's car right outside this house.'

'No way! Mum will kill him if she finds out. We'd better go and say goodnight to her, hadn't we?'

Jess's taxi arrived as they went downstairs. Nathan handed Kate's car keys to Jon.

'Bye, Mum, Nathan,' Jack called.

'Bye, Jack, and you just behave yourself or you'll have your father to answer to,' Jess said as Nathan grunted a goodbye.

'I will.' Jack led Harley back into the lounge, where the rest of the teenagers had paired off and were draped over the sofas with the lights turned low.

'I suppose it's probably a good job Mum and Dad are in,'

Harley said as Jack pulled her close. 'Otherwise, this lot would be in our beds.'

He smiled and planted a kiss on her lips. 'Are we okay now?' He held her tight. She looked tired and pale tonight. Jack felt very worried about her. All he wanted to do was love her and look after her. Not for the first time he wished he was a few years older and they could be married.

'Of course we are, and thanks again for my lovely present.' She fingered the fine gold chain, with a teddy bear sitting on a heart, which Jack had fastened around her neck earlier.

'You're welcome,' he said. 'I've got something else for you too but I want to give it to you privately. The adults are all in the dining room, this lot are in here, so can we sneak back to your room? Your mum and dad have come down now, so it should be safe.'

She nodded and led the way.

Jack pulled her down onto the bed and kissed her long and hard. He reached in his jeans pocket, pulled out a ring box and opened it. 'It's just to be going on with,' he said as she gasped, 'I got it from Argos. It's real gold, but the diamond's a pretend one. When I leave school and get a job, I'll buy you the biggest diamond in the world.' He slipped the ring onto Harley's finger and kissed her again. 'We're secretly engaged now but I expect you'll have to wear it on that chain around your neck unless we're alone.'

'It's gorgeous, Jack,' she said and her eyes filled with tears. 'Mum told me that she and Dad were secretly engaged while she was still at school. I love you and I'll never leave you.'

'I love you, too,' he said. 'Next week, when you're feeling better, we'll go to Pizza Hut and celebrate.'

She nodded. 'Jack, I've got another secret. I'm not allowed to say anything at the moment, not even to you, but it's really massive and you just won't believe it when I tell you,' She finished as Jack's eyes widened.

8

'Close your mouth, Liam, there's a tram coming,' Jon said as the young boy's jaw dropped.

'But that's, err, she's, umm...' Liam stuttered as Jon swept Livvy into his arms and kissed her.

'I thought I'd surprise you,' she said, hugging Jon back tightly. 'Sheena, this is Jon Mellor. I told you about him. This is Sheena, my old school friend from Glasgow.'

'Pleased to meet you, Sheena.' Jon shook her hand.

'Likewise, I've heard a lot about you,' Sheena said, a twinkle in her eye.

'Then it's a wonder you aren't running a mile,' he said with a smile.

'She only told me nice things, well... for the most part anyway,' Sheena said, flirting with him.

'Where's Sean?' Livvy asked, looking around the record department for signs of her old boss.

'Nipped to the hole in the wall,' Liam chipped in. 'Can I have your autograph, please, and will you do one for my mate, Charlie? He thinks you're top.'

'Of course, err, Liam, is it?' Livvy said. 'What's the hole in the wall? A new pub?'

'Cash machine. ATM to you,' Jon said. 'Sean won't be long. Go and hide in the staffroom, I'll make sure he goes in there as soon as he arrives back.'

'Good idea.' Livvy led Sheena towards the door.

* * *

'Take a pew,' Livvy said. 'We used to have our lunch breaks in here in my other life.'

Sheena flopped down on the old armchair, now threadbare from years of wear and tear. 'Oh wow, you never told me how good-looking Jon Mellor is!' she said, eyes wide. 'I've got goose pimples just looking at him.'

'I thought you only had eyes for Gerry?' Livvy raised an amused eyebrow. 'Anyway, forget it. Jon's married to Jess and I think he's probably very happy.'

'I wouldn't dream of making a pass at him – I just think he's drop-dead gorgeous. Why didn't you invite me down here years ago, before Jess got her claws in him and I married Gerry?'

'I'd planned on doing just that,' Livvy replied. 'Then I got involved with Roy.'

'Trust you.' Sheena tutted. 'Putting yourself first and denying your very best friend a date with a hunk like Jon.'

'Sorry. Anyway, Jon's a handful – you'd have been dropping your knickers on the first date. Count yourself lucky.'

Sheena raised an eyebrow and grinned as Jon popped his head around the door.

'He's on his way up,' he said. 'I'll switch off the lights. You don't mind the dark, do you?' He grinned in Sheena's direction.

'Course not,' she said as the windowless room was plunged into darkness. 'And I wouldn't say no to being alone with *you* in the dark,' she added as the door closed.

Livvy stifled a giggle and dug her in the ribs. 'Sheena, behave! What's got into you?'

'*He* has. I could rip his clothes off and I've only just clapped eyes on him.'

'Well, Jess would scratch them out if she heard you, I can guarantee that.'

The door opened slowly as Sean came in. 'Who the fuck's turned the lights out?' he muttered as he stumbled against a chair and banged his legs. He snapped the switch down and jumped out of his skin as Livvy flung her arms around him.

'Surprise!'

'Bejesus, Livvy! You scared the shit out of me.' He swung her round and round, holding her tightly. 'Oh, my little darlin', it's so good to see you again, so it is.' He kissed her on both cheeks and set her down. Jon and Liam crowded into the small room, laughing.

'You look exactly the same, Sean.' Livvy smiled delightedly up at him. Her old boss had always dressed snappily and his brown eyes were twinkling with their usual good humour.

'He's greyer though, don't you think?' Jon said.

'He looks quite distinguished with his Rod Stewart spikes. Oh, it's great to see you both again, it really is. I can't believe I'm here.'

'Can I phone Charlie, tell him to come down the shop?' Liam looked pleadingly at Livvy, who shook her head in alarm.

'Would you mind awfully if I said no, Liam? My visit to Manchester is private and very low-key. I've some private business to attend to, you see. I'll make sure you get photographs before I go back to Scotland, and next year, if Juice plays Manchester Arena, I'll sort out tickets and a backstage pass for the pair of you. How does that sound?' Livvy said, hoping to appeal to Liam's better nature.

'Wow, that would be brilliant! Thank you,' he said, smiling. 'Can I tell him you were here when you've gone back then?'

'Of course. It's just that everyone involved in this visit has been sworn to secrecy and I'm rather hoping to keep it that way.'

'Tell you what, Liam,' Sean spoke up, 'make us all a coffee. While the kettle's boiling, you can nip out to Greggs for chocolate éclairs to celebrate with. I presume you still like them, Liv?'

'Oh, yes,' she said as Liam shot off down the stairs.

'Do *you*, Sheena?' Jon winked at her and she blushed slightly.

'I do,' she replied, looking him straight in the eye.

'Come through into the shop,' Sean said, leading the way. 'It's quiet today and you can sit with your back to the counter, Livvy.'

'I'll put my shades and baseball cap on if it gets busy,' she said, fishing them out of her handbag. 'I always carry them, just in case.'

'You're staying at The Midland, I believe?' Jon asked.

'We are.' Sheena nodded. 'It's incredibly posh. We've got mini bars and Jacuzzi baths.'

Livvy laughed at Sheena's excitement. 'She's planning on drinking hers dry – the bar, that is. Would Tina and Jess have any objections to you having dinner with us tonight?'

'No, they wouldn't,' Sean replied. 'We okayed things with them after you first called, but it's on the condition you make time to visit me and Tina at home.'

'I intend doing just that,' Livvy said. 'How are your mum and dad?' she asked Jon.

'They're great,' he replied. 'Mum never changes, she still looks good. Dad's a bit greyer these days, but still going strong.'

'And Jess and the twins? They'll soon be sixteen.'

'Jess is okay. The boys are sixteen in June. Nathan's a bit of a handful, but Jack's a good lad.'

'And Katie and Dominic?' she asked, referring to Jon's younger siblings.

'Katie's Kate these days and she's engaged to Phil Jackson's son, Zak. Dom's working in Uganda at a school he helped set up.'

'Wow, really? Gosh, all grown up then. I used to babysit Jon's little brother and sister,' she told Sheena. Livvy chewed her lower lip and looked closely at Jon before asking her next question.

'And Roy?' She took a deep breath and swallowed hard as he smiled.

'Still rocking, of course. No changes there.'

'And he's still happy, with Sammy?'

Jon nodded. 'Very happy.'

'And my daughter?' Livvy's eyes filled with tears as she choked on her question.

Sean put his arm around her shoulders and led her into the staffroom, shooing out a puzzled Liam, who had returned from Greggs and was artistically arranging the éclairs on a plate.

'What's goin' on?' he demanded as he joined Sheena and Jon in the shop. 'Why's she crying?'

'Don't be nosy, Liam,' Jon said. 'In fact, you can go downstairs to Instruments for a while and help Shelley behind the counter. And, Liam, keep it buttoned that Livvy's up here, or else.'

* * *

With Liam out of earshot, Jon turned to Sheena: 'I presume you know what happened with Roy and Livvy?'

'I do,' she replied. 'But she only told me last week. Even her husband Danny doesn't know who Harley's father is.'

'Really?'

'Mm.' Sheena nodded. 'She's had quite an eventful last few days. Livvy won't mind me telling you this, but one of the reasons for her trip to Britain was to meet her real father and his family. I helped her trace them. She met them last week for the first time. She needs to see her daughter, Jon. She'll crack up if she doesn't do that soon.'

'I'm sure. Well, Roy and Sammy have told Harley everything. She wants to meet Livvy.' Jon kept it to himself that Harley wasn't well – it wasn't his place to say anything.

Sheena breathed a sigh of relief. 'Thank God for that.' She blinked away a tear and blushed slightly as he looked into her eyes for a long moment.

'What do you do for a living, Sheena?' he asked, breaking the silence. 'Are you a singer, too?'

'I used to sing duets with Livvy years ago,' she replied. 'I'm an interior designer by trade, run a business with my better half. He designs and builds kitchens and fitted bedrooms, while I do the colour schemes and the soft furnishings side.'

'Interesting. Me and Jess are hopeless at that sort of thing. Sammy does all our colour schemes – she studied art and design before she married Roy.'

'What's Sammy like?' Sheena asked.

'She's wonderful,' Jon replied. 'She's a good wife to Roy and a great mum to Harley and Jason. They adore her, we all do. Have you any idea what Livvy's plans are – for Harley, I mean?'

'She just wants to see her. To assure herself that she's okay and that Roy and Sammy are doing the best they can for her.'

'So, she's no intention of removing her from their care?'

'None at all. Harley's old enough to make up her own mind about things,' Sheena replied as the staffroom door opened and Livvy carried through a tray of coffee, Sean following with the éclairs.

'You okay, Liv?' Sheena asked, looking at her pale face.

'Oh, to be sure she is.' Sean ruffled Livvy's curls affectionately. 'And it wouldn't be the first time she's wet my shirt with her tears now, would it, Olivia?'

'True. I've wept buckets on the pair of you in the past!' She picked up an éclair and bit into it. 'Oh... yum.' She closed her eyes as the choux pastry melted in her mouth.

Jon and Sean looked at one another and burst out laughing.

'What's the joke?' Sheena asked.

Livvy blushed and joined in with their laughter.

Jon spoke first. 'We always used to say that no one could eat an éclair as suggestively as Livvy.'

'Oh, I see.' It was Sheena's turn to blush.

'They were a dreadful pair to work with,' Livvy said, 'full of innuendoes. I had to be so careful what I said or did, because they would always find something smutty in even the simplest things.'

'So you can imagine the field day we had when Roy accidentally banged a bun in her oven!' Sean said. 'I'm only teasing.' He looked fondly at Livvy. 'It wasn't the best of times was it, sweetheart? Giving birth in the back of a Cherokee Jeep in the arms of Mr Macho Cantello couldn't have been easy.'

'It was certainly a birth with a difference,' Livvy said, and quickly changed the subject. 'Sheena and I are going shopping this morning – I want to look around some of the new stores. It's certainly changed around here with all the rebuilding that's gone on since the IRA bombing incident.'

'We were very lucky indeed,' Sean said. 'All our shop windows blew, of course, but none of the staff were injured. The Shambles has gone and the old Marks & Spencer's, but they're rebuilding that on Market Street. We've got Metro Link trams now, of course, and there's a new out-of-town shopping complex called The Trafford Centre. You'll have to take a cab and have a wander round if you have the time.'

'Maybe we will,' Livvy said. 'I don't have a current phone number for Roy. Can one of you call him and ask him to contact me at The Midland later? I'm checked in as Mrs Marie McVey.'

'Sure,' Sean said. 'But why Marie?'

'It's the name given to me by my real parents and it's still my middle name,' she replied, smiling.

'You kept that one quiet,' Jon said.

'I only started using it when I made a name for myself. Mrs Marie McVey, housewife and mother. Sounds boring and respectable.'

'Livvy, my darlin', there's never been anything boring about *you*,' Sean said, laughing. 'Now take yourselves off shopping and we'll see you this evening. What time should we arrive?'

'Is seven in the bar okay?' she replied. 'I'll book a table for seven thirty.' She gave them both a hug and a kiss on the cheek.

Jon grinned at Sheena, holding her gaze as she smiled at him. 'I'll see *you* later then,' he said.

* * *

Sheena helped Jon to carry the drinks from the bar and they rejoined Livvy and Sean, who were chatting in a corner of the lounge.

'One for the road, then we should be making tracks,' Sean said. He downed his whisky and yawned. 'I'm not used to being out this late in the week. Thanks for the meal, Liv, I really enjoyed it.'

'It was my pleasure, Sean,' she said. 'I'll see you and Tina on Thursday afternoon then, if that's okay?'

'I'll book a day off work. Tina's really looking forward to seeing you and meeting Sheena, too.' He took Livvy's hand and squeezed it gently. 'Good luck tomorrow with Roy and Harley. You know where me and Tina are if you need us.' He kissed both Livvy and Sheena and slapped Jon on the back. 'C'mon, mate, we'll share a cab. Pick the cars up tomorrow.'

Jon finished his drink and got to his feet. 'It's not often I'm let off the leash, so I suppose I shouldn't push my luck. Good luck tomorrow, Liv.' He kissed her on the cheek and turned to Sheena: 'I'll see you soon,' he whispered as he gave her a hug.

'Hope so,' she whispered back.

'Let's go up to my room,' she said to Livvy as they left. 'I think you may be getting recognised. Those two guys at the bar keep looking across and now Sean and Jon have gone, they may come over and tell you that you look like Livvy Grant. We can have a drink from my mini bar.'

'Okay.' Livvy smiled. 'You're determined to drink that bar dry, aren't you?'

* * *

Livvy jumped up and yawned. 'One last drink and I think we'll call it a night.' She opened two small brandies and poured them into tumblers. 'Sorry, it's the wrong glasses, but I'm too tipsy to care,' she said, handing one to Sheena, who was sprawled on the bed.

'I think this will be the one to throw me over the edge, too. Don't forget, you have to call Danny before you go to bed.'

'I know.' Livvy grinned drunkenly. 'I'll tell him I love him, it'll keep him happy for now. I'm dying to see Harley tomorrow. Sean told me she's lovely – she's got long dark hair, looks a lot like Roy, but has my face shape.'

'When did he tell you that?'

'When you and Jon were standing at the bar, gazing into one another's eyes,' Livvy said. 'He also said, "There'll be trouble there if those two don't watch it!"' She hiccupped and sat down heavily. 'You really fancy Jon, don't you?'

Sheena lowered her gaze and ran her finger around the rim of her glass. 'Maybe.'

'Oh, oh! Don't even think about it, Sheena. Jess will go mental. I remember how jealous she used to be about Nick even *speaking* to me.'

'I'm having lunch with him tomorrow,' Sheena said quietly.

'When did you arrange that?'

'While we were standing at the bar. He told me to call in the store at one – I'm not sure I should, really.'

Livvy sighed. 'Oh well, it's up to you. I don't suppose lunch will do any harm.'

'True.' Sheena grinned lopsidedly. 'I feel so drunk, Liv. We shouldn't have mixed our drinks. Too much wine washed down with brandy doesn't really work.'

Livvy drained her glass. 'Get into bed. I'm going to my room to call Danny. I'll see you in the morning. Sweet dreams, or naughty ones, if you prefer.'

'Definitely. Especially if they include a romp with Jon Mellor! G'night, Liv, sleep tight.'

'Night, Sheena.'

Livvy closed the door and made her way to the next room. She stripped off her clothes and flung them vaguely in the direction of the bedroom chair. She pulled on a towelling robe and flopped down on the bed, thinking back to her telephone conversation with Roy that afternoon. It had been strained at first, both talking stiltedly, with Roy sounding as though he wasn't alone.

He'd told her about Harley and how she hadn't been too well lately, but that he was sure it was nothing to worry about. He and Sammy were taking her to the doctor's in the morning for the results of routine blood tests. They'd chatted about their respective musical careers then he'd finished the conversation with, 'I've really missed you, Liv,' leaving her reeling and assuming that he *must* have been alone, because he would never have dared to say that if Sammy had been in the room with him.

Livvy sighed now, picked up the bedside phone and dialled her home number. Mrs Grayson answered and told her Daniel was in New York. She gave her a contact number.

Livvy recognised the number of the hotel he often stayed in

when visiting the city. She dialled and asked for Daniel's room. After what seemed an age she was about to hang up when a breathless female voice answered. In the background she heard Daniel saying, 'I told you not to answer the damn phone!' Her stomach lurched and the room spun as he said, 'Hello, hello, who is this, please?'

'Your wife, you cheating bastard!' She threw down the phone, burst into tears and ran next door.

Sheena was just drifting off to sleep. 'Livvy, what's wrong?'

Between sobs, Livvy told her.

Through the open door, Sheena could hear Livvy's phone ringing. She jumped out of bed and ran to answer it. 'Danny, what the hell's going on? Livvy said you were with another woman. What are you playing at?' She listened to Daniel's excuses.

'It's a one-off, she's just a business acquaintance.'

'Well then, you should be ashamed of yourself,' she shouted. 'How could you? Livvy's right, you *are* a bastard!'

She ended the call and ran back to her own room. Livvy was still sobbing and Sheena held her until the sobs subsided.

'I wonder how many times *that's* happened?' Livvy sniffed. 'I bet he's always at it. I mean, how would I know? I suppose he tells them his wife doesn't understand him.'

'And maybe he's *never* done it before,' Sheena said.

'You reckon? I always thought Danny was the ultimate in faithful husbands. He's probably screwed half the women who work for him.'

'What are you going to do?'

'What *can* I do? I'm not going home for another two weeks. If he wants to sort it out, he can get on a bloody plane and fly to Glasgow.' Livvy wiped her eyes. 'I need to get some sleep, I don't want Roy to see me for the first time in years looking a mess. Thanks for being here, Sheena. Goodnight.'

'I'm always here for you, Liv, you know that. Goodnight.'

Livvy crept back to her room, head reeling with Daniel's betrayal, when all she really wanted was to think of her meeting tomorrow with Harley and Roy.

* * *

Jon drove down the private lane in his dad's Mercedes sports car. He pulled onto the main road, thoughts whirling through his head. He'd had a lousy night's sleep, disturbed by the totally unexpected feelings he'd developed for Livvy's friend, Sheena. From the minute he'd clapped eyes on her, he'd felt the electricity between them and from the looks she'd given him last night, he was pretty certain she felt it too. He should cancel lunch. What was the point? *More* to the point, why hadn't he told Jess? After all, there was nothing to hide.

Sheena was Livvy's mate and he was just being friendly, taking her for lunch and showing her a bit of the city. Yeah, he thought, like *that* would wash with Jess. He loved Jess and the boys with all his heart, but over the last twenty-four hours, no matter how hard he tried, his thoughts were constantly returning to that cheeky grin and twinkling blue eyes. As he'd tossed and turned next to Jess, he'd imagined taking Sheena to bed. The thrill of slowly undressing her, exploring her and making wild and passionate love to her. The sort of times he and Jess had enjoyed at the beginning, until the twins had put in their untimely appearance and lovemaking had to be slotted in around a hectic timetable of feeding, nappy changing and sleepless nights. As the boys got older, and Jess was conscious of the fact that they were light sleepers and woke at the least little sound, their once-active sex life had dwindled.

At the traffic lights, Jon was startled by an angry tooting as the impatient driver behind pointed out that the lights had changed to green. He glanced in his rear-view mirror at the chubby red face glaring at him and stuck two fingers up. 'Fuck you!' he muttered as he put his foot down and sped away.

* * *

'You okay, Jon?' Sean asked, looking at Jon's troubled face. He passed him a cigarette and a light.

Jon puffed a cloud of smoke in the air and coughed. 'I asked Sheena to lunch today. I'm having second thoughts. Do you think I should cancel?'

'Definitely, you eejit! Roy took Livvy out for lunch. Look what happened there!'

'Ah, but *I've* had a vasectomy,' Jon said with a wry smile.

'Forget it, Jon. Call her – the hotel number's on the pad by the phone.'

Jon thought for a moment then dialled The Midland and asked for Sheena's room. The receptionist told him that Mrs Cotton and Mrs McVey had just taken a taxi to The Trafford Centre.

'I need to contact them urgently,' Jon said. 'Do you have a mobile number?'

He rooted in his pocket for a pen and scribbled down the number. He dialled and was met with a recorded message, asking him to call back later.

'Shit!' He slammed down the phone as Liam sauntered up the stairs, reeking of cheap cologne and cigarette smoke.

'Jesus, Liam! You smell about as inviting as a tart's boudoir,' Sean said. '*And* you're late – again.'

'Sorry.' Liam shrugged. 'Bus didn't turn up till after nine. What's a boo-dwar?' he called as he went into the staffroom.

'Oh, never mind.' Sean shook his head. 'Brew up and be quick about it!' He turned to Jon. 'No reply?'

'They've gone to The Trafford Centre. The mobile's turned

off, I couldn't even leave a message. I'll have to take her out now – I can hardly cancel when she arrives.'

* * *

'Hi, Sheena.' Jon smiled as she puffed up the stairs to the record department.

Sheena grinned nervously. 'I hope I'm not too early. We've been shopping at that new centre. Livvy's gone back to the hotel for a lie-down before she meets Roy and Harley.'

'Your timing's fine. Shall we go then? If Dad pops in for his car keys, tell him I had to go out, please.' He raised a warning eyebrow at Sean.

'Sure I will. Your secret's safe with me. Off you go and have a nice lunch.'

'Thanks,' Jon called as he and Sheena ran downstairs and out onto the street. 'Do you fancy pub grub or a restaurant?'

'A pub will be fine,' she replied.

'Here we are then,' Jon said and steered her into the nearby Swan with Two Necks. 'The food's great in here and the alcoves are private. Go and bag that one.' He pointed towards the back of the pub. 'What would you like to drink?'

'Pint of Stella, please.'

'Ah, a girl after my own heart! I'll bring the menus.'

* * *

From her seat in the alcove, Sheena observed Jon, taking in his tall, slim frame, thick dark curls and smart business suit. He turned to smile, his green eyes twinkling, and she smiled back.

He carried over the drinks and menus and sat down beside her. After taking a long swig of lager, he sighed blissfully: 'Oh, that's good.'

She pushed a ten-pound note towards him. 'Put that in your pocket.'

'No, this is my treat.' He pushed it back and brushed her hand. The contact shocked her as if she'd accidentally touched a live wire and she gasped.

'You okay?' He frowned.

Nodding, she gulped a mouthful of lager. She coughed and spluttered as it went down the wrong way. Jon took the glass from her and banged her between the shoulder blades. She could feel her nose running and her eyes watering. God, how embarrassing. Jon handed her a tissue and she wiped her eyes and blew her nose. She took a deep breath and looked at him. He was trying so hard not to laugh and she started to giggle – 'I feel such an idiot.'

He smiled and raised an amused eyebrow. He held a menu out: 'Well, that certainly broke the ice. Better choose something to eat, before anything else happens. I'm going to have the chilli and rice, it's always good. I can recommend the chicken curry, too.'

'Mmm.' Sheena's eyes lit up. 'Chicken curry for me, please.'

Jon went to order the food and Sheena composed herself and took off her jacket.

'What's Roy like?' she asked when he came back. 'As a person, I mean.'

'He's a real nice guy. He and my dad have been friends since their schooldays. They're as close, if not closer, than brothers.'

'Livvy's nervous about meeting up with him again.'

'I'm not surprised. I tell you, that was some affair. – it knocked everyone for six.'

'Livvy told me that Roy loved her.'

'Oh, he did, I guess. It wasn't just a casual fling, if that's what you're thinking. He was really into her. I mean, he must have been, to be unfaithful to Sammy. Their marriage was supposedly pretty solid.'

Sheena nodded thoughtfully. 'But that's what we all like to think, isn't it?'

'Well, isn't yours?' Jon frowned.

She nodded slowly. 'It wasn't mine I had in mind actually.'

'Well, whose then?' Jon asked. 'Surely you don't mean mine?'

'I don't know anything about the state of your marriage, Jon. I presume you and Jess are very happy?'

'Most of the time we are, yes.' He nodded, lighting a cigarette. He offered her one.

'No, thanks. It's Livvy's marriage I'm thinking about,' she continued. 'She called Danny last night. He was in a hotel room with another woman. She was so shocked and upset, she'd always assumed she had a very faithful husband.'

'So, what's going to happen there then?'

'I don't honestly know. She has such a lot of emotional stuff going on at the moment. What with Roy and Harley and finding her real family, she hardly needs this mess with Danny.'

Jon shook his head as the waitress arrived with the food. 'Poor Liv. Let's just hope things go okay this afternoon when she meets up with Roy and Harley.'

* * *

The heavens opened as Jon and Sheena left the pub. 'Shit!' Jon turned up the collar of his jacket.

'I've a wee folding brolly in my bag,' Sheena said. She took the brolly out and shook it.

'Now if I get under there with you, I'll be on my knees,' Jon said. He took the brolly and she moved closer to him as he held it down on her side and put his free arm around her shoulders.

'Shall we make a dash for it, or do you want to saunter slowly in the rain with me?'

Sheena stared at him for a long moment. 'Saunter slowly in the rain with you. I always liked that old Ronettes' song.'

'"Walking in the Rain",' he said. 'I was brought up on a diet of Phil Spector songs. Mum's a big fan. Well, here we are.' He stopped in front of the shop. 'Back to work for me. How are you going to spend the rest of your day?'

'I may have a lie-down or a long soak in the bath,' she said. 'The world's my oyster, so to speak.'

'Oysters are aphrodisiacs,' Jon said softly, looking into her eyes.

'I've never had the need of aphrodisiacs.'

'I bet you haven't.' He bent to kiss her lips lightly, then pulled her closer and kissed her passionately. 'Oh, Sheena,' he whispered into her hair. 'I've been dying to do that since I first set eyes on you.'

She pushed him away. 'I'd better go.' She grabbed her brolly and shot off down the street without a backward glance.

Jon, his head reeling, stared after her for a long moment, then turned and walked into the shop.

'How was lunch with the lovely Sheena?' Sean said.

Liam's eyes lit up, almost as though he was expecting to hear a bit of scandal.

'Liam, go downstairs and help Shelley,' Sean ordered. 'Tell her Jon will be five minutes and then she can go for lunch.'

''S'not fair,' Liam said as he reluctantly sloped off. 'I miss out on all the gossip. How the heck can I keep Shelley up to date if I only hear the tail end of everything?'

'Lunch was fine,' Jon replied, rolling his eyes at Liam's departing back.

'So, what was wrong with your face when you came upstairs?'

'I kissed her and she ran away,' he confessed.

'What, you mean kissed her properly, or gave her a goodbye peck?'

'I kissed her properly. Real full-on.'

'Fucking hell!'

'It seemed like a good idea at the time and I thought it was what she wanted, too. I've got to apologise before she flies home.' Tonight was late-night opening and he didn't feel like he could face it. 'If it's okay with you, I'll finish at four thirty today, go to the hotel and try and see her.'

'That's fine,' Sean said. 'Ian's in until eight thirty. He and Shelley can manage downstairs and Liam can help me up here. Shelley's always glad of a couple of extra hours' pay. Do you think it's wise to see Sheena alone?'

'I don't want her to think badly of me and if I wait till Livvy's there, it might be embarrassing. Sheena may not want to tell her what happened.'

'Fair enough, mate. I can see you're quite smitten, so be careful – don't get too out of your depth.'

9

Harley breathed a sigh of relief as she left the consulting room. Doctor Carey had asked her to wait in reception while he had a word with Mum and Dad. He'd looked down her throat, into her eyes, checked her gums and nails, studied her bruises, weighed her and generally prodded her about. He'd remained silent throughout, but didn't look too concerned, she thought. He probably wanted to discuss Mum's hot flushes in private. She picked up a copy of *Hello!* and flopped down on the window seat.

* * *

Roy felt his face draining as the doctor told them he needed to admit Harley to hospital, as a matter of urgency, for further tests. The first blood samples had revealed that she was anaemic and had an abnormal increase of white corpuscles in her blood.

'I'll arrange admission for Friday. You'll have a couple of days to prepare her.'

'What sort of tests are you on about?' Roy asked. He could feel sweat on his forehead and his mouth felt dry.

'I'm requesting a bone marrow sample test.'

Sammy sucked in her breath, her face ashen. 'You think she has leukaemia, don't you?'

'No!' Roy exclaimed, his stomach lurching.

'I can't say anything for certain at this stage,' the doctor said. 'When the results are in front of me, I can make a proper diagnosis.'

'This test,' Roy said, 'will it be painful?'

'It's done under a local anaesthetic. They insert a fine needle into the bone at the back of the pelvis. It's not a particularly painful procedure, but she'll be uncomfortable and aware of poking and prodding.'

Roy nodded. 'And then what? Will she be allowed home?'

'You can take her home the same night. We'll be in touch as soon as we have the results, probably Monday or Tuesday next week. She'll be a bit sore, so they'll prescribe painkillers and she'll need to rest over the weekend.'

'And if it *is* leukaemia?' Roy held his breath.

'Let's cross that bridge when we come to it, Mr Cantello. In almost all cases it's treatable *and* curable. Now I'm quite sure you're going to, but *do* try not to worry too much.'

'Easier said than done,' Roy replied. 'We need to think about how we'll tell Harley the news without frightening her.'

'You know her better than anyone else, so I'll leave that to you.' Doctor Carey stood up to shake their hands. 'My secretary will be in touch tomorrow with the admission details.'

'Thank you,' Roy said. He grabbed Sammy's hand as they left the consulting room.

* * *

'Go and lie down for an hour, Harley,' Roy ordered as the family arrived back at Jasmine House. 'Try and have a little nap and I'll come and wake you at half two and we'll go and meet Livvy.'

'Okay, Dad. Are you going over to Aunt Jane's, Mum?'

'In a while. I'm collecting Pat and the three of us are going to have a good old gossip.'

'Mum, if you see Jack, remind him that I'll be out when he gets home from school. Ask him to ring me later, please,' Harley called as she went upstairs.

'Will do,' Sammy called back. 'Enjoy your visit with Livvy.'

'Would you like a coffee before you go out? Then we can talk,' Roy said, lighting a cigarette. On the way home, they'd told Harley that the tests had shown she was anaemic and needed to rest. She hadn't questioned it.

'Please. Instant will do,' Sammy said as Roy made the drinks. 'I think we should leave telling Harley about the bone marrow tests until tomorrow – meeting her mother will be enough to cope with for one day. You'll have to tell Livvy, though God knows how with Harley around. If she goes to the loo, tell Livvy as briefly as you can and that you'll ring her tonight after Harley's gone to bed. You can explain things properly then.'

Roy sighed. 'What bloody awful news to drop on Livvy's toes after all this time! I hope it's not leukaemia. People die from that, don't they?'

'Not everyone. Doctor Carey said there's a good chance of a cure.'

Roy joined her at the table and handed her a mug. 'But it's cancer, Sam. Why the hell would a young girl have cancer?'

'I've no idea.' She patted his hand. 'These things happen.'

'I was a really heavy smoker when she was conceived. Is this my fault?'

'Roy, don't beat yourself up. You were a smoker when Nick and Jason were conceived. They were just fine, it's not because of anything you did.'

'But I could lose her, Sam,' he said, a catch in his voice. 'I couldn't bear it.'

* * *

Sammy sat silently, hands wrapped around her mug. She should comfort Roy, but she *too* had lost a precious child and Harley meant as much to her as her own flesh and blood did. This time, Livvy would also know the agony of having a child possibly at death's door, just as Sammy had suffered when Nick had been taken from her.

She finished her coffee and went to stand behind him: 'Roy.' She slipped her arms around his waist and hugged him. 'Come on, let's try positive thinking instead of this negativity. I love you and we'll get through this as a team, like we've got through everything else life's thrown our way.'

He turned and kissed the top of her head. She held her face up for more and his lips met hers. 'Thought you were going to Jane's when you finished your coffee?' he said, crushing her to him.

'It can wait a while,' she whispered. 'Let's go upstairs while Harley's sleeping.'

He looked into her eyes. 'Okay, you *always* know how to make me feel good.'

'Well... I've had years of practice!'

* * *

'Do I look okay?' Livvy asked as she twirled around in front of Sheena. 'I don't want to look too flash or too mumsy, just somewhere in-between.'

'You look lovely,' Sheena assured her. 'The suit's a good choice and that shade of pale green is perfect for your colouring.'

'What about my hair? Does it look okay loose like this?' Livvy fluffed out her blonde curls for the umpteenth time.

'Yes. It looks all soft and feminine.'

'Am I showing too much leg?'

'Of course not. Anyway, those silky stockings look sexy – Roy won't be able to take his eyes off you.'

'Oh, don't! I feel nervous, like a wee girl going on her first date. What if Harley hates me on sight?'

'Stop it, Liv. You'll work yourself into a right tizzy. Why would she hate you, for heaven's sake?'

'Because I gave her away, maybe!'

'But you gave her to her father, not to strangers.'

'Yes, but I still regret it. I can never forgive myself for that.'

'I know.' Sheena nodded. 'But what's done is done. All you can do is meet her and see how it goes. You forgave your dad on the spot last week and I have no doubt you will feel the same when you meet your mum.'

'But those were very different circumstances,' Livvy said. 'They were forced into handing me over. I willingly gave Harley away and accepted all that money when I signed the agreement.'

'Well, presumably Harley has no knowledge of the deal. You and Roy would be wise in keeping that to yourselves.'

Livvy nodded and sat down on the edge of the bed, smoothing her linen skirt over her knees. 'How did your lunch with Jon go?'

Sheena blushed and smiled sheepishly. 'I made a complete fool of myself.'

'Why? What did you do?'

'First of all, I choked on my drink and he had to slap me on the back. After that... well, we got on really well. We talked about all sorts, our kids and stuff. Then outside the store, he kissed me and I *mean*, kissed me. I scuttled away like a frightened teenager.'

'Sheena! Now what?'

'I don't know. I mean, do I call him, or just let it go?'

'Hell, *I* don't know,' Livvy said. 'We'll talk about it later. I must go now. Will you be okay on your own for a couple of hours?'

'I'll be fine. I'll jump in the bath and then sleep. Good luck, Liv. Enjoy yourself.'

* * *

Livvy chose a seating arrangement of two brown leather chairs and a sofa. She placed her handbag on the oak coffee table in-between and sank into the comfort of one of the chairs. She busied herself by studying the afternoon tea menu, glancing nervously at the entrance doors every few seconds.

At exactly three thirty the doors flew open and she caught her breath as Roy, holding the hand of a khaki-clad teenage girl, sauntered through. He raised his hand in a friendly wave as the pair strolled across the room towards her.

For the rest of her life Livvy would always remember those precious seconds as his eyes held hers and he broke into an easy smile. He let go of the girl's hand and held out his arms. Livvy melted into them. He enveloped her and whispered, 'I've missed you so much.'

She stepped back and looked up at him, searching his eyes for something she knew with certainty would still be there. Her stomach turned over and her legs felt like jelly. 'You look well, Roy. You've hardly changed at all,' she faltered as he squeezed her tightly again.

* * *

Harley observed her parents greeting each other, a shy smile playing on her face. Her mother was beautiful, much nicer than those posed photographs she'd seen in *Hello!*. She looked so young too, almost like a teenager herself. As though remembering the purpose of the visit, her dad composed himself: 'Harley, I'd like you to meet your mother.' He pulled Harley close. 'Livvy, meet your daughter.' Harley shyly stuck out her hand and then as Livvy held out her arms, she walked into them and was hugged tightly, Livvy's tears mingling with her own.

'It's so wonderful to see you, Harley, please sit down.' Livvy gestured to the sofa.

Harley took a seat as Roy hesitated momentarily. 'Sit with me, Dad, please,' Harley said. He sat down and took her hand in his.

* * *

Livvy saw how comfortable and at ease Roy and Harley were together and was assured that her daughter was adored by her father.

They began to talk, all three at once. Livvy asked Harley about school, her friends, her favourite music. At one point she grinned and pointed to the outfit Harley was wearing. 'You won't believe this,' she said. 'I bought exactly the same outfit from Gap this morning for my daughter, Courtney.'

'Cool!' Harley exclaimed.

Livvy smiled. She wanted to ask Roy about Harley's health. Judging by the paleness of her skin and the dark smudges beneath her eyes, her daughter wasn't very well and there was the matter of the blood tests too. 'Shall we order? The menu looks nice.'

'Please.' Harley nodded enthusiastically. 'Do you think they'll have chocolate éclairs, Livvy?'

'I'm sure they will,' Livvy said, remembering back to the lewd conversation in Flanagan and Grey's yesterday.

'I'll have an éclair and Coke, please. Where's the ladies' loo, Dad?' Harley lowered her voice.

Roy shrugged and looked at Livvy.

'Go out to reception and turn right. You'll see a little sign pointing down one of the corridors. It's a bit of a walk, take care that you don't get lost.'

'Thanks. Give me the car keys, Dad. I've left my phone on the dash and I'm expecting a text from Jack. Won't be long.' Harley hurried across the lounge as Livvy summoned the waitress and placed their order.

'So, what do you think of our girl?' Roy asked proudly. 'Stunning, or what?'

'She's beautiful.' Livvy nodded, on the verge of tears again. 'But then, I always knew she would be. Roy, what's wrong with her? Why is she so pale? She looks really ill. You told me she'd had blood tests. Is it serious? Please be honest with me.'

He nodded. 'I'll call you tonight after she's gone to bed, I'll explain everything then.'

She jumped up and grabbed his arm. 'Tell me now! Why can't you tell me now? Why do I have to wait till tonight?'

'It's not very private in here.' He looked around.

'There's hardly anyone about.' She glanced at the handful of people, tucking into afternoon tea. 'What on earth is it? Why all the cloak-and-dagger stuff?'

He looked at her with such a haunted expression and pulled her down on the sofa beside him.

'Roy, please. You're scaring me.'

'There's no easy way to say it.' He took her hands and held them tightly. 'There's a possibility Harley may have leukaemia. She's going into hospital on Friday for a bone marrow test. We'll know the results early next week.'

'No! No, Roy, surely not? Not our girl, not now.'

His eyes were moist. 'Oh, Liv, I'm so sorry. I promise I'll call you tonight and tell you everything, how she's been and stuff.

We haven't told her yet, we only found out this morning. We'll tell her tomorrow.'

'Oh, poor Harley. How on earth is she going to cope with that?' She saw the sadness in his eyes as he shook his head in answer. Thank God she was around to support him. 'Roy, what you said before. Have you really missed me?'

He looked up. 'Yes, of course. I have a constant reminder of you. I could never, ever forget, nor would I choose to.'

'But you're still with Sammy?'

'Well yeah, of course I am. I love her, Livvy, you know that. *We'd* be together otherwise. I'm sure you *also* know that.'

She nodded. 'I still love you,' she said softly. 'My life's been in limbo since the day I gave Harley to you. Danny's given me six months to sort myself out or he wants a divorce.'

She could see the shock on Roy's face. 'I thought you were happy with Danny. Does he know I'm Harley's father?'

'No. The only other person who knows is my friend Sheena.'

'I see.' He stared at her. 'If I'm honest, Liv, I've been dreading this day. I knew once I looked into your eyes again, I'd be lost.'

'And are you?'

He shrugged. 'Change the subject. Harley's just walked in and the waitress is on the way over.'

Harley sat back down next to Roy and handed him his keys. 'The ladies' loo is lovely, very posh with fresh flowers and peach hand cream.' She held her hand up to Roy's nose.

'Smells like cat pee to me!' he said.

'Dad, you've no finesse.'

'That's what your mother's always telling me,' he said as the waitress left a laden trolley. 'Sammy thinks I'm a lost cause,' he said, lifting plates of sandwiches and cakes onto the coffee table. 'But you know what it's like. When you've stayed in as many hotels as the band has over the years, you become blasé. One place is much the same as another and I make a point of *never* using the hand cream.'

Livvy smiled and poured two cups of tea. He hadn't changed. 'Still sweet enough, Roy, or do you take sugar these days?'

He shook his head, accepted a cup of tea and helped himself to a handful of dainty smoked salmon and cucumber sandwiches. 'There's enough to feed an army here,' he said, tucking in.

'What's your house like, Livvy?' Harley asked. 'Mum showed me the magazine photos and it looks very nice, but you could only see bits of it.'

'Well, as you saw, it's a white-painted ranch with a lot of land and a swimming pool,' Livvy replied. 'We have horses too – we all ride. The ranch is in a place called Santa Ana and that's in Orange County, Los Angeles.'

'Are you anywhere near Disney World?'

'Not too far,' Livvy told her. 'Courtney loves to go there, but we get to spend so little time together as a family because of work commitments – we've only managed a couple of visits in the last few years.'

'We've been to Disney World in Florida a few times, haven't we?' Harley turned to Roy. 'But Dad works away a lot too, don't you?'

'Unfortunately, yes. But I'm home for a good few months now, barring recording sessions and a few TV shows.' He helped himself to a scone and spread it liberally with clotted cream and strawberry jam.

'I've taken six months off so I can spend time with Courtney,' Livvy said. 'Would you like to see some photographs of my family and our home, Harley?' She smiled at Roy as he licked his sticky fingers and stood up, brushing crumbs from his black trousers.

'Just popping to the little boys' room,' he said as Livvy

joined Harley on the sofa. 'Back in two ticks to finish off what you pair don't eat.'

* * *

Roy stood by the door. Livvy and Harley made a delightful picture, sitting side by side, heads together, shoulders touching as they studied the photographs that Livvy had produced from her handbag.

He swallowed hard. In spite of the difference in their colouring, they were so alike. Same mannerisms, identical smiles, they could have been teenage sisters, never mind mother and daughter. Livvy was still so beautiful; she'd hardly changed at all. He was fighting the urge to sweep her into his arms and carry her off to her room. It was a good job Harley was with him, because Roy knew that in spite of his promises to Sammy, he'd probably be struggling to keep his hands off Livvy by now if they'd been alone.

He made his way to the gents' and glanced into the lift as the doors were closing. He frowned and stopped. Was that Jon Mellor standing to the back of the lift? The man had his head down, so Roy couldn't be sure, but there was a strong resemblance. The distinctive, thick dark curls for one. But it couldn't have been Jon, he'd be working at this time of day. Ah well, Roy thought, there were plenty of curly-headed men around – he must have been mistaken.

* * *

Harley gazed at the photographs of her half-sister, sitting astride her pony and helping her father sail his yacht. There were pictures of the family at Disney World and of Courtney sitting alone on the steps of the swimming pool at the ranch in Santa Ana. 'How old is Courtney?' she asked.

'Fifteen, in June,' Livvy replied.

'Will I be able to meet her?'

'I don't see why not, if it's what you would like – I'm sure she would too.'

'Is she at your home in America?'

'No, honey, at the moment Courtney's staying at my friend's house in Scotland.'

'Why did she go to Scotland and not come here with you?' Harley frowned.

Livvy told her why they'd flown to Glasgow first. She explained about her past, her own adoption and how she had traced her father and his family.

Harley sat quietly, nodding now and again. 'They'll be my relatives too then. Do you think you'll get to meet your own mother soon?'

'I hope so, Harley, I really do.'

'Why did you give me away? I mean, you weren't a young teenager like your own mum was. Why didn't you keep me with you?'

Livvy sighed and took her hand. 'I wanted you to grow up knowing your father. I knew that if I kept you that wouldn't have been possible. Because of who he is, it would have created too much bad publicity for all concerned. He'd gone back to Sammy and I felt I'd done enough damage to their marriage without staying around to rub salt in her wounds. They'd lost Nick that same year. Your dad and I had caused Sammy so much pain, I wanted to try and ease it a little. Believe me, it wasn't an easy decision, but at the time I felt it was the right one, the only one, in fact, that would give *you* two parents under the same roof.'

Harley nodded. 'They both love me very much.'

'Oh, *very* much, Harley. I don't think I made the wrong choice, do you?'

'No, you probably didn't,' she agreed as Roy rejoined them, pointing to the teapot.

'Shall *I* be mother this time?'

'Please do,' Livvy said, grabbing a handful of paper napkins as he slopped tea into cups *and* saucers.

* * *

Jon asked at reception for Sheena's room number and headed for the lift. He pressed the button for the third floor and stared at his shoes, wondering if he was making a huge mistake. The doors slid together and the lift began to ascend. What if she refused to see him?

He stood outside room 323 for what seemed like forever. He tapped the door lightly and held his breath. Sheena opened the door a fraction. 'Hi,' he said as her mouth fell open. She stepped back to let him in. His eyes searched her face, which was glowing and devoid of make-up. Her hair hung in damp tendrils around her cheeks, her feet were bare and her pink silk robe clung to her contours.

'I've just taken a bath,' she faltered, blushing slightly as he continued to stare.

'I gathered that,' he said. 'I've come to apologise for kissing you without your consent.'

'I see.' She gave him a bashful smile. 'Your apology, although not necessary, is accepted. Err, please have a seat.'

'Where?' He glanced around the room, taking in the chair by the window and the inviting double bed.

'Anywhere you like.'

Jon removed his outer jacket and placed it over the back of the chair. He sat on the edge of the bed, his hands shaking, and his head screaming that he shouldn't be here.

'Can I get you a drink?' Sheena opened the door to the mini bar.

'Is there any brandy in there?' If he didn't calm his churning guts soon, he felt he might throw up.

Sheena emptied a miniature bottle into a glass and handed it to him. He knocked it back in one go.

'That's better.' He smiled and looked at her.

'Would you like another?'

'Better not. I had those two pints at lunchtime and I've got to drive home. Don't want to risk being over the limit.'

She stood in front of him, twisting the ties of her robe nervously around her fingers. 'Jon,' she began, 'why are you *really* here? Shouldn't you be at work?'

'I've taken time off, to see you.'

'Why?'

He shrugged helplessly. 'Don't know. Would you like me to go?'

'No.'

He reached for her hand and kissed her fingers one by one. 'If I kiss you now, will you promise not to run away again?'

'There's nowhere to run to this time.'

He pulled her onto his knee. She put her arms around his neck and looked into his eyes. He kissed her, gently at first and then passionately, pulling her ever closer. She broke away and pushed his suit jacket off his shoulders, her trembling fingers reaching to undo the buttons on his shirt. Jon stood up, pulled her to her feet and undid the ties of her robe. It slid silently to the floor. She was naked underneath and he felt the blood rushing to his groin as he took in her shapely curves, neat waist and pert breasts.

She helped him undress and they tumbled onto the bed. Jon blocked out a mental picture of Jess's trusting face and they spent the next hour, kissing, caressing and exploring every inch of each other. When he sensed her every nerve was at screaming point, he moved up the bed and slid into her. Sheena gasped and lifted her hips to meet him. He thrust enthusiastically time and again until her wild cries sent him crashing to his own climax. They collapsed in a tangle of arms and legs on a bed that was now devoid of sheets and blankets.

He smiled at her. 'Where the hell did that come from?'

She shook her head. 'God knows. I've never made love like that in my life. I've only known you just over twenty-four hours. I feel so wanton and lusty and… well, it's so out of character for me to do something like this,' she babbled, words tumbling over one another.

'Sheena… shut up,' he said and rolled off her. 'I *know* you don't do this all the time. Neither do I, for God's sake. But there was something between us right from meeting yesterday.'

'I suppose,' she said sheepishly. 'Livvy told me that when Roy first made love to her, it was like flying to the moon and back. I couldn't begin to imagine what she meant – but now I know.'

'I haven't been able to get you out of my head,' Jon confessed. 'I mean, I've hardly given a thought to my family. My mind has been totally filled with you.'

She nodded. 'I haven't even called Gerry and the kids today.'

Jon sat up and pulled her up with him. 'Come on, we'll start feeling guilty and it will spoil what we just had. Do you mind if I smoke?'

'Go ahead. I'll make coffee.' She slid out of bed.

Jon's eyes narrowed as they followed her across the room.

'Sheena, you're so beautiful,' he said.

'Thank you.' She switched on the kettle and turned to smile. 'I could say the same about you – you're incredibly fit.'

He leant back on the pillows and blew smoke above his head. 'Two sugars for me. By the way, I know it's a bit late to mention this, but I've had a vasectomy, so we're quite safe.'

She raised an amused eyebrow. 'Very thoughtful of you to mention it, Jon, but I'm sterilised.'

'Ah, well, doubly protected then. I feel brilliant, I haven't felt so alive in ages.'

'I've *never* felt like this, not ever.'

'Where's Livvy this afternoon?'

'Having tea in the lounge with Roy and Harley,' she said, handing him a mug. She climbed up next to him and sipped her coffee.

'Shit, I'd forgotten Roy was coming here today! It's a good job I didn't bump into him in reception.'

'You'll have to wait here until Livvy comes back to her room, then you'll be sure he's gone home,' Sheena said.

'Actually, if you don't mind, I could do with staying here until at least eight. Jess knows it's my late night and she'll wonder why I'm home early if I go now – it's only just after six.'

'Stay as long as you like,' Sheena said. 'Stay all night if you want to.'

'I would, if I could – you temptress.' He put down his drink and stubbed his cigarette out in the ashtray. He removed the mug from her hands and took her in his arms again. 'You've made me feel good about myself.' He pulled her down beside him. 'Shall we...? Before Livvy puts in an appearance.'

'You're insatiable,' she said. 'I thought you'd be worn out after all that.'

'I am a little,' he admitted. 'But I'm sure I could manage it again with a bit of encouragement.'

* * *

Roy checked his watch and turned to Harley: 'Better be making tracks, princess.' He handed her the car keys. 'Go sit in the car while me and Livvy have a private word. Say goodbye first.'

Livvy smiled. 'Before you go, I've something for you.' She rummaged in her handbag and handed Harley a small beribboned package. 'To make up for some of the birthdays and Christmases I've missed.'

Harley tore excitedly at the wrappings. She gasped with delight as she opened a box to reveal a solid gold Tag Heuer watch with a bronze face. 'Oh wow, it's boss! Look, Dad. Everybody wants one with a bronze face.'

Roy smiled at her excitement. 'It's fabulous,' he replied. 'You'll have to be very careful not to lose it.'

'I thought it was something that might last you a lifetime,' Livvy said.

'It's cool, Livvy, really cool. Faye Blackwell at school has a fake one and she's always showing it off. Wait till she sees this, it'll really put her nose out of joint. I can't wait to show it to my boyfriend, Jack.' She hugged Livvy and put the watch in her handbag. 'Can I see you again, Livvy? Perhaps over the weekend?'

'Go and get in the car now, sweetheart,' Roy said, before Livvy could reply. 'We'll organise something soon.'

'But, Dad...' Harley protested.

'Car, now,' he said.

'Okay, okay, I'm going,' she said, poking out her tongue. 'Keep your wig on!' She gave Livvy a kiss and hugged her tightly. 'I'll see you very soon, fix something up with him.'

'I'm going back to Glasgow on Friday, but I'm free tomorrow. Why don't you come with me to Sean and Tina's for tea?'

'I'd love that. They're my godparents. I'll see you tomorrow then. Arrange with Dad about times and stuff.'

Roy turned to Livvy as Harley called goodbye and walked away.

'I wish you could stay with me,' she said. 'I need you so badly.'

He blew out his cheeks and looked at her. 'I hate leaving you after dropping that bombshell on your toes but I have to take Harley home – I can't have her sitting in the car alone for too long.'

'Of course you can't. Good luck with telling her, I wish I could be there for you.'

'I'll be okay, but I don't know what sort of reception you'll get from her tomorrow afternoon.' He hesitated for a minute. 'Come to the house at two and we'll take it from there.'

'What about Sammy? Will she be there?'

Roy sighed. Under the circumstances he didn't feel he had a choice. 'Just come to the house and leave Sammy to me. When did you say you go back to Glasgow?'

'Friday morning. But I'm not going back if Harley's ill – I want to be here for her.'

'What about your other daughter?' Roy frowned. 'Don't you have to get back for her?'

'Sheena could go back to Glasgow and probably drive Courtney down here for me. Oh, I don't know... I'm not thinking straight at the moment. This is so awful, I can't believe it.'

'I know it is. But we'll get through it, you'll see. Harley's a strong character, she'll fight whatever it is. I'll call you tonight. I'll try and speak to you without Sammy being around. But with *my* track record, she'll be watching me like a hawk at the moment.' He pulled her into his arms and kissed her. 'I had to do that,' he said breathlessly as he pulled away.

'I'm glad you did.' Livvy reached up and stroked his cheek. 'I meant what I said – I need you, Roy.'

'So do Sammy and Harley,' he whispered into her hair.

'And what about what *you* need?'

'What I want and need doesn't matter at the moment.' He pushed her gently away. 'I'll call you later and I'll see you tomorrow. Bye, Liv.'

'Bye, Roy.' She watched him walk away, a lone tear sliding down her cheek.

10

Sheena wrestled with the satin bedspread then plumped up the pillows. She jumped as someone rapped on the door. She opened it a fraction and peered out. 'Hi, Liv, come on in. Are you okay? You look really pale. How did it go?' She smiled warily as Livvy cast her eyes over Jon's discarded clothes on the bedroom chair and floor. She looked away from Livvy's questioning gaze. 'I've... err... just been making the bed. What a struggle. I'm used to duvets, not all these blankets and stuff...' Sheena realised she was babbling and stopped.

Livvy raised an eyebrow. 'So... where is he?'

'Taking a shower.'

'You decided to call him after all?'

'No. He just turned up.'

'What have you done?'

Sheena shrugged. 'Sounds like a real lame excuse, but... well, it just happened.'

'Jess will kill him – and probably you as well!'

'She won't know. How can she possibly find out?'

'Wives always do. I wouldn't like to be in *your* shoes when she does.'

The bathroom door opened and Jon strolled out, towelling himself dry. He blushed as he spotted Livvy and hastily wrapped the towel around his middle.

'Caught in the act! Jon Mellor, what on earth are you playing at?'

He shrugged and smiled sheepishly. 'Not a word to anyone, please, Liv.'

'You know I won't. But it's a dangerous game. You've got happy marriages, kids, responsibilities.'

'We won't be doing it again,' Sheena said. 'It was a one-off, well... a two-off actually!' She smiled at Jon, who blushed more furiously.

'Sheena! Behave yourself.' He turned to Livvy. 'How did it go?'

Livvy flopped down on the bed and sighed. 'Really well. Harley's lovely, I'm very proud of her. Roy and Sammy have done a wonderful job of bringing her up and I'm happy with that.'

'So why the frown?' Sheena asked.

'Harley's ill,' Livvy said quietly. 'She may have leukaemia. She's having a bone marrow test on Friday.'

'Oh, Livvy, no!' Sheena sank down beside her and put an arm around her.

'Liv, I'm so sorry.' Jon patted her shoulder. 'How's Harley coping?'

'She doesn't know. Roy and Sammy are telling her in the morning. I'm collecting her from Roy's place tomorrow after-noon. She's coming to Sean and Tina's with us so you'll get to meet her then.'

'And will I get to meet Roy?' Sheena asked.

'Of course.' Livvy smiled wearily.

'How *were* things between you and Roy?' Jon asked, fastening his towel snugly around his waist.

'Fine,' Livvy said. 'I don't want to go back to Scotland on

Friday. If the news is bad, I want to be here for Harley and Roy.'

'What about Courtney and your family?' Sheena said. 'They're expecting you back. There might also be news of your mother.'

'Listen, Liv,' Jon said, 'go home with Sheena, catch up with your family, then fly back with Courtney next week. If Jess agrees, you can stay with us. Then you can visit Harley if she's in hospital for any length of time and we can take care of Courtney for you.'

Livvy smiled gratefully. 'You'd better ask Jess first – I don't think she'll be that keen on the idea. If the news *is* bad, I'll rent a furnished property short-term. I want to be here for my girl. We got along so well today and I'm not about to leave her again at any cost.'

'What about Danny?' Sheena asked.

'I'll call him tonight. I'll call Hank from the band as well. He can tell the others that I may have to stay in England indefinitely.'

'What about your career?' Jon said. 'You can't just abandon ship, the rest of the band depends on you for their livelihood.'

'We've only just finished a tour. Half of them work as session musicians when the band's not touring anyway. To be honest, at the moment I wouldn't care if I never sing again. My daughter is my number-one priority right now.'

'Daughters,' Sheena reminded her. 'Livvy, you have to tell Courtney about Harley. If you're going to be living here for a few months, then she'll need to go to school.'

'I know,' Livvy said. 'There's all sorts to think about. I'll book flights back here tomorrow and if you'll ask Jess if she wouldn't mind putting us up, I'd be very grateful, Jon. Don't worry if she says no.'

'Okay,' he said. 'Well... I suppose I'd better be making tracks. I won't say anything tonight because how would I know that Harley is ill? I'll do it tomorrow after you see Sean and Tina. Jess may already know if Sammy's spoken to Mum.'

'I thought you were staying till eight,' Sheena said.

'I think you both need a little time to talk, I'll go back to the shop for a while.'

Sheena nodded. 'Thanks, Jon.'

Livvy smiled at them. 'I'll leave you two alone to say good-night. Do you fancy room service later, Sheena? I can't face the restaurant.'

'Sure.' Sheena nodded. 'I can't be bothered getting dolled up anyway – I feel worn out.'

'I'm not surprised!' Livvy looked pointedly at Jon. 'I'll see you soon.'

* * *

Left alone, Jon looked at Sheena: 'If Livvy stays in England for a few months, you could come and visit often, couldn't you?'

She nodded. 'Maybe.'

He picked up his clothes and began to dress. 'Do you think there's a chance of us seeing one another again before you go back?'

'Not on our own, Jon.'

'Why not?'

Her eyes filled with tears. 'Because I could so easily fall in love with you and I'm not free to do that.' He stared at the floor as she continued: 'Let's put this afternoon down to a moment of madness.'

He reached out and stroked her cheek. 'Okay, but I don't think I'll forget it in a hurry.'

'Nor me,' she said as he carried on dressing. 'We've too much to lose and too many people would get hurt if we continued.'

'You're right,' he said. 'And you're too bloody sensible for your own good.'

'I always have been,' she said.

'Thanks for a wonderful time.' He pulled her close and kissed her. 'I don't want to go,' he groaned, lips lingering on hers.

'You have to.' She handed him his jacket and pushed him gently towards the door. 'Now are you sure you've got everything?' She reached up and tweaked a curl in place. 'That's better.' She smiled brightly, blinking back a tear. 'Bye, Jon.'

'Bye, Sheena,' he said, his eyes bright.

As he strolled down the corridor towards the lift she called his name and he turned. *'You're the best!'* she called and wiggled her hips, Tina-Turner style.

His face broke into a smile. 'Thanks. So are you.'

* * *

Roy poured himself a single malt and handed Sammy a G&T. He sat down beside her and patted his knees for her to place her long legs across his. He gently massaged her feet and she sighed with pleasure. They hadn't had a minute to themselves since he and Harley had arrived home. Jack had been to visit and stayed for dinner. Then Jason and Jules arrived with the first scan pictures of the expected baby; their excitement had rubbed off on Harley and Sammy.

Roy had done his best to share in their joy, but he'd drawn the line when Jason produced a Mothercare bag and pulled out baby clothes. Claiming an urgent need for the loo, he'd escaped to the music room and spent an hour sitting alone, reflecting on his afternoon with Livvy. Holding her close and kissing her had awakened long-buried feelings. He'd love to spend some time alone with her, but couldn't for the life of him fathom out how to organise it.

During the affair, Sammy had worked full-time in her business and he was free to see Livvy anytime *she* wasn't working herself. But now Sammy was retired, and they did most things together, it wasn't that easy to go missing without his absence being clocked. He couldn't ask Ed to cover for him again, as he'd done in the past – it wasn't right to involve anyone else. He'd called The Midland to speak to Livvy.

'Hi, Liv, how are you feeling? I know. Don't worry, we'll get through it together. No, I'm alone in the music room. Jason and Jules are here and it's all baby talk downstairs. Oh, of course, you don't know. The boys are expecting a surrogate baby – Jason's the sperm donor.

'A shock. Yeah. How the hell do you think *I* feel? They've brought the first scan pictures round. No, you can't tell what it is. Has a look of E.T. to me. They're thrilled to bits, so are Sammy and Harley. It's me that can't get my head around it. I told 'em a turkey baster's no substitute for the real thing. It gives me the heebie-jeebies, if I'm honest. Well yeah, as you say, each to his own. Goodnight, Liv, try not to worry too much and I'll see you tomorrow. No, I haven't told Sammy you're coming here yet – I need a few drinks for Dutch courage first. Just leave it with me.'

He'd ended the call and walked out onto the landing as Jason shouted upstairs that he and Jules were about to leave. 'Okay, son, goodnight and you too, Jules.'

Harley had wandered upstairs, looking pale and weary. 'Night, Dad, I'm off to bed.'

'Night, princess.' He'd followed her into her bedroom and drew the curtains. She sat down on the bed and picked up the box containing her new watch.

'Wasn't it kind of Livvy to give me this? I really like her, Dad. She's so pretty, so very different to what I expected.' She giggled. 'She must have been a right ego boost to an old man of forty-two!'

'Right, monkey, that's enough.' He pulled her close and tickled her ribs.

'Dad, stop, I'll have loads of bruises there now.'

'Sorry, darling.' He let her go and stroked her cheek. 'I didn't think.'

'It's okay, don't worry.'

'Hey, what's that?' He reached for the chain around her neck. 'What's this ring?'

'Jack gave it to me,' she said. 'We're secretly engaged.'

'Engaged?'

'Yes. And before you start having a go and say we're too young, *you* gave Mum a ring when *she* was still at school.'

'You're right, I did.' He wrapped his arms around her and his eyes filled with tears. 'Princess, if it makes you happy, then it's okay with me.' He kissed the top of her head. 'Right, I'm going downstairs now to join Mum for a drink. I'll tell her your news.'

'Okay, Dad. I love you.' Harley smiled as he stood up. 'By the way, I've told Jack about Livvy – I don't want to keep secrets from him. He won't say anything to Nathan or anyone else at school.'

'Okay, love. Jack's a good lad, we can trust him. What did he say?'

'He thought I was kidding him. I told him to ask his dad for confirmation.'

He smiled and nodded. 'Sleep tight.' He'd closed her bedroom door, choking back tears. 'God, why *my* child?' he muttered. 'Didn't you take enough from me when you took Nick, you bastard?'

'Roy,' Sammy had called up the stairs, 'who are you talking to?'

'No one, love,' he replied and made his way down to the hall. 'I was just remonstrating with bloody God over the unfairness of everything.'

Roy continued massaging Sammy's feet and braced himself. 'I told Livvy about Harley's illness and what's going to happen,' he began as Sammy stiffened.

'Oh, did you? And where was Harley?'

'She went to the loo and then as we were leaving, I sent her to sit in the car while I finished telling Livvy. It's not fair to give her that sort of news over the phone. She was very upset, devastated in fact.'

'I'm sure she was. But you shouldn't have been on your own with her, other than if Harley needed the loo.'

'Sammy, don't tell me what to do. You know I can't stand it.'

She swung her legs down and glared at him. 'And *I* can't stand *you* being on your own with *her*!'

'Hell, Sam, it was five minutes! I had to tell her our daughter may have a life-threatening illness. We were in a busy hotel lounge. Why can't you trust me? What on earth did you think we would get up to? Quick shag on the Wilton? Or what about a blow job behind the grand piano?'

She jumped up and slapped him across the face. 'This is no laughing matter. I took you back and brought up *your* child on the understanding you'd have nothing more to do with her mother. Now she's back and we've already had two arguments on the first day you see her.'

'Well, she's coming here tomorrow afternoon to collect Harley. She's taking her to Sean and Tina's for tea so you'd better get your head around that.'

The colour drained from Sammy's face as she stared at him. 'No way! You cancel that this minute.'

'I'm sorry, Sam. I'm not prepared to do that. The situation has changed because of Harley's illness. She and Livvy got on really well today and it would be cruel of me to stop them seeing one another, especially now.'

Tears filled Sammy's eyes as she turned away from him.

'Sammy, love, please try and understand how it is for me,' he pleaded. 'I'm like piggy in the middle with you and Livvy.'

'Well, *you* try and understand how *I* feel, Roy. How would you like it if I arranged to meet up with Stuart Green one day?'

'You know I wouldn't, but then again, it's hardly the same thing. You and Stuart had a one-night stand, Livvy and I produced a child. I want that child to know her mother.' Roy knew Sammy had only thrown Stuart's name into the equation to hurt him. She'd sought solace in the arms of their old friend during his affair. The one-night stand had meant little to Sammy, but Roy knew that Stuart was secretly in love with his wife and had been for years.

Sammy took a deep breath, sat down again and grabbed Roy's hand. 'I'm sorry, Roy. I overreacted. Under the circumstances, Livvy can come to the house.'

'Thanks, Sam.' He took her in his arms and kissed her. 'Shall we call a truce and have an early night?'

'Yeah.' She nodded. 'You lock up, put the alarms on. I'll run a bath and light some scented candles.'

'I'll bring up a bottle of chilled white and we can relax in the tub. Oh, and by the way,' he said with a smile, 'your girl's secretly engaged to Jack.'

* * *

Jon negotiated the large puddles in the private lane leading to Hanover's Lodge and his barn conversion home. Guilty thoughts crowded his head, like how could he look Jess in the eye, and what if she decided she wanted to make love later? He was absolutely spent and would find it difficult to raise anything other than a smile that night.

He parked his car, took a deep breath, straightened his tie and headed indoors. The wonderful aroma of home-made curry met him. The kitchen table was set for two and candles and an open bottle of red wine took centre stage. Jess had been working hard and he wasn't even hungry after the huge meal at lunchtime.

'Jess,' he called, looking into the lounge and finding it empty.

Jack popped his head around the door. 'Hi, Dad. Mum's nipped across to Pops' to borrow some rice.'

'Okay. How was school today?'

'Alright, I suppose. Bit boring. Got loads of homework.'

'Poor you. Where's Nathan?'

'He's at Faye's.'

'Thought he was still grounded till Saturday.'

'Ah, well, he's doing his homework at her place. Faye's dad's bringing him home later.'

'Fair enough.' He lit a cigarette and poured a glass of wine. Jack continued to stare at him. Jon could feel his face warming. Had Jack guessed his secret?

'Something on your mind, son?'

'Yeah. Harley told me something tonight: she said Livvy Grant is her mother and not Aunt Sammy. That Uncle Roy had an affair with Livvy years ago and she was the result. She said to ask you if I didn't believe her. I *do*, but why all the secrecy?'

Jon breathed a sigh of relief. 'It *is* true. Sit down.' He kept the details brief and Jack nodded solemnly.

'Wow! I bet that caused a bit of a scandal.'

'It was all kept very hush-hush but I guess these things have a habit of coming out. Now that Livvy's here, who knows what the outcome will be?'

Jack looked up as Jess arrived back. 'You've been ages, Mum.'

She smiled and bent to kiss Jon. 'I've just been chatting to Mum and Dad. Go and finish your homework, Jack, while I have a quiet word with your dad.'

'What's wrong?' Jon frowned and took a really lengthy drag

on his cigarette. He could feel beads of sweat break on his forehead as he stared at Jess. She was still as stunning as she'd
always been. Slim, but curvy, long dark hair and big blue eyes,
just like their dad's. Why the fuck had he cheated on her? What
if she found out and left him? He felt sick. He couldn't lose Jess,
she was his life. Sheena was right: it had been fun, but a
moment of utter madness and one never to be repeated.

'Sammy called Mum earlier,' Jess said as he poured her a
drink and tried to concentrate. 'Harley's ill.' She told Jon what
he already knew.

* * *

Harley stared at her parents, her eyes wide. 'A girl at school had
leukaemia,' she wailed. 'Her hair fell out. You told me I was
anaemic.'

Roy reached for her hand. 'You are, but the hospital just
wanted to do this test to rule out leukaemia.'

'This girl at school, Harley, how is she now?' Sammy asked.

'She's okay. Her hair grew back, she's been in remission for
ages. She had a bone marrow transplant. Her mum and dad had
to have another baby so she could have the transplant from the
cells in its cord.'

'Did they?' Sammy looked thoughtful. She got up to clear
the breakfast dishes then turned, an over-bright smile on her
face. 'Now just in case you stay in hospital overnight, you'll
need to pack a small bag. It's best to be prepared. You'll probably be too tired tonight after your afternoon out with Livvy.'

'Jack's coming to see me straight after school,' Harley said,
'so I'll do it before I take a shower.' She stood up and put her
arms around her mum. 'Thanks for letting Livvy come here
later. It can't be easy for you.'

'And thank *you*, Harley, for being mature enough to realise
that it isn't.'

'I'll be okay, you know, Mum. Even if I *have* got leukaemia, I'll still be okay. I just want to feel well again, to go back to school and out for walks with Jack. All the things I like to do, but haven't the energy for at the moment.'

Roy nodded and Harley saw him swallow hard. 'We'll be beside you every step of the way, princess. Whatever it takes, we'll do it, won't we, Mum?'

Sammy said yes, but Harley saw her eyes blinking fast as she turned away.

* * *

'You look shattered, Liv. Didn't you sleep well?' Sheena asked as they ate breakfast in Sheena's room.

'Not really. I've been worrying myself sick over Harley and then just as I was dozing off, Danny called. I told him I'd seen Harley, that she's ill and I'm thinking of staying in Britain indefinitely.'

'And?' Sheena tore the lid off a pot of strawberry yoghurt and licked it clean.

'He said... if I want to stay then Courtney has to go back home and he'll come and collect her.'

'Hell, how do you feel about that?'

'I'll give Courtney a choice. I'd like her to get to know her sister. Harley's keen to meet Courtney, too. I don't want Danny interfering with that.'

'Did you tell Danny that Roy Cantello is Harley's father?'

'Umm, no. He asked, rather sarcastically, if I'd seen my ex-lover. I told him he'd brought Harley to the hotel, but we didn't exchange more than a few words. He called me a liar. I ended the call and switched my cell phone off all night.' Livvy drank her coffee and changed the subject. 'I'm going to hire a car for later. We can have a drive to Stockport before we collect Harley and I'll show you where I used to live and the old haunts where

The Raiders used to play. It'll take my mind off meeting Sammy.'

* * *

Following a whistle-stop tour of Stockport and lunch in The Black Lion, Livvy drove to Ashlea Village and stopped outside the old sandstone church. 'I won't be a moment,' she told Sheena, who frowned as Livvy leant into the back of the car and retrieved a bunch of white lilies from the seat.

'Why are we stopping here?' Sheena asked. 'I thought those flowers were for Tina.'

'Come with me,' Livvy said, adding, 'I got perfume for Tina.' She led the way to a grave near the side of the church. The marble headstone bore the legend in gold lettering that Nicholas Roy Cantello rested there.

As Livvy knelt to place the lilies on the well-tended plot, tears filled her eyes with the memory of a good-looking, fun-loving teenager who'd befriended her and welcomed her into his band and his home, but whose friendship she'd ultimately betrayed.

Livvy looked up as Sheena laid her hand on her shoulder. 'Poor Nick, he was such a great guy and I let him down.'

'So did his dad,' Sheena reminded her.

'This graveyard is where I told Eddie I was pregnant.'

'Oh, Liv, come on, let's get it over with,' Sheena said gently.

Livvy got to her feet and they walked to the car. 'The house is only two minutes from here,' she said.

As they approached the entrance gates to Jasmine House, Livvy's hands shook uncontrollably.

Sheena leant across her to press the intercom. 'Wow, this is lovely!' she said as a disembodied female voice said, 'Come in,' and the gates swung open. They drove slowly up the long gravel driveway towards the double-fronted Edwardian house. 'Just look at those daffodils!' Either side of the drive, the sweeping lawns were home to hundreds of nodding daffodils that created golden pools under the willow trees.

'Those security gates are a new addition,' Livvy said, pulling up in front of the garage block.

'Sign of the times.' Sheena clambered out of the car. 'This is fabulous, Livvy. It's almost a mansion.'

'Jasmine House is Roy and Sammy's pride and joy,' Livvy said. 'It's amazing what skipping school, never doing your home-work and always being in trouble of one sort or another can do for you. Plus, a little rock 'n' roll thrown in for good measure, of course. Backstreet boy makes good.' She locked the car. 'It was a familiar story in those days. Now if Roy had been a good student, like we're always nagging our kids to be, he'd have had none of this.'

Sheena chuckled. 'You're probably right. The Oasis brothers are from these parts too, aren't they?'

Livvy nodded. 'The Gallaghers are from Burnage, a few miles away.' She closed her eyes and took a deep breath. 'Right, I'm ready. Come on, let's go for it.' She propelled Sheena up the front steps, rang the bell and stepped back. The door was thrown open and Harley, grinning broadly, welcomed them inside.

Livvy gave her a big hug, then said, 'Harley, meet my friend, Sheena. Sheena, this is my daughter, Harley.'

'Pleased to meet you, Sheena,' Harley said.

'Likewise,' Sheena replied, taking the small outstretched hand. 'She's very like you,' she said to Livvy. 'Apart from her colouring, of course.'

'*I* think she's the image of her father,' Livvy said.

As if on cue, Roy strolled into the hall. 'Couldn't have got away with this one, could I?' He put an arm around Harley's shoulders and hugged her tightly. 'Not that I would have wanted to, princess,' he reassured her as a frown crossed her face.

'Sheena, this is Roy, Harley's father, and Roy, this is my friend, Sheena,' Livvy introduced them and Roy shook Sheena's hand.

'Nice to meet you, Sheena. Come through to the lounge. Sammy's making tea. Harley, pop in the kitchen and give Mum a hand.'

'I need the loo, and anyway, she said you had to help.'

'Okay, I know my place,' Roy said. 'Livvy, you take Sheena into the lounge.' Livvy hesitated momentarily. 'Go on, it's where it always was. We'll be two minutes.'

Sheena followed Livvy into the huge lounge at the rear of the house. 'Oh, wow! Just look at that swimming pool!' She strode towards the French doors at the top end of the room. The pool, set just below the patio area, shimmered in the bright spring sunshine. 'Do you think it will be heated? It looks lovely, but cold!'

'I'm sure it will be,' Livvy said. 'You can't possibly have an unheated pool in this country. They didn't have one last time I was here, which was Nick's eighteenth birthday party. They had a huge marquee in the garden with a stage and I got up and sang with Roy and Eddie that night. It's the only time I've *ever* sung with Roy, in fact.' She gazed wistfully around the room with its cream walls, deep-pile, beige carpet and large, brown leather sofas, placed either side of the marble fireplace. 'It's all changed since then. Everything is new but it's still as tasteful as ever.'

'Who's that?' Sheena was standing beside a small table that held a collection of silver-framed photographs. She pointed to a large photo of a young couple wrapped in one another's arms, gazing lovingly into each other's eyes. 'They're a very handsome pair.'

'It's Nick and Jess,' Livvy said. 'Taken the night of Nick's party, just weeks before he died.'

'Poor wee man,' Sheena said. 'Jess is very beautiful. No surprise Jon fell in love with her.'

'Yes, she is,' Livvy agreed. 'Mind you, that photo was taken in 1984. She may have changed a bit since then.'

'Nick was extremely good-looking.' Sheena smiled. 'The image of his father.'

'You like him then? His father, I mean?'

'I'll say I do! He's even nicer in the flesh. I can't believe I'm standing in Roy Cantello's lounge and my best friend is the mother of his daughter. It's so weird.'

Livvy grinned and pointed to another photograph of two university graduates attired in caps and gowns: 'That's Jason and Jules, they must have got their degrees after I left. And see that other photo at the back there? That'll be the joint christening. There's Jon and Jess and their twins Jack and Nathan, and Roy and Sammy with Harley. That was the last day I spoke on the phone to Roy until this very week.'

'Admiring the rogues' gallery?' Roy said, coming into the room carrying a laden silver tray.

'I was just explaining to Sheena who everyone is,' Livvy replied, smiling at him.

'Well, take a seat and we'll have some tea.' He put the tray on the coffee table. 'I think Harley must have gone to her room. She was rummaging through boxes of photographs this lunchtime and she's made an album for you. She's probably applying the finishing touches before she brings it down.' He looked up. 'Ah, here's Sammy. Come on, love.' He patted the seat beside him as Livvy and Sheena settled on the opposite sofa.

* * *

'So, how are you, Livvy?' Sammy smiled tightly as Livvy smiled warily back.

'I'm fine, thank you, Sammy. Err, this is my friend, Sheena.'

Sammy nodded politely and busied herself pouring tea. She'd been dreading this moment for years and no matter how hard she tried, she couldn't rid herself of the mental picture of Roy romping naked with Livvy. Thoughts of him kissing her, running his hands through her hair, making love and creating a child were torturous.

Bile rose in her throat and she swallowed. Her cool gaze took in Livvy's immaculate white linen trousers, neat, grey leather jacket and her tumbling, blonde curls. She looked so young still. Sammy was suddenly aware that Livvy was speaking to her and that Roy was taking a cup and saucer from her shaking hands as the room started to spin.

'Sammy, are you okay, darling?' Roy was now looking worriedly into her eyes.

'Actually no, I'm not. Would you excuse me, please?' Sammy rose unsteadily, aware that all eyes were on her. She left the room, ran up the stairs and into her bedroom. Leaning against the closed door, she felt a fool for running away. This just wouldn't do. She needed to be stronger, showing solidarity with Roy, not giving Livvy a chance to see any chink in their relationship.

'Why can't I be more cool and collected, like *her*?' she muttered as she flung herself across the bed. She'd have been better going out to Pat or Jane's, showing that she could cope with Roy and Livvy together and wasn't a clingy wife who was scared of losing her man. Truth is, what Harley had said this morning, about the girl at school having a bone marrow transplant from the stem cells of a new sibling, had bothered her and when Roy came into the kitchen to collect the tray, she was sure she'd seen a light in his eyes that wasn't there before.

* * *

'We shouldn't have come here,' Livvy told Roy. 'You could have brought Harley to Tina's. If the boot was on the other foot, I'm quite sure I wouldn't like it either.'

'You're right,' he said. 'I'm an insensitive swine. She'll want a bit of space. I'll go up to her when you've gone. Have you decided yet what you're doing tomorrow?'

'I'm going to Glasgow for the weekend. I'll fly back here on Monday with Courtney and take it from there. I want to be around when the test results come through.'

Roy went to sit next to Livvy. He reached for her hand. 'We'll get through it. We all need to pull together. Sammy will be fine once she gets used to you being around. Whatever it takes, getting Harley well is what matters most.'

Close to tears, Livvy nodded, loving the feel of his hand on hers.

Harley walked into the room, clutching a large red scrapbook. On the front she'd stuck letters cut from shiny gold paper, stating THIS WAS MY LIFE – BY HARLEY NICOLA CANTELLO. The title struck a cold fear in Livvy's heart, but she kept a bright smile on her face as Harley spoke: 'See, Livvy, it's like *This Is Your Life* from the TV. It's some of the bits of me that you've missed. I thought you could show it to my sister then when we meet, I won't be such a stranger to her.'

'Oh, sweetie, it's so thoughtful of you.' Livvy touched Harley's cheek as Roy, his eyes moist, gathered the cups and saucers and carried the tray out of the room.

'I'm glad he's gone.' Harley lowered her voice to a whisper. 'I want to show you something.' She hitched up her short skirt, exposing her thigh. 'See, my tattoo. It's a J for Jack, but it's fading now. What do you think, Livvy? Cool or what?!'

Sheena stifled a giggle as Livvy raised her eyebrows.

'Err, yes,' Livvy spluttered. 'Very cool.' She frowned at the bruises on Harley's thighs. 'Are those bruises painful?'

'No, they're not actually. But they look horrible, don't they? Dad tickled my ribs last night and I've got them there now. You know I have to have a bone marrow test tomorrow? The doctor said I might have leukaemia.'

Livvy nodded. 'Your dad told me. I have to go back to Glasgow tomorrow. I'll be back on Monday and will bring Courtney with me. We'll both be here for you when the test results come through.'

'Oh, cool! That will take my mind off things. I can't wait to meet Courtney, I'm amazed that I've got a half-sister. *You* can meet Jack later; he'll be here when we get back from Tina's. You'll love him, you really will. He's gorgeous, with dark curly hair and big blue eyes and he smiles like this.' She did an impression of Jack's lopsided grin and burst into fits of giggles. 'And look...' She pulled out the chain and ring from down her sweater. 'We're secretly engaged. Mum and Dad know, but Jack's parents don't yet.'

Livvy smiled at Harley's enthusiasm and the fact that she was clearly smitten by young Jack Mellor. She gave her a hug. 'Umm, I guess congratulations are in order, then.'

Roy strolled back into the room. 'Ready to go, girls? Give my love to Aunt Tina,' he said to Harley. 'See you all later.'

11

Jack lolled against the playground wall, kicking the heel of his shoe against the old sandstone bricks. He couldn't stop thinking about Harley. He wished it was home time. If everything went according to plan at the hospital today, he'd be able to see her tonight. He looked up. Someone was calling his name and he saw Faye Blackwell and Jamie Donahue walking towards him: 'Hi, Faye, Jamie.'

'You okay, Jack?' Faye asked.

'Yeah, err no, not really.'

'You thinking about Harls, mate?' Jamie patted his arm sympathetically.

Jack nodded, blinking hard.

'Aw, Jack, she'll be okay.' Faye gave him a hug. 'Are you seeing her later?'

'Hope so,' he said.

'I've got a card and a little gift for her in my desk, I'll give them to you after school,' Faye added.

'Yeah, err, I've got her some chocolates,' Jamie said.

'Thanks,' Jack said. 'She needs all the cheering up she can get at the moment.'

'C'mon.' Faye linked her arm through his. 'Let's go find Nathan and get ourselves a hot drink and a biscuit before break finishes.'

* * *

'Sheena, are you ready to go?' Livvy asked. 'The taxi will be here soon, we need to be waiting in reception.'

'Yeah, I'm ready,' she replied, and dragged her case into the corridor. A passing porter stopped and took their bags and they followed him into the lift. 'Do you think I should call Jon and say goodbye?'

'Why? What's the point?'

'I know... but... well, I can't bear the thought of not saying a final goodbye to him.'

'Call him then,' Livvy said as the lift came to a halt and the porter took their cases to the reception desk. She settled their bill and turned to Sheena, who was dithering by the revolving entrance doors.

'Here.' She handed her the mobile phone. 'Press number two – it'll take you straight through to the shop.'

'Oh, I can't.' Sheena handed the phone back.

Livvy tutted and pressed number two.

'Hi, Sean, it's Livvy. Is Jon there, please? Oh, okay. Well, say bye to him from Sheena and me. Thanks again for a lovely afternoon yesterday. I'll see you next week.' She ended the call and looked at Sheena: 'Jon's popped out for a few minutes.'

'Oh!' Sheena's face fell. 'It wasn't meant to be then.'

The uniformed doorman called their names and announced the taxi was waiting. The porter took the luggage out to the black cab. Sheena was about to clamber into the back when someone tapped her on the shoulder.

'Were you really going without saying goodbye?'

She spun round. 'Oh, Jon.' She threw her arms around him

and gave him a quick kiss. He gave her a squeeze and turned to Livvy, giving her a hug and a kiss on the cheek.

'So, this is where you popped out to?' Livvy said. 'I just called the shop to say goodbye.'

'Ah, well, I called here and they told me your leaving was imminent, so I nipped out. I wanted to wish you a safe trip and I'll tell Jess I've spoken to you, see if she'll agree to your staying with us. Hope things go okay for Harley this morning.'

'Thanks, Jon. I've booked a couple of nights here next week for Courtney and me, so I'll be in touch sometime on Monday.'

'I'd better get back to work. Goodbye then.' He waved and walked away.

'Well?' Livvy looked at Sheena. 'That wasn't as awkward as you were expecting. Jon seems to have put your moment of madness behind him.'

'He does,' she replied and climbed into the taxi, staring wistfully at Jon's departing back.

* * *

'We'll see you later, princess,' Roy said.

Harley lay on the trolley in her blue and white hospital gown, a green blanket tucked around her legs. He squeezed her hand as her anxious eyes searched his face.

'You won't go home, Dad, you promise?' she said, clinging to him as she fought back tears.

'I'll be right here. We'll have a bit of lunch and then we'll be waiting in your room when you come back.'

'I *will* be able to come home tonight, won't I? I'm really scared now.'

'Yes, darling, they did say that,' Sammy said, fighting back her own tears. 'Don't be scared, sweetheart. They'll look after you, or they'll have your dad and me to answer to,' she added, trying her best to make Harley smile. She smoothed her hair from her face and kissed her forehead. 'Now, be a brave girl and we'll see you later.' She waved as a porter pushed the trolley away.

Roy stared after her. 'Please let her be alright,' he muttered.

'C'mon, Roy, let's get some lunch.' Sammy steered him towards the lift.

'I don't feel very hungry,' he said as they entered the busy hospital restaurant. He stopped by the door – he couldn't handle being stared at today, prying eyes and people whispering behind their hands. And what if a staff member had told the press he was there?

'Have a coffee and a Danish pastry,' Sammy suggested. 'You need to eat something, you didn't have breakfast and you've chain-smoked all night. You're going to make yourself ill at this rate.'

'Okay.' He kept his eyes on the floor and made his way to a table at the back while Sammy joined the queue. He felt he really couldn't get his head around anything. Sammy had been strong for him during the last few hours and for that, he was grateful.

Sammy carried a tray to the table. 'Got you an apple and cinnamon Danish, your favourite.'

'Thanks, darling.' He sighed wearily. 'This brings back a time almost sixteen years ago,' he said. 'Sitting around drinking coffee and waiting.'

'Nick?' she whispered as his face crumpled. She reached for his hand, fighting back her own tears.

'How can this be happening to us again, Sam?' he choked. 'Have I been so bad that I deserve to lose two of my kids?'

'Roy, stop! This isn't helping either of us. It's nothing to do with how good or bad you've been. If the diagnosis *is* leukaemia, Harley has a *very* good chance of survival. You need to have hope, we both do.' She cleared her throat and swallowed.

'Think how bad Livvy must be feeling right now, knowing she can't be here.'

He nodded. 'You're right. I'll call her tonight with an update.'

Sammy sipped her drink and squeezed his hand.

* * *

'There's Gerry and Courtney.' Livvy pointed as she and Sheena made their way through the busy arrivals hall. She waved as Courtney leapt up and down and waved back.

'Welcome home, girls,' Gerry said and bent to kiss Sheena. 'I've missed you,' he whispered to her.

'Missed you too,' she said, blushing slightly.

Courtney flung her arms around Livvy. 'Oh, Mom, I'm so glad you're back.'

'Aw, and me too, honey,' she said, hugging Courtney tight.

Gerry loaded the luggage onto a trolley and they followed him out to the car.

'Dad's coming,' Courtney said, beaming from ear to ear.

'Coming where?' Livvy looked at Gerry.

'Danny called this morning,' he said as he lifted the cases into the boot of his Ford Mondeo. 'He's flying in Wednesday.'

'Oh!' Livvy's jaw dropped.

'Thought you'd be pleased,' Gerry said as they climbed into the car.

'Well, yes, I suppose I am but I wish he'd discussed it with me first. Something's come up and I have to go back to Manchester on Monday. I'm taking Courtney with me.'

'I see.' Gerry raised a surprised eyebrow. 'You'd better call him and tell him your plans. He could change his connection then. No point in coming up here if you two aren't around.'

'I will,' Livvy said quietly, staring out of the window as the scenery passed by in a blur. Damn! Having Danny around was the last thing she needed at the moment. She was bracing herself to tell Courtney about Harley tonight and *that* wouldn't be easy.

'By the way, Cassie's off school,' Gerry said as they pulled up outside the house. 'She's been coughing all night. I left her in bed, but she'll probably get up now you're home.' He took the luggage indoors and pecked Sheena on the cheek. 'I'm nipping out to see a client about a kitchen. Back in a couple of hours. Your mum made chicken casserole, it's in the oven on low. See you later.'

'Okay, thanks, Gerry,' Sheena said. 'I'll pop up and see Cassie. Make yourself at home, Liv.'

Livvy kicked off her shoes. Gerry left and Sheena disappeared upstairs. She was back in minutes. 'She's okay and asking for *you*, Courtney. Fancy a cuppa, Liv?' she asked as Courtney went off to see Cassie.

'I could murder one.' Livvy followed Sheena into the kitchen. She sat down on a bar stool and gazed out of the window at Fred and Sandy, who were sleeping by their kennels, tails flicking and paws moving as though running in their dreams. Sheena filled the kettle and stood with her back to Livvy, seemingly staring into space. 'Penny for them?'

'What? Oh... they're not worth a penny.' Sheena turned and smiled. 'I'm beginning to understand how you feel about Danny now. When Gerry put his arms around me, I felt nothing. For the first time ever, I felt nothing – I can't get Jon Mellor out of my mind.'

Livvy shook her head. 'What did I tell you?'

'Ah well, it's my own stupid fault. I'll get over it.'

She brewed two mugs of tea and handed one to Livvy. They sat in companionable silence for a while.

* * *

'Why can't they stay at the hotel?' Jess asked, taking a sip of wine. They'd just finished dinner and Jon had asked if Livvy and her daughter could stay with them for a few days. 'For starters, we haven't got a spare room. Where do you propose we put them?'

He shrugged. 'I thought they could have the boys' room and they could sleep over at Dad's place. It would help if Courtney had somewhere to stay while Livvy visits Harley.'

'Well, she could take her to Sean and Tina's, surely? And they've got the space to put them up.'

'Okay. I just thought it would be a nice gesture, to show a bit of support to Livvy. But if you're going to be unreasonable, forget it,' Jon said.

'I'm not being unreasonable.' Jess frowned. 'Why are you being snappy with me?'

'I'm not.' He lit a cigarette and stared at the ceiling. 'Bit of compassion's all I asked for, no need to get tetchy about it.'

'I'm not getting tetchy, don't try and guilt trip me.' Jess slammed down her wine glass and pushed back her chair. 'I'd feel I was betraying Sammy for one thing. I don't know what's wrong with you this week, you keep picking arguments.' She grabbed her car keys and made for the door.

'Where are you going?'

'To collect Jack from Roy's place. Didn't you notice his absence at dinner?'

'I'll go for him,' Jon said, stubbing his cigarette out.

'You've had too much wine and you knocked back that large brandy when you came in.' She left the house and slammed the door.

Jon followed her outside and watched as she clambered into the Jeep and sped off down the lane. Guilt at sleeping with Sheena was making him snappy, and although it would never be repeated, he still couldn't stop thinking about her. He strode across the gardens towards his parents' place – *might as well have a drink with Dad and put the world to rights.*

* * *

Harley smiled as she looked across at the beautiful vase of roses Jack had brought. Before his mum had picked him up, they'd had a kiss and cuddle in her room that was bathed in a soft glow from the scented candle gift from Faye. They'd also devoured Jamie's chocolates. Jack had told her that no matter what happened, he would always be there for her and they'd made the decision that she would now wear the ring on her finger, except at school. He was going to tell his mum and dad tomorrow that they were engaged. A gentle tapping at the door brought her back to the minute.

'Come in.'

'Hi, princess,' Roy said. 'I've brought you a cup of tea and some biscuits. How are you feeling?'

'A bit tender on my backside, but otherwise okay. Has Livvy called yet?'

'No, love, but I'll ring her later if she doesn't call in the next hour.'

'Do you think she'll be telling Courtney about me tonight?'

'Yeah, that was her plan. Maybe she'll call after that.' He smoothed her hair from her face and gently caressed her cheek. 'Don't forget to take your painkillers before you fall asleep.'

'I won't. I'll watch a bit of telly then have an early night.'

'Ah, the phone's ringing.' He stood up. 'Might be Jason actually, he's not called yet. I'll see you later, sweetheart.'

'Bye, Dad.' She blew him a kiss as he left the room.

* * *

Courtney lay on the bed, staring at her mother, and then back at the red scrapbook she'd been given. Mom had just told her the most amazing tale about a baby she'd had to give away. 'A sister? I've honestly and truly got a sister?'

'You have,' she said, smiling. 'Harley's a year older than you.'

'Wow, I'm collecting a lot of family on this trip, but a sister, that's wonderful, Mom!' Courtney flung her arms around Livvy. 'I don't want to go back to the States. Get Dad to stay in Britain and then Harley can come and live with us and we can be a proper family.'

'I think Harley rather likes living with her father and she's already got a mum – Roy's wife Sammy has brought her up.'

'Yes, but she was *your* baby, Mom. Can't you get her back?'

'It doesn't work that way, sweetie. But Harley wants to meet you and on Monday, we're flying to Manchester and I'll introduce you to each other.'

'What about Dad? He's supposed to be coming to Glasgow.'

'I'll call him later. Now try and get some sleep and I'll see you in the morning.'

'I'm going to have another look at Harley's album first. Anyway, I'm way too excited to sleep!'

* * *

Livvy's conversation with Daniel was stilted. He told her they needed to have a serious talk about things.

'Why can't it wait till we get home?' she asked. 'After the other night, I have nothing to say to you, Danny.'

'That's why I need to talk to you, to explain. Don't forget, we have a daughter to think about.'

'What's to explain? You obviously didn't give Courtney a thought when you were screwing your secretary, or whoever the hell she was.'

'I'm not getting into that on the phone, we'll discuss things next week. When I return to the States, I'm bringing Courtney back with me.'

'Not a chance!' Livvy shouted. 'She's staying with me. We're flying to Manchester on Monday, so we won't be here when you arrive.'

'Why are you going to Manchester again?'

'You know why. Because Harley's had the bone marrow tests done today. I want to be around when the results come back.'

Daniel was quiet for a moment. 'Of course, I'm sorry, I forgot.'

'Well, you would, wouldn't you? Courtney's looking forward to meeting her sister.'

'So, you've already told Courtney about her?'

'Of course, I've told her everything.'

'Everything?' Daniel's voice raised an octave. 'Including the name of Harley's father?'

'Yes, even that. Harley's father is the rock musician, Roy Cantello. Harley lives with Roy and his wife.' Daniel was silent again. 'Are you still there, Danny?'

'Yes. Why have you never told me this before? For God's sake, Livvy, Roy Cantello is old enough to be your father, never mind your daughter's! What on earth were you thinking?'

'I was in love with him,' she said softly. 'The age gap meant nothing to us.'

'I think you've got a hell of a lot of explaining to do.'

'And so have you!' she yelled. 'Now that's it, Danny. I've nothing more to say to you tonight.' She slammed the phone down.

Sheena walked into the lounge and handed her a G&T. 'Get that down you.' She sat on the sofa next to Livvy and took a sip of her own drink.

'Thanks,' Livvy said. 'Where's Gerry?'

'Taking a shower.' She tapped her fingers against her glass. 'I'm dreading going to bed. Do you think he'll be able to tell?'

'Of course he won't. Not unless you give off odd vibes. Try and be as normal as possible.'

'Easier said than done. He's bound to make a move after going without for a few days. I can't even tell him I've got my monthly, because he'll remember that I had one last week.' Sheena stared gloomily into the fire and sighed. 'Oh well, might as well get it over and done with, then it's out of the way for a while. God, listen to me, I sound like my mother. She can't abide my dad in the same room, never mind the same bed!'

Livvy smiled at Sheena's troubled face. 'Get another G&T down you, but for goodness' sake, whatever you do, don't call him Jon.'

They both giggled as the phone rang out. Sheena answered, her face breaking into a wide smile. 'She's here, just hold on, Roy.' She handed the phone to Livvy. 'I'll leave you to talk and top up our glasses.'

Livvy chatted with Roy, who told her Harley was home and that the hospital would be in touch with the test results early the following week.

'Give Harley my love,' she said. 'Tell her that her sister's dying to meet her. I spoke to my dad earlier and we're having lunch with the family on Sunday. They've got some news of my mother. Can you believe it that after all this time, I've actually got roots? I'll speak to you Monday evening then. Yes, The Midland, same as before. See you soon, Roy. Bye.'

Livvy sat back on the sofa, hugging her knees to her chest, wondering how on earth she was going to find the strength to cope with the next couple of months.

12

'Phone's ringing,' Livvy said, passing the gravy boat to Courtney.

'I'll get it.' Leanne jumped up and Livvy saw her half-sister exchange a look with their dad as she hurried from the room. Livvy stared at him as his eyes lit up and a slow smile spread across his face. She cut into a crispy roast potato and wondered what the pair were up to.

'Dad.' Leanne walked back into the room. 'Gina... for you.'

Livvy dropped her knife on her plate and almost choked on the mouthful of food. 'Gina? My mother?' she said as her dad stood up and gave her a pat on the back.

'Pour her a glass of water, Leanne. I'll be back in a minute.'

Leanne sat down and poured Livvy a drink.

She sipped it slowly, then said, 'They're in touch, really?'

'Yes. He wanted to surprise you. Have another sip and compose yourself. They've spoken each day since her sister gave her our number. I think they're besotted. He goes all silly when he talks to her. She wants to come home so they can start again. She can't believe Livvy Grant is her wee girl. She told Dad that she actually saw Juice play Maple Leaf Gardens in Toronto last year.'

'Oh my God!' Livvy exclaimed. 'We did two shows there last April. I was so close to my mother and I had no idea.'

'She also told Dad that she's never stopped loving him,' Leanne continued, touching Livvy's hand. 'And he's said the same to her.'

'Aw, bless them.' Livvy's eyes filled with tears and she smiled at Courtney: 'I've got to bring your grandma home as soon as possible.'

Courtney stood up and put her arms around Livvy. 'Mom, I'm so pleased for you. You'll feel complete now.'

Livvy smiled. Complete. What a lovely word. And she was, almost. She'd found her family, made contact with her long-lost daughter and now her mother would be coming home. A jigsaw puzzle with almost all the pieces fitting neatly together. All... except one. She didn't want to go back to the States, to that big empty ranch. It had never felt like home with just her and Courtney rattling around with only the housekeeper for company when Danny was away. And *there* was the crux: she didn't want to go back to Danny either.

If she made a home in Cheshire, Harley could visit whenever she liked. The girls could really get to know one another. Seeing Courtney's excitement at being told about her sister, she'd mulled the idea over last night and the more she thought about it, the better she liked it. She could put her career on hold for a while, concentrate on being a mum, properly. Her dad, calling for her, broke her thoughts and she got to her feet. Leanne and Courtney wished her luck as she left the room.

'Your mum would like to speak to you,' he said, handing her the receiver. He patted her shoulder and left her to talk.

Livvy's hands were trembling and her voice came out an octave higher than normal: 'Hello, Gina, err, Mum... oh... Mummy.' She sobbed and she heard Gina crying and calling her 'Marie, my baby'. 'Oh, Mum, it's wonderful to talk to you. Leanne said you want to come home. When would you like me to book your flight?'

She was quiet as Gina spoke for a while and then said, 'Leave it with me. Dad will call you with the details, we'll meet you at Manchester Airport. I'm flying down myself tomorrow afternoon. I'll book Dad a flight to coincide with your arrival and then we'll be waiting for you. Dad told me we look like twins.'

She laughed as her mother said she believed they did. Gina went on to tell her a bit about her life and how she couldn't wait to be reunited with her and Peter. How every day she woke up full of hope that something would happen and how she couldn't believe it when her sister had called with the news that Livvy had made contact with Peter.

'I've so much to tell you, Mum,' Livvy said. 'You've two lovely granddaughters to get to know. I could talk to you all day, but I know it's costing you a lot of money to phone here and I'm sure you want to talk to Dad again before you hang up.' She heard her mother give a girlish giggle and her heart soared. Her parents were one couple who were surely meant to be together and she had it in her power to make that happen. 'Okay, I'll look forward to it, too. I can't wait. I'll get Dad for you. Bye, Mum.' She handed the phone to her dad, who was hovering by the door, eyes sparkling and cheeks pink with excitement.

Back in the dining room, she smiled at Courtney and her cousins, who were still tucking into their Sunday roast. They looked up with undisguised curiosity. Leanne said, 'Let's take the wine into the lounge, then we can talk properly.' She turned to the teenagers: 'I'll bring an apple pie and jug of custard through and maybe Courtney will serve up.'

'I'll join you in a while, hen,' Leanne's husband said. 'Give you a chance to talk. I'll bring a pot of coffee through later.'

'Thanks, Jamie.'

Leanne led the way into the cosy lounge. She threw a shovel of coal on the fire and plumped up the sofa cushions. The sunlight streamed in through the large bay window. Shielding her eyes, she drew one of the curtains across. 'Can't see a bloomin' thing in here. It looks a nice day, but it's still a bit cold. Make yourself comfortable while I get their pudding,' she said as Livvy flopped down on the sofa.

Leanne was back in seconds and sat in the chair beside the fireplace. 'So, how do you feel now?' She poured two large glasses of red and handed one to Livvy.

'Wonderful, like I'm in a dream. I'll book Gina... err... Mum a flight in the morning before I fly off myself. I'll book Dad's flight, too. Then I'm going to treat them to a few nights in The Midland, so they can get reacquainted.'

'Oh, that's good of you,' Leanne said, wiping a tear on her sweater sleeve. 'He's so made up, you know. He's had a new lease of life since she first called. He deserves to find some happiness. After all, he's only fifty-three and he shouldn't be on his own. He and my mum never really got on, they were always at one another's throats. I tell you, when they were splitting up and me and Pete were given the choice of who to live with, we didn't even have to think. If I see my mother twice a year, it's twice too much. I can't wait to meet *yours* – she sounds such a sweetie. And if they marry... well, she'll be my mum, too.'

'One step at a time,' Livvy said. 'But I have a good feeling about them.' She took a sip of wine and stared into the fire, a smile playing on her lips.

'What's happening with Danny? You said he was flying in on Wednesday.'

'He is, but I won't be here. He'll have to sort himself out. Actually, I've a few things to tell you all, so shall we give Dad and Jamie a shout and ask them to join us?'

'Of course.' Leanne stood up. '*I'll* make the coffee and tell them to come through when they're ready. I doubt Dad will finish his meal, he's too excited.'

Left alone, Livvy allowed herself to think again about happy families. She'd ask Daniel for a divorce, find a property in Ashlea Village, register Courtney at the same school as Harley – and see how things developed with Roy. If Harley had leukaemia, she could help him take care of her by having her stay over. If her condition was much less serious, maybe she'd actually want to live with them. Her new family could visit whenever they wanted.

The holiday she'd promised them in LA would have to be postponed for a while, but she didn't think they'd mind *too* much. Sheena might visit occasionally when she wasn't busy with work. If by any chance things moved forward for her and Roy and he left Sammy, they could be a proper family with their daughters. Have another child together, one whose upbringing they could share.

And then an unbidden thought crept into her head and made her smile. She could *still* have another child with Roy, even if he stayed with Sammy. Coming face to face in that hotel lounge, the chemistry was still there, even after all these years apart, and she knew with certainty that she could persuade him they should make love at the first opportunity. She could take back what she'd given him all those years ago. And this time she'd be better equipped to cope. She finished her wine and put the glass down on the coffee table as the door opened and Leanne, Jamie and her dad walked in.

'I've a few things I need to discuss with you,' Livvy began as Leanne poured the coffee.

'Fire away.' Leanne passed a mug to Livvy.

'Thanks. First of all, my daughter Harley is unwell.' She explained the situation and outlined her plans to stay in England.

Her dad, visibly shocked, took her hand. 'We'll give you all the support you need, hen. But what about Courtney's education, your career and your marriage?'

'I've thought everything through,' Livvy said, stirring her coffee. 'Courtney can go to Manor Banks, same as Harley. It's a private school, so I shouldn't have a problem getting her a temporary place, especially if I tell them it may be permanent. I'll rent a house for now, my career can go on hold and as for my marriage, well, that's pretty much on the rocks. Danny's having an affair. To be honest, I don't love him any more, I don't believe I ever did – he just made me feel safe when I was at my lowest ebb. That's not reason enough to stay married to him. And we've a long-standing problem that won't go away.'

'Anything I can help you with? Not that I mean to pry...' Leanne faltered.

'I know you don't, Leanne. It concerns Harley's father. He was a married man... still is. He's a lot older than me – older than Dad, in fact. We had a brief affair and Harley was the result. Her father and his wife are the people who raised her. You may as well know his identity, because if the truth ever comes out, the press will have a field day.'

'He's not a politician, is he, hen?' her dad looked worried.

Livvy stifled a giggle as she caught Leanne's raised eyebrows. 'Oh no, Dad, he's nothing quite so boring! He's in the same business as me. He's one of the best rock guitarists in the world.'

'Clapton, Townshend?' Jamie offered.

'No, Jamie, not Eric or Pete. Harley's father is Roy Cantello.'

'Really?' Leanne's face lit up. 'Oh my God... he's so good-looking. Fancy getting to jump into bed with him. Livvy, you lucky girl!' She blushed and looked at Jamie, clapping her hand across her mouth.

Leanne's husband rolled his eyes. 'Remind me to get my old

guitar down from the loft next time you claim to have a headache,' he teased as they all laughed.

'Roy Cantello,' Livvy's dad said, nodding his head slowly. 'Fancy that. I've always been a Raiders' fan. I saw them play Glasgow a couple of years ago and they're still as good as ever. Well... you're certainly going to have plenty to tell your mother when she arrives. I won't be able to get a word in with all you girlies! I hope young Harley will soon be well, hen. What a dreadful shock for you.'

'I feel devastated inside. She's so lovely, Dad. The image of Roy with her dark colouring and brown eyes, but petite, like me. She's a lively character, in spite of being so ill. I can't lose her now, not after all this time.' Tears tumbled down her cheeks as her father's arms enfolded her.

'You won't lose her, hen. If she's anything like her mother and grandmother, she's a survivor. Whatever the diagnosis, I'm sure she'll be fine.'

* * *

Jon frowned as he saw Jess slide something under a table mat. She picked up her glass and took a sip of wine. They were dining with Mum and Dad.

'What's that?' he asked, putting down the bottle of Merlot he'd just brought up from his father's wine cellar. He sat down and stared at Jess as Eddie uncorked the bottle and muttered something about leaving it to breathe for a few minutes. Something was going on; Jane and Jess had been whispering a lot while they'd been preparing the meal.

'What's what?' Jess pushed her glass over for a refill.

'That thing you've just shoved out of sight.' Her cheeks were turning pink, she was definitely hiding something. A trickle of perspiration ran down his spine. Could she have got some evidence of his fling with Sheena? Maybe she'd hired a private detective to follow him and had photos of him leaving Sheena's hotel room. He took a long swig of wine and told himself to get a grip. That wasn't even a possibility, as he himself hadn't known he was going to Sheena's room until the last minute. 'Well, come on, what is it?' Guilt made him snappy and he saw his mum frown.

'Tell him, Jess,' she urged. 'Just like your father, he'll give you no peace until you do.'

Jess handed the envelope over. Jon pulled out a brochure: a social services headed letter was paper-clipped to it. He looked at Jess and handed the brochure back. 'Fostering! Is this some kind of joke?'

'Of course not. I asked you last year if we could foster and you said you'd think about it. Every time I bring the subject up, you change it. I just thought I'd make a few enquiries, see what's involved.'

'Jess, I don't even want to discuss this. Don't you think we've got enough with the boys?'

'But they're growing up. I missed out on having more children because *you* had a vasectomy when they were six months old.'

'Well, we didn't want more kids. You said from the start that two was enough. I thought we were in agreement on that score.'

'I think Jess feels she missed out, Jon,' Mum said, patting Jess's hand. 'I mean, *I'd* be more than happy to help out with foster children – I miss having little ones around the place.'

Jon looked at his father for backup but Eddie just shrugged and topped up the glasses.

'It's up to you two.'

'We don't have the room for starters,' Jon said. 'We struggle to make ends meet and before you even suggest it, Jess, I will *not* accept handouts from Dad. He's given us enough with the house, the cars and the boys' education. We stand on our own two feet, right?'

She nodded. 'Money isn't the problem,' she began. 'Social services pay weekly allowances for each child. Dad said he'd pay for an extension to the bungalow, make it into a four-bedroomed place. We need an extension anyway – the boys should have their own rooms now and we could use another bathroom.'

Jon scraped his chair back and stood up. He could feel anger welling. They'd all been discussing this behind his back. Well, it wasn't on. No way was he being a foster parent. For God's sake, the boys drove Jess mad most of the time. She was always grumbling about one thing or another. Why the hell would she want someone else's ankle-biters round her feet now her own two were growing up?

'I thought you were looking forward to spending more time with me when the boys go off to uni,' he said. 'Don't you think we deserve some *us* time for a change?'

'*Us* time! Chance will be a fine thing,' Jess said. 'If you're not working late, you're gigging with one band or another, or out for a drink with Sean. When we *do* spend time together lately, you're snappy with me – well, you have been this last week.'

'I think you two could do with a short break,' Eddie said, passing a cigarette to Jon. 'Me and your mum can keep an eye on the lads. Get something booked as soon as you can and take a bit of time out together. My treat, an early anniversary present.'

'Dad, that's really kind of you,' Jess said. 'Thank you.'

'Yeah, thanks, Dad,' said Jon. 'I'll try and book some time off work.'

'Well, don't leave it too long. The Raiders are in the recording studios in a couple of months. We're doing the final album and a bit of promo. I'll be away for a few weeks and if you do go for a break, Mum will need my help with the kids.'

'Err, I'm quite capable of looking after the boys, you know,' Jane said. 'I brought these two up almost single-handed while you were working away for months on end. Anyway, Kate will be around to help me.'

Jon sat back down. He sipped at his drink and tried to relax. A long weekend away with Jess would be good. It was ages since they'd done that. No kids, total bliss. She might even be up for a bit of passion. And while they were away, he would try and talk her out of this daft idea of fostering.

* * *

Jon was changing the window display with Sean when Shelley called out, 'Jon, lady wants to speak to you.' He tutted and banged his head on a guitar as he crawled out of the narrow space. It'd better not be Jess, mithering about fostering again, he thought as he took the receiver.

'Jon Mellor.' His face broke into a broad grin. 'Sheena, hi. You okay? Sounds noisy, where are you? Oh... right. I'll call her later then. Do you? I miss you, too.' He turned his back on Shelley, who was staring at him curiously. He lowered his voice. 'Oh great... I'll look forward to that. In spite of what we said, I can't stop thinking about *you* either. Yeah, okay. I'll talk to you soon. Bye.'

Sean raised a questioning eyebrow as Jon crawled back into the window space.

'Sheena,' Jon said. 'Calling from the airport. She's just seen Livvy and her daughter off.'

'And how *is* Sheena?'

'Fine. She's coming down in a couple of weeks – *if* Livvy stays.' Jon busied himself with the display, sensing Sean's eyes on his back.

'And?'

'And nothing,' he said. 'Maybe I'll take her out for a drink.'

'Yeah, and the rest. Jess will kill you.'

'It'll just be a drink. And Jess won't know.' He shrugged as the phone rang out again.

'Your wife, Jon,' Shelley called.

'See, she's on the case already.' Sean laughed.

'Very funny. Don't even joke about it.' Jon clambered out of the window space again. 'Jess? I haven't asked him yet. Okay, that sounds nice. You got any money? I'm skint until payday. Oh, did he? Alright, but we can't keep doing that. I'll meet you in Est, Est, Est at six thirty then.'

'Problem?' Sean asked.

'No, Dad's offered to pay for a meal for me and Jess. He's also treating us to a short break away – no kids. I need to book some time off. Jess was just reminding me to check availability.'

'Take whenever. No one's got anything booked in for the next couple of months.'

'Thanks, Sean. I'll ask Jess later if she's sorted anything. She said last night that she fancies Paris or Rome.'

'Very romantic.'

'Yeah, let's hope so.' Jon sighed.

* * *

'So, what's on your mind?' Jon asked as Jess twiddled the stem of her wine glass while they waited for their meal. They were in their favourite budget-priced restaurant. She'd been unusually quiet since she sat down and had hardly looked at him, focusing instead on a family with a couple of tiny girls, who were seated at an adjacent table. The youngest was chewing a breadstick and staring at Jess with big brown eyes.

'Err,' she began, switching her attention to him. 'A lady from social services called this morning. There's a meeting on Friday night, a sort of introduction to fostering. There's no obligation on our part, but I thought it would be nice to go. Just to see what it entails.'

Jon spluttered into his wine glass and slammed it down. 'No way! I told you last night that fostering isn't an option. Anyway, I've a gig in Oldham on Friday and I can't afford not to do it.' He was aware of people staring as his voice rose.

The waitress brought their starters. 'Garlic mushrooms?'

'That's mine,' Jess said. 'Thank you.'

'Broccoli and stilton soup, sir?'

'Thanks.' Jon nodded. 'I don't want to talk about it any more,' he said as the waitress left. He changed the subject: 'Did you book the holiday?'

'No. I'm going to Stockport for lunch with Mum tomorrow. I'll pop in the travel agent's on Mersey Square and do it then. And if you won't come with me on Friday then I'll go to the meeting with Mum.'

Jon stared at her as she looked down at her plate. He sighed. Here wasn't the place to make a scene, but he was seething inside that she'd spoiled a rare night out and hadn't waited until they got home to talk. After a few spoonfuls, he pushed the soup away.

Jess frowned. 'Don't you like it?'

'I've lost my appetite,' he muttered as she toyed with her mushrooms. 'I'm not in the mood for this, let's get the bill and go.'

'Okay.' She shrugged and pulled on her jacket. The little girl with the breadstick flashed them a big smile. Jon turned away and summoned the waitress, but not before he'd seen the longing on Jess's face as she spoke to the child. He told the waitress they had to leave, but he would pay for the meal they'd ordered.

Outside, he took Jess's arm. 'Fancy a drink? Sean and Ian from Instruments will be in The Swan.'

She shook her head. 'No, thanks. Apart from the fostering thing, is everything okay between us? You're so distant lately.'

He looked into her eyes, saw they lacked their usual sparkle and felt guilty all over again. If he agreed to this fostering malarkey, she'd be smiling and her usual self, but it wasn't what *he* wanted. She'd have less time for him and they'd grow even further apart.

'We're fine,' he said, and bent to kiss her. 'Get that holiday booked and I'll show you how okay we are. Be like the early days.'

She smiled. 'We need it, don't we? Time together, I mean. I'll set off for home. You follow when you've had a drink with the lads.'

He walked her to the Jeep. 'Time together is the exact opposite of what we'd get if we fostered,' he said and kissed her. 'Just think long and hard about it, Jess.'

'I will. By the way, Jack told me earlier that he and Harley are secretly engaged, but they don't want it to be a secret any more.'

Jon smiled. 'Bless 'em! Puppy love. Ah well, if it's meant to be, it'll last.'

'It will.'

Jon waved as she pulled away. He lit a cigarette. Across the road, the lights of The Midland beckoned a friendly welcome. Drawn, he strolled towards them and thought about his stolen hours of passion with Sheena. Livvy should be here and settled in by now. Might as well pay her a flying visit.

The young receptionist looked up as he strolled towards the desk. 'Has Mrs McVey checked in?'

'Yes, sir. Would you like me to call her room?'

'Please, tell her it's Jon Mellor.' He fidgeted from foot to foot as the girl picked up the phone.

'Mrs McVey? I've got Mr Jon Mellor in reception. Okay, thank you. Room 125, sir.'

'Thanks.' He took the lift to the first floor and tapped lightly on the door.

'Hi, you,' Livvy greeted him. 'This is a nice surprise. Come on in. Meet Courtney.'

He stepped inside the room and a young version of Livvy, lying on her front, chin on hands, peeled her eyes from the TV screen and smiled. 'You Harley's dad?' she asked, sitting upright.

'Err, no, I'm Jon,' he replied.

'This is my friend, Jon Mellor.' Livvy introduced them. 'Jon and I used to work together many years ago.'

Seemingly satisfied with the answer, Courtney turned her attention back to *Coronation Street*.

'She's hooked on the *Street*, thanks to Sheena's daughter,' Livvy said. 'Keeps her occupied, anyway.'

'How was your flight?' Jon asked.

'Fine, thanks. Would you like a drink? We can go and sit in Courtney's room if you want to talk. It's through the doors off mine, but the telly's only tiny!' She reached into the mini bar for two bottles of brandy and led the way. 'Sit down.' She gestured to the bed and he took off his jacket and threw it over a chair. He sat down next to her. 'What is it?' she said, tipping the brandy into glasses and handing him one. 'You look troubled.'

He took a sip and smiled. 'I need this.' He told her what had gone on between him and Jess and his feelings of guilt over Sheena, but how he didn't really regret what he'd done.

She nodded slowly. 'Well, I can't say that I blame you about the fostering issue. Your boys are growing up and it will be nice to have time to yourselves. But I do understand Jess's feelings about wanting children around. Although *I'd* quite like to have more of my own.'

'Would you?' He frowned. 'Having *our* own kids isn't an option. There's no way I'm having a vasectomy reversal after so long. It's not just the fostering thing though, it's the fact that Jess has gone behind my back with the whole idea. She seems to have Mum and Dad on her side, too. Dad's offered to pay for an

extension to our house and Mum's as keen as Jess on the issue –
I felt like an outsider in my own family yesterday.'

He took a swig of his drink and continued. 'But that's it,
isn't it? An outsider is exactly what I am. The "outsider" Eddie
thought he'd fathered and got lumbered with for the rest of his
life. His hand's never been out of his pocket since.'

Livvy's jaw dropped and she sprang to her feet. 'Jon Mellor,
where's that chip on your shoulder come from? Eddie would be
devastated to hear you talking like that. As far as *he's* concerned,
you *are* his son. Your mum and dad are two of the nicest people
I've ever met. They've always loved you. You don't know how
lucky you are. I *never* had that sort of love until recently. Now
pull yourself together before you go home. Talk to Jess, don't
fight with her. And don't forget, you owe her one big-time for
what *you've* done.'

Jon stared open-mouthed at Livvy, who faced him, hands
on hips, looking for all the world like Harley when she had an
axe to grind with Roy. 'Sorry, Liv. I guess I was feeling self-pity
because Jess refuses to see my side of things.'

She nodded. 'And *you* refuse to see *hers*. Finish your drink
and go home. By the way, to avoid any more arguments with
Jess, I spoke to Tina earlier and she's offered to put us up for a
while, at least until I know how things are with Harley. If I'm
staying long-term, I'll rent a place.'

'Oh, good,' Jon said. It saved him having to tell Livvy that
Jess had already refused his request. He changed the subject:
'Sheena called me from the airport.'

'Did she, now? I was just about to ring her to let her know
we'd arrived safely when *you* turned up.'

'Were you?' He smiled. 'Why don't you call her now while
I'm here? She told me she's missing me.'

Livvy raised an eyebrow. 'And are you missing her?'

'Very much.'

'Is that why you're so crabby? Raging testosterone and

nowhere for it to go.'

'Something like that,' he said as she reached for the phone.

'I think you're under Sheena's skin more than she'll admit,' Livvy said as she dialled. 'It's me. Yes, we're here. Are you alone? I mean... is Gerry with you? Hang on a minute.' She handed the phone to Jon. 'I'll leave you to talk. Gerry's out.' She left the room, shaking her head.

Jon spoke softly. 'Hi, Sheena. Yeah, I'm *sure* it's a surprise, but is it a nice one?' He grinned into the receiver and told her why he was in Livvy's suite. 'I came to cry on her shoulder,' he finished. Sheena sympathised with his situation and told him she was missing him, even though she was trying hard not to. 'I miss you, too. Madness, when you think we hardly know each other. Try and come back soon, please. I know we said we wouldn't see one another alone, but I really need to. Will you call me tomorrow at the shop? You will? Great, I'll see you soon then. Don't hang up. Livvy wants to speak to you.' He went next door and sat with Courtney while Livvy spoke with Sheena.

'So, you like *Corrie*, do you?' Jon asked Courtney.

'Sure,' she said. 'And *EastEnders* and *Hollyoaks*.'

'My twin sons like *Hollyoaks*,' he told her.

'How old are your sons?' Courtney asked, twiddling a curl around her finger.

'Sixteen in June.'

'Nine months older than me,' she said. 'What are their names?'

'Jack and Nathan,' he replied.

'Cool!' Courtney laughed, wrinkling her cute little nose, just like her mother and Harley when *they* laughed.

Jon looked up as Livvy came back in the room. 'I guess I'd better get going,' he said. 'Thanks for the drink and the ear to bend, Liv.'

'Feel better now?' Livvy asked as she saw him to the door.

She whispered, 'Sheena will call you tomorrow when Gerry's not around. Hopefully, she'll see you in a couple of weeks. *I'll* see you tomorrow. Go and make your peace with Jess.'

'Thanks, Livvy.' He bent to kiss her cheek and waved at Courtney, who waved back. 'Goodnight, girls.'

13

Livvy turned off the light in Courtney's room. After a room-service supper and hot bath her daughter had declared she was tired and going to bed. She was asleep within minutes. Livvy closed the adjoining door.

She sat down on the bedroom chair, poured a glass of red wine, picked up a pad and began to list everything that would need her attention over the next couple of days. Her priority was to call Roy, which she did right away. Sammy answered. Livvy asked to speak to him.

She assumed Sammy must have left the room, because Roy greeted her with, 'Hi, sweetheart, you arrived safely then?'

'We did.' She held her breath for a minute. 'Any news on Harley's tests?'

'No. Maybe we'll hear something tomorrow.' He lowered his voice to a barely audible whisper: 'I was about to nip to Carl's to collect some tapes. Can I call and see you?'

'Of course.' Her heart thudded so loud, she was sure he must be able to hear it. 'Room 125. My daughter's with me, she's asleep in the adjoining room.'

'Be with you in about thirty minutes.'

She said goodbye and put the phone down. Her hands were shaking and her stomach looped. He was coming to see her. They'd be alone. Well... almost. Not much could happen with Courtney in the next room. It wouldn't be right... would it?

She took a quick shower, pulled on white lacy underwear, tight white jeans and a blue silk shirt. She unpinned her hair and fluffed out her curls in front of the bedroom mirror. A slick of pale-pink lip gloss, a quick spray of her favourite L'air du Temps perfume and she was ready. After checking her watch, she peeped in on Courtney. She turned the key in the lock, praying the loud click wouldn't disturb her. She tried to relax with her pad and pen again. A gentle tapping heralded Roy's arrival.

His dark eyes searched hers as she let him in. A slight tick in his left cheek told her he was as nervous as she.

'Hi.'

'Hi, yourself,' he replied and held out his arms. She melted into them. His lips met hers and he crushed her to him. 'I need you,' he whispered into her hair and lifted her, slowly twirling her round and round, before lying her down on the bed. He lay beside her and traced round her face with his fingers.

'I need you, too,' she said.

He kissed her again and undid the buttons on her shirt. 'You never used to wear a bra,' he said softly, unhooking the front fastening and cupping her breasts.

Tears flowed down her cheeks, mingling with his, as he finished undressing her. She helped him remove his clothes and snuggled into him.

'I'd forgotten how hairy your chest is,' she said, smiling through her tears.

'And I'd forgotten just how beautiful you are. You're rounder, curvier.'

'That's what happens when you have children.' She

prodded his stomach gently. 'So are you, rounder, I mean. You used to be flat as a pancake.'

'Well, that's what happens when you have children,' he quipped. 'And *I've* had three!'

'Oh, Roy, I've so missed you and your silly jokes.'

'I've missed you, too. Are you sure about this?'

'Yes... I've waited years.'

'What about your daughter?'

'She's sound asleep, I don't think she'll wake up.' She didn't tell him that she'd locked Courtney in. If she *did* waken, she'd bang on the door. 'We'll just have to make sure we're quiet.'

He raised an amused eyebrow. 'Quiet? If I remember rightly, *you* were a very noisy lover.'

'Well, you weren't so quiet yourself.' She kissed him, sensing his nerves were settling. 'Stop talking now. Make love to me while we've got the chance.'

He held her close. 'I've dreamt about this,' he said softly.

'Mm.' She sighed. 'I've had dreams, too.'

Time stood still as Roy kissed and explored every inch of her. She reacquainted herself with his body, loving the feel of his strong arms around her. When he knelt between her legs and looked at her, she could see the love in his eyes. He shook his head, as though lost for words. She reached for him and they clung together. He whispered that he loved her and she arched towards him as he slid inside. His kisses were deep and probing as he thrust into her. Her orgasm was explosive and she bit her lip to stop herself yelling out while he muffled *his* cries of pleasure into her shoulder. He held her tightly, showering her face with kisses.

'That didn't take long,' he whispered, eventually. 'I was desperate for you. What a homecoming, if you'll pardon the pun. Thank you, sweetheart.'

'Roy, it was my pleasure.'

They lay quietly for a while, murmuring endearments. He

propped himself up on one elbow and smiled at her. 'Presume we were safe, then?'

She nodded. 'Perfectly.' Her cycle had been all over the place just lately – she hoped she *wasn't* safe.

'Sorry, I should have asked.'

'Now that would be a first. Would you like a drink?' She slid out of bed. 'I've got brandy, gin, whisky or red wine.'

'Glass of red would be nice.' He nodded to the side table by the chair, where her glass from earlier stood. 'I see you already hit the bottle before I arrived.'

She smiled and poured him a drink. 'Cheers.' She clinked her glass to his. 'Here's to a good result for Harley.'

'Here, here,' he said, jumping as the phone rang out.

'Who can be calling at this time of night?' Livvy frowned and looked at her watch. She snatched up the receiver. 'Hello! Oh, hi.' She signalled with her eyes for Roy to keep quiet. 'Yes, Dan, we arrived safely, thank you. No, you can't speak to her at the moment, she's sleeping. No, Harley's results are not back yet, but thank you for asking. Yes, I spoke to Roy earlier.' She rolled her eyes in Roy's direction. 'No, of course I haven't seen him, I've been busy making arrangements for my parents to stay at the hotel and looking through estate agent ads for rented property. What for? Well, for me and Courtney, of course. We're not *coming* back, Danny, I told you that. Not until Harley is well. No way, Courtney is staying with me. Oh... have you? Okay... We'll discuss it when you arrive then. I'm too tired now. Goodnight.' She slammed down the receiver.

'Damn him.'

Roy looked at her. 'What's wrong?'

'He's changed his flight to Manchester and booked himself a room here for Wednesday.'

'Does he know that I'm Harley's father now?'

'He does. He's not very happy about it, but there you go. He wants to take Courtney back to the States, I want her to stay here. *She* wants to stay here.'

'That'll be nice for Harley,' Roy said. 'She can get to know her sister and her mum properly. If the worst comes to the worst, she'll need all the family support we can give her. She told me and Sam that a girl at school is in remission from leukaemia. She had chemotherapy and a bone marrow transplant from her baby sister.'

'That sounds promising.' Livvy nodded. 'If Harley needs a transplant, hopefully one of *us* could be a donor and there's Jason and Courtney, too. They might be a match.'

'Yeah, possibly.' He looked at his watch. 'Shit, look at the time! Sam will wonder where the hell I've got to. I promised her faithfully I wouldn't see you alone – I don't want her putting two and two together.'

She nodded. 'I don't want to cause trouble for you. You'd better take a quick shower. Don't use the shower gel. It's that strawberry Body Shop one and it's got a really strong smell. Sammy will be sure to recognise it as something you don't use at home.'

'Good thinking,' he said and leapt up.

She tidied the bed while he was in the bathroom and picked up his clothes from the floor. The citrus scent of his aftershave clung to them and her stomach tightened as she buried her face in his T-shirt. She could feel tears welling as she thought of him going home and climbing into bed with Sammy. She was conscious of him standing behind her and she turned and slipped her arms around his waist.

'I love you, Roy. I always have.'

'I'm sorry I have to go, Liv. I'll call you tomorrow. By the way, you told Danny that you've made arrangements for your parents to stay here. Does that mean your mum's coming?'

'Yes. She's flying in from Toronto on Saturday and Dad's coming down from Glasgow an hour before she arrives.'

'I'm so pleased for you, sweetheart. Will I get to meet them, you know, as the father of your eldest daughter?'

'I hope so, Roy.'

'I'll have to meet Danny too, I expect. He'll want to punch my lights out.'

'Why should he? What happened with us was before I got together with him.'

'Men have a strange way of looking at things,' he replied, putting on his clothes. 'He knows I was your first and no doubt guesses correctly that I'm the reason your marriage is floundering.'

She sighed as he pushed his feet into his boots. 'That, and the fact he's been seeing another woman. Anyway, go, before Sammy starts checking up on you. I bet your phone's turned off.'

'It is. I'll check for messages when I get in the car. Talk to you tomorrow.' He kissed her one last time, grabbed his jacket and left.

* * *

Livvy stared at her reflection in the bathroom mirror. Her cheeks were glowing and her eyes were shining. It had been so easy. Typical of Roy to make love to her without a thought for contraception... until afterwards. She rubbed her hands over her naked stomach and smiled. With a bit of luck... She turned off the bathroom light. Lying on the big bed, she breathed in the scent of him still on the sheets, her mind working overtime with plans for a new future for her and her daughters.

* * *

Roy dropped the phone back onto the cradle and sat with his head in his hands for a long minute. Sammy was outside stringing bags of nuts to the bird table. He lit a cigarette and knocked on the patio window. She looked across and waved. He beckoned her inside.

'Sit down,' he said as she walked into the kitchen.

'What is it?' She pulled out a chair and flopped on to it.

He poured two mugs of coffee and handed her one. 'The oncologist's secretary just called, we have to go to the hospital for one o'clock today.'

'Okay,' Sammy said, her cheeks going pale. She reached for his hand. 'Is that all she said?'

'Yeah, that was it. She's got it, hasn't she? Otherwise, she would have told me the tests were clear and there's nothing to worry about.'

'It's not a secretary's job to do that, Roy. Let's not jump to conclusions until we know for sure.'

'I'd better call Livvy.' He stood up and pushed his chair back. 'She should be with me when I take Harley to the hospital.'

Sammy frowned. 'What do you mean, when *you* take her? We'll both be going.'

Roy felt his cheeks warming. 'Did I say that? I'm sorry, love. Not really thinking straight.'

'You don't want me there, do you? You want to be alone with that slut!'

Roy sighed. 'Of course I do, love. But I have to give Livvy the option to be there.'

Her eyes darkened a little. 'You mean *you* want her there. That's more like it, isn't it?'

'Oh, don't start, Sam. I need your support right now, not petty jealousies. Alright, yes, *I'd* like her to be there, but only because she's our girl's birth mother, no other reason.'

'Sorry, Roy.' She put her arms around him and gave him a hug. She reached up and stroked his cheek. 'Go and call her then. I'll get Harley up and organised.'

Sighing, Roy made his way to the music room and closed the door. He dialled the hotel and waited to be put through to Livvy's room. Sammy had been asleep when he arrived home and slid into bed last night. She had no idea of the late hour, otherwise he would have been subjected to twenty questions that morning.

He could hear the smile in Livvy's voice as she realised the caller was him. To his query, she said she was feeling great after last night. 'So am I,' he told her. 'But listen, the hospital just called. We have to take Harley along for one o'clock today. Do you want to come with us?'

'What about Sammy?'

'You should be there. You're Harley's mum.'

'Okay. So long as it won't cause problems. I'll call Tina, see if I can leave Courtney with her. I'll meet you at the hospital.'

Roy said goodbye and sat at his mixing desk, smoking another cigarette and staring out at the swimming pool, the landscaped gardens and the orchard beyond. The rolling Cheshire countryside stretched ahead for miles, with foot-ballers' favourite, Alderley Edge, to the right. He'd swap it all tomorrow for a tower-block council flat in Stockport if only his daughter could be guaranteed her health.

* * *

'Are you two ready yet?' Roy called up the stairs. Sammy and Harley had been getting dressed for ages. Anyone would think they were going to a party, never mind The Christie Hospital. He returned to the kitchen and paced up and down, puffing agitatedly on yet another cigarette. He'd smoked his full day's quota already.

Harley appeared and slipped her slender arms around his waist, resting her head on his chest. He held her tight, his heart contracting with love, and kissed the top of her head: 'You okay, princess?'

She nodded. 'Mum won't be a minute. She's nipped to the loo, again. Is Livvy meeting us there, Dad?'

'She is, after she's taken Courtney to Tina's.'

'Can I meet Courtney later? Could they come back here and have tea with us?'

'Maybe. But I think we should ask Mum first how she feels about that.'

'How Mum feels about what?' Sammy said, coming into the kitchen behind them.

'About Livvy and Courtney coming for tea,' Harley said. 'I'm dying to meet my sister. Please say it's okay, Mum.'

'Of course they can, sweetheart. I've arranged to take Mum and Tom out later with Pat, but you can invite them along and I'm sure you and Dad can manage to prepare something between you. Actually, there's a lasagne in the freezer, remember? From last week, or was it the week before? I'll get it out now, shall I? And then it won't take too long to cook. You could even have strawberries and ice cream for dessert.'

Roy realised Sammy was babbling with nerves and looked at her stricken face. 'Are you sure, Sam? You never said anything to me about going out later.'

'Didn't I? Must have slipped my mind. We arranged it a few days ago. Pop upstairs and get my handbag, Harley. I've left it on the bed.'

Roy followed Sammy into the utility room, where she reached into the freezer for the lasagne. He pulled her round to face him, took the dish from her and placed it on the worktop. 'I'd rather you were here with us,' he said. 'Can't you cancel your mum and Tom and take them another day?'

'I'm doing you a favour by going out, Roy. I won't deny Harley getting to know her sister, but I don't want to be a party to you and Livvy playing happy families. There's no trip out with Mum and Tom but I'll eat with Pat and Tim and then come back here to say hi before Livvy and Courtney go home.'

He nodded and kissed her long and hard. She was doing her best, which was more than *he* was doing after last night, and it must be killing her inside. 'Come on, let's make a move.'

* * *

Livvy spotted Roy's BMW, with its unique registration number, RC 1, as she searched for a parking space in the overcrowded hospital car park. She squeezed the rented Renault Clio in-between an old red van and a brick wall and climbed out. A hand fell on her shoulder, startling her.

'You okay?' Roy handed her a ticket. 'Saw you searching for a space while I was at the ticket machine – it's pay and display.'

'Oh, thank you.' She placed the ticket on the dashboard and locked the car. 'Where are Harley and Sammy?'

'Gone inside to use the loo. Come on.' He took her arm and led her towards the main entrance.

Tears pricked the backs of her eyes. 'I feel sick,' she muttered. 'How's Harley today?'

'Very nervous,' he said. 'But that's to be expected. She wants you and Courtney to come for tea tonight.'

'We'd love to, but what about Sammy?'

'She's going out. She'll pop back and see you before you leave.'

'That's very kind of her. It can't be easy.'

Roy raised an eyebrow. 'Understatement. Ah, here they are.' He raised his hand as Sammy and Harley walked towards him. 'Ready, princess?' he asked as Harley smiled at Livvy and Sammy nodded politely. Roy took Harley's hand and led the way.

* * *

The consulting room was large and airy and smelt of fresh paint. Roy gripped the edge of his chair as Mr Taylor, the silver-haired oncologist, explained that the test results revealed that Harley was suffering from acute lymphoblastic leukaemia (ALL), an aggressive type of leukaemia.

'Her treatment will begin immediately with induction chemotherapy. This should bring the ALL into remission. The treatment is very intense and lasts about a month. I'm confident Harley will be cured in the course of time and the success rate is very high. Once she's in remission, the next stage will be a bone marrow transplant. In the meantime, we'll start looking for a donor.'

He glanced at Roy and Sammy: 'As her parents, Mr and Mrs Cantello, you will be tested and also, any siblings she has.'

Roy spoke up: 'I'm Harley's father and, err, this woman is her mother, not my wife.' He inclined his head towards Livvy. 'Harley has two half-siblings – my son and Olivia's daughter.'

'Right, well in that case, we'll arrange to take samples from the four of you, see if any are a suitable match. Ideally, a full-blood sibling is often our greatest chance,' the oncologist replied, seemingly unperturbed.

'That's not possible, I'm afraid,' Roy replied, glancing at Sammy, whose face had blanched whiter than the newly painted walls. He squeezed her hand reassuringly. 'But hope-fully one of us can be the donor.'

'I'd like to admit Harley on Monday,' Mr Taylor continued. 'That will give you time to get yourself organised over the week-end, young lady.' He smiled at Harley, who was staring at him, wide-eyed. 'In the meantime, we'll give you some drugs to start the ball rolling. Bring in something to read – you'll be doing a lot of sitting around and a good book helps pass the time. I have it on good authority that the latest *Harry Potter* is excellent.'

'Will I be in for long?' Harley asked, twiddling her hair around her fingers.

'Just for a day or two and then you'll go home in-between the sessions of chemotherapy. You'll feel a bit queasy but it passes and we'll give you something to help with that.'

'You won't let me die, will you? Because my boyfriend Jack needs me and I've only just met my real mum and I'm meeting my half-sister today for the first time,' she urged.

Mr Taylor smiled and patted her hand. 'Harley, my dear, I'm in this business to make people well. I promise I'll do everything possible to make you fit and healthy again.'

She nodded and stood up. 'Well, you'll have my dad to answer to if you don't.'

Roy shook the consultant's hand. 'Sorry about that.'

'She's got fighting spirit,' Mr Taylor said. 'It will help her through the treatment.'

They left the hospital, Livvy promising to bring Courtney to Jasmine House at six.

* * *

Livvy gripped the steering wheel tight as the oncologist's words tumbled around in her head – *Ideally, a full-blood sibling is often our greatest chance.* And then Roy's dismissive – *That's not possible, I'm afraid.* Hadn't he told her he would do anything to get Harley well again – *anything*? Well, thank goodness she'd taken matters into her own hands. Having another child with him was her dream, her mission, but now it was beyond that. Another child, whether it was a good idea or not, could save their daughter's life. She pulled up on Tina's drive and composed herself.

In the comfortable living room, Livvy sat on the sofa in front of the fire and told Tina and Courtney the outcome of the consultation: 'When Harley's finished her chemotherapy, the leukaemia will hopefully go into remission. Then she may need a bone marrow transplant to make her completely well again.' She took a sip from the mug of tea Tina had handed her.

'What does that mean?' Courtney asked.

'It's a procedure to get rid of the bone marrow that doesn't work and replace it with some that will. Roy, me, Jason and you too, Courtney, are all to be tested to see if we match Harley's bone marrow. If one of us does, then the hospital will take enough to use.'

'Can she have mine?' Courtney said. 'I'd really like her to have mine.'

'That's very generous of you, honey, but we'll have to see if you match up first. Right, I'll pop to the bathroom and then we're off to join Roy and Harley for tea.'

'Oh, cool,' Courtney said. 'I get to meet my sister at last. Where are we meeting them?'

'At their home,' Livvy replied, catching Tina's raised eyebrow.

Tina followed her out of the room. 'Is Sammy okay about you going to the house?'

'Apparently. Roy said she's going out. It'll be just me, Roy and our daughters.'

'Happy families then?'

'Something along those lines. Under the circumstances, we all have to do our best for the girls.'

'You watch your step with Roy Cantello,' Tina warned. 'Remember what happened last time you got up close and cosy.'

'I know what I'm doing, Tina,' Livvy replied.

She was sure Tina's eyes were burning a hole in her back as she went upstairs. In the bathroom, she leant on the sink and stared at her reflection in the mirrored cabinet. The oncologist's words reverberated through her head again. If she'd conceived last night, by the time Harley would be needing a transplant, the baby would be almost here. It would be perfect timing. She hardly dared let herself hope...

14

With a million knots tangling themselves in her stomach, Sammy quietly let herself in and put her handbag and keys on the hall table. She could hear girlish laughter echoing through the open kitchen door. She walked slowly, pushed the door open further, and took in the little tableau. A pale-faced Harley and a younger version of Livvy were seated at the table in front of the patio doors, heads together, looking at something in a magazine. Sammy's eyes were drawn to her rival, who was leaning against the sink, hands wrapped around a mug, her eyes shining with obvious love for the man standing in front of her. And Roy... well, he was holding his usual cigarette in one hand and twiddling one of Livvy's curls around a finger with the other. He was talking animatedly and his eyes never left her face. They looked totally relaxed and at ease and in that instant, Sammy realised with certainty that her life was about to change. She felt like a stranger in her own home. She cleared her throat and Roy froze.

He untangled his fingers from Livvy's hair at the same time as *she* slopped her drink on the floor. 'Sammy, hi, love. Didn't hear you come in.' He smiled and moved across to peck her on the cheek. Livvy grabbed a cloth off the sink and mopped the tiles.

Harley called out, 'Mum, come and meet my sister. This is Courtney. This is my mum, Sammy.'

Courtney got to her feet and held out her hand. Sammy smiled and shook it, telling herself that whatever was going on, it wasn't the girl's fault. 'Nice to meet you, Courtney.'

'We've got loads in common,' Harley said. 'You wouldn't believe it. We like the same clothes and music and things. You can tell we're sisters, can't you?' Harley's excitement was infectious, and in spite of herself, made Sammy smile.

'Yes, there's a definite likeness,' she agreed. 'Except for your colouring, of course.' She was fighting the urge to fly across the room, scream and rant at Roy and slap Livvy across her smug little face.

'Courtney wants to be my donor if she's a match for me,' Harley announced. 'We're going up to my room for a while now. I'm going to have a lie-down and Courtney can have a look at my birthday party photos.'

'Courtney, we must be going soon,' Livvy said. 'We don't want to tire Harley too much.'

'But there's nothing to do at the hotel. It's boring, I want to stay here. I'll just sit quietly with Harley.'

'Ten minutes and then we have to leave – I have phone calls to make.'

'Are you calling Dad?'

'Yes, later. *You* can speak to him, too.'

'Cool. You'll like my dad,' Courtney told Harley as they were leaving the kitchen. 'He's called Danny and he's really nice.'

Sammy shook her head after them. 'Well, looks like those two have hit it off and no mistake.'

'It was instant,' Roy said. 'And they haven't stopped talking for a minute.'

'And what about you two? You looked pretty chummy when I walked in, gazing into one another's eyes like a pair of lovesick parrots.' It was hard to keep the sarcasm out of her voice, but at the moment she was past caring.

Livvy blushed and looked down at the floor and Roy frowned.

'There's no need for that, Sam. We were discussing Harley's treatment, that's all.'

'Yeah, it looked like it. Do you fiddle with the hair of every woman you speak to, Roy?'

'What?'

'You didn't even realise you were doing it. It just came so naturally to you.'

'Sammy, I refuse to get into an argument with you while we have guests.'

'Fine. Come and look me up when they've gone.'

Sammy stormed from the room, grabbed her bag and keys and left the house. She sat in her car for a few minutes, composing herself. 'You bloody idiot,' she muttered. Why the hell hadn't she just made a joke of things and tackled Roy about the hair twiddling later? She should have hugged and kissed him and gone into 'Stand By Your Man' mode, instead of the jealous harridan stunt she'd just pulled. Roy wouldn't be very pleased and now, Livvy would be looking for cracks and wheedling her way into their lives even more. Well, there was no way she was going back inside to make an even bigger fool of herself.

She started up the Porsche, drove swiftly down the drive and onto Jasmine Lane, narrowly missing her green-wellied neighbour, who was walking a pair of Golden Labradors. 'Sorry!' she mouthed as the young woman shot her a dirty look.

She gripped the steering wheel as the oncologist's words, about a full-blood sibling being Harley's best chance of a match, came back to her. At the hospital Roy had said that wasn't possible and at that point Sammy had agreed but seeing Roy and Livvy back there had freaked her. She wondered if they'd been discussing the possibility.

Wouldn't they, as parents, do everything within their power to make their daughter well again? She knew *she* would and Harley was *her* daughter too. Well, there *was* something she could do: if Livvy were to donate an egg, Sammy would be willing to try and get pregnant. She was fit and well, apart from the hot flushes, and you occasionally heard of women in their late fifties giving birth to IVF babies. But would Roy agree? It was certainly an option to discuss with him later and the lesser of two evils.

* * *

'Go after her, Roy. She's really upset,' Livvy urged.

'No.' He shook his head. 'She needs some space. She'll be embarrassed to come home while you're still here, she'll go back to Pat's. I'll catch up with her later. I could use a single malt right now. Would you like a drink?'

'I'll just have a Coke, please.' Livvy followed him into the lounge. 'Sammy makes me nervous. My stomach's jumping all over the place.'

'Sit down and relax.' He handed her a glass of Coke and sat beside her on the sofa.

'She has every right not to trust us,' Livvy said.

He raised an eyebrow. 'I know.' He took a large swig of his drink and sighed. 'I thought I'd successfully dealt with my feelings for you, Olivia. I threw myself into the band, my songwriting, bringing up Harley and just generally getting on with my life. I imagined that you were doing the same. That you'd put us down to, well, one of those things – and moved on. But as soon as I set eyes on you it all came flooding back. I never thought I'd want to stray again, that loving Sammy was enough – I mean, it's got to be, hasn't it? I can't do anything about my feelings for you, but I can't be in the same room as you and not want you. What about you? How do *you* feel?'

Livvy ran her finger around the top of her glass and stared at the floor. 'The same as you, I guess. Leaving Harley with you was agony. Marrying Danny on the rebound wasn't right, but it seemed the best idea at the time. Having Courtney and joining Juice were turning points, but everything else was wrong. I've felt like a square peg in a round hole for years.'

He took the glass from her, pulled her into his arms and kissed her long and hard. 'If the kids weren't in, I'd take you here and now on the sofa.'

'Then it's a good job they are,' she said, 'because I'd let you. I'd better get back to the hotel before we get too carried away.'

'Is there any chance of me seeing you alone again before Danny arrives?'

'There might be,' she replied. 'Tina's invited Courtney and Harley for tea tomorrow. I can collect Harley at three, drop them at Tina's and meet you at the hotel at four. Danny won't be there until after eight.'

'Perfect. I need to take an amp into town for repair, so I'll do it tomorrow. I'll make myself scarce before you collect Harley and I'll tell Sam I'm popping in to see Phil Jackson on my way back from Manchester. Call my mobile if you're going to be late.'

Livvy smiled and stood up. 'I've so much to do, I don't know where to start. I suppose finding a house and getting Courtney into school is the priority. I also need to let my band know that I'll be away for a few months.'

'What about Danny?'

Livvy shrugged. 'We need to talk and sort things out. Knowing Danny, he won't stay too long. He'll be itching to get back to the business within the week. What about you and Sammy?'

'Oh... she'll be okay. It'll all blow over in a few days when she gets her head around things.'

Livvy smiled and stroked his cheek. 'For a man of the world, Roy, you really have no idea about women, do you?'

* * *

'Fancy a drink in The Royal Oak, or do you want to go home?' Roy asked. He'd walked to Pat and Tim's to catch up with Sammy and was driving them in her car towards Jasmine Lane. She'd been all over him when he'd arrived, as though the earlier incident had never happened. He'd been ready to have a go at her, but he certainly wasn't bringing the subject up now, especially as it looked like he was on to a promise.

'Home, please,' she said, stroking his thigh. 'There's something I want to discuss with you.'

'What? There's nothing going on, if that's what you're thinking.' He took a deep breath. *Stop being defensive*, he thought, *it makes you look guilty*.

'I'm sure there isn't,' Sammy replied. 'I just got a bit jealous, that's all. It's my own fault for not staying around when you asked me to. I trust you, Roy, and I promise to always be there for you from now on.'

'Good.' He swallowed hard. Did she already suspect and was she being sarcastic? You never knew with Sammy when she had one of her heads on, but he was enjoying the thigh stroking. He groaned as her hand crept further up. They were passing the car park entrance to Norman's Woods. He turned in and stopped the engine. 'Shall we?' The car park was deserted, so chances are they'd have the clearing to themselves.

She nodded. 'Just like old times.'

* * *

Roy lay back in the bubbles and stared open-mouthed at Sammy, who was sitting at the other end of the Jacuzzi. 'So... let me get this right. You want me to ask Livvy if she'll donate an egg so that you can have an IVF baby to give Harley a transplant. You'd really be willing to put yourself through all that?'

'Yes. I'd do anything to save her life, Roy. I thought you would, too.'

'Well, yeah... but a baby... and at your time of life? Sam, I don't know.' He puffed out his cheeks. 'It's too much of a risk, love. What if something happened to you? I'd never forgive myself. Let's wait and see if any of us are a suitable match before we start talking about bringing another life into the world.'

'You heard what the oncologist said: a full-blood sibling is the best bet. And if *I* don't have a child, there's only one other way and I couldn't bear it.' Sammy's eyes filled with tears as she stared at him.

'Well, there's no chance of that happening, is there?' He sat up and shuffled towards her. 'Don't cry, things will be fine. If our samples don't match, there's a donor system and the hospital will try that.'

'And what if there isn't anyone suitable?' Sammy sobbed against his chest. 'It may be too late by the time they've exhausted all their enquiries. If I got pregnant right away, by the time Harley needs the transplant, the baby will be here. Roy, it might be the only way.'

'I appreciate what you're saying and I love you so much for wanting to do it, but I can't get my head around this at the moment. Let's leave it for tonight. *You're* tired, *I'm* tired, and I can't think straight. You've knocked me for six, sweetheart. Come on.' He pulled her to her feet, reached for a towel and wrapped it around her. 'Let's get you dry and into bed. I think we've had enough for today.'

* * *

Livvy lay on her back, staring at the ceiling. Her eyes filled with tears again as she went over the last two hours. Roy had visited the hotel as promised, but had been preoccupied and didn't want to make love. When pushed, he'd taken her hands and told her that Sammy had suggested she donate an egg so that he and Sammy could have a baby to help save Harley's life. Apparently, they'd lain awake most of the night, discussing the subject, and although he admitted he was very worried about her taking such risks, he'd finally agreed that it was the only way.

When she tentatively suggested that there *was* another way, he shook his head. 'It can't happen,' he said. 'It would destroy Sammy and *you* need to patch things up with Danny. Face it, Liv, he's only guilty of the same crime as you. I can't rock the boat at home. Harley needs a peaceful haven, not a war zone. You saw the state Sammy was in yesterday and you and I were only stood talking – she'd kill me if she knew I'd slept with you.'

'But I thought you loved me.'

'You know I do, but I also love Sam.' He stood up and paced the room. 'I can't believe this is happening again. If Harley wasn't ill, you'd just be paying a visit and then going home, wouldn't you?' He stopped pacing and frowned. 'Or did you have a hidden agenda?'

Livvy felt her cheeks warming. 'I guess I thought I'd see how things went between me and Harley and us two and take it from there,' she admitted.

'So, you were hoping to split me and Sammy up again, is that it?'

'Well, if things were right between you and Sammy then you wouldn't have made love to me, would you? You told me you were desperate for me.'

'I was... I am. Shit! I'm going, Liv. I don't want to fight with you. Please think about the egg thing. We should all pull together and do everything we can to save Harley's life.'

With that, he was gone and she'd lain around feeling desolate. She couldn't donate an egg if she was pregnant herself, but how the hell was she going to explain that to Roy? He'd go absolutely mental. She groaned and curled herself into a tight ball.

Tina had dropped Courtney off an hour ago after taking Harley home; she was in her room, reading. Danny had called from Heathrow, while waiting for his shuttle to Manchester, and asked her to book a table in the restaurant for dinner tonight. The last thing she felt like doing was playing happy families. She got off the bed and popped her head around Courtney's door: 'I'm taking a shower. Dad wants us to eat downstairs later.'

'Do we have to? I'm stuffed from tea at Tina's and I was planning to show Dad all the photos Harley lent me. They're of her as a baby and while she's growing up. There's loads of her with her dad. He's really nice, Mom, no wonder you fancied him!'

Livvy turned away and almost choked on the sob in her throat. She hadn't the heart to tell Courtney that photographs of Harley and Roy would be the last thing her father would want to look at tonight.

'By the way, Mom, I'm going to Harley's tomorrow to meet Jack and I can stay the night as well.'

'Has she asked permission?' Livvy frowned.

'Yeah, Roy came in as me and Tina were leaving. He said it was okay and they'll come and pick me up at eleven. They can meet Dad then, can't they?'

Livvy drew a sharp breath. How uncomplicated it all was when you were Courtney's age. Still, Roy and Danny meeting was inevitable and their daughters' presence would help. 'If it's alright with Roy and Sammy then you can go.'

'Oh great, thanks, Mom. I don't ever want to go home. I love it here. Harley said Jack's brother Nathan is coming to tea tomorrow because he wants to meet me. He looks really nice on the photos, just like Jack but with longer hair.'

Livvy's heart sank even further. Jon had admitted his son Nathan was a handful. 'I thought Nathan already had a girlfriend?'

'Yeah, he does. But I can still have him as a friend, can't I?'

'I suppose so.' Livvy sighed and shut herself in the bathroom.

* * *

Daniel hailed a taxi and clambered in. 'Midland Hotel, please.' He sat back in his seat, looking out at the darkening streets. First time he'd been to Manchester. Pity it wasn't a holiday. He'd love to explore some of the narrow streets and the Victorian buildings, and take Courtney to one of the theatres. He wondered what sort of reception awaited him. Unsurprisingly, Livvy had been curt when he spoke to her earlier.

He was looking forward to seeing Courtney again. He'd really missed her warm smile and bright chatter. The ranch was too quiet with only the housekeeper for company. Deep down, he knew Courtney's place was with her mother – after all, he was home so infrequently and it wasn't fair to leave her alone with Mrs Grayson. His daughter had been lonely for too long. The excitement in her voice last night as she'd described her time with her sister had brought a smile to his face.

He wished he'd been firmer years ago and insisted that Livvy have another child. It was too late now and if she wasn't coming back to him, well... he had other plans. He'd spent the weekend with his PA Jodie, who loved him and was prepared to wait till he'd sorted out his problems. He kind of loved Jodie too. She'd shown him more affection in a few short months than Livvy had in over fifteen years of marriage. Jodie had told him she wanted to have kids with him. He wasn't about to start messing her around and making her wait for ages while Livvy decided what *she* wanted to do. This trip was all about make or break. If Livvy wanted to stay in England then so be it, but if he set up home in LA with Jodie, he hoped his daughter would join them at a later date.

'Here you go, mate: The Midland.'

The taxi driver broke his thoughts. Daniel paid the fare, took a deep breath and walked into the hotel.

* * *

Livvy twiddled with the stem of her wine glass and looked across the table at Daniel and Courtney, who were chatting animatedly. He'd hardly spoken to her and had ignored her apart from a brief hug and a peck on the cheek. She wished she hadn't agreed to dine in the restaurant tonight. It was busy; she was conscious of the curious stares from nearby diners and guessed she'd been recognised. Her head was still reeling from Roy's earlier rejection and his suggestion of egg donation.

'Dan, if you and Courtney have finished, would you mind if we go upstairs?' She indicated sideways with her head at two young men who were staring open-mouthed at her.

'Of course.' Daniel nodded. 'I didn't think. Haven't you brought any disguises with you?'

Courtney grinned. 'She's got that dreadful curly red wig and her Dame Edna glasses.'

'Has she?' He smiled. 'I think she'd get *more* attention wearing those. Come on then, let's go up.'

Back in the suite, Livvy sat on the bed and, without waiting to be asked, Daniel sat beside her.

'I want to show you something, Dad,' Courtney said. She went to her room to get Harley's photo album.

'What have we here?' Daniel patted the bed next to him and Courtney flopped down.

'Photos of my sister and Roy and Sammy,' she announced.

Livvy felt Daniel stiffen. 'I really don't think Dad wants to see those tonight, Courtney,' she began.

'It's fine,' Daniel replied. 'Might as well get it over with, eh?'

'If you say so,' Livvy said, looking at the first page of photographs. She felt her eyes fill as she gazed at a smiling Roy holding Harley as a tiny baby, Sammy standing beside him, her arm possessively around his waist. She swallowed hard, it was a lovely family photo but that should have been her. Even in his forties Roy had looked so youthful and could easily have passed for a much younger man. She took a deep breath. Courtney chattered on and on, explaining who was who until Livvy could stand it no longer. She excused herself, made her way to the bathroom and stood swaying in front of the mirror. She gripped the washbasin. The wine had made her light-headed. She shouldn't have drunk any at all, just in case she was pregnant, but she'd needed a bit of Dutch courage to face Danny and was bracing herself for the interrogation she knew she would get when Courtney went to bed. She splashed her face with cold water and patted her cheeks dry with a soft towel.

Back in the bedroom Courtney was regaling her father with tales of tea at Tina's and Harley's and how Harley had a 'J' tattooed on her thigh. Livvy stopped her mid-sentence: 'I think we've had enough for tonight, Courtney. Dad's tired. You can catch up with him in the morning.'

'But I'm going to Harley's in the morning, Mom. Roy's coming to pick me up. I'm staying over, remember?'

Livvy could feel Daniel's eyes searching her face. He must have a million and one questions to ask and she certainly had a few for him. 'We'll breakfast in here and you can spend a couple of hours together before you go out. Bed now, please.'

Courtney nodded and picked up the album. She kissed them goodnight and disappeared into her room.

Livvy poured Danny a brandy. 'Here, you probably need it after all that.'

He nodded and knocked it back. 'She's very lively tonight. It's like someone's plugged her in and we can't find the off switch. She seems very taken with Harley.'

'She is,' Livvy replied. 'They get on so well.'

'You'd better sit down now and tell me everything, including how you managed to get involved with Roy Cantello in the first place. Also, I'd like to know why you never trusted me enough to tell me that he was your daughter's father. That's the bit I have a major problem with, Livvy. And then you'd better tell me what's going on now, because I have a feeling he's back in your life again, and I'll have another brandy while I'm at it.'

Livvy poured him another drink and began her tale, which, with Daniel continually interrupting, took them into the early hours.

When she'd finished, he looked into her eyes and said, 'Now correct me if I'm wrong here, but are you and Roy lovers again? And I'll have the truth this time, Olivia. I think I deserve it, don't you?'

Livvy stared at him for a long moment. 'I'll tell you the truth, but only if you're prepared to be truthful with me about what *you've* been up to, and for how long.'

'I will be. Are you and Roy lovers?' he repeated.

'Yes,' she admitted.

He drew in his breath and got to his feet. 'How many times?'

'Oh, for God's sake, does it matter?'

'To me it does.'

'Once, that's all.'

'When?'

'Bloody hell, Dan! Do you want a blow-by-blow account? Why do you want to know that?'

'When?' he demanded, his face white, fists clenched.

'Monday night. Satisfied now?'

'And where was Courtney?'

Livvy felt her cheeks flaming. 'Asleep in her room.'

Daniel grabbed her arms and brought his face close to hers. She could smell the brandy on his breath and turned her head away. 'You screwed your lover while our daughter was in the next room.' He shook her roughly. 'You're an unfit mother, Olivia. That's all the proof I need to get a divorce and custody of Courtney and if needs be, I'll take you to every court in the land to get it. I'm taking her home with me as soon as I can organise a flight.' He pushed her away and helped himself to another brandy.

'You can't take her home.' She ran across the room and beat him on the back. 'You've been having an affair. I can divorce *you* for adultery.'

'Just try it. You've no proof of that at all.' He turned, a smug expression on his face.

She lashed out at him and knocked his drink flying. 'You absolute bastard! I hate you.' Then she remembered that Sheena had been here with her when the woman had answered her call. 'You promised to be honest with me if I was honest with you,' she yelled. 'And I *do* have proof. Sheena was here that night. You spoke to her, remember? She'll help me. And you can't take Courtney home. I want her here with *me*. Harley may need a bone marrow transplant, Courtney might be her only chance of a match.'

'No way! You're not messing around with *my* kid,' Daniel yelled back.

'But you can't deny Harley a chance of being well again. What sort of a man are you? I should never have married you,' Livvy screamed at him.

The adjoining doors slid open and Courtney stood blinking in the half-light. 'Mom, what's wrong? Why are you both yelling?' She went to Livvy, who put her arms around her.

'Courtney, Dad wants to take you home,' Livvy sobbed.

'No. I'm not going back to America,' Courtney shouted at her father. 'I'm staying here with Mom and Harley. You can't make me, Dad. My new grandparents are coming on Saturday. We're a proper family now. I'm not going back to stay with just you and Mrs Grayson. You should be here to help support Mom through all this.'

'Back to bed, Courtney,' Daniel ordered. 'This is between me and your mother. You're too young to have an opinion on what's right or wrong.'

'I am not!' Courtney yelled. 'I love my mom and my sister. I love you too, Dad, but if I have to choose between you, then Mom and Harley win. I am *not* coming home with you so you'd better get used to the idea.'

Daniel glared furiously at Courtney. 'You do *not* speak to me like that. Now go to bed.'

'No! I'm not leaving you alone with Mom. You're just being a bully now.'

'Fine, I can see when I'm outnumbered. *I'll* go to bed then and I'll speak to you in the morning.' He headed towards the door.

'Well, don't forget that Roy's coming for me at eleven,' Courtney reminded him.

'Ah yes, the wonderful Mr Cantello! Well, I'm sure I'll cope with that one.' He closed the door firmly on his way out.

Livvy and Courtney sank onto the bed.

'You're shaking. Are you okay, Mom?'

'I'll be fine, sweetie.' Livvy pushed the curls out of Courtney's eyes and kissed the tip of her nose. 'I'm sorry you had to hear all that. Go back to bed now and I'll see you in the morning.'

She nodded. 'I love Dad, but I really wish with all my heart that me, you, Roy and Harley could be a family, you know, living together in one house.'

'Honey, so do I, but it won't happen.'

'Maybe if I wish hard enough it might.'

'Well, you can certainly try. Now, bed, go on.' She kissed Courtney, pushed her gently towards the adjoining doors and closed them behind her.

Livvy lay on the bed and curled herself into a tight ball. First chance she got tomorrow she would contact a solicitor for advice on how to prevent Danny removing Courtney from her care. She would also make an appointment at Manor Banks School, get Courtney started there as soon as possible, and find a house to rent. If she could show they had a settled and stable way of life then it might help her case.

15

'You're very quiet, princess,' Roy said as he and Harley travelled along the A6 towards Manchester to collect Courtney. 'You okay?'

Harley shrugged. 'Just thinking. When I called Courtney earlier, she was a bit upset. Her dad and Livvy had a big fight last night.'

'Really?' He glanced at her. 'Did she say why?'

'Her dad wants to take her home, Livvy wants her to stay. Courtney wants to stay too. She also said that she heard *your* name being mentioned a few times.'

'Hmm, okay.' He patted her knee. 'Don't worry; if I know Livvy she'll stand her ground. She won't let Courtney go without a fight.'

'Well, I hope not. She wants to be my bone marrow donor.' Harley folded her arms and sighed.

Roy could feel his eyes filling behind his shades. He blinked the tears away and tooted at the driver in front, who was dawdling at the traffic lights. 'She might not be suitable, love. We'll have to wait and see. Jason might be a better match, or maybe me – or your mother.'

'You mean Livvy?' Harley smiled. 'Sounds odd when you call her my mother.'

'I'm sure it does,' he said, 'but that's what she is.'

Harley nodded and stared out of the window for a while.

'Oh, smell that?' Roy said. They were passing McVitie's biscuit factory and the scent of warm syrup and ginger hung in the air. 'Freshly baked ginger nuts. Marvellous! My Auntie Vera worked there years ago. She used to bring home big bags of broken biscuits on a Friday night.'

'Broken biscuits?' Harley frowned. 'Couldn't you afford to buy proper ones in the olden days?'

'Cheeky madam,' he said, grinning. 'You've never lived until you've dived into a bag of McVitie's broken bits. You're spoilt today with all the fancy stuff Mum gets you from Marks & Sparks.'

Harley smiled. 'Mum was a bit quiet this morning, don't you think?'

'I expect things are getting on top of her. Livvy being here and you being ill, I mean. She'll be fine when she's had her coffee quota and we get back home.' Roy thought back to last night and Sammy's insistence once again that he ask Livvy today to consider egg donation. He'd kept quiet about his visit to the hotel yesterday and the fact he'd already asked Livvy to think about it. There'd be hell to pay if Sammy knew that. He didn't for one minute think Livvy would play ball; he was sure she'd mull over the idea but would prefer to have a baby herself. Well, it couldn't happen. It was down to him and Sammy – or not at all. He'd felt guilty all night for leaving Livvy upset yesterday. It had taken all his willpower not to touch her. Walking out without even a kiss had been agony.

'Here we are,' he said, swinging into a vacant spot in front of the hotel. He wasn't looking forward to this meeting with Danny – he hoped Courtney was ready and they could leave quickly.

Courtney flung open the door at their knock and pulled Harley into the room. Roy followed and took off his shades.

'Come and meet my dad,' Courtney said.

'Nice to meet you, Harley.' Daniel smiled and held out his hand.

Roy stared at Daniel, who was a similar height to himself and as blond as he was dark. He had a golden tan and a confident air, but his smile didn't quite reach his blue eyes. Roy took an instant dislike to him – he'd bet money on it that Daniel was a control freak. He turned as Harley grabbed his sleeve.

'This is *my* dad, Roy,' she announced.

Roy shook Daniel's proffered hand firmly. God, he felt awkward and for once in his life, he was lost for words. *What the hell did you say to a guy whose wife had given birth to your daughter?* He caught Livvy looking at him and she gave him a half-smile. He smiled back and she looked at him with such pain in her eyes that his stomach turned over. He wanted to go to her, take her in his arms and tell her everything would be okay.

'How are you feeling today, Harley?' Daniel broke the awkward silence.

'Not too bad, thanks. A bit tired and I've got more bruises on my legs and stomach, but otherwise I'm okay.'

Roy saw Livvy's eyes fill with tears. He crossed the room to her side. 'You okay, Liv?' He placed an arm around her shoulders, almost challenging Daniel to have a go at him for the gesture. He could feel her slight frame trembling against him.

'I'm fine, Roy, don't worry.' She pushed him away. 'Take the girls now. I'll call you tonight to make sure they're alright.' She held out her arms to Courtney and kissed her goodbye and did the same to Harley.

Roy swallowed hard. He didn't want to leave her alone with Daniel. 'Call the house if you need me. Come on, you two, let's go.' He picked up Courtney's holdall as she kissed her father goodbye. He could sense Daniel's eyes burning into his back as they left the suite. *Shit*, he thought, *why is life never straight-forward?*

* * *

Livvy sat on the bed, her shoulders shaking, as Daniel closed the door behind Roy and the girls. She felt sick and just wanted to lie down; she wished Daniel would go to his own room and leave her in peace for a while. She could feel tears sliding down her cheeks as he stood in front of her.

'He's in love with you, Olivia.'

She shrugged. 'Maybe. But he loves Sammy as well.'

'Who is he kidding? He might *love* Sammy, but he's in love with *you*. Any fool can see that. When are you going to come clean and sort yourselves out? All the years you've wasted, not just your own, but mine and Sammy's too.'

She wiped her eyes on her shirtsleeve and looked at him: 'How on earth can we possibly do that? There's too much going on at the moment. Getting Harley well is our main priority, everything else has to wait.' She got to her feet and paced the room, arms wrapped around herself. 'Roy's trying to do his best for everyone,' she continued. 'Please don't cause problems for us. Sammy's upset because *I'm* here. Having Courtney stay over can't be easy for her. We all need support, Danny, not pulling apart with petty jealousies.'

'I'd hardly call being angry with him after what he's done a petty jealousy. If the kids hadn't been around, I'd have punched his goddamn lights out.'

Livvy stopped pacing and glared. 'Don't even think about it.'

Daniel shrugged and held up his hands. 'Look, I can see how ill Harley is. I'm not an unreasonable guy. If it were Court-ney, I'd be going out of my mind. Fighting isn't helping us, so let's call a truce for now. Courtney can stay here with you but I'd like her home for Christmas, maybe you too.'

Livvy nodded, glad to agree to anything for now. If she were pregnant, the baby would be almost due by Christmas so she wouldn't be flying anywhere.

'I guess we need to find you somewhere decent to live then,' Daniel said. 'Why don't we get ready, have lunch in a pub and check out a few estate agents? I fancy a trek around the city, take in a few of the sights.'

'Okay.' Livvy nodded. 'I'll show you where I used to work and you can meet Jon and Sean. Jon's the son of Eddie Mellor, The Raiders' drummer.'

'I'll go take a shower,' he said. 'Give me a call when you're ready to go.'

* * *

Back in his room, Daniel dialled a number: 'Hi, baby, sorry to wake you, but I won't get another chance to call you until tonight. No, she's staying in England for the foreseeable future, Courtney too, so when I get home you can move into the ranch with me. I'll fire Mrs Grayson as we don't want her telling tales. It'll be just the two of us. Yes, like I promised you, I'll get a divorce as soon as I can – I've enough grounds. I just need a few days to find them a house and get Courtney settled in school. Livvy's involved with her ex again and I can't see her wanting to leave England while their daughter is so sick. I miss you and I love you, too, honey. I'll be back next week to make it up to you. Bye, Jodie, talk to you later.

* * *

With Daniel out of the way, Livvy called directory enquiries for the number of Manor Banks School. She booked an appointment for the following afternoon. When she saw Jon later, she'd ask him if he knew of a good solicitor, or maybe his dad would. She'd start the ball rolling for divorce as soon as Daniel went home. She could do with finding out just who he was involved with, so she could give the solicitor names. She hadn't recognised the voice of the woman who answered her call last week, for the line hadn't been all that clear. She'd bet her life it was the latest secretary to join the company.

It definitely wasn't Maria, who had a distinctive Puerto Rican accent, nor did she think it was Jodie, his PA. Jodie had always been friendly towards her and had even babysat for them on occasions. The rest of the staff were either far too young or male. Ah well, she'd get to the bottom of it one way or another. Maybe she'd call Jodie sometime soon, take her into her confidence and ask her to keep her eyes and ears open. For now, she'd make the best of the time she and Daniel had together, for Courtney's sake. She ticked off school and underlined solicitor on her 'to-do' list, scribbled a reminder to call Jodie and put the notepad back in the bedside drawer.

* * *

Sean greeted Livvy and Daniel with welcoming smiles: 'Well, hello there, Liv.' He gave her a kiss on both cheeks then turned to Daniel: 'And you must be Danny?'

Daniel shook the outstretched hand. 'Sean, I take it. The Irish accent gives it away.'

'And this is Jon.' Livvy introduced Daniel to Jon, who shook hands with him and gave Livvy a hug.

'Kettle on, Liam,' Sean ordered as Liam's jaw dropped.

'S'not fair, I never get to have any fun,' he grumbled, stomping into the staffroom.

Daniel grinned. 'Just like my junior staff back home. So, this is Flanagan and Grey's?'

'Certainly is.' Sean nodded. 'The only branch of the business still open. John Grey closed the others a while back. I guess he felt sorry for Jon and me after all the years we've worked here, so kept this store going.'

'Long time then?' Daniel asked.

'Err, for me, thirty-five years and for Jon, about seventeen.'

'Oh wow, thirty-five years is some time,' Daniel said. 'Wish my staff were as loyal and long-serving. LA's so transient – nobody stays in one place for too long.'

'You've had Jodie a couple of years now, Maria's been with you over ten and...' Livvy stopped and frowned. 'What's wrong? You've gone all flushed.'

'Nothing, I'm fine,' Daniel said quickly. 'Still, thirty-five years...' He shook his head.

'Sean's been part of the furniture since before The Raiders had their very first hit,' Livvy told him.

'That's right,' Sean said. 'I used to work with Jon's parents when Jon was just a nipper.'

'Dad, Roy and Tim used to go in the very first store in Stockport after school in the late fifties,' Jon said.

'And it was downhill from then on,' Sean quipped. 'No, seriously, those were the days. Decent music, bands that could play their instruments, none of that monotonous dance routine stuff they churn out today. Just good, earthy rock 'n' roll.'

'Sounds like fun,' Daniel said as Liam brought a tray of coffee through.

'Seen you on your yacht in *Hello!*,' he said to Daniel. 'Married to Livvy, ain't you?'

'Err, yes, I am.' Daniel shrugged and picked up a mug. He turned away and took a sip.

Sean, sensing a problem, sent Liam downstairs to help Shelley. 'Where's Courtney today?' he asked.

'She's with Harley at Roy's and she's staying over there tonight,' Livvy said.

'Well, in that case, why don't you join Tina and me for a meal at ours?'

'Thanks, Sean, but why don't you and Tina come into town and dine at the hotel with us?' Daniel suggested.

'No, Danny, let's go to Sean and Tina's,' Livvy said quickly. 'I don't really want to be seen too much in public.'

'Okay.' Daniel nodded. 'Thanks, Sean. We'd love to take you up on your offer.' He turned to Livvy: 'If you've finished your coffee, we'll go and find you a house to rent.'

Jon looked up. 'Hey, if you're looking for a place, Phil and Laura have a house to let. It's a four-bedroom cottage near their own home, Apple Tree House.'

'Phil and Laura?' Livvy asked.

'Yeah, you remember Phil Jackson, The Raiders' self-confessed love-machine!'

'Oh, Phil. Of course I remember him. Who wouldn't?' Livvy said, laughing.

'Would you like me to call him and arrange for you to view?'

'Please, Jon. That would be lovely,' she replied.

'I'll show you around the store while Jon makes his call,' Sean said to Daniel. 'As you can see, it's all CDs, videos and DVDs up here, but we've some great guitars in at the moment. Follow me.'

* * *

Jon hung up, smiling. 'Laura said you can go anytime this afternoon. She's gonna prise Phil out of bed and he'll show you around.' He scribbled down the address and phone number and handed it over.

'So, where exactly is Apple Tree House in location to Hanover's Lodge?' Livvy asked. 'I presume your mum and dad still live there?'

'They do. Mum says the only way she'll ever leave The Lodge is in a pine box!' Jon laughed. 'It's a five-minute drive.'

'And how far from Manor Banks School are we talking?'

'Ten minutes, tops. Are you thinking of sending Courtney there?'

'Yes. We've got an appointment to see the head tomorrow afternoon. Also, while I think about it, do you know of a good solicitor?'

'Not offhand, but Dad does. I'll get you the number.'

'Thanks, Jon. You may as well know, I'm planning to divorce Danny.'

'Why? You seemed quite happy together just now.'

'It's all show. We've called a truce until he goes back. You should have heard us arguing last night. He accused me of being an unfit mother, said he wants custody of Courtney. I wouldn't mind, but he's having an affair, except he won't admit it.'

'Why on earth would Danny think you're an unfit mother?'

Livvy shrugged. 'Because of Roy.'

'What's it got to do with Roy?'

'We made love while Courtney was sleeping in the next room. I told Danny last night.'

'Jesus, Livvy, you must have a death wish!'

'I love Roy, Jon. He loves me.'

'Christ, history's repeating itself.'

Livvy changed the subject. 'How are things with you and Jess? She still going on about fostering?'

'Yep. Like a dog with a bone. She's going to that meeting on Friday night with Mum, but we're off to Paris on Sunday for four days, so I'm hoping to talk her out of it. I haven't mentioned the trip to Sheena yet, just in case you speak to her soon. She's calling me later, so I'll tell her then.'

'Okay.' Livvy nodded. 'Sheena won't mind. Jess is your wife, you're entitled to take a break with her.'

'Yeah, Sheena and me, well, we're just friends at the end of the day.' Jon smiled wistfully. 'We had a bit of fun and maybe one day we will again.'

'Well, as long as you both agree not to let it get out of hand.'

* * *

'So, what do you think of the place?' Phil stifled a yawn and ran his fingers through his long blond hair.

Livvy smiled. 'Late night, Phil?'

'Had a bit of a session with my sons,' he said. 'Hence the shades. Can't keep up the pace any more, getting too old for boozy nights and hangovers.'

'I know the feeling,' Daniel said. 'Well, I like the cottage very much. It's really spacious, perfect for Livvy and Courtney. There's room for Harley to stay over and a spare room for when Livvy's parents visit.'

Livvy looked out of one of the lounge windows at a couple of glossy black Cocker Spaniels, who sat staring at the closed front door, expectant looks on their faces.

'I like your dogs, Phil. They're very cute. What are their names?'

'Gene and Elvis,' Phil said, grinning. 'They're Laura's actually, but they follow me everywhere. This place was originally three farm-labourers' cottages. They were derelict when I bought Apple Tree House. We were gonna demolish them, then Laura had the bright idea of rebuilding and knocking them into one big house. The last tenant was here for five years. Bit of a boffin, invented some sort of computer game. Made a fortune and retired to Switzerland a couple of months ago. You came at just the right time. We've had it all redecorated, fitted new carpets, replaced the furniture and Laura was about to advertise it.

'Tell you what, I'll go back home, leave you two to have a good look round on your own and then come on up to the house for coffee and to meet Laura.' Phil let himself out, calling goodbye.

* * *

'So,' Daniel said, 'you're very quiet, what do you think?'

'That it's perfect,' Livvy replied. 'I can see me making a home here. I love the beamed ceilings and just look at that...' She pointed to a herringbone patterned brick fireplace built into the inglenook. 'We can burn logs on cold days.'

'You might be back home when it's cold,' Daniel said. 'Well, Courtney will be, anyway.'

'Hmm, we'll see,' Livvy said. 'I'll take another look upstairs. Why don't you make your way to Phil's? I want to wander round on my own, get the feel of it. I'll join you in a few minutes.'

'Okay, if you're sure.' Daniel let himself out and looked around outside. There was nothing but trees and fields as far as the eye could see, except for the roofline and chimney pots of Apple Tree House, tucked behind the nearby incline. He took out his cell phone as he walked towards the house, and called Jodie: 'Hi, baby, good news. I'll be home sooner than I thought. We've found the perfect temporary home. Livvy's parents are arriving at the weekend but once I've met them I can change my flight and head back so expect me say, Tuesday. I'll call you tonight. Love you too.' He ended the call and with a self-satisfied smile, walked up to Phil's front door.

* * *

Left alone, Livvy wandered from room to room, taking in the far-reaching views from each window. The décor was in keeping with the age of the cottage and Phil's wife Laura had a good eye for detail. The huge sleigh bed in the master bedroom was tucked under a sloping ceiling with a large central beam. Livvy recognised the traditional wallpaper behind the bed-head as William Morris's 'Golden Lily'. The bed was covered with a matching bedspread and piled high with co-ordinating cushions.

The second bedroom was pink and cream, had twin brass beds, stripped pine furniture and an en suite shower room – perfect for the girls. The third was decked out with a blue and white Laura Ashley design wallpaper and a double bed, great for visitors. The smallest room was currently in use as a dumping ground for tins of paint and leftover wallpaper.

Livvy stood in the middle of the floor and hugged herself. The room was at the back of the house, overlooking a neat garden with lawns and colourful flower beds and was crying out to her – nursery. She let out a long breath and shook her head. She was almost bursting with excitement, but she mustn't allow herself to get too carried away with happy family thoughts.

She wanted Daniel to think she was angry and hurt by his betrayal, but deep down, it was the best thing that could have happened. Tomorrow, when she collected Courtney from Roy's, she'd tell him and Sammy that she would think about donating an egg. That would stop Roy from mithering her for a while and keep Sammy off *his* back, too.

Next week she'd do a pregnancy test and take it from there. She peeped into the Victorian-style bathroom, then went downstairs. They could move in straight after the weekend, she thought, as she let herself out and made her way to Apple Tree House. She wouldn't need to buy anything other than linen and towels. The lounge was comfortable, with pine furniture, two cream leather sofas, a TV and a decent hi-fi system. The kitchen was well equipped, with a dining area overlooking the back garden. She was certain that Courtney would love the cottage and couldn't wait to see her face when she told her that it was almost on Roy's doorstep. The girls could spend a lot of

time together and she'd be on hand to help Roy look after
Harley.

* * *

Phil's wife Laura, who, Livvy thought, bore more than a passing
resemblance to Jane Asher, led her into the spacious lounge,
where Daniel and Phil were chatting amicably.

'Sit down, Livvy,' Laura invited. 'I've got the coffee on,
won't be a mo.'

Phil waved his arm in greeting and Livvy sat down next to
Daniel. Phil was stretched out opposite, feet up over the arm of
the sofa. Laura came back in with a tray and placed it on the
coffee table.

'Feet off the furniture, Phil Jackson,' she said. 'Honestly,
you're worse than the kids! He makes more mess than the six of
them put together,' she told Livvy.

'Six kids!' Daniel exclaimed. 'Wow, you have your hands
full.'

'We do.' Laura nodded. 'Well, we did, but they're all adults
now *and*, I hasten to add, they're not all mine. They're all *his*
though,' she said, grinning. 'And they still treat the place like a
hotel.'

'The product of two marriages,' Phil said, sitting up and
offering cigarettes around. 'Well, three really, seeing as me and
Laura are married for the second time.'

'I must have had a brainstorm agreeing to that one.' Laura
laughed, refusing a cigarette. Daniel and Livvy also shook their
heads.

'Oh well, if you're not having one, I'll do without, too. I'm
trying to give up.'

'He's been saying that since the day I met him,' Laura said.
She poured four mugs of coffee. 'Help yourself to cream and
sugar. What did you think of the cottage, Livvy?'

'Oh, it's fabulous, absolutely perfect and beautifully furnished. You have great taste,' she replied. 'When can we move in?'

'Soon as you like,' Daniel told her, waving a piece of paper under her nose. 'Here's the lease. I've given Phil a cheque to cover the next six months. All you have to do is sign this. I've explained our situation to Phil and Laura; that I'm going back to the States soon, and you're staying here for the foreseeable future.'

Livvy nodded and felt obliged to peck him on the cheek. 'Thanks, Dan. I can't wait to tell Courtney and Harley, they'll be so excited.'

'It will be lovely to have you as a neighbour,' Laura said. 'We can have girly chats over morning coffee. Danny told us your mum and dad will be reunited this weekend. How wonderful that you found your parents after all this time and that they found one another again, too.'

Livvy smiled and nodded. 'It's a dream come true to finally have a family and roots.'

* * *

Afternoon break time, Jack was standing in a corner of the playground, keeping an eye out for teachers as Nathan and Jamie Donahue passed a cigarette between them. He spotted Courtney and her parents getting out of a taxi at the school gates.

'Hey, Courtney,' he hollered, waving to catch her attention.

Jamie spun round, his eyes opening wide. 'Fucking hell, that woman looks just like Livvy Grant!'

'Hmm, she does a bit,' Jack said, winking at Nathan as Courtney, flanked either side by her mum and dad, waved back. 'I bet she'd do really well as her on *Stars in Their Eyes*!' No way was he letting on to Jamie that Livvy was exactly who he thought she was – Nathan had also been sworn to secrecy.

'Hi, Jack, Nathan,' Courtney said, as they drew level with the boys. Jamie hurriedly threw the cigarette over the wall and frowned.

'Hi yourself,' Jack said, a wide grin splitting his face as Jamie's puzzled expression grew. 'Good luck.'

'You two know that girl?' Jamie said, mouth hanging open as his gaze followed Courtney into the school building.

'She's a relative of family friends,' Jack told him as Nathan nodded. 'They're moving to the area, so hopefully she'll be starting here next week.'

'Well, she'll certainly be an asset. Prettiest girl I've seen in a long time, apart from Harls and Faye, of course,' Jamie said as Jack punched him playfully on the arm as the bell rang, signalling the end of break. 'I can see me dumping Tash this weekend,' Jamie continued. 'Perhaps we'll catch up with Courtney later.'

16

Gina Carter closed her book and fastened her seat belt as the British Airways 747 began its final approach to Manchester Airport. Her stomach looped, her legs felt like jelly and her palms were sticky. She hated flying and what with the fear, coupled with the excitement of seeing Peter again *and* meeting their daughter, she'd got herself into a right old state. She took several deep breaths and forced herself to look out of the window as the green patchwork landscape quickly gave way to toy town suburbs, liquorice strip roads and Dinky-sized cars.

Her right hand crept into her jacket pocket and folded around a dog-eared, black and white photo of herself, holding a tiny, shawl-clad baby. The photo had been taken by one of the girls at the mother and baby home, shortly before Marie had been taken from her. She'd kept it hidden from her parents' prying eyes for years and it was her most-treasured possession. All that pain she'd endured during the years that followed the adoption. The bottled-up anger and hatred towards her parents, who'd placed her in a mental hospital for months, claiming she was insane when she'd been suffering post-partum depression.

Then there was their disapproval at her short-term marriage

to bartender Jake at the age of eighteen. She hadn't loved Jake; the marriage was merely an escape from her stifling home life. The longing for Marie and Peter never went away. Even the birth of her son Joel didn't quell the pain. She smiled as she looked at the photo again. Her Marie – her beautiful girl. She couldn't believe she was about to see her again after all these years. Not only that, but she was going to share the moment with Peter, the love of her life.

She was so lost in her thoughts that the gentle bumping of tyres on tarmac went unnoticed as she continued to stare at the photo. The plane slowed and taxied to a halt. She pushed the photo back in her pocket, gathered her hand luggage and made her way to the nearest exit.

* * *

Livvy was beside herself with excitement as she, Dad, Courtney and Daniel waited by the barrier, scanning the faces of the passengers as they began to filter through. Dad's flight had arrived from Glasgow earlier and they'd passed the last hour drinking coffee.

'I'll recognise her as soon as I see her,' her father said. 'It's been years, but I'll know her.'

Livvy smiled at his animated face. 'You've waited a long time for this.'

'All my life, hen, all my life. You never forget your first love.'

Livvy caught Daniel's raised eyebrows and wanted to kick his shins for taking the piss out of this special moment. She wished he wasn't with them, but he'd insisted on coming and had hired a big limo. It was waiting outside to take them back to the hotel. Trust him to be so OTT. She was sure her parents would be far more comfortable in a normal taxi. Her breath caught in her throat as a petite, blonde woman struggled through the doors with a laden trolley. That surely must be Gina, she was her mirror image.

'There she is,' Dad called out, waving both arms and jumping up and down. 'There's my angel. Gina, Gina, over here!'

Gina looked up and her face broke into a wide smile. Livvy felt that she would capture that moment in her head forever. Gina let go of the trolley and ran towards Peter, who swept her off her feet and swung her round and round. They were crying and laughing and gazing into each other's eyes, oblivious to the curious stares directed at them. Daniel retrieved the trolley and went to stand beside Courtney.

Peter turned to Livvy and put his arm around her shoulders: 'Livvy, this is your mother.'

Gina held out her arms and Livvy melted into them, crying along with her. 'You have no idea how many times I've imagined this moment,' Gina whispered. 'I can't believe this is really happening.'

'Nor me.' Livvy smiled through her tears. She beckoned Courtney forwards. 'Mom, this is my youngest daughter. Say hello to your grandma, Courtney.'

Gina enveloped Courtney in a bear hug. 'You're so like your mother,' she said. 'Where's your other daughter, Marie, err, Livvy?'

'She's at home. You'll get to meet her later today. As Dad's told you, she's not too well at the moment, but I'll explain everything when we get to the hotel and you've had a chance to rest. You must be exhausted.'

'A little,' Gina admitted. 'But then, I've been too excited to sleep properly for days.'

'Come on then.' Daniel took charge. 'Let's go and get you settled in.'

* * *

Livvy smiled as Peter gazed around the spacious suite, his mouth open.

'Hen, this is pure luxury. Are you sure you can afford it?'

'Dad, I intend to spoil the pair of you something rotten from now on,' she said.

'Well, this is a wonderful start.' Gina ran her hand over the blue satin drapes that hung from the mahogany four-poster. 'I've never seen such opulence in my life. And look, Peter, we've even got our own bathroom.'

'It's actually the honeymoon suite,' Livvy said. 'I hope you don't mind – I want your time here to be really special. The bath's a Jacuzzi and there's champagne chilling over there.'

Peter grinned as Gina blushed prettily. 'You little romantic,' he said to Livvy. He caught Gina around the waist and pulled her close. 'I'm sure Gina won't mind sharing a room with me, unless of course you prefer to sleep alone?' He raised an enquiring eyebrow.

'Peter, I've spent too many nights sleeping alone. We've got thirty-odd years to make up. Now go and run me a bath and I'll have a glass of champagne while I'm soaking in the bubbles.'

'Yes, madam, whatever you say. Still as bossy as ever,' he called over his shoulder as he went into the bathroom.

'Start as you mean to go on, eh, Mom?' Livvy said, grinning.

Gina smiled and tweaked a curl behind Livvy's ear. 'You're so beautiful, but then I always knew you would be. I feel very proud that you're my daughter. When I saw you in concert at Maple Leaf Gardens, I never once considered that you were my flesh and blood and yet we look so alike. I can't get used to thinking of you as Livvy. To me, you've always been my little Marie. You'll have to forgive me if I get muddled on occasion.'

'Oh, Mom, don't worry. Call me whatever you feel comfortable with,' Livvy said as Gina took her hand.

'You and Danny have problems, don't you? I sensed it right away. Do you want to talk about it, honey?'

'Later, Mom. I'm going to leave you and Dad to get reacquainted. We'll talk some more tonight. We're taking Courtney shopping for her school uniform then I'll collect Harley and bring her back here for afternoon tea. We'll meet up at four in the lounge,' she said as Peter announced the bath was ready. 'Have a lovely time. You deserve it.'

'I can never thank you enough for all this,' Peter said, hugging Livvy close. 'I don't just mean this fabulous room, I mean you finding us after all this time. I feel like I'm dreaming some days. I'll never be able to pay you back.'

'Dad, you will, just by supporting me over the next few months. I'll need you both during Harley's treatment time and beyond.'

'We'll be there.' Gina joined in the hug. 'See you later, sweetie, and thank you from the bottom of my heart.'

* * *

Livvy wiped away tears as she went to her own room. If only she and Roy could be like her parents, getting back together, forever. Still, she could dream and who knew what the future held?

'Mom, Roy called you,' Courtney announced, tearing her eyes away from the TV. 'He said to call him back when you're free.'

'Thanks, honey. Where's your dad?'

'Gone to explore Manchester. He'll see you back here for dinner.'

'*Will* he?' Livvy tutted. 'He might at least have waited until I finished settling my parents in. We were supposed to be shopping together.' She went into Courtney's room and closed the door.

Sammy answered her call and in a clipped tone asked if her parents had arrived safely then went to get Roy. 'Hi, Roy,' Livvy began. 'How's Harley?' She listened as he told her that Harley wasn't too good. She'd had a heavy nosebleed and complained of chest pains; she wasn't up to being brought into Manchester to meet her grandparents.

'You could bring them to the house tomorrow afternoon,' he suggested. 'Maybe you and Courtney could pop in for half an hour later.' He was quiet for a moment. 'I don't suppose you've given any thought to the egg donation?'

'Erm, yes,' she replied and took a deep breath. 'I'm still thinking. I need to know what's involved. Could Sammy get some information and then we can discuss the matter when my parents go to Glasgow and Danny goes home?' She heard him sigh and he put his hand over the receiver for a minute, presumably while he spoke to Sammy, who, she was certain, would be giving him no peace over the idea.

'Fair enough, Liv,' he said. 'We'll see you later.'

* * *

'Maybe you should let me talk to her,' Sammy said, as Roy replaced the receiver. 'I mean, it's not something she should even have to think about – it's her daughter's life she could be saving.'

'Sammy, give it a rest, love, please. The more you push, the less likely she is to say yes. And she's quite right. You need to find out exactly what's involved and that means for you as well.'

* * *

Roy and Sammy said a tearful goodbye to Harley on Monday morning. As their daughter lay on her hospital bed, her face as white as the pillows, Roy took her hand.

'You'll be fine, princess. Be brave and it will soon be over.

We'll come and collect you tomorrow morning and take you home for a few days.'

'Now, you've got your book to read and all your toiletries for later,' Sammy said, smoothing Harley's hair off her face. 'We'll be in tonight to see you, even if they only allow us five minutes.'

Harley nodded. 'I just want to get on with it now then I can have my life back. Where are you going when you leave me?'

'Uncle Ed's for coffee and then home,' Roy said. 'I'll call Livvy later to let her know how you've gone on. She'll come and visit you tomorrow night when you're at home.'

Harley smiled. 'Ask her to bring my grandparents, too. They'll be going to Glasgow on Wednesday, so I won't see them for a while. I really like them; they're so romantic with one another. It's such a shame they missed out on all those years and bringing Livvy up together.'

Roy felt Sammy flinch beside him and took her hand.

'Mum, I'm sorry,' Harley said. 'I didn't mean anything by that. I wasn't implying that Dad and Livvy should have been together to bring me up. You've been the best parents in the world and I love you both so much.'

'It's okay, love. We love you too,' Sammy said, her eyes filling with tears. 'We must go now before they throw us out.' She bent to kiss her and backed out of the room, leaving Roy and Harley alone.

'Don't cry, Dad, please, you'll have me at it in a minute. I'm trying to be brave for us all.' Harley looked up as a big tear slid down Roy's face and landed on her hand.

He wiped his eyes with the tissue she passed him and stroked her cheek. 'I'll do whatever it takes to get you well, princess, no matter what. I'll do everything possible. You know that, don't you?'

Harley nodded. 'Give my love to Jack when he calls you later. He's as bad as you are – I had to dry *his* tears last night.'

'Well, we men are not quite as tough as we think we are. But we do our best.'

'I know you do, Dad. Now go, let me rest. I'll see you later.'

Roy bent to kiss her and left the room. Sammy was waiting in the corridor and took his arm.

'She's a fighter, Roy. She'll get through it.'

'I hope so, Sam. She means the world to me. I never thought I could love a kid as much as I love her.'

Sammy's face clouded and she pulled away from him.

'Oh, Sam, I don't mean that I love her more than Nick and Jason, of course I don't. It's just that, well... considering I ordered Livvy to get rid of her, which I've never stopped feeling guilty about, the love I feel for her is incredibly protective. Maybe it's because she's a girl and more vulnerable.'

'Or maybe it's because Livvy is her mother and I'm not.'

'Sammy, don't start, please. Not today. I couldn't handle it right now.'

'Sorry, Roy.' She put her arms around him. 'I feel very insecure at the moment and it doesn't help now that Livvy's going to be a stone's throw away and you'll be taking Harley to her house on a regular basis. And don't you dare insult me by denying you still have feelings for one another. It was written all over your faces the other day when I walked in on you in the kitchen. If I didn't know better, I'd swear you were lovers again.'

'Now you're just being ridiculous,' Roy said. He could feel a blush creeping up his neck as he unlocked the car. 'Get in before we really have a fight and just drop the subject before we get to Ed's place.'

* * *

Jane looked up from loading the dishwasher as the back door opened and Roy and Sammy strolled into the kitchen. 'Hi, you two. How did it go?'

Roy blinked hard. 'One of the worst things I've ever had to do, leaving her there on her own.'

'Sit down, mate.' Eddie patted Roy's hand. 'I'll make a fresh pot of coffee.'

'Actually, I'm popping over to Jess's,' Jane said. 'Come with me, Sam. We'll have our coffee there and leave these two to catch up.'

Jane linked her arm through Sammy's as they walked across the communal gardens.

'What's on your mind? Apart from Harley, of course.'

Sammy sighed and told her about the plan to try and have a baby with Livvy's donated egg.

'Wow!' Jane stopped and stared at Sammy. 'And do you think she'll do it?'

'Who knows?' Sammy shrugged. 'I think she'd be very selfish to refuse. It's the only way we can produce a full-blood sibling and if *I'm* willing to put myself at risk...'

'It's not the only way though, is it?' Jane interrupted.

'It is,' Sammy said. 'We're not going down the other road again – I just couldn't bear it.' Her eyes filled with tears and Jane put her arms around her.

'I know. I'd find it hard to deal with too, I mean, if it were mine and Ed's problem. I guess there's no simple solution, but I think you're being very brave to even consider another pregnancy at your age.'

* * *

'Thanks, Ed.' Roy took his coffee and sat at the table.

'How many sessions of chemo will Harley need?' Eddie asked, sitting opposite Roy.

'They said six. That will hopefully put her in remission. Then pending further tests, they may want to do the bone marrow transplant. And there lies the problem.' Roy outlined his and Sammy's plans. He offered Eddie a cigarette and lit up himself. 'It's not ideal, I know, but what else can we do?'

'Hope for the best, I suppose,' Eddie said. 'I don't envy you. Jane was saying only this morning that she expected life to be simpler now the kids are grown up, but it seems harder somehow. Perhaps we should consider retiring the band after the next album.'

'That's what I've been thinking for a while, to be honest.' Roy nodded. 'It's too much at our ages. We could finish with a final tour and make the next album the last.'

'Well, as long as Tim, Phil and Carl are in agreement, we should work towards that goal. One final big show at Manchester Arena for all the local fans and then bow out disgracefully. In fact, we could make it a charity gig, for cancer research.'

Roy's eyes filled and he nodded.

'How are you getting on with Livvy?' Eddie asked. 'Any sparks still there?'

'Yep,' he admitted. 'She's still in love with me.'

'And you?'

'I guess I still love *her*, Ed. It was like we'd never been apart. I've paid visits to her on my own that Sammy knows nothing about.'

'I thought you might,' Eddie said. 'You shagged her then?'

'It was the most natural thing in the world.' Roy stubbed out the remains of his cigarette and immediately lit another. 'I try and fight it like crazy, but she's always on my mind, day and night. I met her husband Danny when I went to pick Courtney up. There was a lot of tension between him and Liv – I got the feeling he wanted to flatten me.'

'She's told him you're Harley's father at last?'

'Yeah, and he's not a happy bunny.'

'Hardly surprising. So what now?'

'Well, Livvy's renting Phil's cottage while we get Harley

over the worst. Courtney's starting at Manor Banks on Monday, Danny's flying home tomorrow.'

'I meant between you and Sammy. What's gonna happen?'

Roy shrugged. He stared into his coffee. 'We're hoping Livvy will say yes to the egg donation idea.'

'And you'll all live happily ever after?' Eddie drained his mug and stood up. 'Get real, Roy. Livvy's never gonna agree to that.'

'She might.'

'And what happens when Sammy finds out you've shagged her?'

Roy drew a finger across his throat. 'I'm a dead man, or at least a divorced man. I shouldn't be taking risks while Harley's so ill but Livvy's beautiful – I find it hard to keep my hands off her.'

'She was always beautiful. Her beauty was your downfall last time.'

Roy didn't reply.

* * *

Livvy fidgeted on the edge of the bath as a bright blue line appeared in the window of the white plastic stick. She caught her breath and tears slid down her cheeks. She wrapped her arms around herself, closed her eyes and rocked back and forth. Harley's future was now hopefully secure. No matter what anyone would think of her for this, saving her daughter was the most important thing and if her actions finished Roy's marriage, then so be it. She would try not to feel too guilty. After a quick shower and hurried make-up, Livvy woke Courtney for her first day at Manor Banks.

'Toast and cereal, sweetie?' she asked as Courtney sat down at the kitchen table. 'You look really smart in that uniform. Dark green and navy suits your colouring.'

'Cereal, please, Mom.' Courtney stared down at her clothes and pulled a face. 'The sweatshirt's okay, but I hate this skirt. Why can't I wear pants?'

'They weren't on the list,' Livvy said, handing Courtney a packet of Weetabix. 'You'll have to see if any of the other girls are wearing pants. I have a feeling it'll just be the boys – schools over here are a bit formal. Anyway, it's a nice little skirt. No pleats or anything, just plain and straight, and not too long. Grin and bear it, honey, for now anyway.'

'I'm still tired.' Courtney yawned. 'I feel really excited and I could hardly sleep.'

'Well, you were zonked when I got up at seven,' Livvy said and took a sip of orange juice.

'You okay, Mom? You look a bit pale.'

'I'm fine. A bit tired myself – it's been a hectic last few days.'

'You worrying about Harley?'

'I am. And I'm wondering how Mom's getting along with Dad's family. I'll call them tonight.' Her parents had flown to Glasgow a couple of days earlier after celebrating their engagement. As her dad had said, why wait? Daniel had gone back to LA and she and Courtney had moved into Charlecote Cottage. Harley was home with Roy and Sammy for a few days before her next session of chemotherapy. 'I'm also concerned about you, of course. It's a big thing, starting a new school, especially in a different country.'

'I'll be okay. Jack will be waiting at the gates for me. He's going to show me around. I can look after myself, you know.'

'I'm sure you can. But just promise me one thing, Courtney.'

'What?' Courtney frowned, spoon halfway to her mouth.

'Don't go off alone at lunchtime with any of the boys. Especially that Jamie Donahue you've done nothing but talk about since you met him last week.'

Courtney blushed slightly and smiled. 'I won't. Chill, Mom.'

'Chill! You sound more like Harley every day. Hurry up now or you'll be late. I'm going to see Tina for coffee after I've dropped you off.'

* * *

Livvy took the mug Tina handed her. Bursting to say something, she'd just told Tina her news and Tina was staring at her, open-mouthed.

'Congratulations. And is Danny pleased?' She sat next to Livvy on the sofa and offered her a biscuit. 'I remember Jaffa Cakes were always your favourites.'

'Thank you.' Livvy helped herself and took a sip of coffee. 'I haven't told Danny, you're the first to know. I only did the test this morning.'

'I see.' Tina nodded. 'Well, it's a heck of an age gap. You're going to have to take good care of yourself – they seem to class anyone over thirty as an older mother these days.'

'Which, at thirty-eight, I am,' Livvy agreed. 'It's very early days and I don't want anyone to know for a while. I just needed to tell someone I could trust. That's why I chose you.' She smiled at Tina who, along with Sean, had looked after her before and after Harley's birth and had always been supportive.

'So, when will you tell Danny?'

'I'm not sure that I will.' Livvy studied the Jaffa Cake and nibbled around the edge.

'Why not? He'll have to know sometime. Don't you want the baby?'

Livvy's eyes filled with tears. 'Oh, Tina, of course I do. You've no idea how much I want this baby. I *need* this baby.'

Tina put down her mug and wrapped her arms around

Livvy. 'Hey, come on, don't get upset. I don't understand. If you want it so badly, why on earth won't you tell Danny?'

'Because it's not his,' Livvy whispered.

Tina sat back, her mouth agape. 'Not Roy's? Not again? You've got to be having me on?'

Livvy sat silently, tears tumbling down her cheeks as Tina stared at her.

'Oh my God! Sammy will go crazy. Does Roy know?'

'Not yet. But I'll tell him soon.' In-between sobs, she told Tina about the egg donation plan and Sammy wanting to have a baby herself and why.

'Christ! This will devastate Sammy. You know that, don't you? You can never put *this* right by handing a baby over. Why, Livvy? Why have you allowed it to happen again? I thought you were happy with Danny and your wonderful life in LA. I mean, you have everything.'

'Appearances can be very deceptive.' Livvy sniffed. 'I've never really loved Danny. There's not a day gone by that I haven't thought about Harley and Roy. And anyway, this baby may well save Harley's life. What if the egg thing didn't work with Sammy right away? It could take months. Harley hasn't got that sort of time to wait.'

Tina puffed out her cheeks. 'You're crazy. What about Roy's rights? Doesn't he get a say in this?'

'Of course he does. When I tell him, I'm sure he'll agree it's for the best.' Livvy drew a deep breath, not totally convinced by what she was saying. Even to *her* ears it sounded like a mad idea now. But there was no going back. 'Anyway,' she continued, 'if he can tumble so easily into bed with me, then there has to be something seriously lacking in his marriage. The chemistry between us was intense, it was a purely natural act of love.'

'More like lust, knowing Roy Cantello,' Tina muttered. 'I don't know what to say to you.'

'I don't expect you do,' Livvy said. 'Tina, I just want to try and save my daughter's life. To do that, I have to have Roy's child. It's her best and probably her only hope. We've all been tested but it's unlikely we'll be suitable. A full-blood sibling could make the difference between life and death – I haven't a choice.'

Tina shook her head. 'Put like that, I can see your point though God help you.'

Livvy wiped her eyes and stood up. 'I'd better go – I need to do some shopping and then go home. Roy's going to call me later with an update on Harley and whether she's up to a visit from Courtney after school.'

Tina accompanied her to the door and gave her a hug. 'It's not going to be an easy ride for you, but me and Sean will be here if you need us when the shit hits the fan.'

17

Livvy lay on the sofa, reading her horoscope in *OK!* magazine. She felt drained after her confession to Tina, but had been bursting to tell someone her secret. Deep down she knew that not everyone would agree it was good news, but to be carrying Roy's child again was the most wonderful thing that could have happened and not *only* because it could save Harley's life. Two birds with one stone, as they say, and it had been so easy, too. But how to tell Roy that she couldn't donate an egg, and why, was the problem now. She glanced at her horoscope again and sighed. The last sentence – *You will end the week feeling a lot more cheerful and optimistic due to events that are set to put a smile on your face* – sounded positive enough, she thought, but she didn't really believe in all that stuff, although she'd grasp any given straw at the moment.

She jumped as the phone rang. It was Roy's expected call. He kept it brief, just told her he was on his way to see her. He didn't even give her time to ask if everything was okay with Harley. She got to her feet, smoothed out the creases in her linen skirt and made her way to the bathroom, where she stared at her pale reflection in the mirror. She ran her fingers through her curls and swept blusher onto her cheeks. A sweep of mascara, touch of lip-gloss and she looked and felt human again.

Roy's car screeched to a halt and she ran downstairs to let him in. He swept her into his arms, kicked the door closed with his foot and hugged her tightly, raining kisses on her face. It was the first time they'd been alone since the night he'd refused to make love to her at the hotel. He carried her into the lounge and lowered her onto the sofa. She pulled him close, craving his kisses and running her hands through his hair. 'Is Harley alright?' she managed to ask.

'Yes, she's doing okay. We'll talk later. I'm so sorry about the other night...' he began.

'Shh, it doesn't matter, you're here now,' she interrupted. Feeling reassured there was no emergency with Harley, she allowed herself to relax in his arms.

'What time do you have to pick up Courtney?' he whispered, unbuttoning her shirt.

'Three thirty.' She reached to unzip him.

'Just over an hour,' he said, his hand wandering up her skirt. 'No time to waste. I'm so desperate for you, Liv.'

They made quick, passionate love half-on, half-off the sofa, almost fully clothed. Livvy cried out as she came, her shuddering sending Roy to his own climax.

'Oh, Jesus!' He crushed her to him. 'I love you. I've thought of hardly anything but this for days. I know I shouldn't, but I can't keep my hands off you.'

'The feeling's mutual,' she said, stroking his face. 'I want you every minute of every day.'

He kissed her again and rolled onto the floor.

She wriggled into an upright position. 'Zip yourself up, I'll make us some tea.'

Roy followed her into the kitchen, tucking his T-shirt into his jeans. He leant with his back against the sink and rummaged in his pockets. 'Do you mind?' he held up a packet of cigarettes.

'Go ahead. Not for me, thanks. I gave up when I was expecting Harley, remember?'

'I do. I wish I had your willpower.' He lit up and drew deeply. 'Harley's had quite a good day, so far. She's really looking forward to seeing Courtney later.'

Livvy grimaced and he frowned.

'What's wrong?'

'I don't know if I can face Sammy. Not after what we've just done. She'll be able to read it in my face. I don't know how you can go home and be so normal.' She handed him a mug of tea.

'I do it with great difficulty,' he said. 'But you can't disappoint the girls. You don't have to come in. Drop Courtney at the door and I'll bring her back later.'

'But then I don't get to see Harley.'

'If she's feeling up to it, she can come with me when I bring Courtney home.'

'Okay. Let's drink our tea in the lounge.'

Roy followed her, put both mugs on the coffee table and pulled her down beside him on the sofa.

'How are Jason and Jules getting on with their baby plans?' she asked, snuggling into him as he slipped his arm around her waist.

He gave a wry smile and shook his head. 'Fine, I think. I try and keep out of it as much as I can. I've got to be honest here and say that I find the whole surrogacy thing a bit odd but I have to keep my thoughts to myself at home. I mean, how can you top making babies in the normal way?'

Livvy stared at him for a long moment and then looked away. 'You can't,' she said softly.

He placed his finger under her chin and tilted her face to his. 'What's wrong?'

'Nothing,' she replied, feeling her cheeks warm.

'Livvy, I know you too well. Something's bugging you.' He

clapped his hand to his forehead and groaned. 'Fucking hell! I know what it is.'

'What?'

'Shit! I'm sorry, sweetheart. Christ, you should have stopped me! As usual, I just didn't think.'

'Roy, for God's sake! What are you on about?'

'Just now. I didn't use anything. Can you take the morning after pill? Kate Mellor might be able to get hold of some for you – she got them for Harley.'

'Roy, stop. I can't ask Kate. Danny's not here and she'll be wondering who I've slept with.'

He raised an ironical eyebrow. 'Well, she won't have far to look. She'll guess right away.'

'Exactly. I've registered with a GP, I'll go and see him tomorrow. Unless there's a family planning clinic near here?' She played along with him.

'I wouldn't know,' he said, running his hands agitatedly through his hair. 'It's not something I've ever had to think about. Look online, or maybe Phil's missus would know. Although with six kids to their name, I don't think family planning's their strong point either.'

Livvy drew a deep breath and took his hand. 'Roy, stop fussing. I'm not going to do anything.' This couldn't have happened at a better time even if she'd planned it, she thought. Roy would never need to know that she'd been deceptive in conceiving the child and chances are that she'd deliver a week or two early, like she did with Harley and Courtney, and that would be perfect.

'What do you mean?' he said, his voice rising. He gripped her shoulders and she could see the panic in his eyes. 'You have to do something. You won't be safe now, not if you were the other week, that much I *do* know.'

'True,' she replied, as calmly as she could, while feeling like mush inside. 'And if I get caught now, the baby will be a full-blood sibling for Harley, don't you see? There'll be no need for me to donate an egg to Sammy.'

Roy's eyes widened as the realisation dawned. 'Livvy, what are you saying? We can't do this again. Think what it will do to Sammy, not to mention Danny and the girls.'

'*I'm* thinking of Harley,' she said, digging her fingernails into her palms and looking him straight in the eyes. 'It might be her only chance. How could any of us deny her that?' She got to her feet and folded her arms protectively across her stomach. '*You* promised Harley that you would do everything you possibly could to get her well, no matter what it takes. *If* I've just conceived and the baby is a perfect match, then we've created a miracle, Roy, and you'll be keeping your promise to our daughter, *our* daughter,' she repeated. He was watching her every move, looking like the stuffing had been well and truly punched out of him. He seemed incapable of speech. She had to convince him she was right and tried again.

'I don't give a damn about our marriages. Mine's on the rocks anyway and how can yours be working properly when you won't stay away from *me*? And as for Courtney, her wish is that you, me, she and Harley could all live together as a family.' She could feel tears tumbling down her cheeks now and he was still staring at her, dumbstruck. 'I need the loo,' she muttered and ran out of the room.

* * *

Roy sat with his head in his hands, his mind working overtime. How the fuck was he going to get out of this? But then, Livvy was right: Harley should come first, not him and Sammy, or Livvy and Danny. She might not have conceived anyway and he was worrying for nothing and they could still go ahead with Sammy's plan. He looked up as she came back into the room. His breath caught in his throat and his heart thudded. He was in love with her, there was no denying it. She needed him and he should be with her, he knew that too. But how the hell did he make it all happen and make it right for everyone else? It was too much to think about at the moment. His head felt mashed. He would have to give something up for her and it looked like it would have to be Sammy and his home. Livvy sat down beside him and took his hand. He drew her into his arms.

'Olivia, I know what you're saying and you're right, Harley means everything to me and so do you.' He stopped and swallowed hard. 'Are you really willing to give up your marriage, your home and career?'

She nodded. 'Totally. My career's on hold, for now anyway. I've got a home here. I don't want to be with Danny, I don't love him and I've wasted enough of his life. My main worry is losing Courtney to him.'

'Why would you lose Courtney?'

'Well, Danny might say I'm an unfit mother, falling pregnant again by my ex-lover. It would be perfect grounds for a divorce and the tabloids would have a field day.'

'But we don't know that you're pregnant yet. We're jumping the gun a bit here and maybe it's just wishful thinking. *But*, if you are,' he continued, seeing a look of something cross her face, 'I'll be behind you all the way. Whatever it takes, we'll be together on this one.'

'What about Sammy?'

He felt his eyes fill and shook his head. 'Christ knows! My marriage will be over. No matter how good the intention, she won't tolerate me having another child with you. She'll think we've planned it deliberately.'

'So, you'd be willing to walk away from everything, too?'

He could feel her eyes searching his for further reassurance. 'I guess I would, this time. But let's wait and see what happens in the next couple of weeks, then you can do a test and we'll take it from there.'

'Okay.' She planted a kiss on his lips.

* * *

Livvy quickly changed out of her crumpled linen outfit and pulled on jeans and a T-shirt. Roy was taking her to collect Courtney from school. She splashed her face with cold water, scraped her hair into a ponytail and rummaged in her handbag for her shades to hide her red-rimmed eyes. Although she'd won a victory, she felt hollow inside, ashamed at deceiving him. But she couldn't tell him she was already pregnant and would have to play along for the next two weeks until she could do another test.

* * *

Roy sat in his car, his mind doing overtime as he went over the possible life-changing events of the last hour. Maybe fate was intervening and it was all meant to be. There was no denying that his love for Livvy was so strong it was taking precedence over everything, barring his concerns for Harley. This time around he felt powerless to fight it. But how to tell Sammy, that was the problem. He'd need all his strength to act normally at home for the next couple of weeks, stalling Sammy from mithering about the egg thing until Livvy knew for certain. If she wasn't pregnant, then what? Harley would still need a donor. Jesus! He felt like his head was exploding. He looked up. Livvy was running towards the car, her ponytail bouncing up and down. She got in beside him and he revved the engine and drove quickly down the private lane.

'You look like a schoolgirl yourself in that get-up,' he said, smiling at her.

She smiled back. 'We'll be okay, you know, Roy. If the worst comes to the worst, I mean.'

'I'm sure we will,' he said, pulling onto Ashlea Road. 'And hopefully, so will Harley. I've just been thinking of an excuse as to why I'll have Courtney with me when I get home. I'll have to tell Sam I popped in to see Phil and you were just arriving home from the school run, so I offered to bring Courtney with me. That sounds feasible enough, doesn't it?'

'Perfectly.'

He reached for her hand. 'It amazes me how so much can happen in so short a time. You should never take anything for granted.'

'I never do,' she replied. 'But I'm a great believer in fate.'

He pulled up on Manor Banks car park and waved to Jess, who was parked nearby.

'Hell, I forgot about Jess collecting the boys! I thought she and Jon were in Paris.'

'They only went for a few days,' Livvy said.

'Damn it, now I'll have to rethink my excuse as to why I've got Courtney with me.'

'Why?'

'Well, Jess is bound to go home and tell Ed and Jane that you and I turned up at school together and Jane will be straight on the blower to Sammy.'

Livvy nodded. 'Well, people will just have to get used to seeing us together.'

Roy sighed. 'Yeah, but not yet. Oh, oh, look.' He pointed towards the school entrance, where Courtney was emerging. Jamie Donahue steering her by the elbow and carrying her schoolbag, Tasha following in his wake.

'Oh no!' Livvy cried. 'I warned her this morning about keeping away from him. I hope she didn't leave the school premises with him at lunchtime.'

'So do I,' Roy said. 'Or we might not be the only ones with a little problem.'

'Oh, don't! I couldn't cope with that. I'd lose her to Danny for good.'

'I'm pulling your leg, sweetheart,' Roy said and patted her arm. 'Courtney's a good kid, she knows how to behave herself.'

'Yes, she does. But I've heard that Jamie doesn't and she's easily flattered.' Livvy leapt from the car as Courtney sauntered over, Jamie hot on her heels.

'Hi, Mom, hi, Roy.' Courtney bent to wave at Roy, who stayed in the car. She pulled a disappointed face. 'Oh, I thought you might have Harley with you.'

'No, Roy's taking you home with him,' Livvy told her. 'We had a bit of business to discuss.'

'I see.' Courtney raised her eyebrows and took her bag off Jamie as Tasha linked her arm possessively through his. 'See you tomorrow, Jamie,' she said, ignoring Tasha as Jamie winked at her.

'You bet,' he muttered.

Jack yelled, 'Bye, Courtney,' across the playground and she turned and waved at him and Nathan.

'See you tomorrow, boys. I'm going to Harley's for tea.'

'Okay, give her my love. Tell her I'll call her tonight,' Jack said, climbing up into the Jeep beside his mother, who, with a puzzled expression on her face, waved goodbye as she pulled away.

'She'll be dashing straight back to Hanover's Lodge to tell the tale,' Roy whispered to Livvy. 'You alright, Courtney? How was the first day?'

'I loved it,' Courtney enthused. 'You okay, Roy?'

'Couldn't be better,' he replied, glancing at Livvy, who blushed and ordered Courtney to fasten her seat belt.

* * *

'See you later, Liv,' Roy called as he dropped her off back at the cottage.

Courtney waved to her mother and then turned to Roy: 'So, what have you and Mom been up to this afternoon?'

'Up to? What do you mean?' He frowned and pulled up at the traffic lights at the end of the lane.

'Well, she was wearing her shades, it's not sunny and her eyes were all red when she took them off just now. She's been crying. Did you two have a fight?'

'Of course not.' He gripped the steering wheel tight.

'She loves you,' Courtney said in a matter-of-fact way. 'And *you* love *her,* don't you? I heard you telling her.'

'Did you? When was that?' he asked, keeping his eyes on the traffic lights.

'At the hotel. You both thought I was sleeping, but I woke up. You were saying it to her over and over.' Courtney fixed him with a stare that made him feel hot under the collar.

'I see,' he said. The lights changed and he put his foot down.

'I didn't want to disturb you,' she continued, 'so I stayed in my room.'

'That was thoughtful of you.' He glanced at her serious face.

'But you do love her, don't you?' she persisted.

'I do,' he admitted.

She sat back, arms folded, a satisfied expression on her face.

'What about you, young lady? Do you miss your home and friends?'

'No. I miss Dad a bit, but he was hardly ever around and always left me with the housekeeper. I was lonely in LA. I've got everything I need right here. Mom's home all the time. I've got Harley. My granny and grandpa are only a short journey away. I've got my aunts and uncles and cousins and now I've got new friends like Jack and Nathan and Faye – and Jamie,' she finished with a smile.

'Jamie Donahue is trouble with a capital T and you're far too young to be getting involved with the likes of *him*.'

'I'm not getting involved with him. To be honest, Roy, I think it's Mom he fancies. He's never stopped asking me questions about her and Juice and why we're living here. He knows she's Harley's real mum now and I told him we're here because Harley's ill.'

'Good girl. The less he knows the better, for now anyway,' Roy said as the gates of Jasmine House swung open. 'I've got to come up with a good excuse for Sammy as to why you're with me. I don't want her to know that I spent the afternoon with your mother. This really isn't the best way to learn about adult relationships, Courtney. All the secrets and lies and the mess we've made of things, but I'm trying to protect Sammy from being hurt by the truth.'

'I think I understand.' Courtney nodded. 'I guess Sammy will be angry with you, no matter what you tell her.'

'I guess she will,' Roy agreed as he parked in front of the garage block. He patted Courtney's shoulder. The girl was wise beyond her years. Perhaps as well, he thought. She'd need to grow up pretty quickly in the next few months.

Harley flung open the door and greeted Courtney with an air-kiss to each cheek. She shot a wary half-smile in Roy's direction and raised both eyebrows.

'What?'

'You're in trouble!' She slid her fingers across her throat and pointed to the closed door of the lounge. 'Mum's in there with a G&T and it's not her first. She's not a happy bunny, Dad.'

'Okay.' Roy sighed. 'You two take yourselves upstairs and I'll go and face the music.'

* * *

Roy poured a large single malt and turned to Sammy, who was sitting on the sofa, clutching a glass, her face ashen and her eyes staring at him as though he was a stranger. 'Can I get you a refill?'

She shook her head and took a gulp of her drink.

'Want to talk?' he ventured, sitting opposite her. He should go to her, put his arms around her, but he couldn't and he sensed she wouldn't want that anyway. 'How many of those have you had?' He'd noticed the almost-empty gin bottle, which last night had been almost full.

She shrugged. 'Dunno! Don't care.'

'Ah, so you *are* speaking to me?' He knocked back his drink and put his glass on the coffee table. He could do with another, but he had to drive Courtney home later.

She continued to stare at him, her eyes burning with unshed tears. 'Why?'

'Did Jess call you and blab? That didn't take her long.'

'No, Roy. Not in the way *you* mean. Jess wasn't telling tales. She was concerned that something had happened to Harley; that you had picked up Livvy and the pair of you were collecting Courtney to bring her here. She said Livvy had shades on and assumed she'd been crying as there's no sun today.'

'Well, why didn't she think to ask Livvy or me while she was parked beside us?'

'I don't know but that's beside the point. You must have left the house shortly after me and Harley because we came back almost straight away. We'd only got to the top of the lane and Harley felt sick with the movement of the car. You obviously went off in the opposite direction or you would have passed us coming back. Phil's place is in that direction, so I just put two and two together.'

'Why didn't you call my mobile?'

'I didn't want you to think I was checking up on you,' she

cried. 'I trusted you, Roy. Hard though it's been the last few weeks, I gave you the benefit of the doubt. I wasn't wrong about you and Livvy being lovers again, was I?'

'No!' He shook his head and looked down at his feet. Pointless lying now. Might as well get it all out in the open and take it from there. He owed her that much at least.

'Oh, Roy. When?'

'It doesn't matter. What bloody difference does it make?'

'It matters to me. Today?'

He nodded. She didn't need to know about the other time.

'And the rest,' she said, slamming her glass down on the coffee table and slopping her drink over the sides. 'Well, that's it, we're through. I knew this would happen. You promised it wouldn't, but where Livvy's concerned, you don't stand a chance. I won't be made a fool of again.'

'I'm sorry, Sam. I never meant it to happen. I don't know what else to say to you.'

'Do you love her?' she asked, her voice barely audible.

'Yes, I do,' he replied in an agonised whisper.

'More than you love me?'

'It's different, Sammy. I'll always love you. I don't even know if I can live without you.'

'Well, you'll find that out soon enough.' She got up and went to the window, keeping her back to him as she spoke. 'I'm going to go and stay with Jason and Jules for a few days. They don't know that yet, but Jason told me I have a home with him if ever I need one. He's *my* son and my new grandchild will be here in a couple of months. They'll need all the help I can give them.' She turned to face him. 'Much as I love Harley, she's your flesh and blood, yours and Livvy's. You'll need to take great care of her, Roy.'

Tears slid down Roy's cheeks as he stared at her. 'Jason's *my* son, too. And that's my grandchild you're talking about.'

'You hardly show Jason any affection and you've made it

quite clear you couldn't give a toss about the baby,' she snapped. 'You never give him a hug or a squeeze. It hurts him. His gayness isn't going to rub off on you, you know.'

Her sarcasm stung, but he wouldn't retaliate. He realised she was right: he'd fought shy of showing Jason any tactile affection for years and for exactly the daft reason she stated. Well, that would have to change. Maybe his new grandchild, when it arrived, would help bridge that gap.

He wanted to go to her, to hold her. She looked defeated. There were no more angry words or recriminations, just an almighty air of sadness that seemed to be settling on her shoulders. An acceptance, almost. 'Sammy, I'm so sorry,' he sobbed.

'So am I. But this is the end. I want a divorce, as soon as possible.'

'What will I tell Harley?' he cried. 'She needs you, she loves you, Sammy.'

'She has you, her mother and her sister and all those relatives of Livvy's in Scotland. Another thing I've had on my mind is the bone marrow transplant. The egg donation was a mad idea, it could take forever. Harley hasn't got that sort of time. While we fight and argue over it, you and Livvy could be having another kid. It might be Harley's only chance and I'm not going to stand in the way of that.'

Roy felt broken, wrung in two. Seeing Sammy so devastated, he wanted to stay with her, but then he thought about Livvy, waiting alone at the cottage, and knew he should be with her, he *had* to be with her. Sammy was being brave for both of them. He had to let go. He tried one last thing, knowing it was pointless, but feeling he should say it anyway: '*We* could stay together and Livvy and I could still have another child.'

'You're missing the point as usual, Roy. I want to be out of your life when that happens, if it hasn't already.'

He stared at her for a long moment. Could she read his mind? Was 'I might have got Livvy pregnant again' tattooed on his forehead? An overwhelming sadness engulfed him. He went to Sammy and drew her close. She clung to him and sobbed against his chest.

'We should have done this sixteen years ago, Roy. I could have moved on and built a new life with Stuart Green. It wouldn't have been too difficult to fall in love with him. You and Livvy could have been together to bring up Harley. We'd have been so far down the line now and the hurt and pain would have gone away. But it's starting again and I can't bear it. What about Livvy's husband and daughter? There are so many more people who will get hurt this time.'

'I know,' he cried. 'I feel torn in two, Sam.'

'Well, one of us has to make the decision. I've psyched myself up for this each birthday since Harley was ten. I guess I've been lucky to have an extra six years with you, if lucky's the right word!'

Roy wiped his eyes with the back of his hand. '*I've* been the lucky one. You took me back and brought up my girl. The ball's always been in your court, Sam. You could have chucked me out ages ago and you didn't. I don't want you to leave our home. Stay here, it's yours. You chose it and designed every inch of it – I can't live here without you anyway.'

'I don't want it, Roy. It's too big without a family, I couldn't bear to stay here alone.'

'It's too soon to make decisions like that,' he said, 'but you could sell it when you're ready and buy whatever you want. Wait till you come back from Jason's and then have a think.'

'I'll leave in the morning.' She smiled wistfully through her tears. 'At least we'll part as friends, almost.'

'I'll always be your friend,' he whispered, stroking her hair. 'Come back when you feel ready. I'll stay here for now with Harley. Try and keep things as calm as possible for her sake.'

As if on cue, the lounge door opened and Harley peered in,

a worried frown creasing her brow. 'Can we come in? We're hungry. You both look upset. Are you okay?'

Courtney followed Harley into the room and stood by the door, twiddling her thumbs.

'We're fine,' Sammy answered brightly. 'Dad will take you for a pizza if you feel up to it and then he'll take Courtney home and you can pop in and see Livvy. He needs to have a chat with you both and he can do that while you're at Livvy's.'

'Okay, Mum.' Harley smiled. 'But aren't you coming out for tea with us?'

'I'm not really hungry,' Sammy replied. 'I've got lots to do and I need to make a few phone calls. I can do that while you're all out of the way.'

Harley nodded and crossed the room. She flung her arms around Sammy. 'I love you, Mum.'

Sammy kissed the top of her head. 'I love you too, sweetheart.'

Roy saw Sammy signalling to him with tear-filled eyes. 'Come on, Harley.' He took charge. 'Let's go, Mum needs a bit of space. Are *you* ready, Courtney?' She nodded and he tossed his car keys to Harley. 'Go and get in the car. I won't be a minute.'

He turned to Sammy as the girls left. 'You sure you'll be okay on your own for a while?'

'Yes, positive. Feed the kids and then go and put Livvy out of her misery. I'll call Jane and Pat, tell them what we're doing.'

He nodded. 'Okay, if you're sure.' He walked towards the door and turned. 'Sammy...'

'Don't make it harder, Roy. I'll see you later.'

* * *

Livvy lay on the bed and stared up at the oak-beamed ceiling. Roy had called her briefly to tell her he was taking the girls out for tea and would be with her by seven. He'd also told her things had come to a head at home and that he would explain later. She ran her hands over her flat stomach and sighed. She'd spoken to Sheena, told her the news. Sheena said she would come down for a visit very soon. Kate Mellor had popped in on her way to Apple Tree House. She'd excitedly told Livvy that she and Zak had decided to get married this Christmas.

'Send the girls up to Laura's later,' Kate had said. 'They can help us look through the books of wedding dress designs.'

When Roy and the girls arrived home just after seven, she sent Courtney to change out of her school uniform then told them they could go up to Laura's if Harley felt well enough. Harley followed Courtney after Livvy had given her a hug and a kiss. Livvy expressed her concern to Roy at their daughter's pale face.

Roy sat down and took her hand. 'You look pale yourself,' he said, and stroked a curl from her eyes. 'Harley felt a bit sick in the car, but it seems to have passed now. Apparently, the same thing happened this afternoon when Sammy took her out and I came here.' He told her the events of the last few hours.

She stared at him as he finished. 'And that's it?'

'More or less. Now *you* have to tell Danny and ask him for a divorce.'

Livvy nodded slowly. 'I'll call him after midnight. That way he'll probably be home, rather than at the office. I was going to check my rights with regards to custody of Courtney, but I've still not got around to doing it. Jon gave me Ed's solicitor's number. I'll do it tomorrow.'

'He's my solicitor, too,' Roy said, 'so we'll go and set the ball rolling.'

He pulled her into his arms. 'I feel numb, Liv. I wasn't expecting any of this to happen today. It's all so quick.'

Livvy thought back to this morning's *OK!* horoscope. For once it was right.

'This *is* what you want, isn't it?' Roy whispered. 'You, me, our daughters and maybe Roy Junior in there?' He gently patted her stomach.

Her eyes filled with tears. 'More than anything in the world, Roy. I always have done.'

'Well, that's settled then.' He held her tight. 'We need to tell the girls tonight. I don't know how Harley will take it. It's the wrong time to be upsetting her, but there's never going to be a right time.'

Livvy nodded. 'Please don't mess me around like before. Back and forth between me and Sammy for weeks on end. I couldn't bear all that again.'

'I won't. It's not like last time,' he reassured her. 'I realise my place is with you and our girls and so does Sammy. I'll walk up to Phil's and bring them back, then we can tell them.'

* * *

Roy chewed his lower lip as Harley stared ashen-faced at him.

'So, are we all going to live at Jasmine House?' she asked, lips trembling.

He knelt in front of her and took her hand. 'No, darling. For the time being, me and you will live there. Livvy and Courtney will stay here, but we'll spend lots of time together. There are things to sort out and your mum, Sammy, needs time to decide what she wants to do. Jasmine House is hers. I signed it over to her years ago for tax purposes. She can sell it when she needs to. She'll stay with Jason and Jules for a few days and then she'll come home and we'll talk some more but we won't be living as a husband and wife.'

Harley nodded and wiped her eyes.

'Mum will still want to be involved with you, princess, and you can spend as much time with her as you like.'

Roy looked at Livvy, who was seated opposite, her arm around a tearful Courtney.

'Cheer up, Courtney,' he said. 'It will work out for us.'

'But it's my fault,' she sobbed. 'I wished we could be together and happy as a family, but we're all sad and crying now.'

'Sweetheart, we will be happy one day, I promise you,' Roy said. 'But it's a very difficult time for everyone and things are sometimes worse before they get better.'

18

Sammy swirled her drink around the glass, leant back in the chair at Roy's mixing desk and stared at the photograph in her hand. It had been taken in Mauritius almost seventeen years earlier. Roy was gazing lovingly into her eyes; they'd just retaken their wedding vows and celebrated with a second honeymoon. The previous week, Livvy had agreed to hand over her expected baby and after the loss of Nick, they'd had a rosier future to look forward to. Now it had all gone to rat-shit – again. No doubt Roy was looking into Livvy's eyes right now and swearing his undying love to *her*. 'How could you, Roy!' She hurled the picture at the wall. The glass smashed into fragments and the broken frame lay forlornly on the carpet.

She finished her drink, tipped the last of the gin into her glass and hurled the bottle at the wall, too. The shards joined the picture frame. She got unsteadily to her feet, looked out of the window at the gardens and the far-reaching view in the evening gloom, and burst into tears. How could she bear to give up her lovely home and all her memories? It would be so empty without Roy and Harley. Forty-two years she'd been with him, thirty-six of them married. How on earth would she begin to live without him? She didn't know any other life. She'd spoken to Pat and Jane after Roy had left with Harley and Courtney. Both urged her to go to them or they would come to her, but she told them she wanted to be on her own for a while: Roy would be coming back with Harley later and no doubt they would talk some more.

She picked up a guitar case and opened it. His pre-CBS pink Fender nestled in the faded-satin lining. She felt like smashing it too, but something stopped her. One of his first guitars, it was a prized possession and rare as rocking horse shit now, he'd told her. The first time she'd seen him with The Raiders, he'd played this guitar. Strutting his stuff on stage in tight black leathers, sexy as Elvis. She'd fallen in love with him that night and they'd been inseparable until Livvy came along. She took the guitar out of the case, strummed it and smiled through her tears. Roy had tried to teach her to play during their first few months together, but she'd never quite got the hang. She felt sick, her chest felt tight, her whole world was crumbling and she didn't know what to do. Letting him go was right, because she couldn't share him, but it had broken her heart to say it. The phone rang. She ignored it for a while, then thinking it might be Roy or Harley, she grabbed the receiver: it was her friend Margaret Grey, John's wife, wanting a chat.

* * *

A week later, Jane and Pat stared at Sammy, mouths wide open.

'Oh my God, that's a bit *too* quick!' Jane exclaimed.

They'd met for lunch in Number 14, the brand-new chrome and glass wine bar in Alderley Edge. Sammy had just told them about her visit to the solicitor's and how it would only take six months to get a quickie divorce.

'There's no reason to drag it out,' Sammy said. 'Roy's not

contesting, obviously. He's admitted adultery and that's all there is to it.' Her eyes filled with sudden tears and she blinked them away. 'I vowed not to cry today, so come on, you two, cheer me up.'

Jane took a sip of wine and made a face. 'There's not much cheerful going on,' she began. 'Mum's old next-door neighbour died last week, so I've just dropped her and Dad off at the funeral. My Uncle Jack in Ireland's been diagnosed with terminal bowel cancer and Jess and Jon are still at one another's throats over this fostering malarkey.'

'For God's sake, Jane, I said cheer me up!' Sammy shook her head and Pat went to get them a refill. As she came back with a bottle of Chardonnay and the menus, Sammy continued: 'I spoke to Margaret Grey last week and told her about me and Roy. No point keeping it to myself. Actually, I was very drunk and I think she got more of an earful than she was expecting, but it helped me and she really understood. She's invited me to join her and John at their villa in Portugal next month so I've accepted. It's a two-week break and I could do with getting away. I'll think about selling the house when I get back.'

'That'll be a wrench,' Jane said. 'After all those years. You love Jasmine House. I couldn't bear to part with Hanover's Lodge.'

Sammy shrugged. 'I can't stay there on my own. It's bad enough with Roy and Harley still around, everybody walking on eggshells, but without them...' She picked up her drink and took a sip.

'Will Harley be okay while you're abroad?' Pat asked.

'She's got Roy and Livvy and her sister to look after her. I'll only be a phone call away if she needs me and I can get a flight home soon enough if there's an emergency.'

'Have you decided what you want to eat?' Jane asked, studying the menu. 'It's suddenly got busy in here. We'll be ages getting served if we don't make a move.' She looked up as the door swung open and a young couple, wearing matching black leather coats and shades, strolled in. 'Bloody hell, it's the Beckhams,' she whispered.

Sammy nodded and swallowed the lump in her throat. She and Roy had always worn matching leather coats in their youth. 'Yeah, they've bought a place round here. Same road as John and Margaret. They've heard them outside in the garden talking to the little boy, what's his name?'

'Brooklyn,' Pat replied.

'That's right,' Jane said. 'Strange name for a child. Apparently, it's where he was conceived. Can you imagine if *we'd* done that? Jon would be called Stockport and Jess – Wilmslow!' She laughed at her own joke. 'Ed saw Posh and Becks shopping in Tesco at Handforth Dean last week. I think they're only in residence up here when he's playing at Old Trafford.'

'She could do with a bit of meat on her bones,' Pat whispered as the Beckhams were shown to a table at the back of the wine bar. '*They* get escorted to a table and we had to find our own. Go and tell the young girl at the bar we're The Raiders' wives,' she finished with a grin.

'Yeah, like she'll know who The Raiders are.' Jane laughed.

'She might have heard her mother playing their records,' Sammy smirked.

'More like her grandmother,' Jane said. 'Right, I'm having a ham and turkey panini with a tomato salad.'

'Sounds good.' Sammy nodded. 'I'll have the same. Pat?'

'Make mine cheese and tuna with a green salad.'

Jane went to place the order and came back smiling. 'Fifteen minutes, they said.' She topped up their drinks. 'Cheers, here's to a new start for Sammy.' They clinked glasses. 'So, will Stuart Green be in Portugal? I believe he has an apartment near the Greys' villa.'

Sammy spluttered into her glass. 'I've no idea. Nothing's

been said. I haven't seen Stu for months – I always feel really uncomfortable whenever I bump into him.'

'That's because you've never stopped feeling guilty at letting him down after your one-night stand,' Jane said. 'I wonder what would have happened there if you hadn't got back with Roy.'

'I don't know,' Sammy said. 'But I did and it's far too soon to be thinking about matchmaking, Jane Mellor. I can see the way your mind's working.'

'Stu married a girl from London after your fling, but he's divorced now,' Jane said. 'Just thought I'd mention it,' she added as Sammy rolled her eyes.

* * *

'You sure you'll be alright while I'm gone, princess?' Roy asked Harley, who was lying on the sofa at Charlecote Cottage.

'Dad, I'll be fine. Livvy's here. Stop fussing.'

He nodded. 'It's just that you're looking really pale.' He'd arranged to have lunch with Jason and Jules and had brought Harley to stay with Livvy as Sammy wouldn't allow Livvy into Jasmine House. After Sammy's recent accusations that he neglected his son, he'd called and asked Jason to meet him and to bring Jules too. Jason said they could only spare him an hour or two as they were very busy at The Gallery. That was better than nothing and Roy was determined to make an effort to build bridges. After all, at thirty-four years of age, Jason was unlikely to change his sexual preferences so Roy thought he might as well start getting his head around it once and for all. 'I'll be back in time to collect Courtney from school,' he said to Livvy.

She saw him to the door and kissed him. 'You look really smart in those clothes.' She picked a speck of fluff off the collar of his black linen jacket. 'Good luck.'

'Thanks. *You* look a bit pale, too, never mind Harley. You okay?' He stroked her cheek.

'I haven't had time to put any make-up on yet,' she said. 'And I'm really tired. When you come back, we'll do a pregnancy test.'

He frowned. 'Isn't it too soon?'

'You can do a test almost immediately after conception now,' she said. 'And that could have been anytime this last week.'

'True. But do you feel pregnant?'

'Not sure, maybe,' she replied, looking away. 'It's probably wishful thinking.'

'Okay.' He hugged her tight. 'If it makes you happy, we'll do it when I come home.'

* * *

Roy ordered a single malt while he waited in The Olive Grove in Wilmslow. Jason had suggested they meet there as it was close to work and the Italian food was the best in town. Roy would have preferred a pub lunch, a decent pint and his jeans and leather jacket, but today wasn't about what *he* wanted.

The young waiter, snake-hipped, with hair as dark and shiny as his own used to be, showed Roy to a reserved table. Roy wondered if the waiter was also gay. It was the way he wiggled his arse when he walked and fluttered his hands with excitement when Roy told him he was meeting his son, Jason Cantello. The name seemed to bring the lad out in a nervous tremor and his cheeks flushed pink.

'He designed this interior – your son,' the waiter said, waving his arms around. 'He is very clever.' He pointed to two tall bronze sculptures of near-naked women; both of them water features, their reflections in the mirrored walls, seemingly endless. 'Jules made those.'

Roy smiled a pleasant smile and wished the waiter would go away. He sat down. The waiter left and Roy stared at the sculptures, trying to fathom out how Jules, who created such perfect images of women, and must have had models posing naked in front of him, could not be turned on by them and would choose to sleep with a male. He shuddered and knocked back his drink. He wasn't even aware that Jason designed commercial interiors. He'd assumed his commissions were mainly domestic. He'd always closed his ears when Sammy brought up the subject of Jason and work. He felt bad now that he'd taken so little interest in his career and relationship.

He summoned the waiter and ordered another single malt. He fiddled with the red napkin on the table and crumpled it in his fist without realising what he was doing then picked up a bread stick and nibbled the end. He checked his watch: ten minutes late. Where were they? One thing Roy hated was bad timekeeping. The door opened and four young women came in. Thirty-something, office workers, judging by their smart clothes, he thought. In for the lunchtime special: pasta, side salad and a glass of house plonk for a fiver.

The women were shown to a table. Roy smiled as they looked at him with almost recognition. One of them smiled back. He winked at her and she whispered to her friend, who turned and stared. Nice to know he wasn't losing his touch. The door opened again and Jason and Jules strolled in, wearing stylish suits: Jules in cream, accentuating his tan and his blond hair, and Jason in chocolate brown that matched his eyes. Jason waved. Roy held up his hand.

The young waiter accompanied them to the table and Roy got to his feet and gave his son an awkward hug. Jason, looking surprised, then pleased, hugged his dad back and air- kissed both cheeks. Jules shook hands with Roy.

'Nice to see you, son, and you, too, Jules.' He summoned the waiter and ordered a bottle of the best red.

'Good to see you too, Dad.' Jason smiled as he and Jules took a seat. 'You look a bit rough. Not sleeping? How's Harls?'

'She's not too bad, son, coping well enough. I've left her with Livvy while I'm here. Your mother's dining out with Jane and Pat, and no, I'm not sleeping well at all.'

'Hardly surprising. You've a lot on your plate. Mum told me last night that she was meeting Jane and Pat today. Bet your ears are burning.' Jason smiled and patted his dad's hand. 'Listen, Dad, I've heard Mum's side of the story and I understand what's going on, but please, don't mess either of them about this time. Make your decision and stick to it. Me and Jules will stand by you whatever you decide and we'll support you all.'

'Thanks, son. Your mum made the decision for me: I'm with Livvy and once things are sorted with Danny, I'll move me and Harley into the cottage. Danny can't prove there's anything going on between us at the moment and she's paranoid about losing Courtney to him, so we're treading very carefully for now. How *is* your mum, Jason? I mean, *really*. She's spending a lot of time with you two, but she hardly talks to me at home, only when she has to and mainly about Harley.'

Jason shrugged. 'She seems to have accepted things unless it's the calm before the storm. She said her decision to let you go is best all round for Harley. She's been helping us get the nursery ready for Daisy. She's really excited, it's keeping her mind focused.'

'Daisy?'

'Your expected granddaughter.' Jason grinned and Jules dug in his pocket, producing a scan picture and gave it to Roy.

'There she is, in all her glory,' Jules said. 'Bit different from E.T. a few months ago, wouldn't you say?'

Roy took the picture and stared at the perfect little being that sucked her thumb and seemed to be staring directly at him. The picture was 3D effect, in colour, and as clear as an actual photo. Little chubby cheeks and a button nose. 'A girl,' he whispered and felt the hairs on his neck prickle and his eyes fill. He looked at Jason and shook his head. 'She looks like Nick, you and Harley as babies, a real Cantello. I'm so proud of you, son, of you both. I didn't know you could get such clear scans, it's wonderful.' He was tempted to tell them that he and Livvy were trying for a baby, but decided it could wait till he knew for certain. He couldn't bear to have Jason looking on him with scorn, a fifty-nine-year-old bringing more kids into the world.

'We had the scan done privately in London,' Jules said. 'Expensive, but worth it. Actually, Roy, we've been thinking, we can get Daisy's stem cells checked after she arrives. They may be a match for Harley. Let's face it, anything's worth a try, although I suppose the further down the generations you go, the less chance there is.'

Jason nodded. 'Maybe you and Livvy should get down to business and try and produce a full-blood sibling, Dad. Fuck Daniel, Harley's well-being is what counts now.'

Roy smiled. 'We'll see. Right, let's order some grub. I'm bloody starving. I must say, son, this place is very classy,' he said, indicating the gleaming black marble floors and the cream chandeliers that cast a subtle light over everything. 'It's... it's... well, it's fucking amazing.'

* * *

Livvy gripped the edge of the sink, drew a deep breath and closed her eyes. The pregnancy testing stick was sitting on the window sill with the inevitable blue line. Harley was sleeping downstairs on the sofa and Roy was waiting in their bedroom. She could hear him pacing anxiously. Keeping up the pretence was almost over. It had been such a strain. She felt heartsick at deceiving him and thought she might throw up at any minute. When she looked in the mirror, her cheeks were flushed and she was sure he'd see the guilt in her eyes.

She splashed her face with cold water and told herself this was the best thing that could have happened, for all of them. She had to hang on to that belief and give the best performance of her life. It was now or never. She grabbed a towel and patted her face dry. The baby would probably arrive early anyway, like the girls had, and that would be perfect. Roy would never need to know about the deception. She just hoped and prayed now that nothing would go wrong; that she wouldn't miscarry and that the child would be Harley's perfect match. Her hand shaking, she opened the bathroom door.

'Roy, you can come in now.'

He hurried to her side. 'Is it?'

Livvy picked up the white stick. 'Take a look.'

'It's blue,' he said. 'Does that mean?'

She nodded, tears in her eyes. Roy's face lit up as he stared at the stick. He let out a yell and swept her into his arms, crying with her. He carried her to the bed, lowered her down and covered her face with kisses.

'I can't believe it,' he cried, shaking his head. 'I just can't believe that we've been so lucky the first time we try. But thank God we have. Right, that's it, you're doing nothing for the whole nine months except be waited on hand and foot.'

She leant against him, feeling the tension slip away. She smiled through her tears. 'I'm not an invalid, Roy.'

'I don't care. This is it now, Liv,' he said, his excitement mounting. 'We can start to think of a future for Harley, a positive future.'

'You're happy then? About being a daddy again, I mean?'

'Very happy,' he said, tears still streaming down his cheeks. 'I love you, woman.'

Her head started to spin. The feelings of guilt were diminishing as she saw how excited he was. She found herself smiling and crying at the same time. Her heart no longer pounded and she felt overwhelmed with love for him. 'I love you too, Mr Cantello, so, so much. Let's just pray the baby's a good match.'

'I'm sure it will be,' he said, stroking her stomach. 'Will we tell the girls?'

She shook her head. 'Let's leave it for a few weeks, give them time to adjust to everything else first. I'd rather we waited a while before we told anyone, actually. Certainly, let's keep it to ourselves for the next few months. We don't want Danny finding out, it will only give him further ammunition.'

'Okay.' Roy nodded. 'How do *you* feel?'

'Very relieved, but nervous of course. It's such a big age gap and a life-changer for us all.'

Roy nodded and hugged her so tight, she could hardly breathe. 'We'll be fine,' he said. 'All you need do is take it easy and let me look after you.'

* * *

Livvy straightened the guest room duvet and plumped up the pillows. She folded a set of towels, placed them at the foot of the bed, threw open the window and leant on the sill, taking in the view of rolling fields and the tip of White Nancy in the distance. Sheena was coming to stay tomorrow. She already knew about the baby, as did Tina, but Livvy knew she could trust them not to say anything to Roy. She still felt a bit uneasy about deceiving him, but it was done now and Harley's future seemed more positive. She wandered into the little spare room, which was now clear of paint tins and clutter, drew a deep breath and began to plan the nursery.

* * *

Sheena drove though Ashlea Village, window open and singing along to Jackson Browne's 'Everywhere I Go', blasting from the car stereo. The lovely words reminded her of Jon and her feelings for him. She spotted a faded wooden sign to her right, declaring that Apple Tree House was down the lane she was just passing.

'Damn!' She braked hard and backed up slowly along the main road, praying that no one would come hurtling up behind her. She indicated right and turned into the narrow lane. The tall, dense hedgerows of holly and hawthorn bushes formed a tunnel almost and she drove slowly, keeping her eyes open for further signs or gateways. Livvy had told her the house was tucked away and not easy to find. With her friend's predicament, it was maybe as well.

About a quarter of a mile further on the hedges thinned out and Sheena spotted another sign creaking back and forth on rusty hinges in the breeze. The sign indicated that her destination was to the left and she turned into a rutted private lane, bumping carefully over potholes and through puddles. Several farm buildings came into view and to the left, standing alone, was a large, detached stone-built cottage. A tall, blond-haired man stood with his back to her. He appeared to be talking animatedly to someone hidden from view.

As she slowed to a stop, the man turned and smiled. Livvy's head popped around the doorframe and she waved enthusiastically. Sheena leapt from the car and ran towards them. The blond man stepped to one side and grinned in a friendly manner – he looked familiar.

'Sheena!' Livvy shrieked and threw her arms around her. 'Glad you found us okay. It's so lovely to see you.' Then, as if remembering, she turned and introduced the blond man: 'This is Phil Jackson, my landlord, and The Raiders' rhythm guitarist.'

Sheena smiled and held out her hand. Phil clasped it, raising it to his lips.

'How very nice to meet you, Sheena. I've heard a lot about you.'

Sheena felt her cheeks warming and hoped that Livvy hadn't mentioned her fling with Jon.

'I've only told him nice things,' Livvy said pointedly.

'Thank goodness for that,' Sheena said and grinned. 'It's lovely to meet you too, Phil. I've seen you many times on TV, but it's nice to see you in the flesh, so to speak.'

'And there's plenty of that these days.' He laughed, patting the beginnings of a beer belly. 'Mind you, I don't do too badly when you look at other chaps in their late fifties.'

'You look wonderful, Phil,' Livvy said. '*And* you know it. This one's always had an eye for the ladies,' she told Sheena.

'Not any more,' Phil said, then lowered his voice, although there was no one around to hear. 'Not until the next tour, anyway! And you know what they say...'

'What happens on tour stays on tour!' Livvy echoed with him. 'That's strictly a man mantra,' she said, laughing.

'I'll leave you girls to catch up and I'll see you soon,' he said.

'Bye, Phil,' they chorused.

'Come on in,' Livvy said and Sheena followed her into the spacious kitchen.

'Wow, Phil's fit.'

'Just a bit.' Livvy nodded. 'But randy as they come, *and* he's married with six kids!'

'No way! I'll steer clear of him then and stick to Jon Mellor.'

'You'd be as well to stay clear of him, too,' Livvy said. 'It'll all blow up in your face if you're not careful.'

'I know. I promised I'd meet him tomorrow night. Just a one-off.' Sheena changed the subject. 'So, how are you feeling today, Livvy? You look pale.'

'A bit grim,' she replied. 'I can't understand why I feel sick so early on. I didn't feel like this with Harley and Courtney at first, it took a few weeks for it to kick in.'

'No two pregnancies are the same and maybe it's to do with you being older this time.'

'Maybe,' she agreed.

'Where are the girls?' Sheena glanced around the empty kitchen.

'Courtney's at school and Harley's at the doctor's with Roy. They shouldn't be too long now. Let's get your bags out of the car and I'll show you to your room then we'll put our feet up and have a coffee. You did really well for time.'

'I left Glasgow at seven,' Sheena said, following Livvy outside. She handed her a small holdall. 'I'll get the heavy bag. I brought extra clothes in case we go out anywhere posh. I'll call Jon in a minute, let him know I've arrived.'

* * *

Livvy dropped the phone onto its cradle. Her hands were shaking and she clasped them together on her knee. She was alone in the lounge. Sheena was out with Jon for a meal, Roy and Harley were at Jasmine House and Courtney had just gone up to bed.

Livvy had called Jodie on her cell phone and Daniel answered. Courtney had spoken to Daniel only ten minutes earlier and he'd been at home. So that could only mean one thing: Jodie was at the ranch. Daniel wouldn't have realised it was Livvy calling as the landline number wouldn't have appeared on Jodie's screen, maybe *number unavailable*, or something like that. As soon as she'd realised it was Daniel saying *hello, hello*, she'd hung up. But why hadn't Jodie taken the call herself? And why was she with Dan? And then it dawned. She thought back to the afternoon in Flanagan and Grey's when he'd gone pink at the mention of Jodie's name. Could she be his bit on the side? Well, there was one sure way of finding out.

She grabbed her cell phone off the coffee table, texted *You bitch* and sent it to Jodie's number. A call came within minutes.

'*Livvy?*' Jodie's voice wavered.

'You know damn well it's me!' Livvy yelled. 'What the hell are you doing in my home and why did my husband answer your cell?'

She heard Jodie gasp and then Daniel's voice came next: 'Livvy, I didn't realise it was you calling. Jodie was expecting a call from her mother and she was in the bathroom. I guess—' He paused and then continued. 'Well, I guess it's time for the truth.' There was silence for a minute. 'Me and Jodie, we're in love. She's moved in with me, we're making a home together here for Courtney.'

'Over my dead body!' Livvy yelled. 'You devious bastard! Why didn't you just come clean and tell me it was Jodie? And you dared give me a hard time over Roy. Well, that's it. Now I've got the name of your tart for my solicitor, I can get the divorce sorted as soon as possible and marry Roy.'

She ended the call before she was tempted to blurt out that she was pregnant. She felt sick and angry; angry at Daniel for not admitting his love for Jodie earlier and angry at Jodie for betraying their friendship.

The lounge door opened and Courtney popped her head in: 'Mom, why are you shouting? Are you okay?'

Livvy shook her head as her cell phone rang again: 'Ignore it.' She cancelled the call and switched the phone off. 'Come and sit with me.' Courtney curled up beside her and Livvy put an arm around her shoulders. 'Your dad's having an affair with Jodie, she's moved into the ranch with him.'

'What?' Courtney stared at her. 'Jodie... from the office? Well, if Dad's living with her, I'm not even going to visit in the school holidays now,' she said, folding her arms mutinously.

'Don't be too cross with him, sweetie,' Livvy said. 'I don't want you to fall out with him. We can't expect him to stay alone forever. *I'm* lucky, I've got Roy and you girls and I wouldn't wish your dad to be lonely. But I'm very angry because it's

Jodie, who I considered to be my friend, and because *he* could have made things easier by being honest with me when he was here.'

Courtney nodded. 'He talked to Jodie quite often when you were away. *And* she came over to see him. He always sent me off to bed early – I thought they were having business meetings.'

'Well maybe they were, some of the time,' Livvy said, thinking of Daniel having Jodie in their bed. God, if she'd known what he was up to, she'd never have made love with him that one last time before she left for Glasgow. The thought made her cringe now. And him going on at her, telling her he wanted another baby with her when all the time he was screwing Jodie. She swallowed the bile as it rose in her throat. 'Well, at least we know where we stand now,' she said to Courtney. 'In a few months we'll all be together and hopefully Harley's leukaemia will go into remission. By Christmas you might get your "Happy Family" wish.'

'Please don't let Dad make me go home, Mom. I couldn't bear to be away from you and Harley.'

'You're not going anywhere, sweetie, except back to bed. I can hear a car engine – I expect it's Sheena being brought home.' She kissed Courtney, who ran back upstairs, calling, 'Don't forget to switch your phone back on in case Roy calls you later.'

The front door opened and closed and Sheena popped her head around. Her eyes filled with tears and her lips quivered. She looked at Livvy, who held out her arms.

Sheena threw herself down on the sofa. 'I so didn't want to say goodnight to him,' she wailed. 'He can't even see me again this week, he's got stuff on with Jess and his family. I don't know when I'll next get to see him.'

'Maybe when me and Roy get married,' Livvy ventured. 'You can come down here and help me plan everything. I'm hoping you'll be my bridesmaid, along with the girls.'

'Oh, I will.' Sheena smiled through her tears. 'But it'll take ages for your divorce to come through, even if Roy gets *his* quickly, and Jess will be with Jon at the wedding.'

'There'll be odd days when you can get together. And my divorce might not take as long as you think, although I'd prefer us to marry next year after the baby arrives. I don't want to be a waddling bride,' Livvy said and told Sheena the events of the last hour.

19

SEPTEMBER 2001

Livvy hurried into the lounge. Courtney was calling her but she couldn't hear what she was saying above the noise of the microwave. 'What do you want, a drink of juice or something?' She looked at her daughter who, recovering from a bout of tonsillitis, was tucked up under her duvet on the sofa.

'New York's on the news,' Courtney said. 'It's on every channel. Something's happened.'

'Like what?'

'I don't know. You need to turn up the volume.'

Livvy picked up the remote control. 'This is live news from New York City,' she said, turning up the sound. 'Oh my God, look, there's a huge fire in one of the World Trade Center towers.' As she spoke, a plane was making its way across the television screen and, to her horror, crashed headlong into the upper part of the second tower. 'Jesus Christ! What's going on?'

Courtney clapped her hands to her mouth and stared. 'Dad's in there.' She turned wild eyes to her mother.

'What?'

'Dad's at the Trade Center for a meeting today. He called

me last night and told me he's in New York all week on business. Mom, what if he's been hurt?'

'Don't worry, I'm sure he'll be fine.' Livvy felt her voice wavering. 'They'll evacuate the towers and get everyone out safely.'

'Call his cell phone, or the hotel,' Courtney pleaded.

'Which hotel is it? He may not even have left there yet, it's only just gone nine in New York.'

'He didn't say. Call Mrs Grayson or Jodie's cell, they'll know.'

'Jodie's probably with him.' Livvy rang the ranch but there was no reply. She tried Daniel's cell phone. There was no connection, nor was there one when she tried Jodie's number. She shook her head at Courtney, who glanced up from the screen, tears running down her cheeks.

'They're saying that a plane also crashed into the North Tower,' Courtney cried. 'It's not just a fire.'

Livvy ran to answer a knock at the door.

Laura Jackson greeted her with a smile. 'I'm popping into Wilmslow for some groceries,' she began. 'Can I get you anything, Livvy? You're looking very pale. Are you okay?'

Livvy grabbed Laura by the arm. 'Come in, please. Something terrible is happening in New York and I can't get hold of Danny. He's in the towers,' she said, feeling herself shaking uncontrollably.

Laura caught Livvy's arm as she swayed and she led her into the lounge. She sat her beside Courtney, who was sobbing wildly and gesticulating at the television screen.

'My dad might be in there,' she howled as Laura frowned.

'What's going on?'

Livvy shook her head in bewilderment. 'Two planes have crashed into the World Trade Center – I don't understand it.'

Laura stared open-mouthed at the TV as the horror

unfolded. 'Jesus Christ! Is it a terrible accident with air traffic control?'

Livvy shook her head again. 'I don't know. It must be, it can't be deliberate. Who would be so wicked?'

Laura shrugged helplessly. 'Why would Danny be in there anyway?'

'Courtney said he's got a meeting today. He rang her last night. I didn't speak to him, so I don't have any details. I've tried calling home to find out where he's staying and I've also tried his cell phone.' Livvy ran her hands agitatedly through her curls. 'God, Laura, I don't know what else to do.'

'Ring Roy,' she suggested. 'Ask him to come over.'

'He can't,' Courtney wailed. 'Harley's not allowed to come near me 'cos of my throat infection and her weakened immunity and he can't leave her on her own.'

'Isn't Sammy at Jasmine House?' Laura frowned. 'She could take care of Harley, surely?'

'No, she's at Jason and Jules' place today, looking after the lady who's having their baby,' Courtney replied.

'Well look, call Roy anyway. Get him to bring Harley to ours and I'll look after her. Then Roy can come here and help you locate Danny.' Laura sat down beside Courtney and put her arm around the distraught girl's shoulders while Livvy called Roy, who agreed to come right away.

* * *

'Give me the number of Danny's office in LA,' Roy said as he picked up the phone for the umpteenth time. 'There should be someone there by now.'

Livvy wrote down the number and went to sit beside Courtney, who was crying hysterically. Almost an hour had gone by since the second plane had crashed into the South Tower and harrowing scenes of terrified people, running for their lives, and others, trying to escape the inferno by jumping from the burning skyscrapers, filled the TV screen, alongside reports that a third plane had hit the Pentagon building in Washington DC.

Livvy had tried Daniel's cell phone, and the ranch, continuously to no avail. Now Roy had taken over, but so far was having no more luck than she.

He stuck up his thumb as his call was finally answered and spoke for a while then scribbled down a number. He hung up and turned to Livvy and Courtney: 'The staff have been trying to contact Danny, but the phone lines in New York are out of action. Maria, the girl I spoke to, said that he and Jodie were due to attend a meeting with a bank at eight thirty this morning in the North Tower. She's not sure which floor. I've given her the number for here and she's given me his hotel number for later. She said she'd call as soon as Danny makes contact. He's apparently fired your housekeeper, so that's why there's no one at the ranch. There's nothing more we can do now, Liv, other than sit tight and wait.'

She nodded. 'I guess you're right but I feel so helpless.'

'I'm so sorry, Courtney.' Roy put his arms around the girl's shoulders and held her while she sobbed against his chest. He felt lost for words at the sadness in her blue eyes.

'I can't take it in,' Livvy whispered. 'It's like some horrible nightmare. Did Maria say *why* Danny was having this meeting with the bank?'

'Something to do with a merger – the meeting was to finalise the financial details.'

'Why on earth does he want a merger? He works 24/7 as it is. How on earth can he juggle all his businesses *and* expect to take proper care of Courtney in school holidays now that he's fired Dolores? Danny's priorities have always been work, work, and *then* us.'

Roy shook his head, signalling with his eyes to Livvy as

Courtney stiffened in his arms and turned to stare at her mother.

'He might have chosen his work over us, Mom, but he's still my dad. Now I may never see him again and I feel real bad for saying I don't want to live with him.'

'Courtney, I didn't mean anything... I was just saying...' Livvy tailed off.

'Go and make us a pot of tea, Liv,' Roy suggested as the phone rang. He put Courtney gently aside and leapt up to answer it. 'Hello. Nothing concrete as yet, Laura. I've spoken to a member of Danny's staff. She'll call us as soon as they have any news. Is Harley still okay with you for the time being? Great. Oh, you have? Well, thanks for that, Laura. I'll speak to you soon.'

He hung up as Livvy carried a tray of mugs through to the lounge. 'That was Laura.' He took the tray from her and placed it on the coffee table. 'She rang Jane and Ed to tell them the news and they're watching it on TV. Oh... Jesus Christ!'

'What?' Livvy followed his gaze. They stood in shocked silence as the South Tower of the Trade Center began to collapse. Courtney leapt up, her mouth a silent O.

'It's okay, Courtney, it's okay.' Roy pulled her close. 'Your dad's in the North Tower, they've already evacuated people from there.'

'Try his cell phone again,' Courtney pleaded. 'If he's outside now he may have a signal.'

Livvy redialled. 'Still no connection.' As she replaced the receiver, the phone rang out immediately. It was Eddie, for Roy, wanting to know if there was any news and to say that Jess was on her way to see if she could help by taking Harley for the rest of the day. Within five minutes of Roy hanging up there was a knock at the door and Livvy ushered in a worried-looking Jess.

'Livvy, I don't know what to say,' she began as Livvy shook her head.

'There's still no news,' she told Jess. 'We've tried and tried Danny's phone but there's no connection.'

'I guess you'll just have to wait till he contacts you. He must be frantic by now, knowing that you'll be seeing it all on TV.'

'Maybe he's tried to text me,' Courtney cried. 'My phone's in my bag.' She shot out of the room as Roy looked at Livvy and Jess.

'If anyone gets out of there alive it will be a bloody miracle,' he whispered. 'But let's keep that from Courtney, she needs to have hope.'

'Sit down, Jess. Would you like a cup of tea?' Livvy offered.

Jess nodded and flopped down on the sofa. 'She's very together, very composed,' she said as Livvy left the room.

'She's in shock,' Roy replied. 'She's pregnant, Jess. I'm worried sick about her.'

'Really?' Jess raised her eyebrows. 'Yours or Danny's?'

'Mine,' he replied. 'We've been keeping it under wraps because of the divorce and custody thing. But she's nearly six months, we can't hide it for much longer. I'm surprised nobody's commented on her weight gain, actually.'

'I hadn't noticed.' Jess frowned. 'But then again, we've hardly seen anything of her this summer with you both keeping a low profile. I presume Danny doesn't know?'

'No,' he replied. 'Apart from Livvy's folks and her mate Sheena, we haven't told a soul, not even the girls or Sammy. I haven't even told your dad and he and I never keep secrets from each other.' He went on to tell Jess how important the baby was to him and Livvy and why.

Livvy strolled back into the lounge carrying a mug of tea.

'I've told Jess about Roy Junior...' he began as Courtney ran into the room. Livvy silenced him with a warning look.

'There was nothing from Dad, but I've sent him a text asking him to get in touch,' she said. 'It went off alright.'

'Okay, honey. Well maybe he'll contact us soon. Go and lie

on your bed for a while. Give Harley a ring or send her a text to see if she's okay. Tell her that Jess will pick her up later.'

'Sit down, Livvy,' Jess said as Courtney left. 'You look wiped out, you should be resting. Are you okay?'

'Numb!' Livvy replied. 'It's unreal. They suspect terrorism. A fourth plane's come down in Pennsylvania. When's it going to end?'

'They've halted all domestic flights in the US,' Roy told her, 'so there's nothing in the air as we speak.'

'Just look at all those frantic people.' Jess stared at the TV screen as hordes of New Yorkers huddled in groups, staring in disbelief at the debris and the remains of the South Tower. 'Oh my God, no!' Her hand flew to her mouth as the North Tower began to collapse, one floor at a time.

Roy pulled Livvy close as they stared at the terrifying scene. She grew heavy in his arms and he realised she'd fainted. He swept her up and lay her on the sofa, kneeling on the floor beside her. 'Call the doctor, Jess,' he said as he patted Livvy's pale cheeks. 'The number's on the pinboard in the kitchen. Come on, Liv, open your eyes, please, darling.'

Livvy's eyes flickered open and she stared blankly. Roy turned as Courtney ran back into the room. 'It's okay, sweetheart,' he reassured her. 'Your mom's fainted but she'll be fine.' He stroked Livvy's hair back from her face as Courtney threw herself onto the sofa.

'The North Tower has collapsed,' she cried. 'I heard it on the radio. What if Dad's trapped in there?'

Roy looked on helplessly as Jess pulled Courtney up, held her with one arm and dialled the surgery with her free hand.

'Ask him to come right away,' Roy said as Livvy struggled upright. 'Stay where you are, Liv.'

'He'll be here as soon as he can,' Jess said and hung up.

'Call Ed and get him to come over,' Roy said. 'Ask him to bring a bottle of brandy, we've no alcohol in the house.'

Jess nodded and went to answer the door to frantic knocking.

'Harley's with Phil so don't worry about her,' Laura began, hurrying inside. 'Can I do anything here?'

Roy shrugged helplessly, still kneeling on the floor.

'I'll make more tea.' Laura gathered up the tray. Jess let in Doctor Shaw, who was closely followed by Eddie and Jane.

Jess ushered them into the kitchen. Roy explained the situation to the doctor, who gave Courtney a sedative and suggested Roy put her to bed while he examined Livvy.

'I know this is a very difficult time for you. I can't begin to imagine what you and your daughter are going through at the moment, but you must rest or I'll need to admit you to hospital,' he warned Livvy. 'Your blood pressure is too high.' He turned to Roy, who had come back into the room. 'Even though she's extremely traumatised, I'm reluctant to give Mrs McVey a sedative in her condition. But she must rest, it's vital for the sake of the baby.'

Roy nodded. 'Whatever you think best. A drop of brandy in her tea, perhaps?'

'Just a drop on this occasion will do no harm. I'll pop in tomorrow morning. If you need me in the meantime, don't hesitate to call the surgery.'

He saw the doctor to the door then called to the others: 'You can come out now.'

Laura carried a tray of mugs into the lounge, while Eddie followed with the bottle of brandy, Jane and Jess on his heels.

'Are you okay, Livvy?' Jane asked.

'The doctor said her blood pressure's too high. She needs to rest or he'll have her in hospital. Oh shit, none of you know of course, apart from Jess,' Roy said as they all looked puzzled. 'Livvy's pregnant. Not the best of times to be announcing our news, I'm afraid.'

'Oh, Livvy, I know congratulations sound a bit odd at the moment,' Laura said, 'but you know what I mean.'

'Thanks, Laura, I'm sorry we've kept it quiet,' Livvy said. 'But it's a difficult situation, what with our divorces and stuff.'

'We've kept everything as low-key as possible because of the girls, too,' Roy added. 'They don't know about the baby yet and this isn't a good time to tell them but we have to do that soon, for obvious reasons. Also, I haven't told Sammy yet. I'd be grateful if you keep this to yourselves until I get the chance to speak to her.'

'Does Danny know you're pregnant, Livvy?' Jane asked.

'No,' she replied, her eyes filling. 'Now it looks as though he never will. He's gone, I just know he has.'

'They evacuated a lot of people from the North Tower before the collapse. Maybe he got out safely,' Eddie said, pouring brandy into the mugs.

'Just a drop for Livvy, please,' Roy said. 'Before Courtney closed her eyes when I put her to bed, she said the same thing as Livvy... Dad's gone.'

Jane and Laura blinked back tears as the phone rang. Roy answered it and spoke briefly then turned to the others: 'That was Maria from Danny's office. They haven't heard anything officially yet, but she confirmed the meeting was on the eighty-fifth floor. If he and Jodie were in the building at the time the plane hit, it's unlikely they'll have got out alive. She'll keep us informed.'

'I'll take Harley home to stay with me tonight, Roy,' Jess announced. 'I've arranged for Jon to collect Jack and Nathan from school, so I don't have to worry about them.'

'Thanks, Jess. I'll stay here, of course. Harley has her pills with her in her pillbox. She takes quite a cocktail, but she knows exactly what to take and when.'

'She'll need a nightdress and something to wear for tomorrow. I'll get her some of Courtney's things,' Livvy said, struggling to get up off the sofa.

'Don't you dare move,' Roy said. 'I'll see to all that.'

Eddie stared after Roy as he left the room. 'We've had some stuff to deal with in our lives, but never anything quite as shocking as this. You let Roy take care of you, Livvy, and look after that baby. It will mean a lot to you both, I'm sure.'

'It does,' Livvy replied. 'You do all realise that this baby could be a perfect bone marrow match for Harley?' She gently patted her bump. 'Roy Junior might save our daughter's life someday.'

'Roy Junior?' Jane smiled tearfully. 'It's a boy then?'

'It is.' She nodded. 'When we had the twenty-week scan they asked us if we wanted to know. I wasn't bothered, but Roy was so excited at seeing his baby wriggling around on the screen that he couldn't wait to find out. He's thrilled to bits. It's such a shame we couldn't announce our news on a happier occasion, but sometimes there's never a right time.'

* * *

Livvy's family in Scotland were in constant touch to see if there was any news and Sheena and Gerry offered to fly out to New York, but Livvy begged them not to go.

'I'd be terrified at the thought of you flying at the moment,' she told Sheena. 'There's little you can do if you *did* go. Danny isn't in any of the hospitals, nor on the latest list of survivors. His office is in daily contact with us and I'm afraid we have to assume the worst until we're officially informed.'

* * *

On 20 September, Livvy received the news she'd been expecting: Daniel and Jodie were listed amongst the missing. She was told there'd been no survivors from above the point of impact in the North Tower. All the stairways and elevator shafts had been destroyed prior to the building's collapse, leaving no escape routes.

She granted permission to the authorities for them to take both Daniel's hair and toothbrushes from the hotel suite to help with DNA identification, although, as of yet, his remains had not been recovered. Livvy felt numb with grief. Although any love she'd had for Daniel had waned during their marriage, she *had* cared for him. He'd been a devoted and loving father to Courtney and his loss would leave a gaping hole in their lives. She felt sad that he'd not had the chance to marry Jodie and have his much longed-for son and heir.

'I don't know what to do about the businesses, Roy,' she said after speaking to a concerned Maria. 'The staff are understandably worried about their jobs. There are good managers, like Maria, in each real estate office, so they'll carry on as normal for now, but it's the future I'm concerned about. I can't fly home at the moment to deal with anything. There's the ranch too, of course, *and* the horses. I'll try and speak with the stable manager later today. He's already been on to Maria, voicing his concerns.'

Roy nodded. 'Once the baby arrives and Harley's in remission, we'll fly to LA as a family and sort everything out. *I* don't know anything about real estate, but when The Raiders retire, maybe we could divide our time between here and LA and try and run the businesses ourselves.'

Livvy shook her head. 'I don't want to do that. The girls are settled in school here and can you imagine the protests from Harley when she has to leave Jack for any length of time, not to mention Courtney and that Jamie Donahue? I'd rather try and float the whole lot and sell up.'

'It's up to you, sweetheart, but you don't have to make any big decisions just yet. Danny's lawyer can earn his living by doing some of the worrying for you. Courtney inherits the bulk of his assets anyway, so it's *her* future we should be concerned with. The kid's a multi-millionaire before she's even sixteen. There's *your* career too. I know you told me you don't ever want to sing again, but believe me, Liv, once Roy Junior arrives, you'll feel differently. When I called Hank the other day he was wondering if he shouldn't fly over to see you. I told him you'd speak to him as soon as you're feeling up to talking to people. He said he'd let your other band mates know what's happening.'

Livvy sighed and rested her hands on her wriggling bump. Roy Jnr was getting so big and he was very active. He was never still for a minute and with all the stress she'd hardly slept a wink since 9/11. She couldn't face speaking to anyone at the moment, not even her parents and Sheena. She'd had the press on the phone, though God knows how they'd got her number, wanting her comments on Danny's death and asking why she was still in England when her husband was missing in New York. She'd responded with 'No comment' and now there were reporters and photographers hanging around the lane. Livvy felt like she wanted to hide away with her daughters and Roy and never have to face the world again. There was no closure for her. Without a body there was no funeral to arrange, just this surreal feeling of limbo.

Courtney had quietly accepted the fact that her father had passed away and to everyone's surprise, had calmly announced at the beginning of October that she was going back to school. Livvy knew her daughter's pain was bottled up and her calm exterior was just a front. She reminded her so much of herself. If only she would cry and scream and give vent to her feelings, but since Doctor Shaw had administered that sedative, Courtney had been dignified in her grief, retreating into a private shell that only Harley and Jamie Donahue seemed able to penetrate.

Livvy had spoken in depth to the head of Manor Banks, who had assured her that Courtney would receive the utmost support from him, his colleagues and pupils. So she felt that she had no choice but to allow her daughter to return.

* * *

'Are you quite sure you're ready for this, Courtney?' Livvy asked as they all sat around the breakfast table. Two weeks on from hearing that Daniel was confirmed as missing, Roy and Harley had moved into Charlecote Cottage, now that there was no reason not to.

'Yes.' But Courtney's smile didn't reach her eyes and her lower lip trembled.

Harley, who was seated opposite her sister, caught her eye and nodded. 'Don't bottle out now,' she mouthed silently.

'What's with you two?' Roy frowned, catching the look that passed between the girls.

'Life has to go on,' Harley announced philosophically. 'I'm doing well with my chemo, even though I have to wear this stupid bandanna round my head, Courtney's coping as well as she can and Jamie's being supportive, so don't you go giving her earache about seeing him, *and...*' she tailed off, looking sternly at her parents, 'it's about time you two came clean. Honestly, you're behaving like a pair of kids with a guilty secret.'

'What?' Roy gasped, a blush creeping up his neck.

'Mom's pregnant!' Courtney announced bluntly.

'*Very* pregnant,' Harley chipped in. 'Why didn't you tell us? We're not idiots, we guessed ages ago.'

Livvy glanced at Roy, whose mouth was twitching with the beginnings of a smile. 'Role reversal,' he said. 'Okay, girls, you win. Roy Junior is due in January.'

'Roy Junior? So, it's a boy?' Harley exclaimed. 'Really? You've had a scan?'

'Two scans,' Livvy said. 'The second scan shows quite clearly that the baby is a boy.'

'With all the necessary Cantello equipment!' Roy beamed proudly.

'Dad!' Harley exclaimed. 'Do you have to?'

'When did you guess?' Livvy asked.

'When Courtney found a pregnancy testing kit in the bath-room bin,' Harley smirked. 'Months ago, in fact. Didn't take you two long to make another mistake.'

'Roy Junior isn't a mistake,' Livvy told her, 'he was planned for a very good reason: I wanted another child with your dad.'

Harley nodded slowly. 'It *had* dawned on me that the baby would be a full-blood sibling. Maybe he'll be a perfect match for me.'

'Hopefully,' Roy said. 'They told us at the hospital that they can take stem cells from his umbilical cord after his birth and they can tell from that apparently. Clever stuff.'

'So!' Harley patted Livvy's stomach gently, 'I can't wait to make your acquaintance, little brother.'

'No objections to our being too old then and showing you up at school?' Roy smiled.

'I guess not,' Harley replied with a shrug.

'What about you, Courtney?' Livvy turned to her daughter, who was staring silently into space.

'What? Oh, I'm okay about it, Mom. I'm just glad it's out in the open and we can all be honest from now on. No more secrets. I've always wanted a brother anyway. Did Dad know about the baby?'

Livvy shook her head. 'No, we hadn't got around to telling him.'

'Perhaps as well!' Courtney scraped back her chair on the flagstone floor. 'He always wanted a boy, but *you* would never have another baby with *him*.'

'Courtney!' Livvy frowned as she grabbed her school bag and flounced towards the hall.

'You three and Roy Junior will be a proper family now,' she

called over her shoulder. 'Will you take me to school, please, Roy?'

Roy stood up without a word and picked up his car keys. He turned to Livvy and said, 'She's hurting. It'll take time. Now that the girls know, when I've dropped Courtney at school, I'll call on Sammy and tell her the news.' He followed Courtney out to the car as Livvy nodded.

Harley patted Livvy's hand across the table. 'Dad's right, Courtney has a lot to deal with at the moment.'

'I know she has, honey, but so have you – we *all* have.'

Harley smiled. 'I tell you what, Mom. Do you mind if I call you that now?'

Livvy's eyes filled with tears. 'If you want to – it would make me very happy.'

'Good. I'll still call Sammy Mum, of course, because she is. But I'll call *you* Mom, like Courtney does, then there's no confusion. What I was going to suggest was that we go out shopping and buy some things for Roy Junior. You can wear one of your wigs and sunglasses while we get past the pressmen on the lane and then no one will recognise you.'

'I think shopping's a wonderful idea. It'll get us both out of the house, we can't stay hidden away forever. We can have lunch out too. I haven't bought a single thing for this baby yet. My mom's knitted lots of outfits, but I've asked her to keep them until after he's born.'

'What are we waiting for then? Leave Dad a note on the table. He'll probably go and see Uncle Ed after visiting Mum anyway. Tell him we'll pick up Courtney from school on our way home.'

* * *

'What's bugging *you*, Courtney?' Roy asked as he headed towards Manor Banks after running the gamut of pressmen and snap-happy photographers on the lane.

'Nothing,' she muttered and stared out of the window. Her phone bleeped with a message. She looked at the screen, a smile crossing her face.

'Jamie?' he asked.

'Yep.' She nodded. 'He's waiting for me by the gates. Is it okay to tell him about the baby?'

'Err, I'm not sure that's a good idea at the moment. Leave it a week or two. Your mom's thinking about doing an interview for *Hello!* to put the record straight before the gutter press put their own spin on the whole affair.'

'So, she'll tell them about Roy Junior too?'

'Yes, everything. My divorce will be through soon and maybe we'll marry before the baby arrives.'

'Why don't you wait till afterwards?'

'It would be much nicer to have him born into wedlock, don't you think?'

'Sounds a bit old-fashioned.' Courtney smirked.

'Well, maybe it does, but at least it's put a smile on your face. Are you worried that you're not going to feel a part of the family when I marry your mother?'

She nodded. 'I'll be the odd one out, the outsider, because *you're* not my dad,' she replied quietly, her eyes filling with sudden tears.

Roy swallowed the lump in his throat. He pulled the car over to the side of the road. 'Courtney, sweetheart, I'm so sorry.' He held her tightly while she cried. When her sobs subsided, he tilted up her chin and looked at her: 'Would you like me to take you home?'

'No.' She shook her head. 'I want to see Jamie. I've really missed him and he said he's missed me too. I'll be okay, Roy, honestly.'

'If you're sure.' He sighed. 'Courtney, you're not an

outsider, you never will be. You're Livvy's child just as much as Harley and Roy Junior are. If anything, *I'm* the outsider here.'

Courtney smiled and wiped her eyes. 'I feel better for crying, I'm calmer inside now.'

'You needed that, sweetheart. You've been bottling it up for ages. Now let's get you to school and you can see Jamie. But don't forget what your mother and I have told you. Make sure you're never alone with him, because he's a handful and you're not quite ready to cope with all that just yet.'

'I can take care of myself,' Courtney retorted as Roy pulled up at the school gates. She leant across and pecked him on the cheek, then clambered out of the car.

Roy watched as she ran across to Jamie, who grabbed her hand and kissed her on the lips. He shook his head and returned her wave as she smiled defiantly at him from the confines of Jamie's arms.

'She's a little madam and that one's so bloody cock sure of himself,' Roy muttered to himself as he drove away. 'Oh well, what will be, will be, and all that crap. If he makes her happy, and God knows she needs it, then so be it.'

20

Sammy stepped from the en suite shower and heard someone calling her name, then footsteps on the stairs: Roy. She grabbed a towel, wrapped it around herself and went through to the bedroom.

He was standing in front of the wardrobe with at least a day's growth on his chin, his face pale and gaunt, hair untidy and an expression of immense sadness in his eyes that she hadn't seen there since Nick's death.

'Roy, what on earth are you doing here? You look dreadful. Is something wrong?'

'I've just dropped Courtney at school. I need to talk to you, Sam. If it's convenient, that is?'

'Of course. Sit down.' She gestured to the bed, then wondered if she should have told him to sit on the chair instead. Too late, he'd flopped down with a huge sigh. 'I'm so sorry to hear about Courtney's father,' she said. 'Jane told me what's happened – I'm surprised you didn't call me yourself.'

'I've been looking after Livvy and Courtney, not to mention Harley,' he said. 'I haven't had a minute.'

'How's Livvy taken it, given that she and Danny were in the throes of divorcing?'

'How would *you* feel if it were me?'

She stared at him for a long moment. 'Devastated.'

'There's your answer. She's in bits, won't go out of the cottage because the flamin' press are on our tail. She's worried to death about Courtney, who's insisted on going back to school today. Then there's Danny's business empire and even her horses at the ranch. It's a nightmare and there's no closure. She can't lay him to rest because there's no body. I'm worried sick about her, Sam. She appears to be coping on the outside, but it's her mind and the...' He stopped and stared at her, then averted his gaze.

'And the what, Roy?' She reached for his hand and squeezed it. He laced his fingers through hers.

'She's pregnant,' he admitted.

She nodded thoughtfully. 'I know.'

'Did Jane tell you?'

'Of course not. When I took Harley to the cottage a few weeks ago I had my suspicions then. Livvy just had that look about her and when she turned, I could tell by her profile. How far gone is she?'

'Just over six months.'

Sammy pursed her lips and frowned.

'I'm sorry, Sam.'

She shrugged. 'How does Harley feel about it, and Courtney too, of course?'

He told her what had happened at breakfast that morning.

'I felt like a teenager whose mother's giving him earache for getting his girlfriend in trouble,' he said. 'Harley's so outspoken at times.'

'I wonder where she gets that from.?'

'How's Jason, by the way?' Roy changed the subject. 'I've

been so caught up in the aftermath of 9/11, I haven't called him for a couple of weeks.'

'He's fine. Daisy's due next week. He and Jules are so excited. Promise me you'll make time to go and see them after the birth.'

'Of course I will. She's my first grandchild, I'm looking forward to her arrival.'

'So am I. I can't wait. Do you know what sex yours is yet?' Sammy held her breath. How could she possibly be having this conversation with Roy? Like it was a normal thing to do.

'It's a boy,' he announced proudly. 'We saw him on the scan.'

Sammy looked down at their hands, still entwined. She blinked away the sudden rush of tears and smiled. 'That will be nice for you and a first boy for Livvy after two girls.'

'You're thinking about Nick, aren't you?' he said softly, lifting his hand to stroke her cheek.

She nodded again, tears running freely now. '*Our* first boy. We were so happy then.'

'Don't, Sam, please.' He choked on a sob. 'I can't bear to see you crying like this. I shouldn't have come, I'm so sorry.'

She looked at him. 'I love you, Roy. I always will, but you belong to Livvy now. You'd better go before I make a bigger fool of myself and beg you to stay.'

He stood up and pulled her into his arms, holding her tightly. 'I wish I could have two wives and then I wouldn't have to choose,' he whispered into her hair.

She pulled away and punched him gently on the chest. 'Now you're just being bloody greedy, Cantello! You'd better get back to Livvy before we do something we'll regret.'

'I'm going. Holding you like this with just a towel wrapped around you is asking for trouble.'

'I know. I can feel it!' She raised an eyebrow. 'In spite of everything, I still turn you on?'

'That was never in doubt. Have you made any decisions about the house yet?' he asked, following her down the stairs.

'I've had three valuations. I'm putting it on the market with Fraser-Hamptons for one point five million.'

'Fucking hell!' he exclaimed. 'I paid twenty grand for it in 1966 and that was a king's ransom, when you consider the average property was around a thousand.'

'*I* was gobsmacked myself. I thought about one point two maybe, but never that much.'

'Ah well, it's the Cheshire stockbroker belt.' Roy nodded. 'It's all yours, too. What will you do?'

'I've found a lovely detached cottage in Alderley Edge, near Jason and Jules. The vendors have accepted my offer and I've also paid a deposit on a villa in Portugal on the same road as John and Margaret Grey's place. Stuart Green's got an apartment in the same complex so we'll all be neighbours abroad,' she concluded with a smile.

'I see.' Roy frowned. 'So, you're seeing Stuart?'

'We're just good friends, nothing more, yet. He's divorced now and taken early retirement, like me. We plan on spending quite a lot of time in Portugal. Stop frowning like that, Roy. I'm moving on and this time it's easier. I wasn't ready to let you go when Livvy was expecting Harley and we lost Nick. I needed you then; we needed each other. But I'm stronger now and I know I can do this and build myself a new life. I'll always love you, that won't go away, but I *can* live without you now.'

He nodded. 'I just hope that Livvy and I can move on. I think she cared more for Danny than she realised.'

'But she was determined to win *you* back and this time she wasn't going to let anything stand in her way.' Sammy folded her arms and looked at the ceiling for a moment before continuing: 'Right or wrong, this is my theory. I believe Livvy came to the UK with an agenda. She wanted another child with you, and you, of course, fell right into her trap.'

'What a crazy thing to say, Sam. Livvy didn't have a plan, she isn't that devious.'

'Isn't she? Just you wait till the baby arrives. I bet you anything it's born before its due date. She planned that pregnancy from day one, knowing your aversion to contraception, and how easy it would be to tempt you into bed. I bet she told you the first time was safe, didn't she?'

Roy's face fell and Sammy knew she was right. 'She did, didn't she?' she repeated. 'For a man of your age, you're so gullible, Roy. Hasn't it dawned on you that it's payback time for her giving Harley to you?'

'I don't have to listen to this,' he snapped. 'I'm going. Give me some credit where it's due.' He stormed out of the house, leaving Sammy staring thoughtfully after him, guessing that her theory was probably right.

* * *

Sammy made a mug of coffee, laced it with brandy and went to sit at the table in front of the patio doors. She didn't usually drink this early in the day, but she needed it. She'd known Livvy was pregnant, but to hear Roy confirming it had affected her more than she'd anticipated. It would have been so easy to coax him into bed and she'd been tempted, *very* tempted. She was pretty sure he wouldn't have refused. But what purpose would it serve, other than to upset her and confuse him even more than he seemed to be already?

She hadn't been entirely truthful with him about Stuart either. She'd seen a lot of her old friend since her trip to Portugal, where he had helped her choose a property and they'd got on so well. He'd also spent a couple of nights with her at Jasmine House, but Roy didn't need to know that.

* * *

As Roy drove away from Jasmine House his thoughts returned to a conversation he'd had with Eddie, following the first time he'd slept with Livvy. 'Never trust a woman who tells you it's safe!' his mate had said, but Roy had laughed it off. Then this morning Livvy had told Harley that she'd wanted another child with him. *Had* she deliberately planned from day one to get pregnant then? Surely not? But Sammy had planted the doubts firmly in his mind now.

Back at Charlecote Cottage, he found the scribbled note on the table from Harley and Livvy. He smiled. At least those two were bonding well and that made him happy. He decided a visit to Eddie's place was long overdue and set off for Hanover's Lodge.

* * *

Eddie was in the music room when Roy arrived. Jane told him to go straight up.

'Morning, Ed,' he called out as he ran upstairs.

'Morning, mate. God, you look rough! Take a pew. Do you fancy a coffee?'

'Actually, Ed, I could use a smoke.' Roy ran his hands over his bristly chin. 'Not to mention a shave. I haven't had a joint for weeks and Lord knows I've needed one.'

Eddie reached for the tin of supplies he kept on the shelf above the mixing desk. 'Help yourself. You roll up or you'll be losing the knack. How's things?'

'Oh, you know, so-so,' Roy replied, rolling a fat joint and lighting up. He took a long toke and sighed blissfully. 'I haven't had a chance to get any stuff from Mac since, well, since 9/11.'

'I don't know how you've managed then. You should have called me.'

'Livvy doesn't approve, so Christ knows how I'll cope. I've almost given up the fags, too. We're keeping the house a smoke-free zone for Harley and the baby. I have to go up to Phil's place or for a stroll down the lane, but the press are still hanging around at the moment, so that's out.'

'How are the girls?' Eddie asked as Roy handed the joint over.

'Courtney's gone back to school today. She's a bit wobbly, but she's a tough little cookie, so I think she'll cope. Harley has her final chemo next week, so fingers crossed that she goes into remission. The girls confronted us about Livvy's pregnancy this morning. Said they'd known for ages and Harley's pointed comments made me and Liv look like complete idiots.'

'I can just imagine.' Eddie chuckled. 'I bet she gave you some stick. Well, at least now you can relax and Livvy can stop hiding her bump.'

'Yeah!' Roy said. 'I've just been to see Sammy, told her about the baby. She said she already knew. She'd sussed it when she saw Livvy the other week because she had a look about her. She also said something strange that's got me thinking, Ed.'

'What's that?' Eddie took a long toke and passed the joint back to Roy, who told him of Sammy's suspicions about Livvy.

'Does it matter? At the end of the day you were probably always going to get back together, baby or no baby.'

Roy shrugged. 'Maybe. But I feel a bit cheated if she did dupe me.'

'Are you going to say anything?'

'I don't think so. She's enough going on in her head at the moment. I'll wait and see what date Roy Junior arrives and work it back from there.'

'Wisest thing. Anyway, it's only a matter of two or three weeks when all's said and done.'

* * *

Livvy cursed under her breath as she negotiated the rain-filled potholes and the handful of pressmen on the lane. She and Harley were on their way back to the cottage, the car laden with packages. Harley's phone bleeped with a message.

'Who's that from?' Livvy asked as Harley studied the screen.

'Courtney. She's having dinner at Jamie's. Can someone collect her about nine thirty?'

Livvy pulled up outside the cottage. 'Do you have Jamie's address?'

'Of course. I'll text her back then, shall I? Tell her it's okay.'

'I suppose so. I would have liked her home straight after school today to see how she's coped.'

'You know something, Mom? Courtney needs a bit of space and time away from us and all the discussions you and Dad keep having about what's happening with Danny's businesses and if they'll ever find any of his remains. It's really screwing her up. I couldn't bear it if it was *my* dad. He's always been there for me. I couldn't stand to lose him. Just because Courtney's not weeping and wailing all over the house doesn't mean that she's okay. I think she's being very brave. Jamie takes her mind off all the problems.'

'I'm sure he does,' Livvy said. 'I just worry about her getting into a situation with him that she can't handle. Jamie's very mature for his age and he's got such a reputation.'

'She'll be fine, she knows when to say no. Now let's go indoors and find a space for Roy Junior's new things. You should be happy for Courtney, that she's settled and made some good friends.'

'You're right.' Livvy gave Harley a hug.

They took the bags indoors, where Roy greeted them with a smile.

'You two have been busy,' he said as they dumped their shopping on the hall floor.

'It's all for Roy Junior,' Harley announced.

'Good. So, you've had a nice day then?'

'We've had a *very* nice day, thanks,' Livvy replied. 'It was good to get out of the house. What about you? How did Sammy take the news?'

'Okay, I guess. She was a bit tearful when I told her we're having a boy. It brought back memories of her being pregnant with Nick.'

He took a deep breath and Livvy saw that his eyes were red, he'd been crying.

'She's putting Jasmine House on the market. It's the end of an era,' he finished quietly.

'Dad.' Harley ran to him and flung her arms around his neck. 'Don't be sad, please. There's enough going on without you breaking down. We need you to be strong for us.'

'And I will be, princess.' He stroked her back gently. 'I've never let you down and I don't intend to start now.' He smiled at Livvy, who was looking tearful too. 'Where's my other girl? I thought you were picking her up from school?'

Livvy yanked off her red curly wig and tossed it onto the sofa. 'She's having dinner at Jamie's.'

'I see. Right, well, let's hope his parents are home then.'

'Roy, don't. I'm worried to death as it is.'

'She'll be fine,' Harley said. 'I'll come to Jamie's with you later, Dad. We have to collect her at nine thirty.'

'Okay, if you're not too tired. Shall we make something to eat then?' Roy looked hopefully in the fridge. 'We need to get our act together, Livvy, and do some serious grocery shopping. This fridge is almost empty and I, for one, am starving. We've no beer in the house, no single malt. Sod all, in fact!'

'Let's order a curry,' she suggested. 'Saves cooking and clearing up. Anyway, I'm too tired for all of that. I feel like I've walked my legs off at The Trafford Centre. By the way, we've ordered a pram, cot and high chair – Selfridges will deliver next week.'

'Okay! You girls can choose some paint and we'll get the chap who decorates Jasmine House to give the small room a wallop. Feels real now, doesn't it? Now that we're getting his room ready.'

Roy Jnr gave a hefty kick of approval and Livvy grinned. 'Ouch! Little monkey. He says yes, get a move on.'

Roy smiled and ran his hands over her bump. 'Have you got footballers' feet, son? We'll get you trained, signed up by Man United, then your old dad can put down his guitar and retire.'

* * *

Courtney's eyes sparkled as she joined Harley in the back of the car.

'Alright, Courtney?' Roy greeted her.

'Fine, thank you, Roy,' she replied with a grin.

'Well?' Harley whispered.

'I had a great time,' Courtney whispered back, 'Tell you all about it later.'

Harley grinned as Roy caught her eye in the mirror. 'There's a lot of whispering and giggling going on.'

'Nothing for your ears, Dad,' Harley said.

He shook his head with mock disapproval. It was good to see the girls enjoying themselves after the traumas of the last few months. No kids should have to go through what those two had endured recently, he thought as he put his foot down. They deserved some normality for a change.

* * *

Courtney brushed her mass of tumbling blonde curls as Harley, tucked up in bed, stared enviously at her.

'I wish I still had my hair.' She sighed wistfully, rubbing her hand over her bristly scalp.

Courtney smiled. 'It's growing back, Harley. You can see it coming through already. Your hair's lovely and grows so quickly that it'll be down your back again in no time *and* it's straight. I hate having curls.'

'I'd settle for curls at the moment,' Harley said. 'So, come on, now we're on our own, tell me all. What's he like to snog properly and did you...?'

Courtney blushed prettily and grinned. She bounced onto the end of Harley's bed, her eyes twinkling. 'He's a brilliant kisser.' She sighed dreamily.

'Tongues?'

'Oh yeah!'

'And?'

Courtney twiddled a curl and rolled her eyes. 'We were, you know, making out and I wanted to, but Jamie said I'm too young and we should wait till I'm sixteen.'

'Wow! That doesn't sound like the Jamie Donahue I know. Age has never stopped him, maybe he's changed.'

'I was relieved,' Courtney admitted. 'I'd like to wait, too. But I like him so much and he told me he's never felt so close to any of the girls he's had before and I really need to feel as though I belong to someone.'

Harley frowned. 'You belong to us, we're a family now.'

'Well, you've got Jack, and Mom has Roy.'

'And you have Jamie – eating out of your hand by the sound of it. Don't rush things. He's obviously got some respect for you, which is more than he had for Tasha. How's she taking you two being an item?'

'She's sulking. Texts him all the time, but he ignores them. She gives me the evil eye each time I walk past. She's told everyone that now my dad's dead, I'm a spoilt little rich girl and Jamie only wants me 'cos I've got money.'

'Jealous cow!' Harley retorted. 'Jamie's family are jewellers, they're absolutely minted. He'll be rolling in it himself one day. Tasha's a bitch. You should ignore her.'

'I try. I'll be glad when you can come back to school.'

'So will I,' Harley said. 'Maybe next week but one I might go back part-time.'

'That would be great,' Courtney said. 'Jack really misses you. Jamie has a mixing desk in his bedroom and he plays keyboards and guitar. We sang together and he said I sound like Mom. He says we should form a band with you, Jack and Nathan. What do you think?'

'It's a brilliant idea. Jack plays bass and Nathan sings well and plays lead guitar. We'd need to find a drummer.'

'Well, maybe we can get together at the weekend at Jamie's place and have a jam session,' Courtney suggested. 'That's if you feel up to it, of course.'

'I should be okay. Next week, I have my last chemo. I'll be out of action for a few days, but do you know, I actually feel as though I'm winning. If I *do* need a transplant in the future, then I'm in with a good chance now, thanks to Roy Junior.'

'Well, if *he* isn't a match, they can always have another,' Courtney said. She plumped up her pillows and slid under the duvet.

'Oh God, don't encourage them. We'll end up with a houseful of screaming brats!' Harley laughed.

* * *

Roy frowned as Livvy dropped the phone onto its cradle and turned slowly to face him. 'Something wrong?'

'That was Sean Grogan,' she said. 'Liam's arrived in work with a copy of *The Daily Mirror*.'

'And?'

'The headline says, "SECOND CHILD FOR LIVVY

GRANT AND ROY CANTELLO", and then there's a report about us and the girls and Danny.' Her eyes filled with tears as Roy strode across the room and took her in his arms.

'Someone's blabbed. They'll be like fucking vultures out there now. I wonder who it is? No one close to us, I'm sure. What name did you give to the salesperson at Selfridges the other day?'

'Mrs McVey, of course,' she said. 'I always do. I've kept my bump under such restrictive clothing on the rare times I've left the house that no one could possibly tell. Even at the antenatal clinic I'm known as Mrs McVey and I always wear a disguise there too. Do you think it might be Sammy?'

'Absolutely not,' he said. 'Sammy hates the press more than I do. I'll nip to the village store and grab a few papers. We can see exactly what's been said and then we can act on it.'

Roy was back within minutes, dropping an armful of dailies onto the kitchen table. '*The Mirror*'s the main culprit, given that we're plastered across the front page. But there's something in all of them. I've nearly mown down a handful of bloody photographers out on the lane.'

Livvy picked up *The Daily Mirror* and stared at the front page. Two separate publicity photos of her and Roy had been cleverly spliced to look as though they were smiling into each other's eyes. She read aloud:

'*In spite of the recent death of her property tycoon husband, Daniel McVey, who perished in the terrorist attack on The World Trade Center, singer Livvy Grant remains in England with her lover, Raiders' frontman, Roy Cantello. The couple are believed to be living in a Cheshire village with their sixteen-year-old daughter, Harley, who is undergoing treatment for leukaemia, and Miss Grant's fifteen-year-old daughter, Courtney, from her marriage to Mr McVey. It has been confirmed by a source known to the family that the couple are expecting a second child.*'

'What source known to the family?' Livvy frowned.

'Christ knows,' Roy replied. 'We need to air our side of the story by giving an interview. I'll call The Raiders' manager. Frank will sort it. The sooner we do something, the better.'

'Do we have to?' Livvy sighed wearily. 'They haven't really said anything that isn't true, have they?'

'No, but tomorrow there'll be all sorts of made-up tales to contend with. I'd rather get this out of the way while Harley's in hospital for the next few days. She'll need peace and quiet when she comes home. You're almost a recluse. We have to do it, Liv. This can't go on, I want our lives back. We don't have to prove anything to anyone, but if we don't get rid of those fucking guys on the lane soon, I might just end up killing one of them! It's difficult enough coping with things on a day-to-day basis without all this crap in the papers. I've only seen Ed a couple of times in weeks. I haven't written a song for months. I'm losing my creativity stuck in here all day. I need some space to call my own, a studio and music room. We need to look for a house to buy soon. I'll get us a big place where we can spread out a bit more.'

* * *

Livvy stared at Roy as though seeing him properly for the first time in weeks. He looked gaunt and ill and she felt guilty for not noticing that he was suffering too. It had all been about her and the girls recently, them leaning heavily on Roy for support, but who was supporting him? Like he said, he'd hardly seen Eddie and if there was one person Roy could depend on, it was his best friend. They hadn't even made love since Danny's death and that was her fault too. Every night Roy reached for her and she'd seen the disappointment in his eyes when she'd told him she wasn't feeling up to it. He hadn't said anything, but she could sense the frustration in him and knew she needed to rectify that particular situation very soon or he'd be running back to Sammy – the thought put the fear of God into her.

'I didn't realise you were feeling so hemmed in. I'm sorry. I've taken away all your freedom and I didn't mean to do that. I've become too dependent on you. I'll give you space, if that's what you want. I might take a trip up to Glasgow at the weekend to see my parents and Sheena and Gerry. I'll take Courtney too. I'd like to take Harley, but she really needs to rest when she comes home.'

'Why don't you wait till she feels up to travelling and then all three of you can go?' Roy suggested.

'Okay. I'll speak with the girls when Harley's home. What about you? What will you do while we're away?'

'Spend some time with Jason and Jules. I've got all my stuff to pack at Jasmine House, too. I'm also going to get to grips with my career. We still have to plan The Raiders' final album and farewell tour. Everything's been on hold since Harley was diagnosed. It's time to dust it all off again. Phil, Carl and Tim have voiced their concerns to Ed.'

Livvy was silent for a long moment. 'You're right, Roy. Let's look to the future. I'll speak to Hank tonight, tell him I'm pregnant and that as soon as I've given birth he can come over and we can begin working on some new songs for Juice. It's time I stood on my own two feet again, instead of expecting you to prop me up all the time.'

'Livvy, I don't want you to have to stand on your own two feet, I need you to need me. I want to look after you. But there are times when I feel overwhelmed by the responsibility of everything. It's happened so quickly. I feel like it's all spinning out of control and I don't know how much more I can take.'

She nodded as he took her in his arms. 'You've almost given up smoking, too – maybe that's why you're so tetchy at times.'

He smiled and planted a kiss on her lips. 'I know what

would make me feel better right at this moment,' he whispered, nuzzling her neck.

'What's that then?' she teased, knowing full well what he was about to suggest.

'That I carry you off to bed and those bloody peasants won't have a clue that we're doing it right under their noses, so to speak! Boy, that would make some front-page photo!'

'Okay,' she giggled. 'It's a deal, Mr Cantello.'

'You feel up to it?'

'I do at the moment. I'm always so tired at night and Harley's usually here during the day. It's not that I don't want you – believe me, I do. But we're going to have to pick our times, like now, while the house is empty and *before* you call Frank James and get into a lengthy conversation.'

Needing no further encouragement, Roy swept her into his arms and carried her upstairs. He dropped her gently onto the bed and strode to the window to close the curtains. 'I don't believe it!' he exclaimed and opened the window. 'Fuck off, you moron or I'll call the police! This is private land.' He stuck two fingers up at whoever he was yelling at and yanked the curtains across before turning back to Livvy: 'That told the cheeky bastard!'

'Who is it?'

'A bloody guy in the tree opposite, taking photographs of the cottage and my Beamer.' He stripped off his clothes and lay down beside her. 'No doubt there'll be a picture of my angry face on all the front pages tomorrow.'

21

Livvy leant back on the sofa and smiled. She'd outlined her plans to the girls, waiting for the enthusiasm that was sure to come. 'It will do us good to go to Scotland. Be nice to catch up with my family.'

'Do we have to go?' Harley's voice held a note of dismay. 'We've got plans of our own. Invite Gran and Grandpa down here instead.'

Livvy shook her head as Harley shifted her position on the sofa. It was her first day home following her final chemotherapy treatment, but she'd refused to go to bed in case she missed something. 'That's not an option. The idea is to give Roy some space – he's climbing the walls holed up in here with us.'

'Well, *we* don't have to go away for Dad to have some space,' Harley said. 'Tell him to go and stay with Uncle Ed, they've got plenty of spare rooms. Anyway, he shouldn't need his own space. We're supposed to be a family, he should enjoy being with us. Where is he now?'

'Gone to Phil's for a cigarette,' Livvy replied wearily. 'I'm worried about him. He's not looking well – it's the stress.' She was bothered that Roy was missing Sammy more than he let on.

He'd been upset when he came back from Jasmine House the other day, telling her that packing up his old life made him feel very sad.

Harley nodded. 'I suppose so. Do you think he's missing Mum? They'd never have split up if you hadn't come back to find me.'

Livvy swallowed hard as Harley voiced her own thoughts. 'That makes me feel bad,' she said, knowing that she didn't really mean it. 'I didn't know things would end up like this – you ill, Danny dead and... him.' She caressed her bump gently and brushed a tear away.

'Sorry for upsetting you, Mom. Will Courtney run up to Phil's and get Dad?'

'No, leave him for a while. Perhaps you two could tell me what *your* plans are.'

'We've started a band,' Courtney announced excitedly.

'Really? That's great. When did this happen and who's we?'

'Me, Harley, Jamie, Jack and Nathan. We had a jam session the weekend we went to Jamie's place. As soon as Harley's feeling up to it, we're having another.'

'Good luck to you. If you need help, you can always ask me and Roy.'

Harley grinned. 'Give us a break, Mom! We're planning on being more Green Day than Juice or The Raiders. But thanks for the offer.'

'All popular music has its roots in country and rock 'n' roll, so don't you knock it, young lady,' Livvy said.

'So now you see why we can't go,' Courtney continued. 'Anyway, I don't want to leave Jamie.'

'And I don't want to leave Jack,' Harley chipped in.

'Fair enough. I know when I'm outnumbered. I'll suggest Roy goes to stay with Ed for a while. Good idea, Harley.'

* * *

The Raiders' manager Frank James had advised Roy and Livvy to issue a statement exclusive to *The Daily Mirror* and put the record straight about their relationship. This eased the situation with the pressmen on the lane. Livvy had also agreed a deal with *Hello!* magazine to do an interview following the birth of their son.

Harley ventured back to school for half-days. Her latest test results revealed that her red blood count was significantly improved, but there was still the possibility of needing a bone marrow transplant and she was pinning all her hopes on the new baby being the perfect match.

Roy and Eddie had revived their shelved songs for The Raiders' final album and the band was planning a trip to the Abbey Road Studios during the first week of December.

* * *

December arrived, cold and frosty, and with Roy off to the recording studios, Livvy's parents were on their way to keep her and the girls company. After running Courtney to school, Livvy set about preparing the spare room. She shivered and turned the radiator thermostat to a higher setting – getting used to the cold after LA took some doing and she was glad she'd bought new winter-weight duvets.

'Harley, will you bring me the cream bedding set, please?' she called above the music blasting from behind the girls' bedroom door. No reply. She got the linen from the airing cupboard and, arms laden, glanced out of the landing window. She smiled at the antics of Laura's Cocker Spaniels as they frolicked in half-frozen puddles, glad that they wouldn't be bringing their muddy paws onto *her* kitchen floor.

As Harley's music faded, she heard a faint bleep, bleep noise. It seemed to be coming from her and Roy's room and sounded like a cell phone message. In the room she couldn't see

Roy's phone lying around. Her own cell phone was switched off and in her handbag. The bleeping noise sounded again from the direction of the wardrobes. She dropped the linen on the bed and opened the doors, rooted in the pockets of several jackets and found Roy's mobile.

'Damn it! How the hell am I supposed to get in touch with him now?' The last thing she'd said to him as he'd packed that morning was, 'Don't forget to take your phone.' Honestly, his memory was rubbish. Still, Ed would be bound to have *his* phone and if there was an emergency, she could always ask Jane for the number. No doubt Roy would call her tonight from the hotel.

She opened the phone and checked in case there was anything urgent she could pass on to him. There were two messages, both from Sammy. The words leapt out and Livvy felt her legs turn to jelly. She slumped down on the bed with a moan and reread both messages. The first stated: *Thanks for a wonderful time last night. I can still taste your champagne kisses. Xxx.* The second was *PS: Good luck at Abbey Road today. All my love, S. xxx*

Last night Roy had told Livvy he was meeting up with Eddie at Carl's house to go through some songs for today. He'd left at seven and rolled home, worse for wear, just after midnight. Livvy had had no cause to doubt his tale. She felt sick that he appeared to have betrayed her again. How could he possibly cheat on her with Sammy, just a couple of weeks before his divorce was due? Roy Jnr gave her a kick in the ribs to remind her that *he* was due very soon, too.

She went over the last few weeks in her head. Roy had spent a fair bit of time at Jasmine House, sorting and packing things. Sammy had received an asking price offer from a couple of members of a successful boy band, who were looking for a country retreat. The recording studio and music room had clinched the deal and she'd asked Roy to help her prepare for the move. Also, the arrival of Daisy Cantello-Young had been a recent cause for celebration. Roy was both enthralled and besotted with his new granddaughter and Livvy hadn't objected to him spending further time in Sammy's company on his visits to Jason and Jules' home. Tears filled her eyes now and she placed her hands protectively over her precious bump and took several deep breaths. 'Your daddy is a cheating bastard,' she muttered.

Harley popped her head around the door. 'Did you call me, Mom? Sorry, I was in the shower.' She joined Livvy on the bed. 'You okay? Is it the baby? Shall I call Dad, get him to come back?'

Livvy saw the panic in Harley's eyes. She shook her head. 'It's not the baby, honey, and no, I don't want you to call Roy. I'm okay. I'll finish making the bed before Mum and Dad arrive. You need to get ready for afternoon school.' She tried to stand, but her legs weren't working and she flopped back down again. Tears welled in her eyes and she stared at Harley, unable to stop them tumbling down her cheeks.

'Mom, what is it? Please tell me,' Harley cried, dropping to her knees. 'Why have you got Dad's mobile?'

'He's forgotten it.'

'Well, that's no reason to cry. He'll call you from his hotel, or use Uncle Ed's.'

'I'm not crying because he's forgotten it. Sammy sent him text messages.' She showed them to Harley, who frowned and chewed her lower lip.

'I don't know what to say, Mom,' she faltered. 'I mean, it only mentions kisses, doesn't it?'

'Oh yeah,' Livvy retorted, 'not to mention the wonderful time. He lied to us last night. Told us he was going to Carl's place, while all the time he was alone with Sammy, presumably at Jasmine House.'

'Maybe they were with Jason and Jules, perhaps that's what

she means, that they had a wonderful time with them. You know how much Dad loves Jules' cooking and...' Harley tailed off as Livvy shook her head.

'If that's the case, why on earth did he tell us he was going to Carl's? I've never had *any* objections to him spending time with Jason, or Sammy for that matter.' Livvy clutched her stomach as a wave of pain shot through her. 'Oh, God!'

'Right, I'm not going to school. I can't leave you on your own.' Harley sprang up and grabbed the telephone from the bedside table. She dialled a number and babbled into the receiver: 'Mum, it's me. Can you come over, please? Dad's gone to London and Livvy's getting pains. I don't know what to do. I'm really scared the baby will come while we're alone.'

Sammy replied that she'd be with them in ten minutes. Harley helped Livvy downstairs and made her comfortable on the sofa.

* * *

Fresh out of the shower, Sammy dashed around, pulling on jeans and a sweater. Harley had sounded so worried on the phone that her heart had gone out to her daughter. She missed Harley with all her being but hoped to God that Livvy wouldn't give birth in front of her.

She quickly dialled Stuart, cancelled their lunchtime date and set off for Charlecote Cottage. Harley let her in and led her through to the lounge, where Livvy was lying on the sofa, her face pale and her cheeks tear-stained.

'Has the baby started?' Sammy asked, taking in Livvy's pained expression.

Livvy shook her head and tried to speak, but only succeeded in sobbing loudly.

'What is it then? Why the tears?'

Harley picked up Roy's phone and handed it to Sammy.

'Dad's forgotten his phone. Livvy read the messages you sent him. What have you two been up to, Mum?'

Sammy gasped at Harley's directness and felt her cheeks warming. 'You weren't meant to see those, they were for Roy.'

'Obviously!' Livvy snapped. 'And I'd have been none the wiser. How could you, Sammy? You know how much I love Roy. Me and the girls, we really need him.'

'And *I* don't, I suppose,' Sammy retorted, angry tears springing to her eyes. Damn it, she mustn't lose control now but it served Livvy right to get a dose of her own medicine. Sammy knew that if she clicked her fingers, Roy would come running back to her without too much persuasion. She also knew that although he loved Livvy, he felt trapped – he'd told her so last night. She blinked the tears away. 'We didn't mean it to happen. We cracked open a bottle of bubbly to celebrate me selling the house. We agreed it was for old times' sake, that's all. We shouldn't have done it, but then again, we are still married and *you* weren't supposed to find out.'

Livvy glared at Sammy. 'You're divorcing him. Roy told me he was going to Carl's last night but he must have known that he was coming to you.'

'Well, of course, he knew. We arranged it the day before. *I* wasn't to know he'd lied to you. We sorted through our record collection. Can you imagine how painful it was? There were records there that we bought together when we first started dating. All that history and loving we shared, until *you* came along.' Sammy wanted to grab hold of Livvy and shake her head off. It was so hard to stay cool and she knew she should keep her mouth shut, but she had to say what was on her mind.

'You've no idea how much I dreaded seeing you again. Each year, Harley's birthday was spoilt with the worry that you'd show up and demand her back. Roy felt the same, which is why he put off telling her the truth. He was terrified of losing her. I suspect that when you arrived in February, it was with an agenda. You were determined to have another child with my husband, weren't you? You didn't give a damn about me or our marriage. I told Roy my feelings about that.'

Livvy gasped and Sammy was satisfied to see a blush creeping up her neck. It gave her the courage to carry on: 'Roy believes that Roy Junior was conceived *after* you moved into this place but I would stake my life on it that he was conceived at the hotel within the first few days of your visit. If Harley hadn't been ill, and you'd gone back to LA, would you ever have told Roy that you'd taken back what you gave him sixteen years ago? Apart from seeing Harley, that *was* what you came for, wasn't it? And my poor, gullible fool of a man hasn't a bloody clue and nor, I presume, did yours.'

'Mum,' Harley cried, 'stop it! She wouldn't do that, would you, Livvy? Dad said they planned Roy Junior to help me get well.'

Sammy wiped her eyes and looked at Harley as Livvy hung her head. 'Those are just my personal thoughts on the matter. Whatever, I'm putting the divorce on hold until I've spoken to Roy.'

'You can't do that, Mum. What about all your plans? And Dad said he wants to marry Livvy before the baby arrives.'

'He'll have a job,' Sammy said. 'That baby will be here much sooner than you think. Isn't that right, Livvy?'

'With all this upset, he'll probably arrive early anyway,' Livvy said. 'I can't believe Roy's let me down again. I'll admit that I hoped to get pregnant and I've lied about my dates, but I'll tell Roy as soon as he comes home. I don't think he'll be *too* bothered. It's only a few weeks anyway and I *would* have told him about the baby. I had no real plans to go home, whether Harley was ill or not.' She gasped and clutched at her bump. 'It's okay, honey,' she reassured Harley as the girl's face registered alarm. 'It's just a pretend contraction. Wee Roy is practising, that's all.'

Sammy wished she'd recorded that confession. 'So, what date *are* you due? Officially, I mean, not the date you've told Roy.'

'Next Tuesday,' Livvy replied. She took a deep shuddering breath and screwed up her face. 'Hell, I think he's coming now! God, I'm not ready.'

'Do something, Mum,' Harley cried. 'Phone the doctor, phone Dad.'

'I'll have to try and get hold of Ed,' Sammy said, rummaging in her handbag. 'Let's hope he's got his phone switched on.' She scrolled down the numbers listed in her phone until she found Eddie's. 'Come on, come on,' she muttered as she waited for a response. 'Harley, you call Laura, ask her to come over. Ring the doctor's number and tell the receptionist we need him to come straight away.'

Sammy recalled Harley's birth, when Livvy went into labour and the baby arrived in no time. She left a message for Eddie and turned her attention back to Livvy, who was clutching her bump and panting.

* * *

'Damn it, I've left my bloody phone in the car,' Eddie said to Roy as they ate breakfast at Leicester Forest Services. 'I promised to call Jane when we stopped.'

'Use mine.' Roy reached into his jacket pocket. 'Shit! I haven't got mine either. Oh damn, *I* know where it is. I wore my leather jacket when I went out last night and it's in the pocket. Livvy will go mad. Last thing she said was don't forget your phone.'

'I'll nip out to the car and get mine. Won't be a tick,' Eddie said.

* * *

Roy lit one of Eddie's cigarettes and drew deeply. Bliss! He so missed smoking, but had to admit that he felt healthier for cutting down to a couple a day. Ah well, he could make up for what he'd missed while they were in London. He was looking forward to a few days of much-needed freedom and could think of nothing better than hitting the studios again and partying with the lads when they'd finished recording for the day. Nothing better, that is, than making love to Sammy for one last time last night. He took another long drag as Eddie strolled back towards him, a puzzled expression on his face.

'What's up, mate?' he said as Eddie sat down.

'There's a voicemail from Sammy. Wants you to call her urgently.'

Roy grabbed the phone and pressed Sammy's number: 'Hi, Sam, what's up?' He smiled into the receiver and then frowned as he listened to what she was telling him. 'What... now... this very minute? Shit! You sure it's not a false alarm? Christ, well look, call me back on Ed's phone when the doctor's seen her. I've left mine at home – well, you obviously know that or you wouldn't have called Ed's.

'We're at Leicester Forest. I'll either get Ed to drop me at a station or grab a taxi if she definitely is. I'll see you later and, Sam, thanks for being there for Harley – *and* for last night.' He ended the call and passed the phone back to Eddie.

He ran his hands through his hair. 'Jesus Christ! Livvy certainly picks her moments to drop our sprogs! The doc's on his way. Sam's calling back shortly. This baby is weeks early. I hope they're going to be okay.'

'They'll be fine,' Eddie reassured him. 'How come Sam's at your place? And what's that about last night?'

'Harley called Sam and got her round because she was scared. Last night, Sam and I sorted out our record collection. We were both in tears at the memories, drank a bottle of Moët and ended up in bed.'

'Fucking hell, Roy! You don't half take some chances – you could jeopardise your divorce.'

'Nobody knows, except me, Sam and now you. It was just one of those things.'

Eddie shook his head. 'You shouldn't be sleeping with your soon-to-be ex.'

Roy sighed. 'I know. But like I said, it was a one-off – it won't be happening again.'

'I thought Sammy was seeing Stuart?'

'She is. I reckon she'll marry him when she's free.'

'You're as bad as each other.' Eddie took a sip of coffee. 'How would you feel if she *did* marry Stu?'

Roy looked down at his plate of congealing egg and bacon. He pushed it away. 'Gutted. But what can I do? I'm not allowed two wives. Neither will tolerate me seeing the other, so I had to make choices. I love them both to bits, but there's Harley to consider *and* the new baby. Courtney looks on me as a dad now, too. Face it, Ed, I'm trapped. I'd love to spend lovely long weekends with Sammy and be with Livvy and the kids in the week, but it doesn't work like that.'

'No, indeed,' Eddie said as his phone rang out. 'Okay, Sam, one minute.' He passed the phone to Roy.

'She is? Right, I'll grab a taxi. This is a big ask, but will you go with her to the hospital? Great, thanks, Sam. See you later.'

Eddie raised a questioning eyebrow.

'I need to go home, Ed. He's definitely on his way. Liv's waiting for an ambulance. Hopefully the baby will hang on until I get there.'

'You usually pass out at your kids' births, so it won't make much difference,' Eddie said. 'Good luck. I'll make your apologies to the lads and you can catch us up tomorrow.'

* * *

Sammy was waiting outside the hospital as Roy leapt out of the taxi and stuffed a wad of notes into the driver's hand. 'How is she?' he asked and gave her a hug.

'Hanging in,' she replied. 'I called Jess for backup and she's with her at the moment. I felt a bit awkward without you there. She's well underway, so it shouldn't be too long before your son puts in an appearance.'

'He's early,' Roy said. 'I hope to God he's gonna be okay. I can't believe she's in labour. She was fine when I left her. A bit grumpy, but that's par for the course with Liv in the morning. Fancy forgetting my bloody phone and at a time like this too.'

Sammy chewed her lip. 'Ah, yes, your phone. Before we go in, there's something I need to tell you.'

'What's that?'

'I sent you a couple of text messages this morning. Erm, one was to thank you for our wonderful time. The other was harmless enough, just to wish you luck in the studio. Livvy found your phone and read them. She was very upset because you'd lied to her about where you were last night.'

'Shit!' Roy exclaimed.

'I'm sorry,' Sammy said.

'It's not your fault. God knows why I told her I was going to Carl's place – I must have had a premonition about what would happen with us. But why would she go into labour because of that? It's too soon.'

'Shock,' Sammy replied. 'Maybe it's not too early. You know my theory on that score.'

'You're wrong. She wouldn't do it to me.'

'Like *you* wouldn't cheat on her with *me*?'

'Touché,' he said.

'Do you want me to come in with you?' She touched his hand gently. 'I know births terrify you.'

'Would you, Sam? Thank you.' He squeezed her hand.

'Here we go again, Roy,' she said. 'Another of those weird

situations where your lover is about to give birth to your kid and your wife's holding your hand. Very rock 'n' roll – bet even Jagger can't top this one!'

'I really appreciate it,' he said. 'It was agony leaving you last night when I had to go home.'

'I know, but you're a big boy now.' She tried to keep the mood light.

'I'm scared, Sam,' he admitted, looking into her eyes. 'I keep letting people down that I care about. I've no backbone, I'm ruled more by what's in my pants than my head. I want to run away and hide, but I can't – Livvy and the girls depend on me. You were always my rock, always there for me. But you do understand that last night was a one-off, don't you?'

Sammy swallowed hard and grabbed his hand. 'I do. Come on, let's get ready to introduce that boy of yours to his crazy, mixed-up daddy.'

* * *

Sammy and Roy were shown to the delivery suite. Jess was holding Livvy's hand and Livvy was sucking on the gas and air mouthpiece. A midwife and team of nurses stood chatting in the corner of the room.

'Liv.' Roy kissed her forehead, pushing damp curls from her eyes. 'How are you doing?'

She reached for his hand as a mighty contraction racked her. She dug her nails into his palm: 'Aaaggghhhh!'

'Ouch! Bloody hell, that hurt!' He yanked his hand away.

She took a deep breath of gas and air and glared at Roy. 'Good,' she spluttered. 'That's for last night, you bastard! And why is *she* back in here?' She looked wild-eyed at Sammy.

'She met me outside,' he said as Livvy's eyes popped and the veins in her neck bulged.

'Aaaggghhhh!' she screamed again. 'I want to push!'

Roy looked panic-stricken as the nurses sprang into action around the bed.

'Come and stand over here, Roy,' Sammy advised, pulling him out of the way. His colour drained and beads of perspiration stood out on his brow. 'You'll be no use to anyone if you pass out.'

'I hate this side of things,' he groaned. 'It's enough to put you off sex for life!'

'Well, it's never put *you* off,' she said, shaking her head.

He smiled weakly as the midwife called out, 'Here comes the head!'

Livvy screamed wildly, clutching Jess's hand. Roy's eyes rolled up into his head and Sammy half-dragged, half-carried him to a nearby chair.

'He's going,' she said as he passed out completely.

Jess shook her head. 'Pathetic,' she mouthed to Sammy, who nodded, a half-smile playing on her lips. She forced Roy's head down between his knees. Livvy was instructed to pant while the baby's shoulders were delivered. Seconds passed and a protesting wail rent the air as Roy Jnr emerged.

'He's got a good pair of lungs.' The midwife cut the umbilical cord and laid the baby on Livvy's stomach. Livvy was silent now, staring at the top of the baby's head. 'Now this cord has to be sent immediately for stem cell analysis to see if this little chap is a match for his sister,' the midwife said as she delivered the placenta.

'He's a bonny boy. We'll get him cleaned up and weighed and then you can have him back, Mum,' she said to Livvy. 'Dad still out cold, eh? Ah well, it happens.'

'He always faints at his children's births,' Sammy said, looking closely at Roy Jnr as he was weighed. 'Wow, he *is* a big boy!'

'Eight pounds ten ounces,' one of the nurses declared. 'And she's such a tiny mummy, too.'

'He's huge, considering he's early,' Sammy said, staring at Livvy as Roy stirred slightly and groaned.

'Early?' The midwife frowned and wiped the baby's face. He puckered up his lips with disapproval, his chubby fists already finding their way into his mouth. 'This little chap isn't early. If anything, he's a couple of weeks overdue. See how he's peeling on his arms and legs. He's dry –that's what happens when a baby's late.'

Sammy stared at the baby, who was looking at her now with bright blue eyes. His head bore tufts of blond hair, still streaked with blood, but blond, nevertheless. He looked nothing like she'd expected him to look. He wasn't even like Livvy, yet his features were somehow familiar. Nick, Jason, Harley and even baby Daisy had all been identical at birth, with the Cantello thick dark hair and brown eyes. This little fellow was a stranger.

As Livvy took her son into her arms, her puzzled expression was back. 'This isn't Roy Junior,' she told the midwife, 'he's blond!'

'He's like you, dear,' the midwife replied, her eyes twinkling. 'Same blue eyes too. You new mummies do come out with some gems – it must be the gas and air.'

Livvy pushed the baby away. 'Take him, Jess. This isn't my baby.'

Jess looked startled, but took hold of him. 'Of course he's yours – you just gave birth to him. Come on, Livvy, he's beautiful. Look at his lovely blue eyes. He'll probably have curls eventually, like you and Courtney.'

Livvy shook her head as the tears came. 'My baby should have dark hair and brown eyes, like Harley. He shouldn't look like Courtney,' she wailed.

As Roy opened his eyes and looked around bemusedly, Sammy knelt beside his chair. 'Roy.' She patted his cheeks gently. 'Are you okay? You fainted.'

He nodded slowly. 'Is it over?'

She smiled. 'The baby's here. He's a fine big boy, but Livvy seems very disappointed somehow. He's blond-haired and blue-eyed and she keeps saying he's not hers.'

He shook his head in bewilderment. 'Well, *she's* blonde-haired and blue-eyed. He doesn't have to look like me, does he? Have they sent the cord for analysis yet?'

'Yes,' Sammy replied, 'they did that right away. Come and see the baby now.'

He stood up and walked unsteadily across the room to Jess, who handed him the tightly wrapped bundle. The child stared unblinkingly for a moment, yawned and closed his eyes. 'Been a busy day for you, young man,' Roy said softly, smiling down at the little face, whose brow was creased in a worried frown. 'Livvy, what is it? Why do you say he's not your baby? He looks like you and Courtney. Come on, love, hold him – he needs his mommy.'

'No!' she mumbled into the pillow. 'Take him away. You have him, Jess – I don't want him.'

Roy turned to Sammy, his eyes filled with despair. 'What's wrong with her, Sam? Apart from being angry with me over last night, I mean?'

Sammy took the baby from Roy and sat down, cradling him in her arms. As she studied his features she saw what Livvy had seen. This baby was most definitely not Roy's. He was the living image of Danny McVey and he was full-term, not four weeks early, not even two. By Sammy's quick reckoning, Livvy must have been in the very early stages of pregnancy when she arrived in the country, but with no clue to her condition.

Sammy looked across at Jess, who was staring at her, eyebrows raised. A sharp nod told her that Jess had also put two and two together. Roy seemed bemused by the whole situation and was still trying to get Livvy to acknowledge him.

Sammy quickly took charge: 'I think we should let Livvy and this little man get some rest now, Roy. She's exhausted.

We'll be back in the morning, Livvy, and we'll bring the girls in to meet their brother.'

There was no response from Livvy. Roy bent to kiss her goodbye and she pushed him away. He shrugged as Sammy handed the baby to one of the nurses.

'Livvy's booked into a private suite,' Roy told the midwife, who smiled reassuringly.

'Everything's ready for them, Mr McVey, don't worry. Your wife is tired, she'll be just fine by the morning.'

Roy followed Sammy and Jess outside and smiled half-heartedly. 'That felt weird, being addressed with a dead man's name. I noticed that Roy Junior had Baby McVey on his name tag.'

Sammy raised an ironical eyebrow in Jess's direction. 'It makes it easier for Livvy to use her married name,' she said. 'They're just being PC with you. You're not telling *me* that they're the only ones in the area who didn't see you both splashed all over *The Sun* and *Mirror*.'

* * *

Sammy stared at Roy's retreating back as he left the kitchen to use the bathroom. 'Who's going to tell him?' she whispered to Jess, who had arrived at her parents' home just before Roy and Sammy and given a stunned Jane the details of the baby's birth.

'You should,' Jane said. 'You're closer to him than anyone else.'

'I'm very tempted, believe me, but it's not my place. I don't think for one minute Livvy realised she was carrying Danny's baby. She probably hadn't a clue that she was already pregnant when she slept with Roy. The shock on her face when she looked at that child was genuine, I've no doubt about that. Livvy will have to tell him that he's not the father.'

'God, what a messy situation!' Jane exclaimed. 'If, as you

say, she had no idea, then to see her dead husband's child staring at her must have come as a horrendous shock.'

Jess nodded. 'He's a beautiful baby, Mum. He weighed eight pounds ten ounces, so he's really bonny and he's got big blue eyes and tufts of blond hair. It's awful to think that Livvy's rejected him because he's not Roy's. She actually said *I* could have him. I mean, I would, but...'

Jane and Sammy stared at one another and Sammy clapped her hand to her mouth.

'Shit, I've just thought of something else! The cord's gone for analysis, to see if the baby is a match for Harley. Of course, he won't be, no more than Courtney was. Poor Harley, she was pinning all her hopes on that.'

Roy strolled back into the kitchen and sat down at the table. Jane poured him a mug of coffee and laced it with brandy. He knocked it back and looked at them.

'That's not my kid, is it?' he directed at Sammy.

She touched his hand. 'What makes you say that?'

'Somewhere in that faint I heard the midwife telling you he was overdue, not early. I couldn't bring myself round and then when I did, the baby was handed to me and I thought I must have imagined her saying it, but it makes sense now. I just worked it out that Livvy wasn't even in the country when he was conceived, so he has to be Danny's.'

Jess nodded. 'Sammy and I had already worked that out. So had Livvy, judging by her reaction.'

'Were you going to tell me, Sam?' He looked at her with such a pained expression that her heart went out to him. She put her arms around him and hugged him.

'Oh, my love! My poor Roy.' Tears poured down Sammy's cheeks as he clung to her and she sobbed against his shoulder. 'We really thought Livvy should tell you herself.' She choked on her sobs, her tears mingling with his. 'Come on home with me, you need to be somewhere quiet to get your head around this.

Jess will call Livvy's parents and the girls to tell them it's a boy and that they can visit tomorrow. You don't need to speak to anyone until you feel ready.'

He nodded and took a deep shuddering breath. 'There's nowhere on earth that I'd rather be at the moment than Jasmine House with you.'

'Come on then. Get in the car while I have a quick word with Jane. She'll speak to Ed for you and then you can call him later.'

Roy shuffled out of the kitchen as Jane stared after him. 'Jesus Christ, it never rains but it pours! How did *you* get involved, Sam? I thought you were seeing Stuart today?'

She nodded. 'I was, then Livvy picked up a text message I sent to Roy earlier, but he'd left his phone at home, you see.'

'And?' Jane prompted.

Sammy sighed and brought her up to speed.

'Would you have him back, in spite of everything?' Jane asked, putting her arms around Sammy.

'What do *you* think, Jane?'

'I don't *think*, I *know*.'

'It's madness, but I still love him,' Sammy admitted. 'And I know he still loves me, but he's got all these responsibilities now. Even though that baby isn't his, it still needs a father and he's promised to marry Livvy. That little family needs stability.'

'She might not want to marry him now,' Jane said. 'Go home and sort things out. Talk to him, help him come to terms with it. At the end of the day this was all for Harley. I guess Livvy's carried a torch for him all this time, but not for one minute do I think Roy ever meant things to get so out of hand. Once Livvy gets used to the fact that the child is Danny's, she'll love it as much as she loves the girls. She may decide to stay single and go back to the States with the kids.'

'Roy won't let Harley go, so we'd be back to square one,' Sammy said. 'By the way, Jess, thanks so much for being there.'

'Think nothing of it,' Jess said. 'Tell you what though; if she decides she really doesn't want the baby, maybe me and Jon could foster him.'

'It's not going to happen, Jess.' Jane gave her a hug. 'Don't get your hopes up, love. Anyway, I thought you two had drawn a line under that subject for now.'

'Just a thought,' Jess said wistfully.

22

Livvy stared at the luminous hands of the wall clock, eyes wide and unblinking. The time was ten thirty. She glanced around, puzzled, no thick oak beams on the ceiling, no comfy sleigh bed with its William Morris quilt, just a small single bed with a plain navy bedspread. Not her bedroom at home then. The pale-blue painted room was quiet and dimly lit by an over-bed lamp. For a long moment she felt confusion then was conscious of stillness about her body. She ran her hands over her flattened stomach and wriggled into a sitting position. So, it hadn't been a dream: she'd given birth. As she reflected, hazy snippets of the last few hours came back and she caught her breath.

Text messages for Roy from Sammy. Then Roy's anxious face and Sammy and Jess in the delivery suite. She glanced around, but there was no sign of her baby, no cot in the room. Had something awful happened? A wave of panic washed over her and she pressed the buzzer by the bed. A minute ticked slowly by before her summons was answered by a stocky nurse who greeted her with a wide smile.

'Well, *you've* certainly had a long sleep, Mrs McVey.'

'Have I?' Livvy pushed herself further up the bed.

'Let me adjust your backrest and pillows. You've been out cold for four hours. We've had to give your hungry young man a bottle to keep him going. Maybe you'd like to try and feed him now? I'll go and fetch him from the nursery.'

The nurse left as Livvy ran her hands through her tangled curls. Roy Jnr was here, but where was Roy Snr? Shouldn't he be with her? There was a telephone on the bedside table. She grabbed the receiver and dialled her home number. Her dad answered and she recalled being told that her parents had arrived from Glasgow earlier. He congratulated her, asked how she was feeling, and then Courtney's excited voice came down the line.

'Mom, congratulations! Are you okay? We're coming to see you tomorrow. I can't wait! Jess called and told us about the baby but she said you were very tired and probably wouldn't want visitors tonight.'

'Jess told you? Where's Roy?' If he wasn't at the hospital with her, then he should be at home with the girls.

'I'm not sure where he is. Jess said he's due to go to London to meet up with the group but he hasn't been home to collect his car and phone yet.'

Courtney's next words brought the events of the whole day clearly into focus for Livvy and struck a chill in her heart: 'Jess said that Roy Junior looks just like me. Isn't that nice, Mom?'

'I have to go now, Courtney,' she said abruptly. 'I'll see you tomorrow, honey.' Livvy hung up, hearing the bewilderment in her daughter's goodbye. She drew a deep breath. Roy was with Sammy, she just knew it.

Tears started as the nurse came into the room, pushing a small crib: 'He's wide awake and raring to go.' She reached into the crib and lifted the baby, handing him to Livvy, who couldn't even look at her son, although *his* bright blue eyes were firmly fixed on *her* face.

Livvy shook her head and held him at arm's length as he started to whimper. 'I can't do it, I'm sorry.'

The nurse took him back and sat on the edge of the bed. 'Are you still feeling groggy? Don't worry, I'll bottle feed him again. But if you want to breastfeed, you'll need to start soon to encourage your milk supply.'

'Don't you understand?' Livvy yelled, startling the baby, who began to cry. 'I don't want that baby. He isn't mine! Where's Roy? Where's my partner? He's not here and he's not at home either.'

The nurse looked puzzled. 'This *is* your baby, Mrs McVey. I'll get Sister, she may be able to tell you if your partner left any messages.' She placed the baby back in the crib and hurried out of the room. The child's cry was now a loud, angry wail and he was sucking hungrily on his fingers.

'Shut up! SHUT UP!' Livvy screamed, and carried on screaming as the nurse and the ward sister dashed into the room.

'Get me the duty doctor, quickly,' Sister instructed. She took hold of Livvy and held her while she sobbed against her shoulder. 'Mrs McVey, I'm Sister Munro. Calm down and tell me what's wrong.'

'That baby isn't mine,' Livvy sobbed. 'My baby should have dark hair and brown eyes, like his father.'

'Well, maybe he takes after you,' Sister Munro suggested gently. 'He has your colouring, dear.'

'But he has Danny's face,' Livvy cried. 'How can that be? Danny's dead! I was carrying Roy's child, not Danny's. Please get Roy for me, he'll tell you that this is not our son.'

Sister Munro shook her head in bewilderment. The young nurse hurried back in the room and announced that Doctor Brierly was on his way.

'Stay with Mrs McVey for a few minutes while I make some

phone calls,' Sister Munro said. 'I'll take Baby back to the nursery for now and get someone to feed him.'

* * *

Back at her desk, Sister Munro went through Livvy's file. Mrs McVey was obviously hallucinating. Maybe she'd had an adverse effect to the gas and air. Roy Cantello was listed as next of kin and father of Baby McVey. There was a mobile and home telephone number for him. A young lady answered the home number immediately.

'Dad's not here at the moment. Would you like to speak to my grandpa Peter instead?'

'Please, dear,' Sister Munro replied. A man with a Scottish accent came on the line, announced that he was Mrs McVey's father and asked how he could help.

'I'm trying to contact Roy Cantello,' Sister Munro told him. 'Mrs McVey is asking for him and we do need to speak to him as a matter of urgency.'

'Is there a problem? Are Livvy and the baby okay?'

'They're fine, there's nothing to worry about,' Sister Munro assured him. 'Mrs McVey is a little confused and we really could do with speaking to Roy.'

'We honestly don't know where Roy is at the moment. All I've been told is that he's due in London tomorrow. Just one moment, please. My granddaughter is trying to tell me something.'

Sister Munro waited patiently while Peter exchanged words with his granddaughter.

'His daughter thinks Roy may be at his old family home. Would you like the number?'

'If you wouldn't mind,' she said and scribbled it down on a pad.

'Would it be okay if I came along to see Livvy? I know it's

late, but her mother and I have driven down from Glasgow today to look after her and the girls. The baby arriving unexpectedly has thrown all our plans out of kilter.'

'That would be most helpful. I'll explain the situation in more detail when you arrive.' She hung up, breathing a sigh of relief. Mrs McVey needed to see a familiar face and in the absence of the errant partner, who better than her own father?

She tried the number she'd been given. A softly spoken woman answered the call and told her that Roy was sleeping. She asked if she could help. Sister Munro raised her eyebrows: *men!* 'We'd like Mr Cantello to come to the hospital. His partner's very distressed and asking for him. It would help us greatly if he could be here when the doctor arrives.'

There was silence for a moment and then the woman spoke again: 'I don't think it would help if Roy came to the hospital tonight. He's not the father of Mrs McVey's baby, her late husband fathered the child.'

'I see,' Sister Munro replied. 'And who shall I say I have spoken to, if Mrs McVey asks?'

'Mrs Cantello,' the woman replied. 'Roy's *wife!*' The line went dead and Sister Munro stared at the receiver, confused.

'You okay, Carol?' Staff Nurse Connor, returning from her tea break, asked.

'Not sure, Maggie.' She related the latest news on the McVey baby.

Staff Nurse Connor nodded and sat down. 'You're obviously not up to scratch with our local celebrities and their shenanigans.' She proceeded to explain the situation, as reported in the newspapers, between Livvy McVey, Roy Cantello and the late Daniel McVey.

'Well, I never!' Sister Munro exclaimed. 'Mrs Cantello, Roy's wife, who he's with at the moment, has just thrown a rather large spanner into the works. Apparently, Roy is *not* the father of Baby McVey. It's Livvy's late husband.'

'Get away,' Staff Nurse Connor said. 'Under normal circumstances, I would have thought that was a wonderful thing. At least her late hubby lives on in his son.'

'I don't think Livvy would agree with you at the moment. She obviously thought she was carrying Roy Cantello's child.'

'Roy's the father of her eldest daughter, who has leukaemia,' Staff Nurse Connor said. 'The family were hoping Baby McVey would be a bone marrow match.'

'Maybe that's what's at the bottom of the rejection,' Sister Munro said.

'Quite possibly, and if that's the case, no wonder she's hysterical. But poor little baby, it's not his fault, bless him.'

* * *

Sammy dropped the receiver onto its cradle and finished her coffee. Roy was upstairs in their bed. She'd lain with him until he'd dropped off. Although they'd held one another and kissed, he hadn't touched her and she'd felt him distancing himself until he eventually rolled away and turned his back. She'd crept downstairs as soon as she heard him snoring softly.

'I heard the phone.' Roy strode into the kitchen, yawning and scratching his head. 'Who was it?'

'The hospital,' Sammy replied. 'I told them you were sleeping.'

'What did they want?' He sank onto a kitchen chair and lit a cigarette. Sammy poured him a coffee and pushed it across the table.

'They said they want you there when the doctor arrives and because Livvy's asking for you.'

He was silent for a minute and took a sip of coffee. 'I suppose I should be with her, and I don't need this.' He stubbed out the cigarette. 'I've almost given up.'

'You're going then?' Sammy felt her stomach turn over. Of

course he was going. Last night was a one-off, he'd already told her that. And he had to sort out this mess with Livvy. 'You need to talk. Every woman's vulnerable after giving birth, but Livvy must feel like she's in the middle of a nightmare.' She tried her best to sound reasonable.

'I'm sure she does, and you know what, Sam? She'll be devastated more for Harley than for her and me. She was so hoping for a perfect match. Now we'll be back to the vagaries of the donor system.'

Sammy took his hand and gripped it tightly. 'There's nothing to stop the pair of you having a child together at a later date.' It tore at her heart to say it.

'Oh yeah,' Roy snapped, yanking his hand away. 'Like that's gonna happen. She won't want to know me now. Not after last night. I'll be surprised if she even speaks to me again. She's probably only asking for me to give me an earbashing about us.'

'Can you blame her?' Sammy said, taking his hand again. 'We've agreed that we made a mistake. You have to try and make her understand that. She'll forgive you – in time. But you've got to do a lot of begging first and make her see that you're really sorry, and mean it. Go on, Roy, get it sorted.'

She handed him her car keys and watched him walk out of the house. She wanted to run after him, grab him and not let go. But she couldn't do that, not now: Roy had to take his own path.

* * *

Peter arrived at the hospital while the doctor was with Livvy. Sister Munro invited him into her office. She made him a mug of coffee and explained the situation.

He shook his head sadly. 'My daughter's had a traumatic life,' he began and told her the sorry tale.

Sister Munro listened and nodded sympathetically as he continued: 'Livvy and Roy got back together and tried for another child to save Harley's life. Then Danny, who she was divorcing, was killed in the terrorist attacks on The World Trade Center. And now *you* tell me she's had his baby. She must be feeling so distraught after thinking she was carrying Roy's child. It must seem like Danny's reaching out from beyond the grave.'

Sister Munro nodded. 'I have to admit it's quite spooky but it's the rejection of the child I'm concerned with. Livvy and the baby could go home in a couple of days, but I have this feeling she won't want to take him with her.'

Peter sighed. 'When her daughters see their baby brother and *she* sees how delighted they are with him, maybe it will get through to her. Her mother and I are staying at the family home, so we'll all muck in to help. I know he's not going to be a life-saver for Harley, but surely we can love the wee laddie for his own worth?'

'Would you like to see the baby? Then I'll take you to Livvy.'

'Aye, hen, I would that,' Peter said and followed her to the nursery.

Sister Munro scooped up the squirming child and placed him in Peter's arms.

His eyes filled with tears as he looked down at his new grandson. 'This is a very special moment for me. I only got to know my wee girl recently. It's the first time I've held one of her children as a baby.'

Sister Munro nodded, looking tearful herself. 'Bring Baby with you to Livvy's room,' she suggested.

'Is that wise?'

'Let's just see.'

The doctor was leaving Livvy's room as they approached and he smiled at Peter. Sister Munro introduced them.

'How is my wee lassie?' Peter asked, adjusting the baby in his arms.

'Very confused,' the doctor replied. 'She's convinced the baby isn't hers. She's asking for the father. Where is he?'

'The one she thought was the father is keeping a low profile. The actual father passed away in September. He died in the 9/11 attacks in New York,' Peter replied. 'This wee boy is his living image. There's no doubt he's Danny's child.'

'I see.' The doctor frowned. 'No wonder she's in such a state. I've given her a very mild sedative to help calm her down but it won't make her sleepy. I don't want to prescribe anything too strong in case she accepts her son and wants to breastfeed.'

Sister Munro nodded. 'We'll keep a very close eye on her and we'll bottle feed Baby for now.'

'I'll pop in tomorrow morning. We should have the stem cell results back then, but I don't expect that will be an issue now.' The doctor took his leave and Sister Munro turned to Peter, her hand on the door handle to Livvy's room.

'Are you ready?'

Peter nodded and followed her in.

'I'll leave you alone for a while. Press the buzzer if you need me.'

* * *

'Hello, hen,' Peter said as Livvy stared bemusedly at him. 'How are you?'

'Dad!' She sat up and he bent to kiss her. 'Where on earth did *you* spring from?'

'Sister Munro called the house in search of Roy. I suggested I come and pay you a visit. We were leaving it until tomorrow, but it seems you need the company now.' Peter sat down on the bed and turned the baby to face her. 'You know something, hen? This wee laddie has a look of you as a baby.'

Livvy turned her face away. 'He looks like Danny. I can't

believe this has happened, Dad. How on earth have I managed to give birth to Danny's child?'

Peter shrugged. 'You must have got caught before you left LA.'

'What are the chances of that happening?' Livvy cried. 'For years I refused to have another baby with Dan. Now he's gone and he'll never know that he has the son he always wanted. And Roy, Dad, how on earth must *he* be feeling? He was so looking forward to this baby. No wonder he doesn't want to see me. I've lost him. He's gone back to Sammy, I just know it. And another thing, the baby *won't* save Harley's life.'

Peter nodded thoughtfully. 'No matter, this is a grand wee laddie and we should all love him for himself. What with *you* and Harley, don't you think we've had enough of babies being pushed from pillar to post in our family? Won't you even look at him, hen?' he cajoled. 'Here, take him.'

Livvy's eyes filled with tears at her father's words and she held out her arms. The baby snuggled into her and she traced a finger along his cheek and around the dimple in his chin, so like Daniel's. She smiled as he wrinkled his brow and his eyes shot open to stare accusingly at her for waking him. Her tears dripped onto his face and he pouted. 'I'm so sorry, Baby,' she sobbed, holding him tightly. 'It's not your fault. It's really not your fault.'

Peter hardly dared breathe as Livvy cried heartbrokenly. He moved to sit beside her and held her in his arms, rocking mother and child. 'See, hen,' he whispered into her hair, 'it's not so difficult, is it? At the end of the day it doesn't matter who fathered him. He's yours, he's absolutely perfect and that's all that counts.'

'Thank you, Dad, for being here with me. It means such a lot.' She smiled through her tears as the baby grunted and aimed his fist into his mouth. 'He's hungry again. This one's going to take some filling. I probably won't be able to keep up with him.'

'Well, there are two willing mother hens back at the house to help you, three if you count your mother!' Peter laughed.

'How on earth am I going to explain to Harley that Roy isn't his father?' she groaned. 'I've let her down so badly.'

Neither heard the door open until Roy's deep voice disturbed them.

'You've let no one down and don't you worry about Harley – *I'll* be explaining things to her.'

'Roy!' Livvy stared open-mouthed as he strode purposefully across the room and sat down on the bed opposite Peter. 'Oh, Roy, I'm so sorry. I had no idea...' she tailed off, sobbing.

'Stop beating yourself up, Liv. I know you didn't.' Roy took the baby from her. He smiled as he looked at the child, who was sucking on his fingers. 'Hungry, are you, little fella? Is your mother starving you? Well, are you going to feed him, or what? I can't do it – I don't have the equipment!'

Livvy smiled through her tears as her father coughed and stood up. 'I'll just nip out and find Sister Munro while you give Baby his supper.'

* * *

As Livvy settled back to feed her son for the first time, she looked closely at Roy. His eyes were red-rimmed and she knew he'd been crying. He had a defeated air about him and in spite of her anger and sorrow at last night's betrayal, her heart went out to him. He must be feeling so disappointed. 'Why are you here?'

'Why do you think?' he said as the baby latched onto her breast and sucked noisily. 'Blimey! He knows what to do and *no* messing.' He ran his thumbs down her tear-stained cheeks and kissed the tip of her nose. 'I'm here because I love you, simple as that.'

'But he's not yours, and after last night, I thought you wanted to be with Sammy.'

'So did I,' he said softly. 'But it really was a one-off. As for the baby not being mine... well, he is in a way. I've watched him grow while you've carried him. I've sung to him through your tummy and talked to him about what we'll do when he arrives. I saw him on the scans and I've been with you every step of the way. I'm sorry I fainted at his birth. I'm crap at that sort of thing. I want us to be together, Liv, if *you* still want *me*, that is, and if you can forgive me for last night.'

'Oh, Roy. Can *you* forgive *me* for having Danny's child? I feel like *I've* cheated on you.'

'You haven't.'

She smiled. 'We'll be okay, Roy. We'll make it work.'

'We'll try,' he said huskily. 'Do you still want to marry me?'

'Yes. The sooner the better, and then you're mine.'

He nodded. 'I've been having a think on the way here in the taxi. Once you've recovered from *this* birth, we can try right away for Roy Junior – for Harley.'

She grimaced and punched him on the arm. 'You'd never want sex again if *you'd* just given birth to *him* this afternoon!'

He held out his right hand, showing her the wheals left by her nails earlier. 'I've got my own war wounds from the delivery.' The baby stopped sucking and let go of her nipple with a contented sigh. 'He's had enough. I'll put him in the crib and then I can hold you properly before your dad comes back. By the way, we can't keep calling him Baby and Roy Junior doesn't seem appropriate somehow.'

Livvy nodded. 'We'll save that for *our* son. We should call him Daniel after his dad and Peter after *my* dad.'

'Sounds okay to me,' Roy agreed. 'I'll bring the girls in the morning. I have to go to London for recording later in the afternoon, but I'll be back at the weekend.'

'Okay,' Livvy said as her father and Sister Munro came into the room.

'Well, *he* seems a happy little chap,' Sister said as she gazed down at the sleeping baby.

Livvy nodded. 'He fed very well. This is Roy, my husband-to-be,' she introduced him to Sister Munro. 'We've named our son,' she announced proudly.

'Daniel Peter,' Roy told them.

Peter nodded delightedly. 'That's a grand name! Gina will be thrilled to bits when I go home and tell her. Talking of home, I suppose I'd better be making tracks. What about you, Roy? Where will you be spending the night?'

'At Charlecote Cottage,' he replied. 'That *is* my home. Will you follow me, Peter? I'll drop Sammy's car off and come back with you. When you and Daniel are ready, we'll go house-hunting,' he said to Livvy. 'We're bursting at the seams now and when Roy Junior *does* finally grace us with his presence, well...'

Livvy grinned as her father and Sister Munro looked on with puzzled amusement.

'Don't push your luck, Cantello. Now go home and leave Daniel and me in peace. We both need some sleep. I'll see you tomorrow.'

23

Livvy looked out of the kitchen French doors, over the gardens and to the hills beyond. There was nothing getting in the way of *this* particular view. Not like the last place they'd looked at, a spacious old farmhouse, where the kind, elderly vendor had given them tea and home-made cakes, but the busy A34 running right behind the back garden had put them off. *This* fabulous house was set well back from the road. It had electric gates and a long driveway. Livvy ran her hand over the black marble worktop. It felt cool to the touch. The glossy white units and appliances were top of the range. She could picture herself cooking their first Sunday lunch here. The house was neutrally decorated but still retained original features and it was ready to move into. They'd soon put their own stamp on the place. She turned as Harley and Courtney came into the kitchen, all smiles.

'Well, what do you think, girls?'

'We love it,' Harley enthused. 'We can have an en suite bedroom each. There's a great room upstairs, like a man's play-room with a snooker table and a bar, but we thought it would make a fabulous sitting room for us and our friends.'

Livvy laughed. 'You'll have to wait and see what Roy says. He might have that one earmarked for his music room if the outside building isn't right.' She looked out of the window again and waved at Roy, who was standing on the patio, talking to the estate agent, with eight-week-old Daniel strapped to his front in a harness. The man pointed to a two-storey red-brick outbuilding further down the garden. In the brochure it had been described as an artist's studio, but Roy was hoping it would be big enough to convert to a recording studio and rehearsal room. He came back indoors, the eager agent on his heels.

'Everybody happy with what they've seen so far?' Roy asked.

'Yeah,' the girls chorused.

'Liv?' He put his arm around her shoulders and gave her a squeeze. 'Do you think this is the one?'

She nodded. 'Let's go home and talk about it. We'll give our decision tomorrow.'

They said goodbye to the agent and Roy promised to call him the next day with an answer. They piled into the BMW and Livvy looked back at Ashlea Grange as they swept down the drive. It was perfect. With its Tudor frontage, lofty gables and tall chimneys, it was the sort of grand old house she'd always dreamed of living in. The seven bedrooms would soon be filled; four immediately, another when Roy Jnr put in an appearance and a couple of spares for visitors. She could picture them living in it already and hugged herself with excitement. The house was only a ten-minute drive from the girls' school and not too far from Jane and Eddie's place, which would please Roy.

Courtney and Harley were talking animatedly in the back, with Daniel in his car seat, between them – her perfect little family. Never in her wildest dreams had she thought this would ever be possible. She looked at Roy's profile, as he negotiated a right turn onto Ashlea Road, and felt her heart swell with love. He'd aged a bit these last six months and his thick dark hair was being overtaken by more silver threads, but it was hard to believe he'd be sixty this year. He still had a boyish charm and the ability to make her stomach flip and her legs turn to jelly when he took her in his arms.

'Shall we eat out, early doors?' he said, smiling at her.

'I need to feed Daniel,' she said. 'Drop me at the cottage and take the girls for a pizza or something.'

'We want to go straight home, Dad,' Harley told him. 'Jack and Jamie are coming over later, we've got important stuff to talk about.'

'Okay, just a thought,' Roy said. 'I'll send out for pizzas when the lads come round.'

'You and I need to talk on our own, too,' Livvy said. 'There's a lot to discuss.'

* * *

Livvy looked up as Roy placed a mug of tea on the bedside table. Daniel had just finished feeding. Roy picked him up, tucked him into the swinging cradle and joined her on the bed.

'Give me a cuddle,' he said, snuggling up to her.

'I smell all milky and mumsy.' She laughed and kissed him.

'You don't, you smell wonderful, like you always do.' He leant up onto one elbow and looked into her eyes. 'So... Ashlea Grange. Is it a yes... or what? The girls have been mithering me to death in the kitchen. They've mentally moved in already. They want the games room for their own sitting room, if I can get that studio sorted for *my* playroom.'

She nodded. 'It's a yes from me. It's the most perfect house. My dream home, in fact. But it's enormous – it'll take some filling.'

'I'll call the agent tomorrow, put in an offer of one point four million and we'll start choosing furniture,' Roy said. 'We're lucky the builders have done a good job. It couldn't have been better if we'd designed it ourselves. We can probably be in within the month if the agent and solicitors get their finger out. Not like we need a mortgage, is it?'

'I don't suppose they get many cash sales on properties over a million.' Livvy laughed. 'That agent was practically on his knees. He'll move heaven and earth if we ask him.'

'Once we're in and sorted, we'll get married before The Raiders go on tour,' Roy said, twiddling her curls around his fingers. He looked across at the crib and smiled. 'And then...'

She grinned. 'We'll definitely start Roy Junior.' She patted her stomach. 'If we haven't already!' She looked closely at Roy: 'Are you happy? I mean, truly happy? It's been a horrible last twelve months for us all. I hope we've turned a corner at last. Do you have any regrets?'

He shrugged. 'A few, but now that I've finally got my head together, I'm happy enough, sweetheart. The icing on the cake for me will be Harley in remission.'

'What about Sammy?' she asked, knowing they needed to talk about Sammy's recent announcement that she and Stuart were tying the knot in Portugal at the end of the month. Roy had been a bit withdrawn and reluctant to talk about it since Jason had called him with the news.

He was quiet for a long moment before replying. 'If I'm honest, I think she's rushing it a bit, but it's not really my business and as long as she's happy, that's all that matters. Jane, Ed, Pat, Tim and the Greys are going to the wedding and Jason, Jules and Daisy, of course – we're not invited.'

'Well, that's hardly surprising. Surely you weren't expecting an invite?'

'I thought she might have asked Harley.'

'She did. Harley wasn't sure she'd feel up to flying. She didn't tell you because she thought it might upset you.'

'Oh... well that makes me feel better actually. I felt as though Sam was rejecting Harley and after bringing her up all these years... well, I guess the least she can do is invite her to the wedding.'

Livvy stretched her arms above her head and smiled. 'I'm gonna jump in the shower while Daniel's sleeping. Why don't you go and see the girls and get the pizzas ordered?'

* * *

Roy and Livvy were curled up on the sofa watching TV, with Daniel asleep in his Moses basket on the coffee table, when Harley and Jack popped their heads around the lounge door.

'Hi, you two,' Roy said. 'What's up? You look a bit anxious.'

'Can we talk to you for a minute?' Harley said as they slid into the room, hand in hand.

Roy swung his legs down and sat up. 'Sure. What's on your mind, princess?'

'Well,' Harley began, 'as you know, I'll soon be seventeen.'

'Bloody hell, that year's gone quick!' Roy exclaimed, picking up his glass and taking a swig of single malt. 'And?'

'Well, you know me and Jack have been engaged for a year now and with me being ill, and everything... and... well, we don't know if I'm ever going to be really right again, do we? I mean, my next blood tests might not be good ones and we haven't got a donor yet, until you two—'

'What Harley's trying to say,' Jack interrupted, his cheeks flushing bright red, 'is that we want to get married.'

'What?' Roy spluttered on his drink. Livvy took the glass from him and slapped him between the shoulder blades. 'Married?' he continued. 'For God's sake, you're far too young!'

'We love one another,' Harley said. 'I don't know how long I've got left, Dad. If I don't go into remission or get a transplant,

I might not be here this time next year. You'll regret not saying yes then.'

'Harley, don't blackmail me. This is serious stuff. Jess and Jon will never agree to it.'

'I've already talked it over with Mum,' Jack said. 'She says I've to ask Dad later, depending on what you and Livvy say. Pops and Grandma think it's a nice idea too.'

'Oh, they do, do they?' Roy raised his eyebrows. 'So we're the last to know... apart from Jon?'

'Roy...' Livvy grabbed his hand to stop him gesticulating wildly. 'Take it easy. Harley and Jack have gone through a lot for such a young couple. Listen to what they have to say before you go off on one.'

'Thanks, Mom,' Harley said. 'Dad, if we get a couple of years of marriage it's better than nothing and it would mean everything to us.' She went to sit on Roy's knee and wound her arms around his neck. 'Don't you want me to be happy? Please, you said you'd do anything for me.'

Roy looked at Livvy, whose eyes were filling. He took a deep breath. 'Jack's not even seventeen until June,' he said, grasping at straws and feeling outnumbered. 'I can't believe that Jess thinks this is okay. I'm damn sure Jon won't. Have you thought about where you'll live and what you'll do for money? You're still at school until July and then you were supposed to be going to college.' He narrowed his eyes and looked closely at Harley. 'I hope you're not pregnant, young lady. Is that what this is all about?'

'Of course not,' Harley said indignantly. 'We haven't even done anything since the condom split last year – I've been too ill. Anyway, I might never be able to have babies after all the chemo.'

Livvy put her arms around Harley and hugged her. 'You will one day, darling. At least they saved some of your eggs, and in time, you and Jack can have IVF, if necessary.'

Roy swallowed hard and looked at his daughter's face. There were still dark circles under her eyes. Her hair was growing back thick and dark, but her new urchin cut made her look vulnerable, like a little girl. The thought that he might lose her in a year or two filled him with dread. He just hoped and prayed that Livvy would soon announce she was in the club. Oh, what the hell! Who was he to stand in the way of Jack and Harley's happiness, for however long it lasted? 'Okay,' he said, nodding slowly, 'you have my permission, on two conditions: that you live with us in the new place until you're older and you both finish your education.'

Harley and Jack whooped and hugged each other.

'Thank you, Dad,' Harley cried, tears running down her cheeks. Jack nodded, his lips trembling.

'So... that's two weddings to organise,' Livvy said, smiling. 'Three if you count my parents, who also want to get married this year.'

'Oh, wow! We could all get married at the same time,' Harley said. 'One big family wedding. Three generations. That would be a great spread for *Hello!*, Mom.'

'What a wonderful idea,' Livvy said, her face animated. 'Not so much the *Hello!* spread, but the family wedding. I'll speak to Mum and Dad tomorrow.' She looked across as the door opened again and Courtney and Jamie walked in.

'Well?' Courtney said to Harley.

'They said yes,' Harley yelled, sticking her thumbs up.

'I can be your bridesmaid,' Courtney yelled back, jumping up and down with excitement and waking Daniel, who screamed loudly.

'Now see what you've done,' Roy said above the racket. He picked up Daniel, who stared at everyone, blue eyes wide. 'I'm not surprised you look shocked, son. We're surrounded by mad women. And don't you even think about it,' he directed at Courtney.

'Not yet.' Courtney laughed. 'Jamie and I have plans to travel the world when we've finished school. We want to try and visit nearly every country.'

'Well, thank God for that,' Roy said. 'Three weddings at once are more than enough. Four would put me in an early grave.'

'Four weddings and a funeral,' Harley quipped. 'Sorry, Dad. I shouldn't even joke about such things,' she said as Roy frowned at her.

'All we've got to do now is convince *my* dad,' Jack said, changing the subject. 'That's not going to be easy.'

'Tell you what, Jack,' Roy said, 'we'll invite your mum and dad over tomorrow night for a meal. Get a few drinks down them and discuss it then.'

Livvy nodded and smiled. 'Good idea. And if anything, Jack, Roy can be very persuasive when the fancy takes him. You might just get a positive response.'

'Thanks,' Jack said, looking relieved. 'We thought the end of April would be nice and then I'm only a couple of months off being seventeen.'

* * *

Sammy stepped onto the deck, leant against the rail and stared out across the vineyards. The day was clear and the late April sun felt warm on her lightly tanned legs. She turned as Stuart came up behind her and slipped his arms around her waist.

'You okay, Sam?'

She kissed him, looking into his kindly green eyes. 'Yeah, just getting my head together to call Harley and wish her good luck for today. Then I'll sort out the bedroom for her and Jack. I can't wait to see her again. Can't believe my little girl is getting married. Doesn't seem five minutes since she learned to walk and talk.' She tried to keep her voice bright, but it cracked and she could feel tears welling. She choked on her next words: 'I'd love to see her taking her vows.'

Stuart wiped her eyes with gentle fingers. He held her close. 'We could have gone to the wedding. After all, they *did* invite us. It was you that refused.'

She shook her head. 'I couldn't do it. It's Roy's wedding day, too. Don't want to freak Livvy out. Better I keep away. But we'll make sure Harley and Jack have the best honeymoon ever.'

'And they will,' he said.

The newly-weds were arriving on Monday.

'I'll pop out and get the flowers and bubbly while you make the place all fancy for them. See you later. Love you.' He kissed the tip of her nose and ruffled her hair.

'Love you, too.' She went back inside and poured herself a glass of wine. Bit early, but still, it would help relax her. She ran her finger over the bottle label and smiled. Vida Nova Tinto, from Cliff Richard's own estate. She remembered going to see Cliff and The Shadows play the ABC Ardwick with Jane and Pat while they were all still at school. The Mersey Square girls... Who'd have thought that forty years later, she'd be his near neighbour on the Algarve? Life was certainly strange. She sat at the kitchen table and flipped open her mobile phone. Damn, a missed call. She hadn't heard it ring. Must have been while she was taking a shower and Stuart was out for his morning run.

The call had come from Roy's landline. No doubt Harley, but she hadn't left a message. Sammy dialled the number her heart drumming so loud, she felt her ears might explode. 'Please let Harley answer,' she muttered. She didn't want to speak to Roy. Not today, anyway. She couldn't bear it. She was finding it so hard to accept that their marriage really was over and that after all those years, and everything they'd meant to each other, they could be no more than civil at family get-togethers.

It hadn't been easy at Daisy's recent christening, which she'd hosted at her new cottage. But she'd done her best to smile, be pleasant to Livvy and make a fuss of baby Daniel. It hadn't been too difficult; he was a gorgeous baby with his big blue eyes and sunny smile. Whenever she'd tried to speak to Roy alone, Livvy had loomed into view and stuck to his arm like Velcro. Sammy had given up in the end and kept her distance for the rest of the afternoon. She'd caught Roy staring at her a few times, but she'd ignored him and thrown herself into Hostess with the Mostess mode.

She loved Stuart, but it wasn't with the fierce intensity and passion that she loved Roy. Stuart had been thoughtful and kind since their marriage, leaving her alone when he sensed she needed it, being there and strong for her when she'd cried. They were fairly compatible between the sheets, but he wasn't her soulmate and she knew deep down that she shouldn't have married him. She wished he'd argue with her now and again; disagree occasionally, instead of hanging onto her every word. *Anything* to arouse a bit of full-on passion when making up. She was going to have to try very hard to make things work and she didn't really know that she'd got it in her. She'd even faked an orgasm the other night for the first time in her life. She was about to hang up when the phone line clicked and she caught her breath.

'Ashlea Grange, Roy Cantello.'

'It's me,' she said, her stomach flipping as she heard Roy's deep voice. There was an awkward silence for a minute before he responded.

'Hi, you. Tried to get hold of you earlier.'

His voice had a friendly edge and she relaxed. 'I saw the missed call, thought it might have been Harley. Didn't hear the phone ring. What... err... what did you want me for?' Was he going to tell her it was all a mistake with Livvy and he wanted her to come home and start again? Her head was a in a whirl. She shouldn't be thinking like this. She held her breath, waiting for those life-changing words. *Get a grip, stupid mare*, her inner voice mocked. You *gave Roy his marching orders in the first place. Now you're married to Stuart, who loves you, and Roy's marrying Livvy – today – so get used to it.*

'You need to be sitting down, Sam.'

He had changed his mind. She knew he would. He wanted them to try again. Her heart thudded louder still, deafening her, and she almost missed his next words.

'The hospital called earlier. It's fantastic news: Harley's last tests show that she's in remission.' Roy's voice wavered as he spoke. 'It's the best news we could have hoped for, especially today. Sam, are you there? Sam?'

She swallowed hard. 'It's wonderful news, Roy.' Tears tumbled down her cheeks.

'She may still need a transplant, but it's a huge weight lifted from our shoulders. She and Jack can get on with enjoying their day now. Look after her while she's with you, Sam. Make sure she doesn't exhaust herself. It's really good of you to have them stay. I'd have been worried to death if they'd gone off somewhere on their own.'

'It's our pleasure, Roy. She *is* my daughter, and of course we'll look after her.' She drew a deep breath and forced a half-smile. 'I'm not quite sure what to say to you now. Will Happy Wedding Day do?'

'It'll do just fine. I'll call you Monday when we've seen their flight off.'

'Okay.' She forced herself out of courtesy to ask, but not really wanting to know: 'You and Livvy jetting off anywhere yourselves?'

'Not until after the tour. No time before that and then there's Daniel to consider. Livvy's parents said they'll come and stay whenever we're ready to take a break. They're off to Paris for their honeymoon.'

'Of course, I forgot that her parents are getting married

today as well. Blimey, it must be some sort of record! Have a good day then... and Roy?'

'Yeah?'

'Congratulations. I'll see you when we bring Harley and Jack home.'

'Thanks, Sam. Are you staying in Cheshire long enough to see a gig or two?'

'Definitely. Stu's looking forward to reliving his youth.'

'And what about you? Are you looking forward to reliving yours?'

He caught her off guard and a loud sob choked her next words: 'Maybe, but it won't be the same.'

'I'll catch up with you then. I'll get Harley for you. I'm keeping out of the way – I'm not allowed to see anything until they're all ready.'

'I'm surprised you're even allowed in the house. It's bad luck to see the bride.'

'I'll clear off to the music room in a minute, but I have to be here. I'm travelling to church with Harley, and Livvy's dad's travelling with her to give her away, so he's dodging around as well, to avoid seeing Gina.'

Sammy smiled, picturing the two of them getting under feet. 'Who's giving Gina away?'

'Livvy's brother, Peter.'

'It's quite a feat to pull it all off and have everything go smoothly. Well... goodbye, Roy, and good luck to you all.'

Roy said goodbye and she heard him calling for Harley and the sound of running footsteps and then Harley's breathless voice.

'Mum, hi. How are you? Oh, Mum, I so wish you were here!' Harley's voice broke and it took all of Sammy's strength not to cry and upset her daughter further.

'It's best I'm not, darling. It's Livvy's special day too and I don't want to spoil it. I'll see you and Jack on Monday, I'm really looking forward to your visit.'

'Me too, Mum. I can't wait to see you. Did Dad tell you the good news?'

'He did. I'm thrilled to bits, sweetheart.'

'And me. I can't wait to tell Jack. I'm saving it as the best wedding present of all. You should see my dress, Mum. It's white silk and long and floaty and Courtney's bridesmaid's dress is blue and matches her eyes. The hairdressers are here at the moment and the lady to do our make-up and nails.'

Sammy smiled as she pictured Harley, excited, cheeks flushed and waving her hand in the air to describe things, just as she'd done as a little girl. 'Make sure there are lots of photos.'

'Oh, we will. Dad's having it all filmed so you'll be able to see it when we get copies done.'

Sammy grimaced as she thought about the likelihood of press invasion, or maybe not, if they'd kept things as secret as she and Stuart had. But a triple wedding would be impossible to keep quiet. Especially with Roy and Livvy being front-page news and splashed all over *Hello!* last month with young Daniel and the girls. That would be Livvy's doing, no doubt: showing the world they were now officially an item. Roy had always hated that sort of celebrity stuff. 'Well, you have a great day and we'll see you Monday. Bye, darling, love to Jack. And, Harley, I love you so much.'

'I love you, too, Mum.'

Sammy ended the call. She'd give her right arm to be at her girl's wedding, but knew for a fact that she'd be unable to stop herself shouting out during Roy and Livvy's vows, like Benjamin Braddock during Elaine's marriage in the film *The Graduate*. She looked up as Stuart walked into the kitchen, arms laden with tightly furled pink and red rose buds.

'Those are lovely,' she said as he placed them on the table. 'Right, I'd better get on with things. The roses can sit in the bathroom in buckets until tomorrow. We'll transfer them to the vases tomorrow night.'

'Did you speak to Harley?' he asked, following her into the utility room, where she rummaged in a cupboard for buckets.

'I did. *And* I spoke to Roy. And guess what? Harley's in remission. They got the call from the hospital this morning. How wonderful is that? On her wedding day, too.'

Stuart's face broke into a wide smile and he took the buckets from her and waltzed her round the room. 'Bloody marvellous,' he said. 'What a relief. I'm so pleased. I bet Roy's relieved too. It can't have been easy for him this last twelve months.'

'It hasn't. But things are taking a turn for the better at last.'

'Good.' He kissed her. 'I love you, Mrs Green.'

'Who?' Sammy looked over her shoulder with a mock-puzzled expression. 'Oh... you mean me!' she teased. 'I keep forgetting I'm Mrs Green now.'

Stuart laughed and raised his eyebrows. 'Do you indeed? Then maybe I can think of a way of reminding you!'

* * *

Livvy flapped her hands in the air to dry her nails. She wished she'd opted for something simpler, but the nail artist had suggested decorative diamond chips and the glue was taking a while to set. She wondered how Jess was getting along, looking after Daniel. She was sure he'd be fine, but her arms ached for her baby boy. It was hard to believe now that she'd rejected him; she loved him so much. Jess had insisted she take him for the day and keep him until tomorrow so that Livvy and Roy could have an undisturbed first night of marriage.

Roy had booked the honeymoon suite of a hotel in the Cheshire countryside and Jane had told her that she and Eddie had spent their honeymoon in the same place thirty-eight years ago. Well, those two had been blissfully happy all their married life, so Livvy was hoping it was a good omen. They'd hardly spent a night together since moving into the new place. Daniel was a light sleeper and Roy woke him constantly, coming to bed late, banging around and snoring. She planned on putting Daniel in his own room soon; otherwise, Roy was going to be getting fed up of being packed off to the spare room. She couldn't believe that she was about to become Mrs Cantello, that she'd got him at last. It was a dream she'd carried since she'd first met Roy in 1984.

Her sister Leanne popped her head around the door, a big grin splitting her face. She was followed by Sheena, also grinning. Both bridesmaids were dressed in full-length, jade-green silk, hair and make-up immaculate.

'Wow, you two look fabulous!' Livvy exclaimed.

'We've come to help you get dressed,' Sheena announced. 'Harley and Courtney are ready. Your mum's all sorted and the men are ponced up in their suits, except for Roy. Bit of a nightmare, reminding them who's supposed to be where and who's doing what, but I think they've got the gist.'

'Is Roy okay?' Livvy asked, wondering why he hadn't got his suit on.

'Haven't seen him for a while,' Sheena replied. 'Think he's gone down the garden to his music room. Thought we'd leave him in peace – he looked like he could use a wee bit of space.'

Livvy frowned. 'Why?'

Sheena shrugged. 'Don't know. He was talking on the phone for ages, then he called for Harley and disappeared.'

Livvy felt a shiver run down her spine. 'Was he speaking to Sammy?'

'Not sure. I didn't stay in the room with him.'

Livvy told herself not to be stupid. What did it matter if he *had* spoken to Sammy? He was hers now, well almost, and Sammy was no threat, married to Stuart, and far away in Portugal. She went back to talking wedding plans. 'Yeah, Roy's got to escort Harley first, then take his place as a bridegroom and then Dad's escorting me and taking *his* place as bridegroom. It's simple enough for Jack, he'll already be there and waiting. The rehearsal went okay the other night, so fingers crossed. The one thing I'm sad about is that I can't watch Harley walk down the aisle on Roy's arm, because I'm next with Dad, and Roy can't see *me* until then. Ah well, I'll have to watch the recordings.'

'Who's first for the ceremony?' Sheena asked as she lifted Livvy's ivory silk dress from the hanger.

'Jack and Harley, then Mum and Dad and Roy and me are last.' Livvy took off her bathrobe and Sheena and Leanne slipped the dress over her head. They fastened the row of tiny covered buttons down the back and stepped away to look. The full-length gown had a sleeveless, tight-fitting, boned bodice, a straight skirt at the front and a fish-tail train at the back.

'Oh my God, you look fantastic,' Sheena said.

Livvy looked in the mirror and put her hands over her mouth. 'I look like a princess,' she whispered, close to tears. 'Oh, don't let me cry, I'll ruin my make-up. Tell me something funny, make me laugh.'

But Sheena and Leanne were lost for words and just stood there smiling.

'Why aren't you and Roy getting married before your mum and dad?' Leanne broke the silence, smoothing out the fish-tail train. 'Like... youngest first, oldest last.'

'Because *Hello!* wants us to be last,' Livvy replied. 'And actually, Roy *is* the oldest. Right, that's me ready. Just need a few minutes to myself, if you don't mind.'

'Not at all.' Sheena smiled. 'We'll go and get Jason to organise his dad. He's just arrived with Jules and Daisy. Have you got your something borrowed, something blue, etcetera?'

Livvy nodded. 'Yep. See you soon. Shout me when the cars arrive.'

As Sheena and Leanne left the room, Livvy hurried into the en suite. She glanced in the mirror and fluffed out a couple of soft curly tendrils around her face. She reached on the windowsill for a white plastic stick, lifted her skirt and slipped the stick down the side of her blue garter. Roy would have such a surprise when he found it later – her little bit of something blue. Not only would they be celebrating their first night together as Mr and Mrs Cantello and the knowledge that their daughter was in remission, but also the fact that Roy Jnr or whoever, was on the way.

24

Roy rolled a fat joint and sat with his feet up on the mixing desk, his favourite position for thinking. He shouldn't be doing this. He was supposed to be getting dressed up, but stuff it. He took a long toke and closed his eyes, waiting for the hit. Speaking to Sammy earlier had left him feeling very unsettled. Perhaps as well she'd refused her invitation to Harley's wedding. Seeing her again, and on Stuart's arm, would have been too much to cope with. He'd got enough on his plate. Strange that, *his* wedding day too, but the only invite to go out to Sammy and Stu was from Harley and Jack – Livvy refused to add them to their list of friends.

His mind went over the few weeks since they'd moved into Ashlea Grange. The girls had settled well, loving the freedom of having their own sitting room. Arrangements for the triple wedding had taken precedence over everything. Livvy had turned into wedding-planner obsessive, constantly on the phone to dressmakers, caterers *and* her mother. And if it wasn't the wedding plans, it was seeing to Daniel.

He was feeling a bit neglected and surplus to requirements. Whenever he'd made a suggestion she'd smiled sweetly and told him it was all in hand. He'd been sent to the spare room a lot lately – Livvy had told him that his snoring kept her awake and disturbed Daniel. He'd suggested Daniel be put in his own room with a monitor, but Livvy said he was too young. Roy couldn't ever recall Nick and Jason in the same room as him and Sammy. But he'd been on the road a lot when they were babies and maybe Sam had shipped them out to their own rooms on the rare nights he was home. Sammy had never complained that he snored, or made him sleep alone, except at the start of his affair with Livvy, years ago. He could picture her now, all excited, getting ready to have Harley and Jack to stay. She should be here, she had as much right as Livvy to be here – all daughters needed their mums on their wedding day.

He rooted in his desk drawer and took out a framed photo of him and Sammy as teenagers, dressed in jeans and matching long leather coats, taken after a local gig. He refused to part with it, but kept it out of Livvy's sight. Sammy, her waist-length hair hanging down her back, was looking lovingly into his eyes and he had his arms around her. He took another lengthy drag and smiled. Sweet bliss. First dope he'd had since moving in with Livvy, and boy, did he need it. He'd spent a lot of time lately with Ed and the lads, and plans for the final tour were complete. The first gig, at Manchester Arena, was the charity gig to raise funds for leukaemia research. He couldn't wait to get back on the road and wished now that it wasn't for the last time.

He'd been dying for a good reason to call Sammy this week, just needed to hear her voice. This morning's news about Harley had been the perfect excuse. When she didn't pick up his call, he'd wondered if she was ignoring him on purpose. She'd almost ignored him at Daisy's christening and that had hurt. But then she'd called him back and it had taken him by surprise. He'd felt a bit strange talking to her at first. Weird that, how he could feel awkward, talking to a woman whose every inch he'd kissed, explored and loved for over forty years.

He sometimes felt like he wanted to run screaming into her arms, just to get away from all this responsibility. It was too much at his age. Not that he didn't love Livvy and the kids; they were very important to him and he was pretty sure Livvy was pregnant again. He'd heard her throwing up a couple of times and she had that certain look about her. Although she hadn't said anything to him yet, all being well, Harley's match was on the way. He'd fulfilled his responsibility on that score, at least.

Probably wouldn't matter a jot to Livvy now if he slept in the spare room for the rest of his life. She'd got what she came for. Sammy had been right in her assumptions, even though Daniel had arrived instead of Roy Jnr. There'd been a bit of a change in his and Livvy's relationship when he'd asked her for the truth a few weeks ago. He felt betrayed in a stupid sort of way and had sulked for a while and started smoking again, although he'd forgiven her eventually, because he couldn't stand atmospheres.

As the cannabis worked its magic he picked up an old acoustic and began to strum. His eyes filled with sudden tears as he realised he was playing the opening chords to 'My Special Girl'. His phone rang out and he glanced at the screen and saw Ed's name.

'Hi, mate,' he said, picking up.

'You okay, Roy? You sound a bit choked. I called the house and Livvy's dad told me you're in hiding. Poor guy sounds like he needs some space too.'

'I'd ask him down here,' Roy said, 'but I'm chilling with a joint and I don't think he'd approve.'

'I'd come and join you, but we need to be making for the church shortly. Jane's just upstairs, talking to Sammy on the house phone.'

'I spoke to Sammy this morning,' Roy said, a strange feeling creeping down his spine. 'I miss her like crazy, Ed. I can't tell anyone else that.'

Eddie was quiet for a moment, as though considering his reply. 'I'm sure you do. But she's fine and seems happy enough with Stu. And you're gonna have a stunning new wife in less than a couple of hours. So, cheer up, mate, and stub that joint out. It's making you maudlin. You don't wanna be stoned, walking your daughter up the aisle. Go back to the house and wait for the cars. I'll see you at the church and before you ask, yes, the rings are in my pocket. Strange really, I never thought I'd be best man to you again.'

'No, quite,' Roy said softly.

He said goodbye, feeling even more despondent as he thought back to his and Sammy's wedding day, all those years ago. The Raiders had just finished their first European tour and Sammy had been pregnant with Nick. They'd been totally in love with so much to look forward to. Now he was due to marry Livvy in the very same church where he'd married Sammy, and then buried Nick, eighteen years later. He'd also retaken his marriage vows there that same year.

Why on earth had he allowed Livvy to book the same church? Had she done it on purpose? Mind you, there wasn't another church for miles, so maybe not. But it was a bit insensitive if she had. He should have put his foot down and insisted that he got more involved with the plans. Too bloody late now. He took another couple of lengthy tokes and stubbed the end out in the ashtray. He shoved it on a high shelf out of reach. Hide the evidence from Livvy, or she'd be giving him earache, something Sammy never did. He'd better stop this comparing or he'd drive himself nuts. His shoulders shook and tears ran down his cheeks. Everything was his fault and it was impossible now to put it all right.

There was a gentle tap at the door and Jason popped his head around.

'Dad, what's wrong?' Jason moved to his side and put an

arm around his shoulders. 'Are you feeling okay? You look really pale.'

Roy looked up through his tears. 'I don't know that I can do this, son. I need your mum.'

Jason shook his head and wafted his hands in the air to dispel the smoke. 'Oh, Dad, come on, pull yourself together. You shouldn't have had a spliff. It won't help your state of mind. Mum's married to Stu now. You've got to let go. She's moved on. It's time *you* did too. Livvy loves you and Harley's waiting for you to escort her to church. Wait till you see her, Dad, she looks amazing. You'll be so proud of your little girl.'

At Jason's words, Roy sat with his head in his hands, his body convulsed with sobs.

Jason continued. 'Come on, Dad, please. You can't let them down. Come indoors and put your suit on.'

Roy got unsteadily to his feet and allowed Jason to lead him inside the house by the side door. Jason took him upstairs and pushed him into the spare room, where his morning suit was hanging.

'I'm going to go and find Jules and Daisy now,' Jason announced. 'You get ready and I'll come back in ten minutes. Wash your face first, you're all red and blotchy.' His phone began to ring. He dug it out of his jacket pocket and glanced at the screen. 'Mum,' he said, rejecting the call. 'I'll call her back downstairs.'

'Let me speak to her,' Roy said.

'No, Dad, not a good idea. Now get dressed. The cars will be here at one, you've got fifteen minutes.'

As Jason left the room, Roy flopped down heavily on the bed. There was a bottle of single malt hidden away in the bedside cupboard and he grabbed it and took a long swig. He wiped his mouth with the back of his hand and sighed. Must be suffering those wedding-day nerves they talk about. He couldn't cope completely sober. A bit pissed and slightly stoned, that was the way to do it. Minty mouthwash and plenty of aftershave and no one would be any the wiser. He stared at his suit, hanging on the front of the wardrobe. He'd look ridiculous in it, like a fucking penguin. He didn't do formal, never had. Why couldn't he have just got married in linen or leather, like he'd done before? Well, there was no way he was wearing that bloody top hat! He threw it on the floor and stamped on it.

* * *

Jason went back outside and called his mother. 'Hi, Mum. Yeah, everything's fine. Harley looks just amazing. I haven't seen anyone else yet except for Livvy's friend Sheena, who let us in. Well yeah, I've spoken to Dad. He's busy getting ready. No, he's fine. Coping well. You know Dad, takes it all in his stride. I'll call you tomorrow, tell you how it went. I'd better go now and see to Daisy. Love you, Mum.'

Jason ended the call and went back indoors. He had this strange feeling, deep down, that he should have told her Dad wasn't coping at all. But what was the point in upsetting her? Jason knew that his mum wasn't as happy as she should be. He really wished she'd not rushed into marrying Stuart. What on earth had she been thinking?

Stu was a lovely guy, but not the right one for Mum to spend the rest of her life with. It was almost as though she'd wanted to prove to Dad that she could get along without him and that Livvy was welcome to him. If it hadn't been for the baby, Mum probably wouldn't have started divorce proceedings in the first place. She'd have forgiven Dad for cheating on her eventually and blamed everything on Livvy. And to cap it all, the bloody baby, when it arrived, hadn't even been Dad's, yet he still acted as though he was responsible. Ah well, Dad was old enough and daft enough to sort himself out.

'You okay, Jason?' Jules interrupted his thoughts.

Jason nodded. Jules was holding Daisy, who looked a picture in her tiny, blue silk bridesmaid's dress and matching headband. Courtney was going to carry the youngest bridesmaid down the aisle, following Harley. Daisy gave Jason a wide gummy grin and held her arms out. He took hold of her and said a silent prayer of thanks, that although unconventional, he, Jules and Daisy were the happiest little family he knew.

* * *

Sammy put down the phone and poured another glass of Cliff Richard's wine. The bottle was almost empty now and she felt quite tipsy. Why didn't she believe Jason's insistence that Roy was okay? She had a gut feeling that he was far from right. Stuart had gone off to play a round of golf with John and Margaret Grey and wouldn't be back for hours. As soon as Sammy was alone, she'd called Jane, who told her that Roy had been a bit odd lately. Nothing she could put her finger on, Jane said, but he wasn't quite himself. That was why Sammy had called Jason, guessing he and Jules would now be at Roy's place.

She couldn't settle to doing anything and got out her laptop. A quick check showed that there was a flight from Faro to Manchester in two hours. She could be in Manchester for 6 p.m. She booked a return journey. Whether she'd use it or not was anyone's guess, but she dug her passport out of the kitchen drawer, scribbled a note for Stuart, saying she was going home for a couple of days, and hurried to the bedroom to pack an overnight bag. She called for a taxi, then sent a text to Jane.

* * *

Roy heard Sheena calling, 'The cars are here.' Then, 'Right, Harley, you go out on the landing and your dad will be at the bottom of the stairs, waiting for you.'

He dashed downstairs and stood in the hall. He felt an immense sense of pride as Harley swanned downstairs, clutching a bouquet of white roses tied up with blue ribbons, Courtney and baby Daisy following.

'Wow! You look like a real princess today,' Roy said, taking a deep breath. 'Truly stunning.' He kissed her and she took his arm as he led her out to one of the waiting vintage Rolls. Harley waved to Courtney and Daisy, who got into the one behind with Jason and Jules.

'You ready for this, sweetheart?' Roy asked as the car pulled away down the drive on its short journey to Ashlea Church.

'Yes.' Harley nodded. 'But I'm feeling a bit nervous. You okay, Dad? You don't look too clever, you're very pale.'

'I'm fine,' he replied. 'Like you, a bit nervous, I guess.' He was bloody terrified, but he couldn't admit that to his daughter. He felt like jumping out of the moving car and legging it down the road to the nearest pub.

'Where's your hat?' Harley asked, frowning.

He looked at her, one eyebrow raised. 'I stamped on it.'

She started to giggle. 'Dad, why? Mom will go mad.'

He laughed with her. 'Can you honestly see me wearing a top hat? Come on, Harley, I'm Roy Cantello, The Raiders' frontman. I don't wear hats and I'd never live it down once the photos were published. I'll tell Livvy I sat on it by accident.'

'Your secret's safe with me,' she said, grinning.

He smiled and gently stroked her cheek. She snuggled into him and he put his arm around her. He wouldn't let her down. If he did nothing else right today, he'd make sure he handed his daughter over to Jack's safekeeping.

'Here we are,' Roy said as the car pulled up outside the church.

'There's Faye, Nathan and Jamie with Jess, Jon and Daniel.' Harley waved as Roy helped her out. The second car pulled up behind them and Courtney hurried over to help straighten

Harley's dress. Jason handed Daisy over and he and Jules followed Jess and everyone else into church. Daniel was smiling over Jess's shoulder at Roy and he waved his arms about and called something that sounded like Dadda.

'Did you hear that?' Roy said. 'He called me Dadda – he's never said it before.'

'He's been saying it for a few days,' Harley whispered. 'You should spend more time with him then you'd know.'

'Chance'd be a fine thing,' Roy muttered. 'Livvy never lets me do anything for him. Right, that's our cue,' he said as the throaty rasp of Enrique Iglesias declared, 'Let me be your hero', lyrics to the song that Harley and Jack had chosen for her walk down the aisle.

Jason and Jules, in their ushers' positions, gave Harley a kiss each and shook Roy by the hand. Jason also gave his dad a quick hug. Harley tucked her arm through Roy's and they began the slow journey. He nodded at Phil and Laura, Carl and Cathy, and Sean and Tina. He could see Ed standing at the front next to Jack with Nathan, who was Jack's best man. Jane was in the second pew with Pat and Tim, Kate and Zak, and Jess, Jon and Daniel. Harley smiled at everyone as she passed, as regal as a true princess. Roy didn't think he'd ever felt so choked and proud all at the same time.

The press gang from *Hello!* were assembled in the left front pew, cameras at the ready. *Bloody hell, Livvy*, he thought, *this is difficult enough without the whole world knowing their every move.* He couldn't believe how camera- and reporter-shy she'd been when she first moved into Phil's place. Alright, so it was to make sure she got custody of Courtney, but that had changed rapidly once Danny had passed away and they'd moved in together. It wasn't like any of them needed the money for the exclusive. Even her parents were living a comfortable lifestyle now, thanks to their daughter. Maybe he'd suggest the money went to The Christie Hospital for cancer research.

Jack turned and caught Harley's eye. He was beaming, his dark curls neatly trimmed, blue eyes sparkling. She smiled back and took her place beside him.

Roy moved to stand by Eddie. 'One down, two to go,' he muttered as Eddie nodded.

'Soon be over,' Eddie whispered. 'Think of tonight. Right, get ready... Here's your future wife.'

Roy felt the lump in his throat threatening to choke him as Livvy walked down the aisle on Peter's arm. She'd chosen the traditional 'Wedding March' and was smiling and looking straight at him. She looked beautiful, but there was a steely glint of determination in her eyes and it was something he'd never seen before. He didn't like the look of it – he felt like a rabbit caught in headlights. Peter led her to stand beside him and then turned to wait for Gina, who had also chosen the same music.

The vicar asked who was giving Harley to Jack and Roy stepped forward. As the service progressed, he couldn't look at Livvy, who kept pulling on his arm, concentrating instead on his daughter and Jack. When Gina and Peter took their place in front of the vicar to say *their* vows, Roy thought his head might explode. He felt sick and the banging noise in his ears was getting louder. Each breath he took didn't seem to be reaching his lungs. He turned to look at Eddie.

'You okay, mate?' Eddie whispered. 'You look dreadful.'

Roy shook his head and turned to face the congregation. He felt panic-stricken, gulping in great breaths of air. He saw Jane staring at him and shaking her head. She was mouthing something to him, but he couldn't tell what. He missed the vicar asking him and Livvy to move forward as he keeled over beside Eddie. The last thing he was conscious of was the vicar's shiny shoes and Livvy's anxious face, her voice seeming to come from a distance, asking was he alright, as he slipped into peaceful oblivion.

* * *

Eddie yelled to Jane to call an ambulance. He rolled Roy into the recovery position and loosened his tie and undid his shirt. Everyone was panicking and Livvy and Harley were crying and crowding round. 'Get back and give him some air,' Eddie ordered as the photographer from *Hello!* started flashing. 'Livvy, get rid of them! He doesn't need it.'

'Oh my God!' Harley cried. 'Dad, Dad! Is he dead?' Tears streamed down her cheeks and she clung to Jack. 'He wasn't very well earlier, he looked so pale in the car.'

Jason sprinted up the aisle and whispered to Eddie that his dad had been smoking dope earlier and had no doubt had a drink or two. Eddie nodded, but told Jason he thought it was something more than that. He was worried that Roy had suffered a stroke or a heart attack. He wasn't coming round, but Jane was checking his pulse now and he was still breathing – a bit erratic, but breathing nevertheless.

'He said he couldn't do this earlier,' Jason whispered to Eddie, out of earshot of Livvy, who was weeping in her father's arms. 'But he didn't want to let Harley down.'

'Well, he didn't,' Eddie said. 'Nor Livvy's parents. It's just he and Livvy that didn't quite make it.'

The paramedics arrived and Jules led them to Roy. The congregation left the church at the vicar's request and made for the church hall next door, with the promise of a cup of tea and an update as soon as there was one.

The paramedics checked Roy's vital signs, gave him oxygen and he began to come round.

'Have you got any chest pains?' he was asked.

He shook his head, looking totally bewildered. 'Just feels a bit tight when I breathe. What happened?'

'You passed out,' a paramedic told him. 'Might be a panic attack, but we're gonna take you to hospital and get you checked

over. Can you walk to the ambulance, or shall we get a
stretcher?'

'I can walk, I think,' Roy said as they helped him to his feet.
'I feel a bit groggy, but I'm okay.'

'I'll come with you,' Livvy cried, grasping his hand.

'No.' He pulled quickly away, which didn't go unnoticed by
Eddie. 'No need. Ed will come with me, you stay here and look
after the girls. In fact, don't let *me* being ill spoil the day for
everyone. Get them all to the hotel for the reception and I'll join
you later.'

'But, Roy, we're not married yet,' she yelled, more tears
spilling down her cheeks.

He stared at her and slowly shook his head. 'I'm sorry, I
didn't do this on purpose. Look on it as an omen. Maybe the
marriage was never meant to happen.' He turned to Eddie, who
gripped an arm, one of the paramedics held the other and they
walked him back down the aisle towards the door, leaving Livvy
looking stunned. She made to run after them, but her dad
pulled her back.

'Leave him be, hen. Let them sort him out. I thought he was
a goner then – you can talk later when he comes home.'

* * *

Jane followed Roy and Eddie out of the church. She took out
her mobile and dialled a number: 'Are you at the airport? Good!
Get on that plane, Roy needs you.' She went back in church and
spoke to Harley and Jack: 'Your dad will be okay, love. He has a
habit of passing out when he gets a bit stressed. He's done it on
tour a few times and frightened us all to death. I think everything just got too much for him today but at least he gave you
away, Harley, and heard you take your vows.'

Harley nodded. 'I couldn't bear it if anything happened to
him.'

'He'll be fine, love, you'll see.' Jane gave her a hug. 'He just needs a bit of space. Maybe they'll keep him in hospital overnight so he can get some rest.'

* * *

Eddie felt a bit of an idiot in his morning suit, sitting in the hospital waiting room while the doctors checked Roy over. A nurse came out of the curtained-off cubicle and told him they were sending Mr Cantello for an ECG as his heart rate and blood pressure were high. She said he could go in and see him for a few minutes.

Roy was still pale-faced and very anxious-looking as Eddie popped his head around the curtains.

'Come in, Ed. Bloody hell, what a time to faint! She'll think I've done it on purpose.'

Eddie smiled. 'And did you? Jason told me you didn't think you could go through with the marriage. Well, ending up in hospital is one sure way of getting out of it.'

'She'll hate me now, she'll say I fucked it up on purpose. If that stupid magazine hadn't wanted us to take our vows last, we'd have been married now. Not my bloody fault she wanted to flaunt it to the world.'

'No, but it's your fault you got stoned and had a drink on an empty stomach. You should have had some breakfast.'

'I did. Black coffee and two sneaky fags, my usual. Do you think it's fate? That I wasn't meant to marry her after all? It didn't feel right, Ed. Maybe someone is looking after me up there.' He raised his eyes to the ceiling. 'I was thinking about Nick and Sammy earlier and I realised I couldn't do it. I should have said something then, but I didn't want to let Harley down.'

* * *

Jane met Eddie in the hospital waiting room and handed him a small holdall. She told him the wedding parties had done as Roy suggested and moved on to the reception. Jess had taken Livvy and Daniel back to Ashlea Grange and it was Jess who'd let Jane in when she'd arrived to get some clothes for Roy. Livvy had begged to come to the hospital with her, but both Jane and Jess had persuaded her to wait until Roy asked for her.

'He doesn't want her here,' Eddie said. 'He was freaking out about the marriage, that's why he passed out. To be honest, I think he's on the verge of a breakdown. Hardly surprising, considering the last twelve months. They're gonna do some tests on him. I think we'll take him back to our place if they let him home tonight.'

Jane nodded. 'If that's what he wants. Can I go in and see him?'

'Yeah, come on.' He took her hand and led her to Roy's cubicle.

Roy smiled wearily as she bent to kiss his cheek.

'How's Liv?' he asked.

'Okay. She's waiting at home for you to get in touch and tell her what's happening.'

He nodded. 'I'll call her when I know. I can't face seeing her just yet. I need some peace and quiet, not her going on about the bloody non-wedding. Christ, it'll be front-page news tomorrow. Me lying prone at the vicar's feet!'

Jane smiled and patted his shoulder. 'Not to worry. It'll be a five-day wonder.'

Roy grasped her hand. 'When I turned to face you in the church you were mouthing something at me. I couldn't tell what it was.'

Jane felt her cheeks heating and she looked away for a moment. 'You looked so panic-stricken,' she said. 'I just knew it was wrong for you to marry Livvy. I was saying, "Don't do it. Sammy still loves you."'

'Does she?'

'You know she does.'

'But she's married to Stu.'

'That was as big a mistake as if you'd married Livvy,' Jane said. 'Anyway, Sammy can tell you that for herself. I'm picking her up from the airport at six.'

'She's coming here?' Roy's face lit up.

'She's in the air as we speak,' Jane replied. 'I called her earlier and she was sitting in Faro Airport, dithering about whether to board the plane. I told her to get on it because you needed her.'

'What about Stu?' Eddie asked.

'I expect she's left him a message and no doubt she'll call him later.'

'I can't believe she's coming,' Roy said, looking more animated than Jane had seen him for weeks. 'Somebody up there is definitely listening to me today. She's still Stu's wife though. Shit, what a fucking mess I've made of everything, again! I just don't know how I'm going to put all this right.'

Jane shrugged. 'What will be will be.'

Roy nodded. 'Now you sound just like your mother!'

* * *

Livvy, still in her wedding dress, accepted the cup of tea Jess handed her. She was propped up on her bed, Daniel by her side. A far cry from the wedding night she'd envisaged. She'd called the hospital half an hour ago; they'd told her Roy was having some tests done and to call back later. The girls were still at the reception with her parents, although Harley had called several times for updates. Livvy told her to call Eddie or Jane as they were the only ones Roy seemed to want with him. She felt in limbo. Did Roy still want to marry her? Had he faked the faint to get out of it? Although in fairness, he'd looked waxen on the floor and at first, she thought he'd actually died.

Something deep down told her the marriage wasn't going to happen. Maybe they were better off just living together. She certainly couldn't cope alone, not with another baby on the way. She needed Roy's emotional support, if nothing else. If he decided to leave her, she couldn't stay here with the kids. Nor did she want to go back to LA. Her mum and dad would no doubt step in to help her. Maybe the best thing all round would be for her to move up to Scotland to be with her family and be near Sheena. That thought cheered her slightly; at least she wouldn't be alone. She thought about Sheena and how this unexpected turn of events meant that she, at least, could have a chat with Jon while Jess was here at Ashlea Grange.

'Do you want me to get Daniel ready for bed?' Jess asked, disturbing her thoughts.

Livvy nodded. 'Please, Jess. He'll need a bath. I think I'll try and have a little sleep. I should think I'm going to be up most of the night looking after Roy if they let him home.'

'You do that,' Jess said and left the room with the baby tucked under her arm.

* * *

Sammy flung her arms around Jane, who was waiting for her in arrivals at the airport.

'So, what's happened, Jane? Why does Roy need me?' she asked as Jane hurried her towards the car.

'He collapsed at the wedding,' Jane said. 'He's in Stockport General, having an ECG.'

'Oh my God! Has he had a heart attack?'

'Don't think so, but his heart rate's erratic and his blood pressure's high, so they're taking precautions. He's very stressed, Sam. He'll be so glad to see you.'

'But what about Livvy? *She's* his wife now. I shouldn't think *she'll* be too pleased to see me.'

Jane stopped walking and grabbed Sammy's arm. 'That's just it. She isn't! His wife, I mean. He passed out before they took their vows.'

'No way! That's so spooky. I had a feeling on the plane that something had stopped the wedding, but I thought that was just me being weird.'

'If you ask me, it's the best thing that could have happened,' Jane said as they got in the car. 'He was only doing what he thought he ought to because of the kids and because *you* didn't want him. There's just one thing, Sam, and I don't think Roy knows this yet. He certainly hasn't mentioned it anyway. Livvy's pregnant again. I just called Jess to see how Livvy's doing and she's told Jess. She was saving the news as a surprise for him.'

'Well, it doesn't surprise me,' Sammy said. 'Nor does it bother me too much. I knew they were trying because of Harley, Jason told me. At least she'll have a match. But it leaves a lot of mess hanging in the air. I wonder what they'll do now.'

Jane shook her head as she pulled out into heavy traffic. 'You and Roy need to have a good talk, see if you can salvage anything out of all this mess. And then there's Stuart...'

'I know. I've dashed off to come to my ex's rescue and left him a scribbled message on the kitchen table. That's not the act of a loving wife, is it?'

'Not really. But it's the act of a woman in love if you ask me.'

Sammy nodded, tears pouring down her cheeks. 'What if he'd died today, Jane? I couldn't bear it. I'll take him back, baggage and all, if it's what he wants.'

* * *

Roy had been moved to a small private room and was wired up to a heart monitor. He felt better than he'd felt earlier. He pushed himself up the bed as Eddie came back into the room. 'Any news from Jane?'

'Yeah, she and Sam are on their way here,' Eddie replied. 'Are you sure you can cope with any more excitement today?'

'I'm fine, they think it was a panic attack. This machine is just a precaution. The nurse who came and checked it earlier said everything looked okay. My blood pressure's back to normal. Just waiting for a doctor now to discharge me. I don't want to go home though, I'm not ready to face Livvy just yet.'

'Okay.' Eddie nodded. 'You can come back with me and Jane tonight. Sam can stay with us, too. That way you can have a bit of space to talk.'

* * *

Roy and Sammy lay side by side on top of the big bed in the spare room at Hanover's Lodge. The same room that had been theirs when they'd all lived together at the height of The Raiders' fame during the sixties. They'd held each other and talked for over two hours and Sammy was concerned that Roy looked tired and should get some sleep. 'I'm going to go downstairs now and talk to Jane and Ed while you have a rest,' she told him. 'And I need to call Stuart, although I don't know what I'm going to say to him. There's Jack and Harley's honeymoon to think about, too.'

He nodded. 'We'll make it up to them. Take them on a cruise or safari or something after the tour. Tomorrow, I'll go and see Livvy, make my apologies and tell her it's not going to happen. She'll probably stick a knife in my back as I'm leaving.' He paused for a minute. 'I think she's pregnant, Sam.'

'She is,' Sammy said, stroking his cheek. 'She told Jess. She got what she wanted, didn't she? Man not included.'

'You make me sound like a toy without the batteries. Will you be able to cope with everything over the next few months? Livvy won't make it easy and I don't even know where to start sorting things out. I'll have to help out with the kids when she resumes her career and goes back on the road.' His eyes filled with sudden tears. 'Daniel called me Dadda today.'

'Did he? Bless him. I know you've bonded with him.'

'Well, I have, in as much as Livvy lets me. I treat him as my own.'

'I'll help you with everything. We'll get the strength to cope from each other. It's a brand-new start for everyone. Maybe not quite the one Livvy wanted but you can't have everything and she'll have two kids of yours, which is more than *I've* got now.' She stared up at the ceiling and half-smiled.

'What's so amusing?'

'Just thinking,' she said. 'We're right back where we started. Nick was conceived in this room, and we got married from here, too. We're back to square one.'

Roy leant up on one elbow and planted a kiss on her lips. 'As far as *I'm* concerned, after the last twelve months, square one is the best place, in fact, the *only* place I want to be right now.'

A LETTER FROM PAM

Dear reader,

I want to say a huge thank you for choosing to read *Secrets on Mersey Square*. If you did enjoy it, and want to keep up to date with all my latest releases, just sign up at the following link. Your email address will never be shared and you can unsubscribe at any time.

www.bookouture.com/pam-howes

To my loyal band of regular readers who bought and reviewed all my previous stories, thank you for waiting patiently for another book. Your support is most welcome and very much appreciated.

As always, a big thank you to Beverley Ann Hopper and Sandra Blower and the members of their Facebook group, Book Lovers. Thanks for all the support you show me. Also, thank you to Deryl Easton and the supportive members of her Facebook group, Gangland Governors/NotRights.

A huge thank you to team Bookouture, especially my lovely editor Maisie Lawrence. As always, it's been such a pleasure to work with you again and thanks also to copyeditor/line editor Jane Eastgate and proofreader Jane Donovan for the copy edits and proofreading side of life.

And last, but definitely not least, thank you to our amazing media team, Kim Nash, Sarah Hardy, Jess Readett and Noelle

Holton, for everything you do for us. You're 'Simply the Best' as Tina would say! And thanks also to the gang in the Bookouture Authors' Lounge for always being there. As always, I'm so proud to be one of you.

I hope you loved *Secrets on Mersey Square* and if you did, I would be very grateful if you could write a review. I'd love to hear what you think and it makes such a difference helping new readers to discover one of my books for the first time.

I love hearing from my readers – you can get in touch on my Facebook page or through Twitter.

Thanks,

Pam Howes

facebook.com/Pam-Howes-Books-260328010709267
x.com/PamHowes1

ACKNOWLEDGEMENTS

As always, for my partner, my daughters, grandchildren, great granddaughters and all their partners/spouses. Thanks for being a supportive and lovely family.